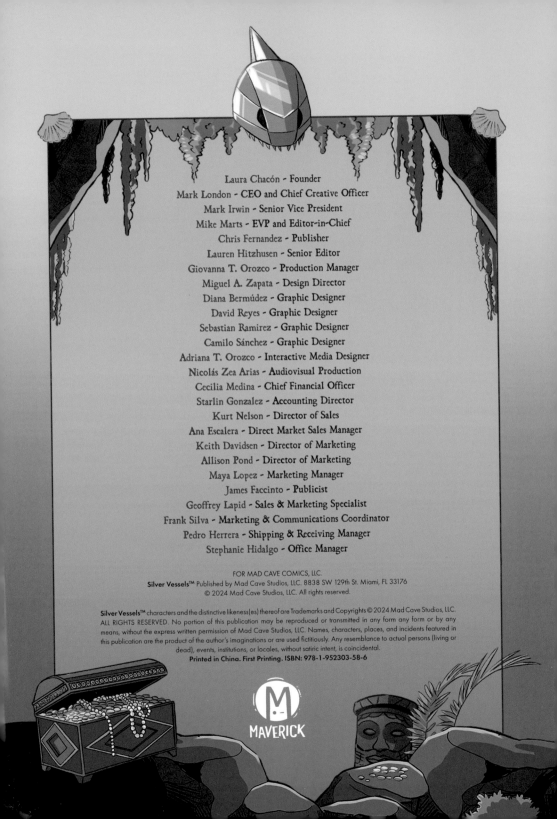

FOR MAD CAVE COMICS, LLC.
Silver Vessels™ Published by Mad Cave Studios, LLC. 8838 SW 129th St. Miami, FL 33176
© 2024 Mad Cave Studios, LLC. All rights reserved.

MAVERICK

SILVER VESSELS

STEVE ORLANDO - WRITER
KATIA VECCHIO - ARTIST

DAVE LANPHEAR - LETTERER
LAUREN HITZHUSEN - EDITOR
CHRIS SANCHEZ - CONSULTING EDITOR
CAMILO SÁNCHEZ - LOGO DESIGNER
SEBASTIAN RAMIREZ - BOOK DESIGNER

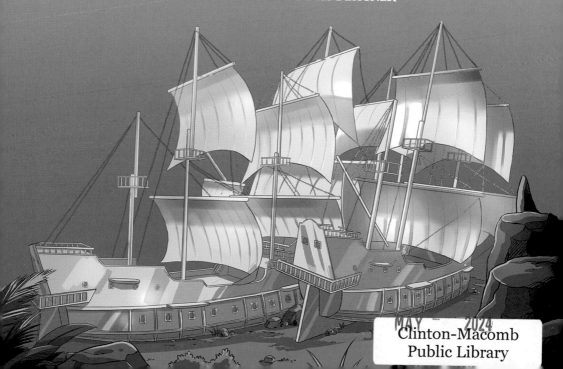

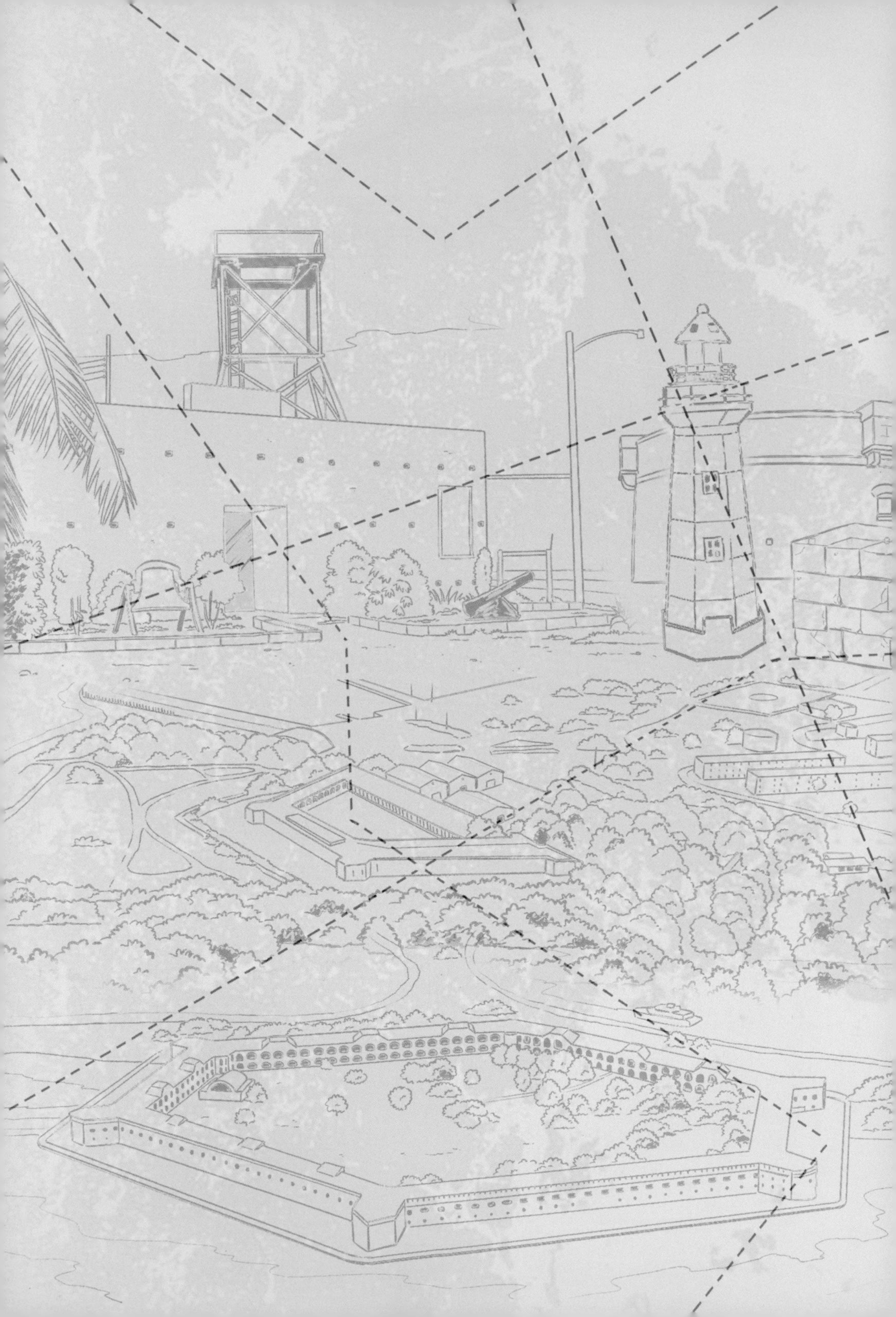

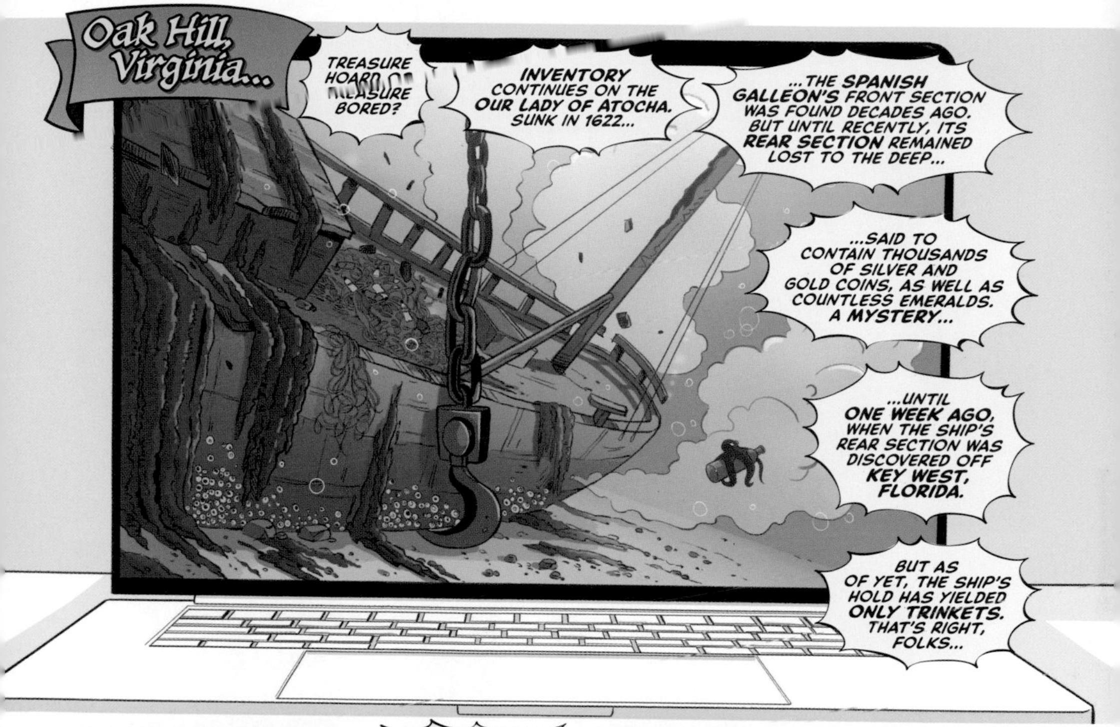
Oak Hill, Virginia...
TREASURE HOARD ... BORED?
INVENTORY CONTINUES ON THE OUR LADY OF ATOCHA. SUNK IN 1622...
...THE SPANISH GALLEON'S FRONT SECTION WAS FOUND DECADES AGO. BUT UNTIL RECENTLY, ITS REAR SECTION REMAINED LOST TO THE DEEP...
...SAID TO CONTAIN THOUSANDS OF SILVER AND GOLD COINS, AS WELL AS COUNTLESS EMERALDS. A MYSTERY...
...UNTIL ONE WEEK AGO, WHEN THE SHIP'S REAR SECTION WAS DISCOVERED OFF KEY WEST, FLORIDA.
BUT AS OF YET, THE SHIP'S HOLD HAS YIELDED ONLY TRINKETS. THAT'S RIGHT, FOLKS...

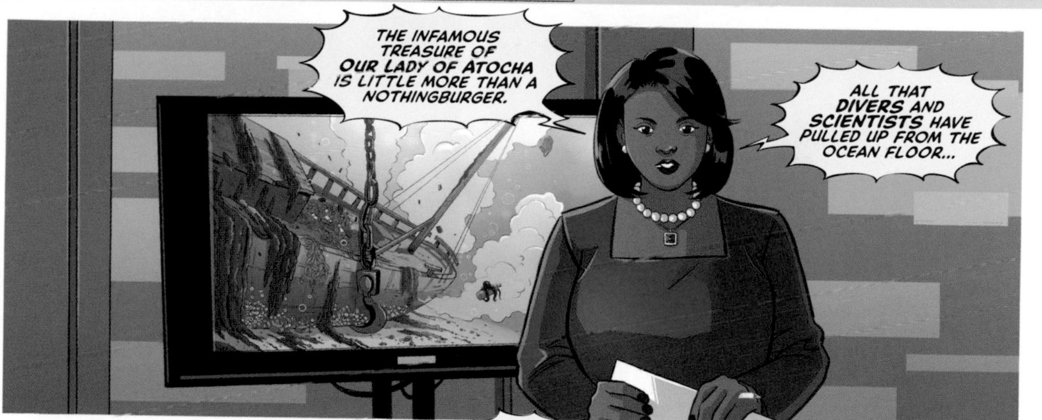
THE INFAMOUS TREASURE OF OUR LADY OF ATOCHA IS LITTLE MORE THAN A NOTHINGBURGER.
ALL THAT DIVERS AND SCIENTISTS HAVE PULLED UP FROM THE OCEAN FLOOR...

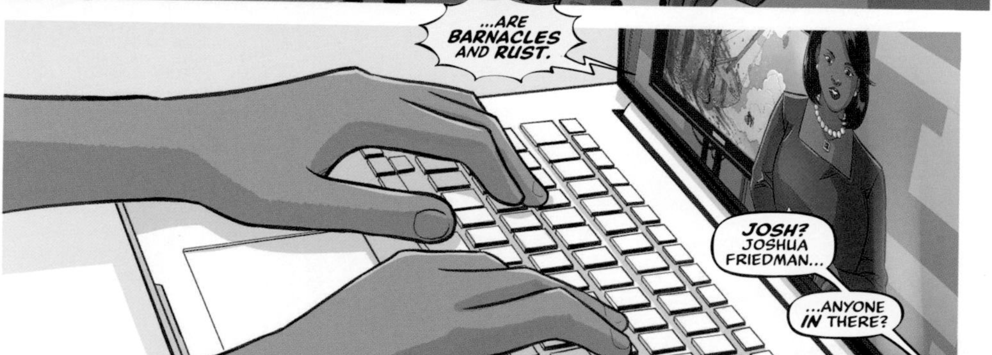
...ARE BARNACLES AND RUST.
JOSH? JOSHUA FRIEDMAN...
...ANYONE IN THERE?

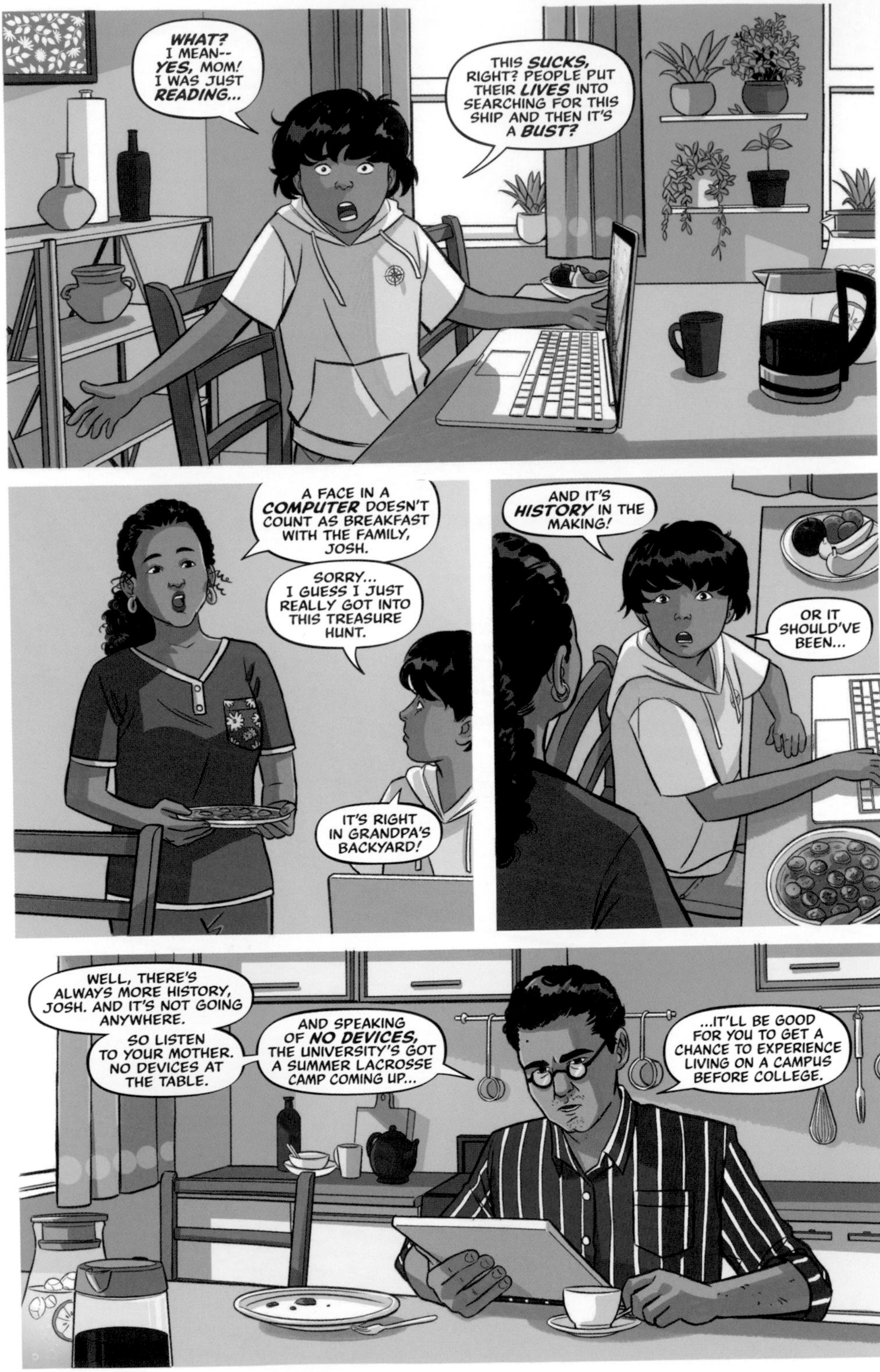

WHAT? I MEAN-- YES, MOM! I WAS JUST READING...
THIS SUCKS, RIGHT? PEOPLE PUT THEIR LIVES INTO SEARCHING FOR THIS SHIP AND THEN IT'S A BUST?
A FACE IN A COMPUTER DOESN'T COUNT AS BREAKFAST WITH THE FAMILY, JOSH.
SORRY... I GUESS I JUST REALLY GOT INTO THIS TREASURE HUNT.
IT'S RIGHT IN GRANDPA'S BACKYARD!
AND IT'S HISTORY IN THE MAKING!
OR IT SHOULD'VE BEEN...
WELL, THERE'S ALWAYS MORE HISTORY, JOSH. AND IT'S NOT GOING ANYWHERE.
SO LISTEN TO YOUR MOTHER. NO DEVICES AT THE TABLE.
AND SPEAKING OF NO DEVICES, THE UNIVERSITY'S GOT A SUMMER LACROSSE CAMP COMING UP...
...IT'LL BE GOOD FOR YOU TO GET A CHANCE TO EXPERIENCE LIVING ON A CAMPUS BEFORE COLLEGE.

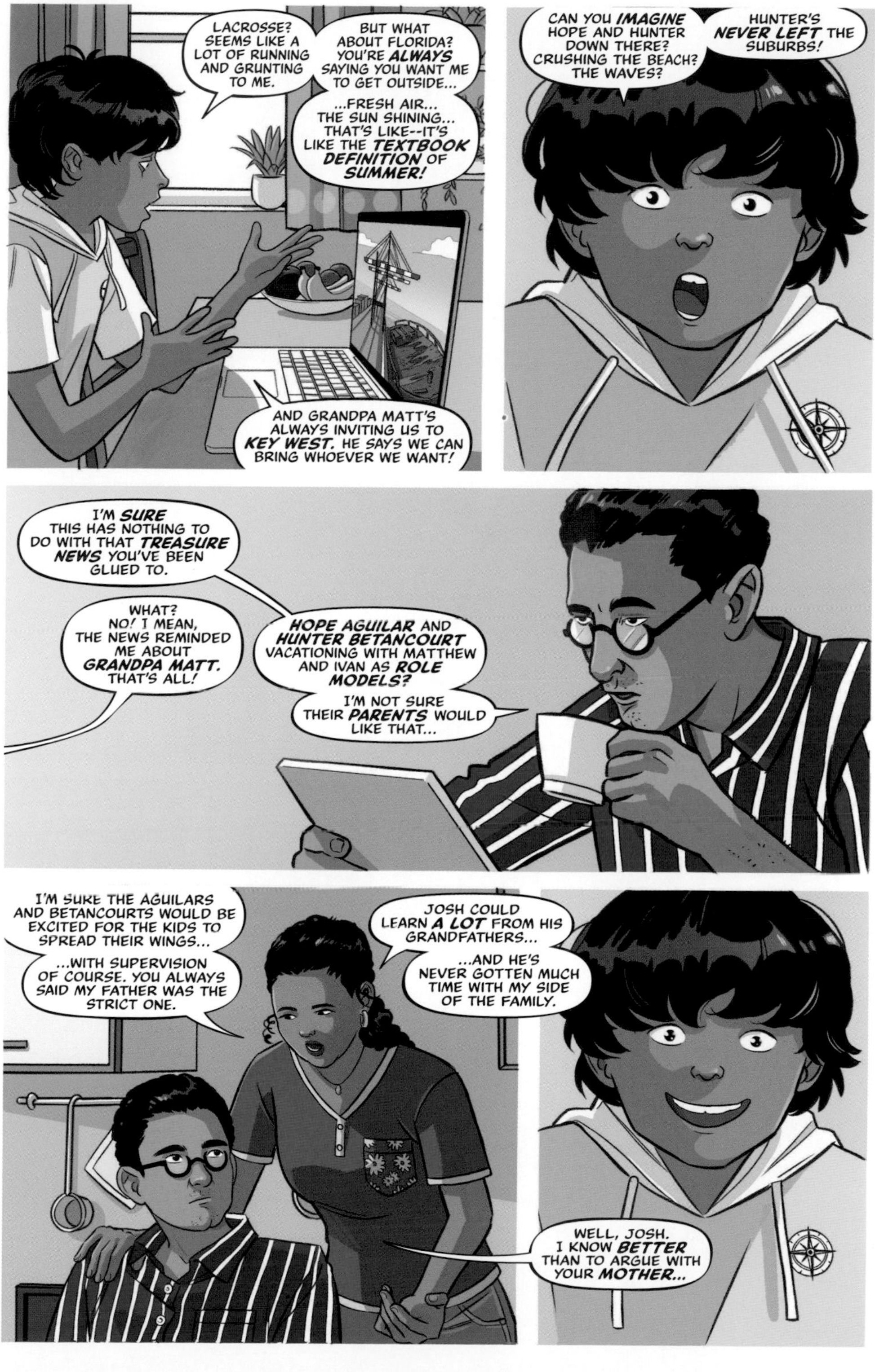
LACROSSE? SEEMS LIKE A LOT OF RUNNING AND GRUNTING TO ME.
BUT WHAT ABOUT FLORIDA? YOU'RE ALWAYS SAYING YOU WANT ME TO GET OUTSIDE...
...FRESH AIR... THE SUN SHINING... THAT'S LIKE--IT'S LIKE THE TEXTBOOK DEFINITION OF SUMMER!
AND GRANDPA MATT'S ALWAYS INVITING US TO KEY WEST. HE SAYS WE CAN BRING WHOEVER WE WANT!
CAN YOU IMAGINE HOPE AND HUNTER DOWN THERE? CRUSHING THE BEACH? THE WAVES?
HUNTER'S NEVER LEFT THE SUBURBS!
I'M SURE THIS HAS NOTHING TO DO WITH THAT TREASURE NEWS YOU'VE BEEN GLUED TO.
WHAT? NO! I MEAN, THE NEWS REMINDED ME ABOUT GRANDPA MATT. THAT'S ALL!
HOPE AGUILAR AND HUNTER BETANCOURT VACATIONING WITH MATTHEW AND IVAN AS ROLE MODELS?
I'M NOT SURE THEIR PARENTS WOULD LIKE THAT...
I'M SURE THE AGUILARS AND BETANCOURTS WOULD BE EXCITED FOR THE KIDS TO SPREAD THEIR WINGS...
...WITH SUPERVISION OF COURSE. YOU ALWAYS SAID MY FATHER WAS THE STRICT ONE.
JOSH COULD LEARN A LOT FROM HIS GRANDFATHERS...
...AND HE'S NEVER GOTTEN MUCH TIME WITH MY SIDE OF THE FAMILY.
WELL, JOSH. I KNOW BETTER THAN TO ARGUE WITH YOUR MOTHER...

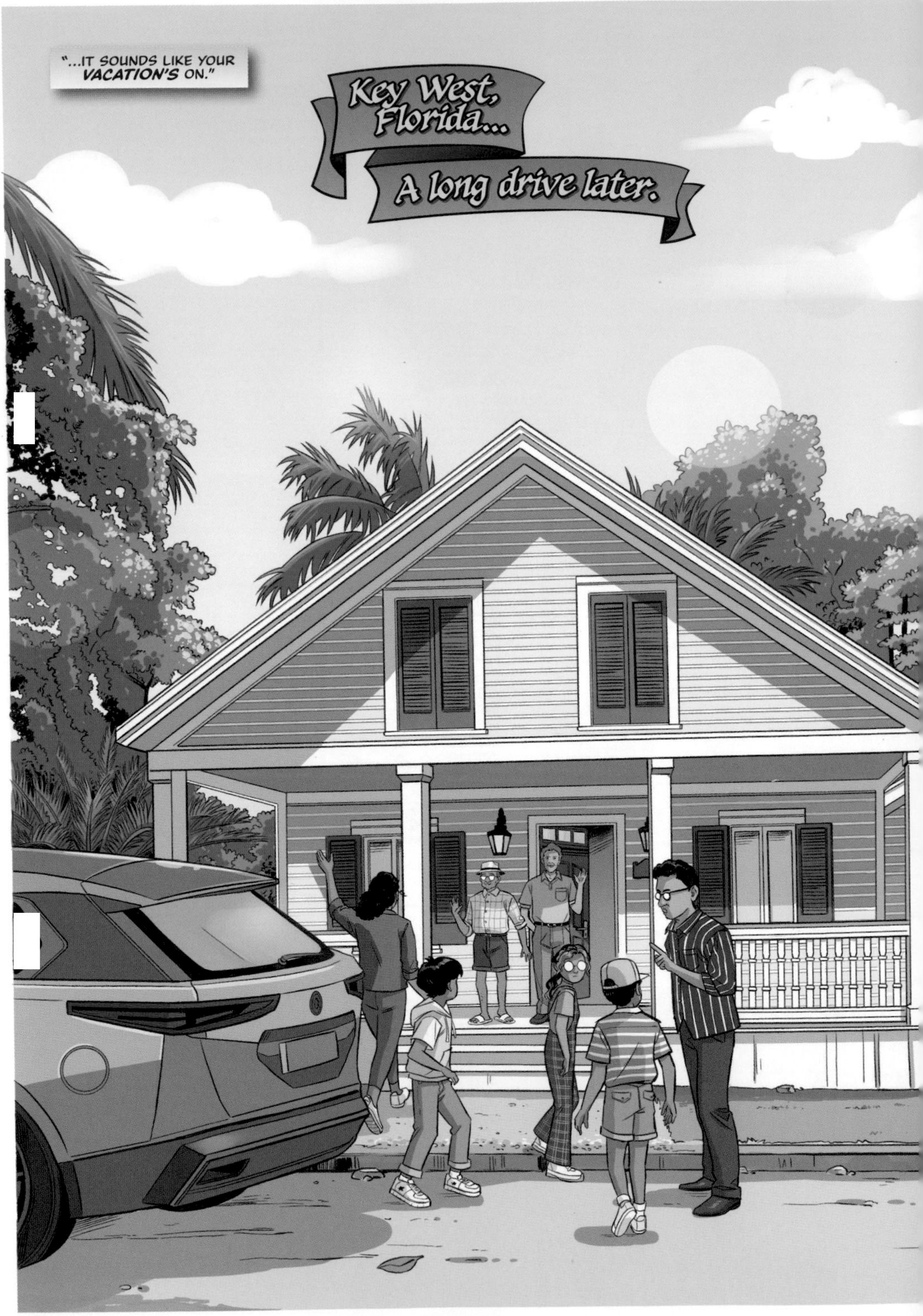
"...IT SOUNDS LIKE YOUR VACATION'S ON."
Key West, Florida...
A long drive later.

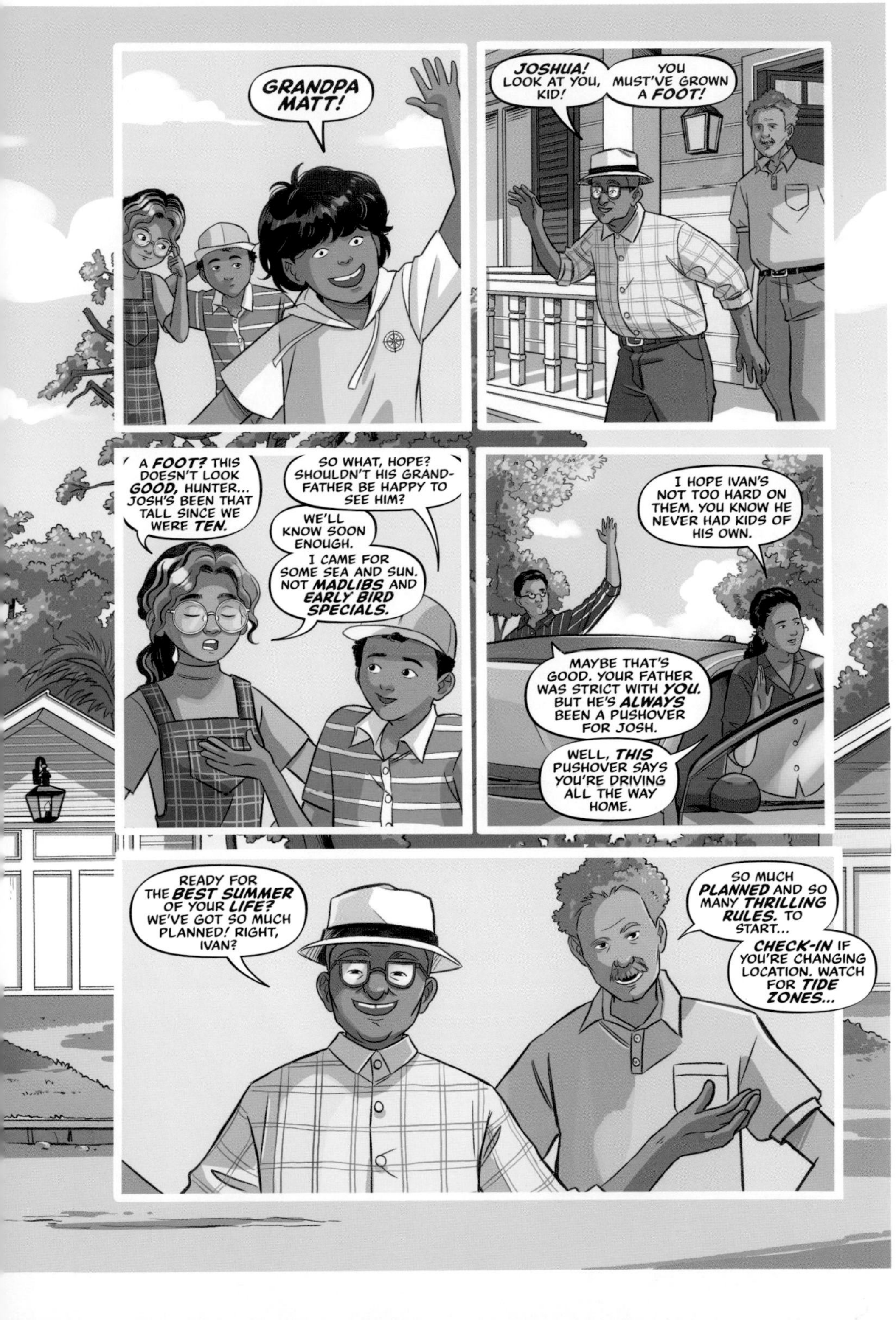
GRANDPA MATT!
JOSHUA! LOOK AT YOU, KID!
YOU MUST'VE GROWN A FOOT!
A FOOT? THIS DOESN'T LOOK GOOD, HUNTER... JOSH'S BEEN THAT TALL SINCE WE WERE TEN.
SO WHAT, HOPE? SHOULDN'T HIS GRAND-FATHER BE HAPPY TO SEE HIM?
WE'LL KNOW SOON ENOUGH.
I CAME FOR SOME SEA AND SUN. NOT MADLIBS AND EARLY BIRD SPECIALS.
I HOPE IVAN'S NOT TOO HARD ON THEM. YOU KNOW HE NEVER HAD KIDS OF HIS OWN.
MAYBE THAT'S GOOD. YOUR FATHER WAS STRICT WITH YOU. BUT HE'S ALWAYS BEEN A PUSHOVER FOR JOSH.
WELL, THIS PUSHOVER SAYS YOU'RE DRIVING ALL THE WAY HOME.
READY FOR THE BEST SUMMER OF YOUR LIFE? WE'VE GOT SO MUCH PLANNED! RIGHT, IVAN?
SO MUCH PLANNED AND SO MANY THRILLING RULES. TO START...
CHECK-IN IF YOU'RE CHANGING LOCATION. WATCH FOR TIDE ZONES...

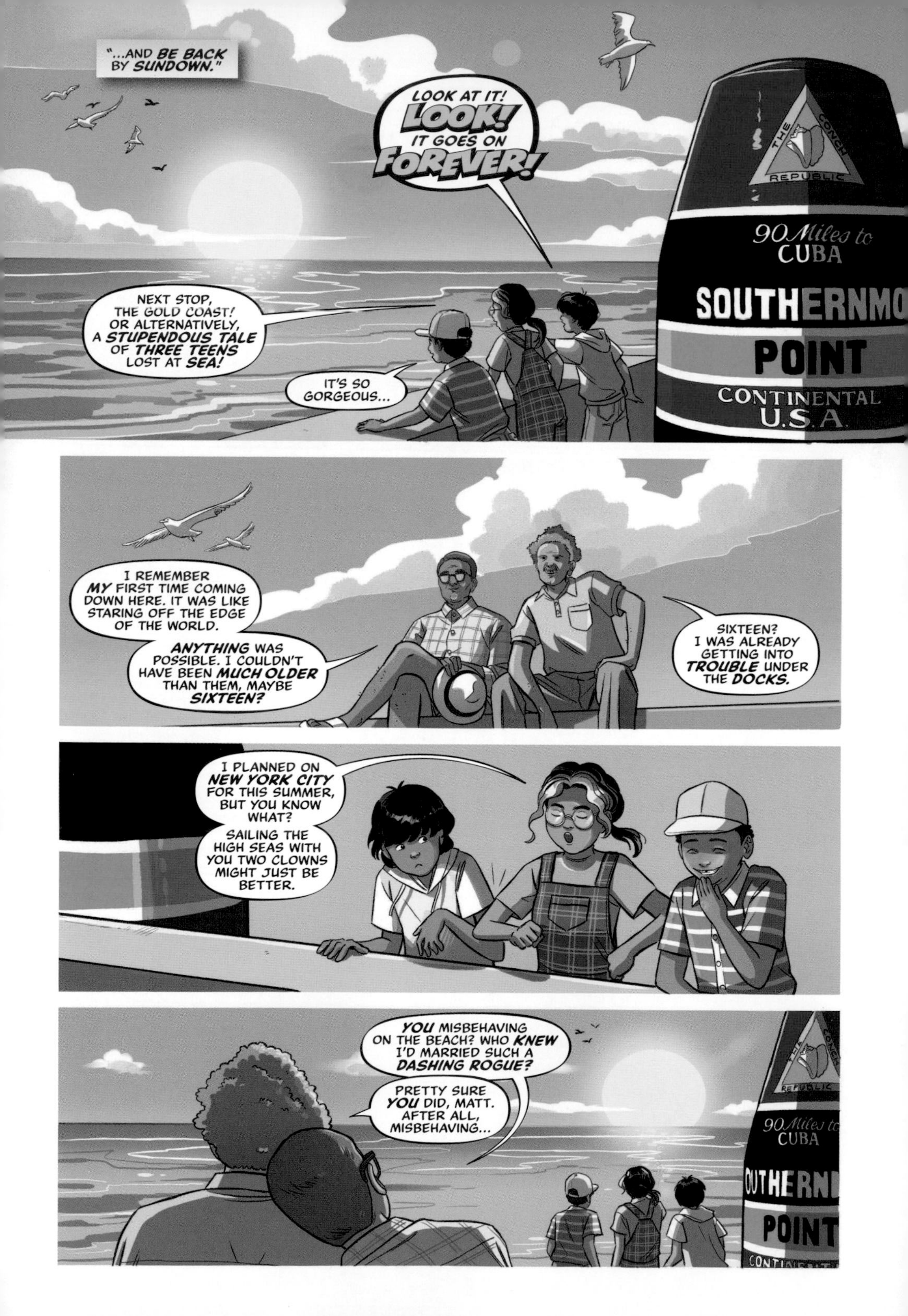
"...AND BE BACK BY SUNDOWN."
LOOK AT IT! LOOK! IT GOES ON FOREVER!
THE CONCH REPUBLIC
90 Miles to CUBA
SOUTHERNMO
POINT
CONTINENTAL U.S.A.
NEXT STOP, THE GOLD COAST! OR ALTERNATIVELY, A STUPENDOUS TALE OF THREE TEENS LOST AT SEA!
IT'S SO GORGEOUS...
I REMEMBER MY FIRST TIME COMING DOWN HERE. IT WAS LIKE STARING OFF THE EDGE OF THE WORLD.
ANYTHING WAS POSSIBLE. I COULDN'T HAVE BEEN MUCH OLDER THAN THEM, MAYBE SIXTEEN?
SIXTEEN? I WAS ALREADY GETTING INTO TROUBLE UNDER THE DOCKS.
I PLANNED ON NEW YORK CITY FOR THIS SUMMER, BUT YOU KNOW WHAT?
SAILING THE HIGH SEAS WITH YOU TWO CLOWNS MIGHT JUST BE BETTER.
YOU MISBEHAVING ON THE BEACH? WHO KNEW I'D MARRIED SUCH A DASHING ROGUE?
PRETTY SURE YOU DID, MATT. AFTER ALL, MISBEHAVING...

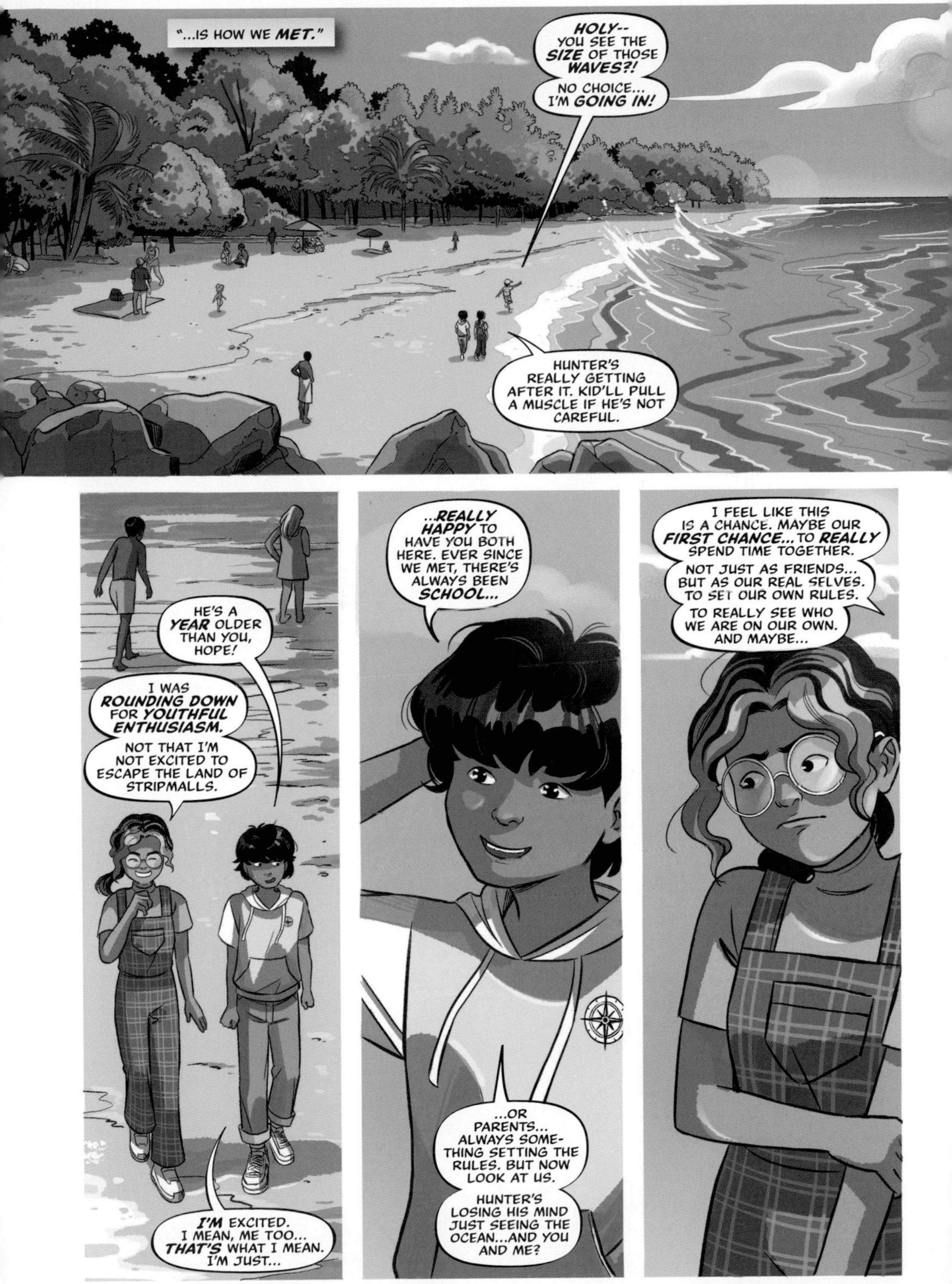
"...IS HOW WE **MET.**"
HOLY-- YOU SEE THE **SIZE** OF THOSE **WAVES?!**
NO CHOICE... I'M **GOING IN!**
HUNTER'S REALLY GETTING AFTER IT. KID'LL PULL A MUSCLE IF HE'S NOT CAREFUL.
HE'S A **YEAR** OLDER THAN YOU, HOPE!
I WAS **ROUNDING DOWN** FOR **YOUTHFUL ENTHUSIASM.**
NOT THAT I'M NOT EXCITED TO ESCAPE THE LAND OF STRIPMALLS.
I'M EXCITED. I MEAN, ME TOO... **THAT'S** WHAT I MEAN. I'M JUST...
...REALLY HAPPY TO HAVE YOU BOTH HERE. EVER SINCE WE MET, THERE'S ALWAYS BEEN **SCHOOL...**
...OR PARENTS... ALWAYS SOME-THING SETTING THE RULES. BUT NOW LOOK AT US.
HUNTER'S LOSING HIS MIND JUST SEEING THE OCEAN...AND YOU AND ME?
I FEEL LIKE THIS IS A CHANCE. MAYBE OUR **FIRST CHANCE...** TO **REALLY** SPEND TIME TOGETHER.
NOT JUST AS FRIENDS... BUT AS OUR REAL SELVES. TO SET OUR OWN RULES.
TO REALLY SEE WHO WE ARE ON OUR OWN. AND MAYBE...

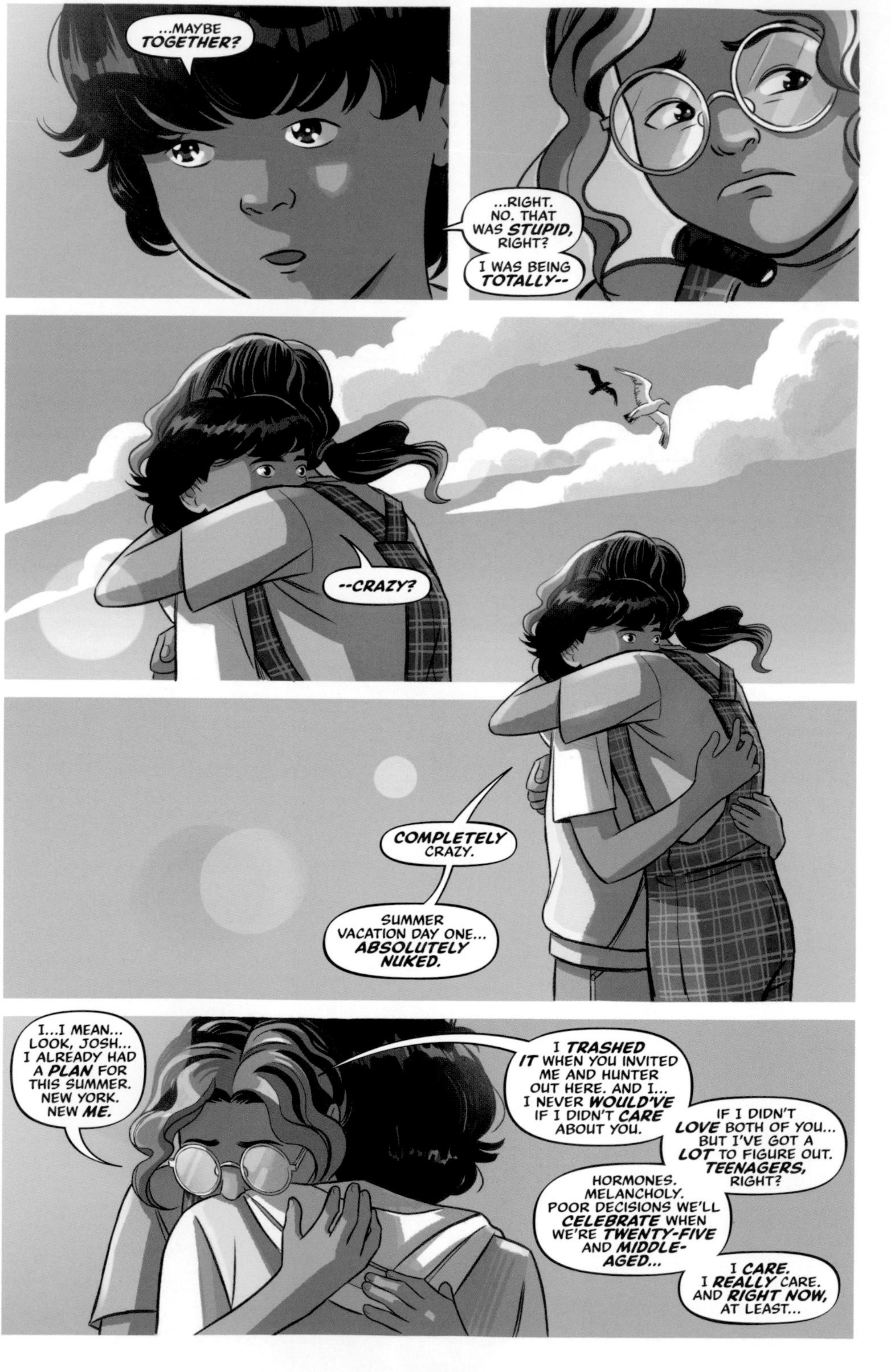
...MAYBE TOGETHER?
...RIGHT. NO. THAT WAS STUPID, RIGHT?
I WAS BEING TOTALLY--
--CRAZY?
COMPLETELY CRAZY.
SUMMER VACATION DAY ONE... ABSOLUTELY NUKED.
I...I MEAN... LOOK, JOSH... I ALREADY HAD A PLAN FOR THIS SUMMER. NEW YORK. NEW ME.
I TRASHED IT WHEN YOU INVITED ME AND HUNTER OUT HERE. AND I... I NEVER WOULD'VE IF I DIDN'T CARE ABOUT YOU.
IF I DIDN'T LOVE BOTH OF YOU... BUT I'VE GOT A LOT TO FIGURE OUT. TEENAGERS, RIGHT?
HORMONES. MELANCHOLY. POOR DECISIONS WE'LL CELEBRATE WHEN WE'RE TWENTY-FIVE AND MIDDLE-AGED...
I CARE. I REALLY CARE. AND RIGHT NOW, AT LEAST...

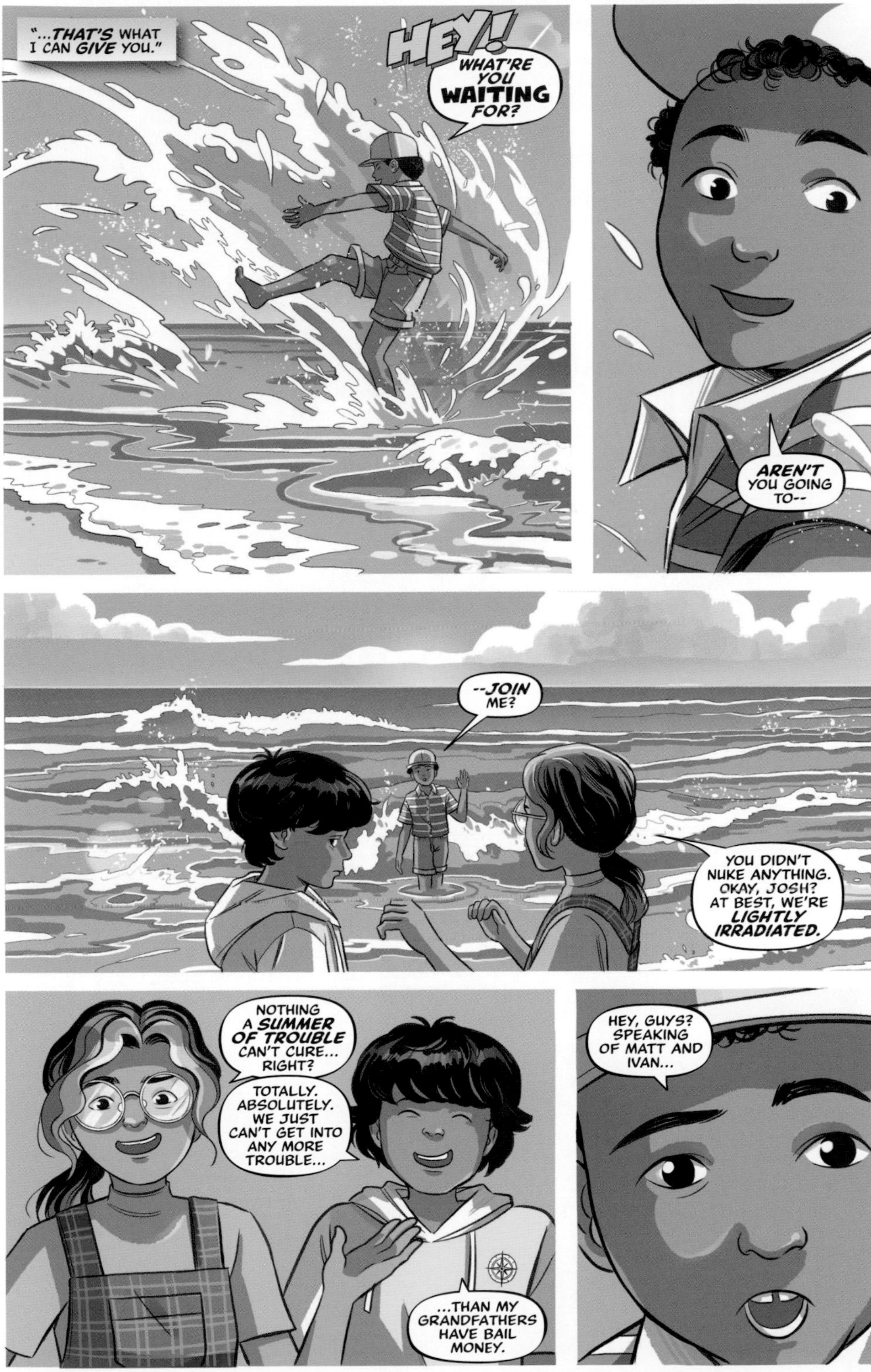
"...THAT'S WHAT I CAN GIVE YOU."
HEY!
WHAT'RE YOU WAITING FOR?
AREN'T YOU GOING TO--
--JOIN ME?
YOU DIDN'T NUKE ANYTHING. OKAY, JOSH? AT BEST, WE'RE LIGHTLY IRRADIATED.
NOTHING A SUMMER OF TROUBLE CAN'T CURE... RIGHT?
TOTALLY. ABSOLUTELY. WE JUST CAN'T GET INTO ANY MORE TROUBLE...
...THAN MY GRANDFATHERS HAVE BAIL MONEY.
HEY, GUYS? SPEAKING OF MATT AND IVAN...

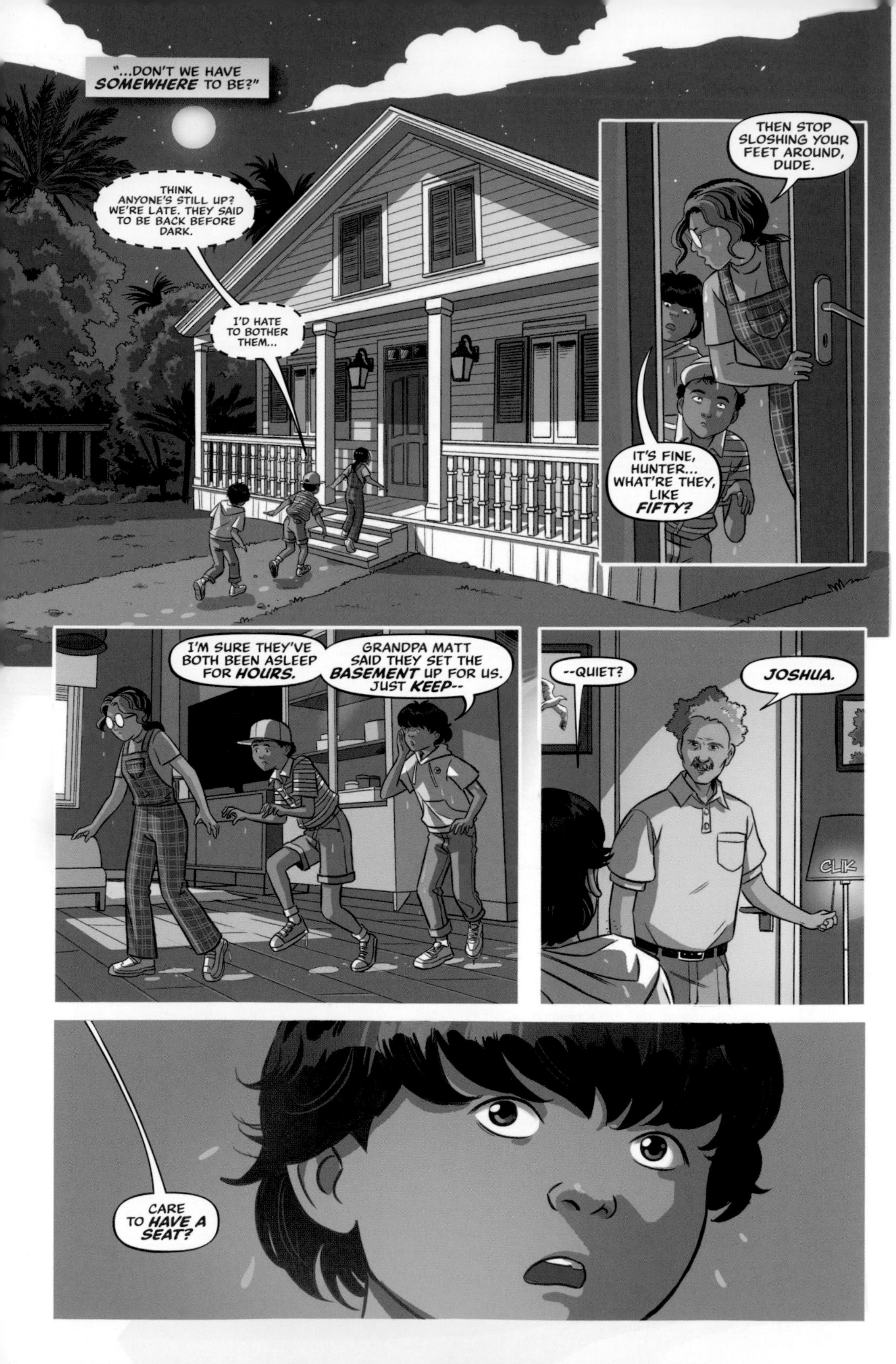
"...DON'T WE HAVE SOMEWHERE TO BE?"
THINK ANYONE'S STILL UP? WE'RE LATE. THEY SAID TO BE BACK BEFORE DARK.
I'D HATE TO BOTHER THEM...
THEN STOP SLOSHING YOUR FEET AROUND, DUDE.
IT'S FINE, HUNTER... WHAT'RE THEY, LIKE FIFTY?
I'M SURE THEY'VE BOTH BEEN ASLEEP FOR HOURS.
GRANDPA MATT SAID THEY SET THE BASEMENT UP FOR US. JUST KEEP--
--QUIET?
JOSHUA.
CLIK
CARE TO HAVE A SEAT?

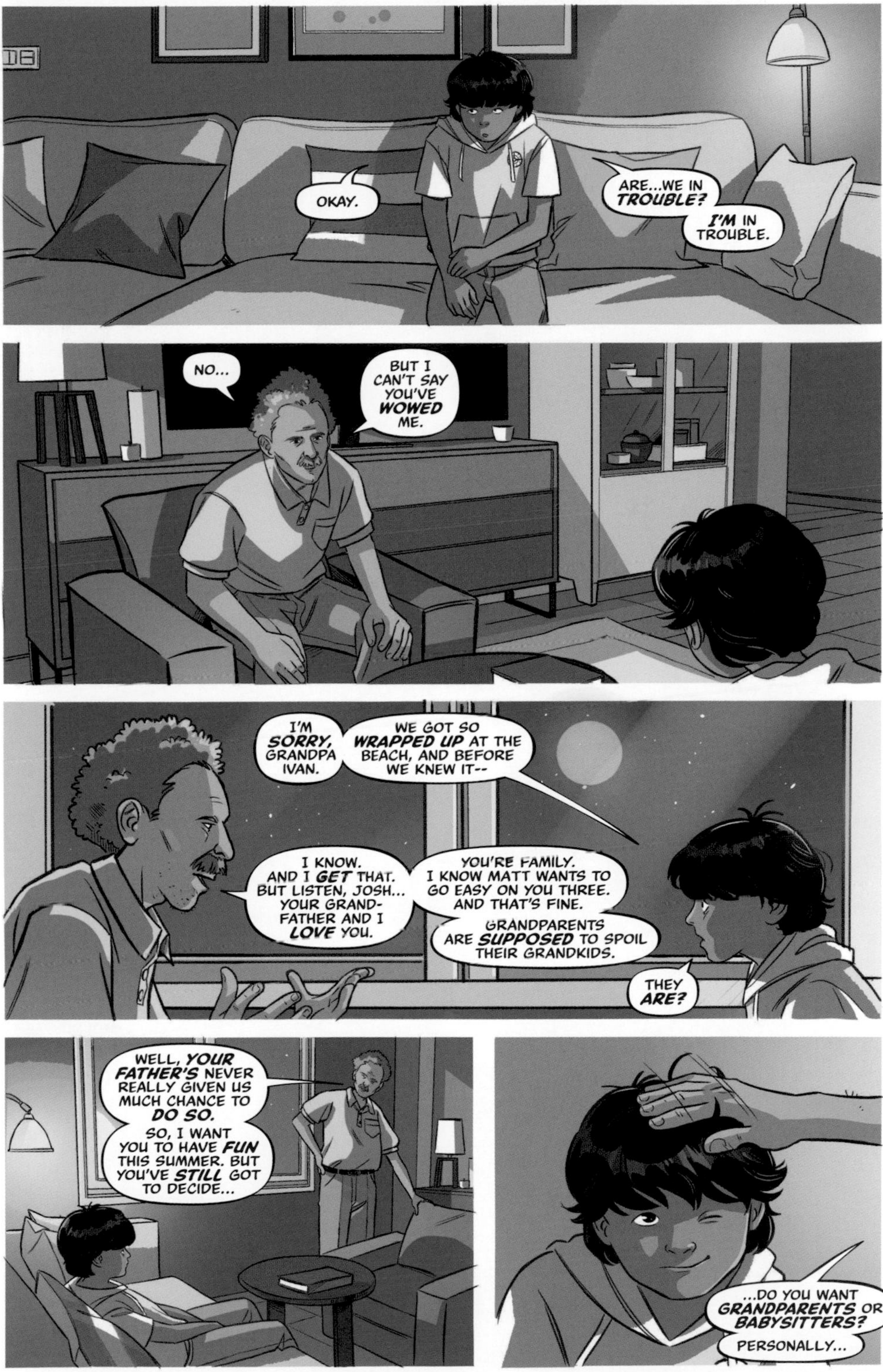
OKAY.
ARE...WE IN TROUBLE?
I'M IN TROUBLE.
NO...
BUT I CAN'T SAY YOU'VE WOWED ME.
I'M SORRY, GRANDPA IVAN.
WE GOT SO WRAPPED UP AT THE BEACH, AND BEFORE WE KNEW IT--
I KNOW. AND I GET THAT. BUT LISTEN, JOSH... YOUR GRANDFATHER AND I LOVE YOU.
YOU'RE FAMILY. I KNOW MATT WANTS TO GO EASY ON YOU THREE. AND THAT'S FINE.
GRANDPARENTS ARE SUPPOSED TO SPOIL THEIR GRANDKIDS.
THEY ARE?
WELL, YOUR FATHER'S NEVER REALLY GIVEN US MUCH CHANCE TO DO SO.
SO, I WANT YOU TO HAVE FUN THIS SUMMER. BUT YOU'VE STILL GOT TO DECIDE...
...DO YOU WANT GRANDPARENTS OR BABYSITTERS?
PERSONALLY...

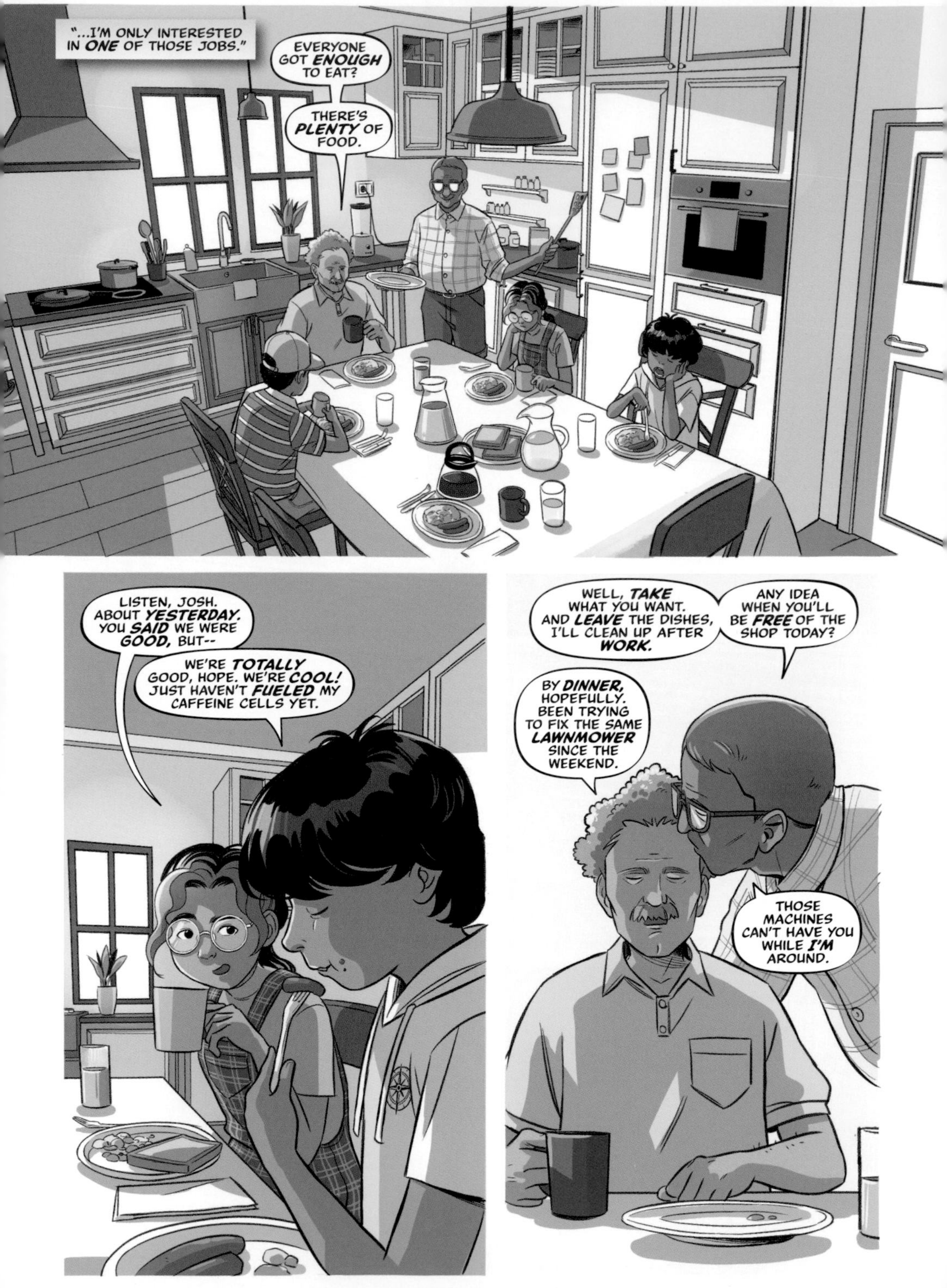
"...I'M ONLY INTERESTED IN ONE OF THOSE JOBS."
EVERYONE GOT ENOUGH TO EAT?
THERE'S PLENTY OF FOOD.
LISTEN, JOSH. ABOUT YESTERDAY. YOU SAID WE WERE GOOD, BUT--
WE'RE TOTALLY GOOD, HOPE. WE'RE COOL! JUST HAVEN'T FUELED MY CAFFEINE CELLS YET.
WELL, TAKE WHAT YOU WANT. AND LEAVE THE DISHES, I'LL CLEAN UP AFTER WORK.
ANY IDEA WHEN YOU'LL BE FREE OF THE SHOP TODAY?
BY DINNER, HOPEFULLY. BEEN TRYING TO FIX THE SAME LAWNMOWER SINCE THE WEEKEND.
THOSE MACHINES CAN'T HAVE YOU WHILE I'M AROUND.

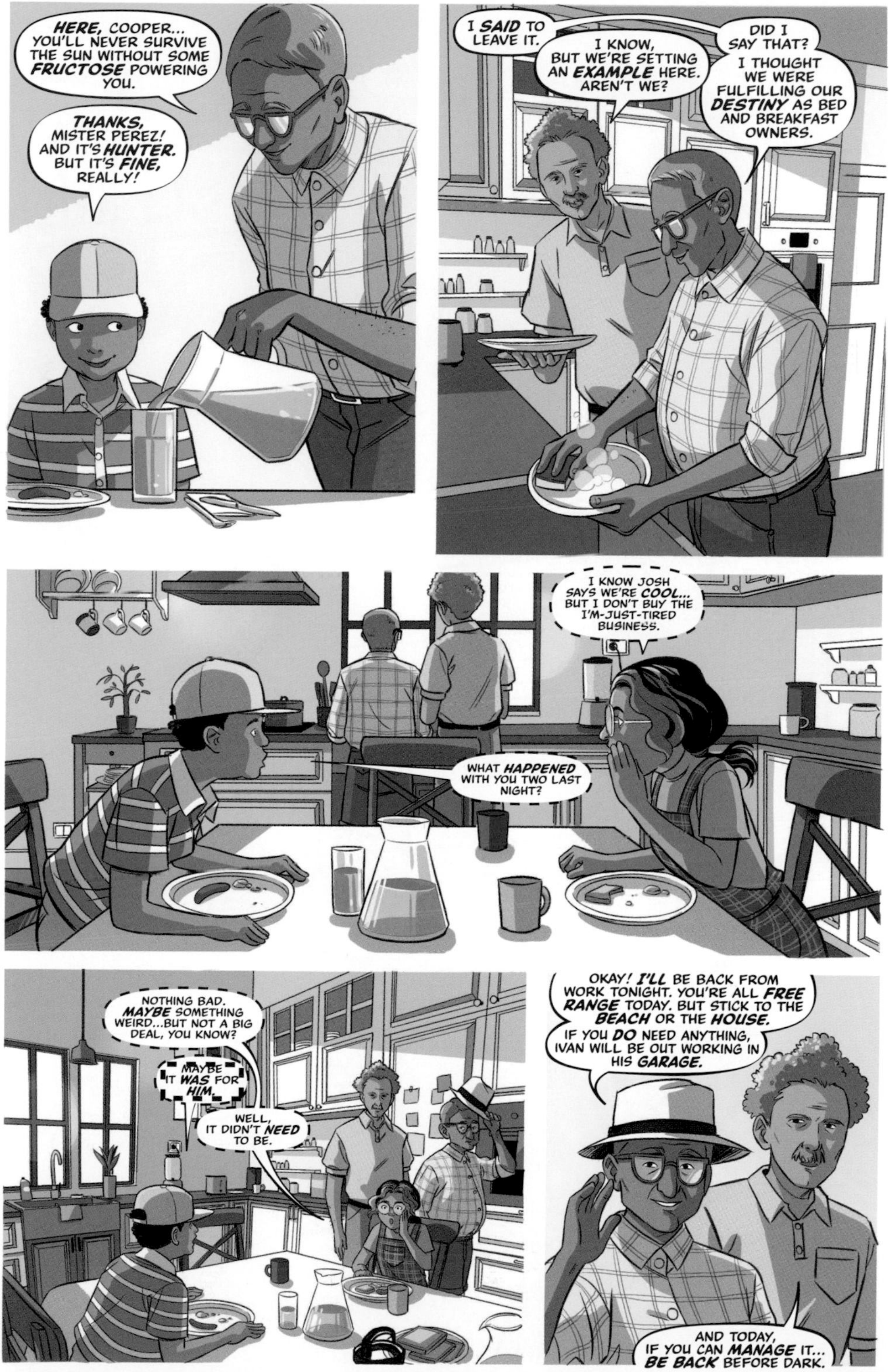

HERE, COOPER... YOU'LL NEVER SURVIVE THE SUN WITHOUT SOME FRUCTOSE POWERING YOU.
THANKS, MISTER PEREZ! AND IT'S HUNTER. BUT IT'S FINE, REALLY!
I SAID TO LEAVE IT.
I KNOW, BUT WE'RE SETTING AN EXAMPLE HERE. AREN'T WE?
DID I SAY THAT? I THOUGHT WE WERE FULFILLING OUR DESTINY AS BED AND BREAKFAST OWNERS.
I KNOW JOSH SAYS WE'RE COOL... BUT I DON'T BUY THE I'M-JUST-TIRED BUSINESS.
WHAT HAPPENED WITH YOU TWO LAST NIGHT?
NOTHING BAD. MAYBE SOMETHING WEIRD...BUT NOT A BIG DEAL, YOU KNOW?
MAYBE IT WAS FOR HIM.
WELL, IT DIDN'T NEED TO BE.
OKAY! I'LL BE BACK FROM WORK TONIGHT. YOU'RE ALL FREE RANGE TODAY. BUT STICK TO THE BEACH OR THE HOUSE.
IF YOU DO NEED ANYTHING, IVAN WILL BE OUT WORKING IN HIS GARAGE.
AND TODAY, IF YOU CAN MANAGE IT... BE BACK BEFORE DARK.

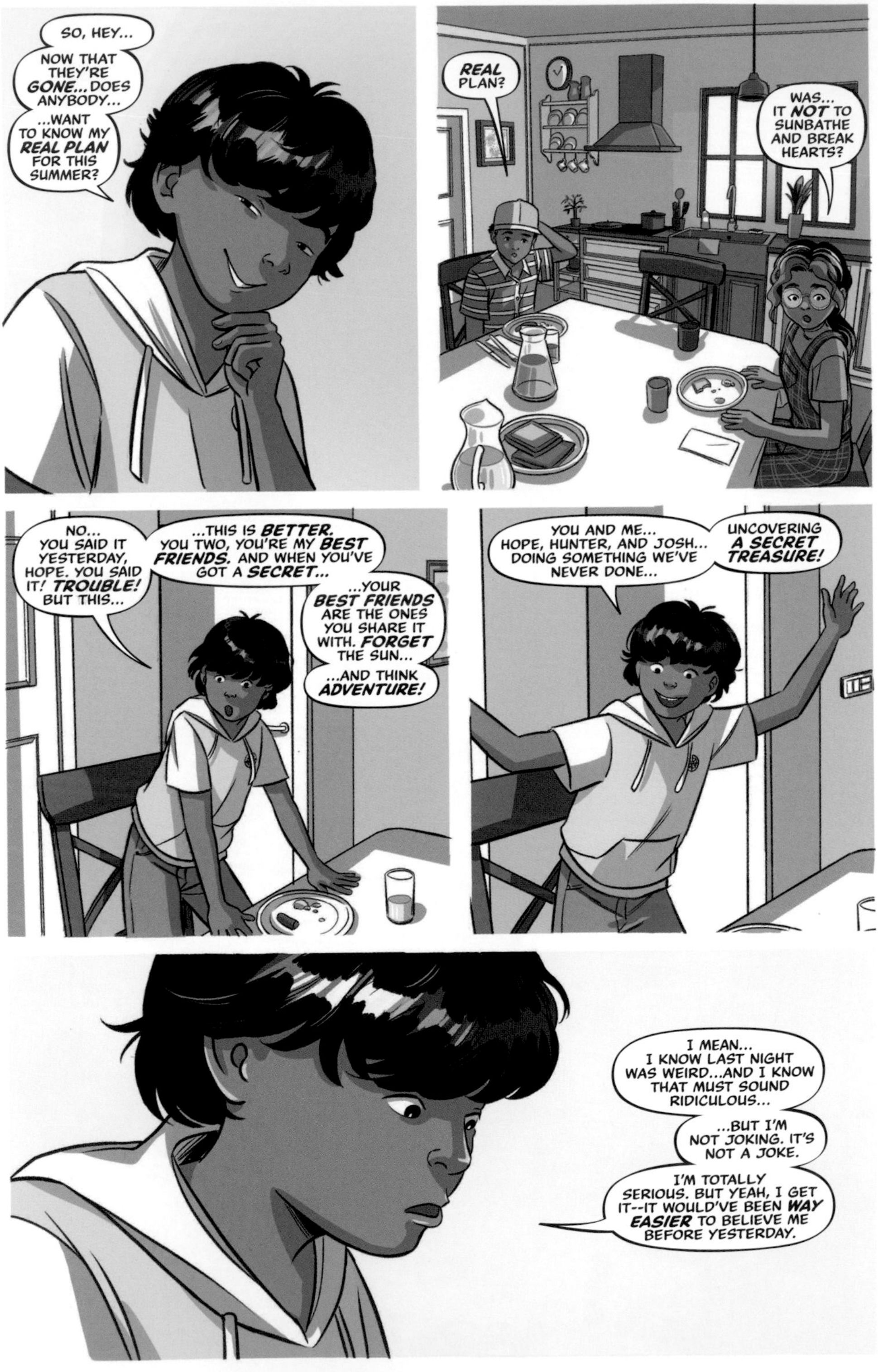
SO, HEY...
NOW THAT THEY'RE GONE... DOES ANYBODY...
...WANT TO KNOW MY REAL PLAN FOR THIS SUMMER?
REAL PLAN?
WAS... IT NOT TO SUNBATHE AND BREAK HEARTS?
NO... YOU SAID IT YESTERDAY, HOPE. YOU SAID IT! TROUBLE! BUT THIS...
...THIS IS BETTER. YOU TWO, YOU'RE MY BEST FRIENDS. AND WHEN YOU'VE GOT A SECRET...
...YOUR BEST FRIENDS ARE THE ONES YOU SHARE IT WITH. FORGET THE SUN...
...AND THINK ADVENTURE!
YOU AND ME... HOPE, HUNTER, AND JOSH... DOING SOMETHING WE'VE NEVER DONE...
UNCOVERING A SECRET TREASURE!
I MEAN... I KNOW LAST NIGHT WAS WEIRD...AND I KNOW THAT MUST SOUND RIDICULOUS...
...BUT I'M NOT JOKING. IT'S NOT A JOKE.
I'M TOTALLY SERIOUS. BUT YEAH, I GET IT--IT WOULD'VE BEEN WAY EASIER TO BELIEVE ME BEFORE YESTERDAY.

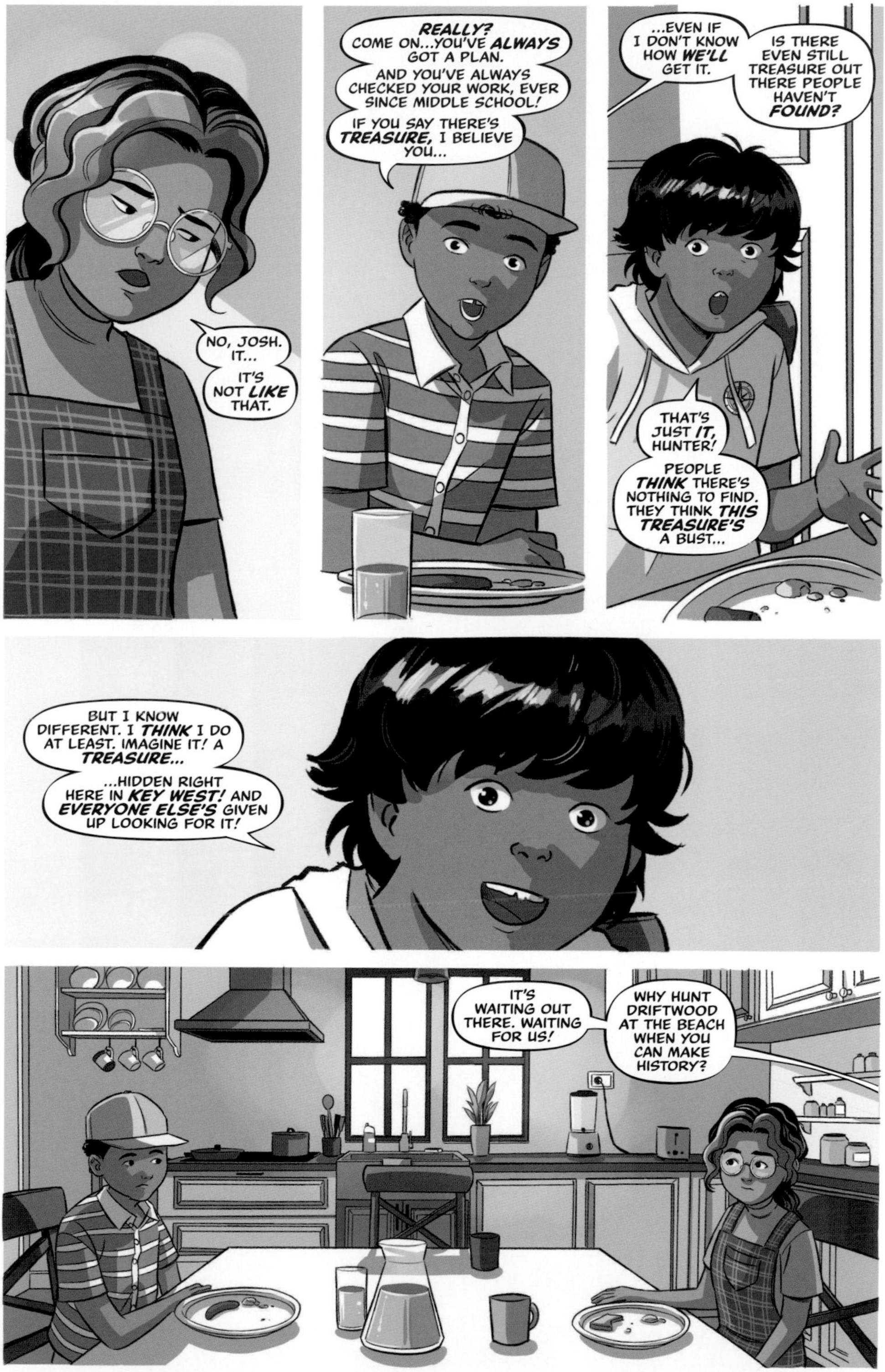
NO, JOSH. IT...
IT'S NOT LIKE THAT.
REALLY? COME ON...YOU'VE ALWAYS GOT A PLAN.
AND YOU'VE ALWAYS CHECKED YOUR WORK, EVER SINCE MIDDLE SCHOOL!
IF YOU SAY THERE'S TREASURE, I BELIEVE YOU...
...EVEN IF I DON'T KNOW HOW WE'LL GET IT.
IS THERE EVEN STILL TREASURE OUT THERE PEOPLE HAVEN'T FOUND?
THAT'S JUST IT, HUNTER!
PEOPLE THINK THERE'S NOTHING TO FIND. THEY THINK THIS TREASURE'S A BUST...
BUT I KNOW DIFFERENT. I THINK I DO AT LEAST. IMAGINE IT! A TREASURE...
...HIDDEN RIGHT HERE IN KEY WEST! AND EVERYONE ELSE'S GIVEN UP LOOKING FOR IT!
IT'S WAITING OUT THERE. WAITING FOR US!
WHY HUNT DRIFTWOOD AT THE BEACH WHEN YOU CAN MAKE HISTORY?

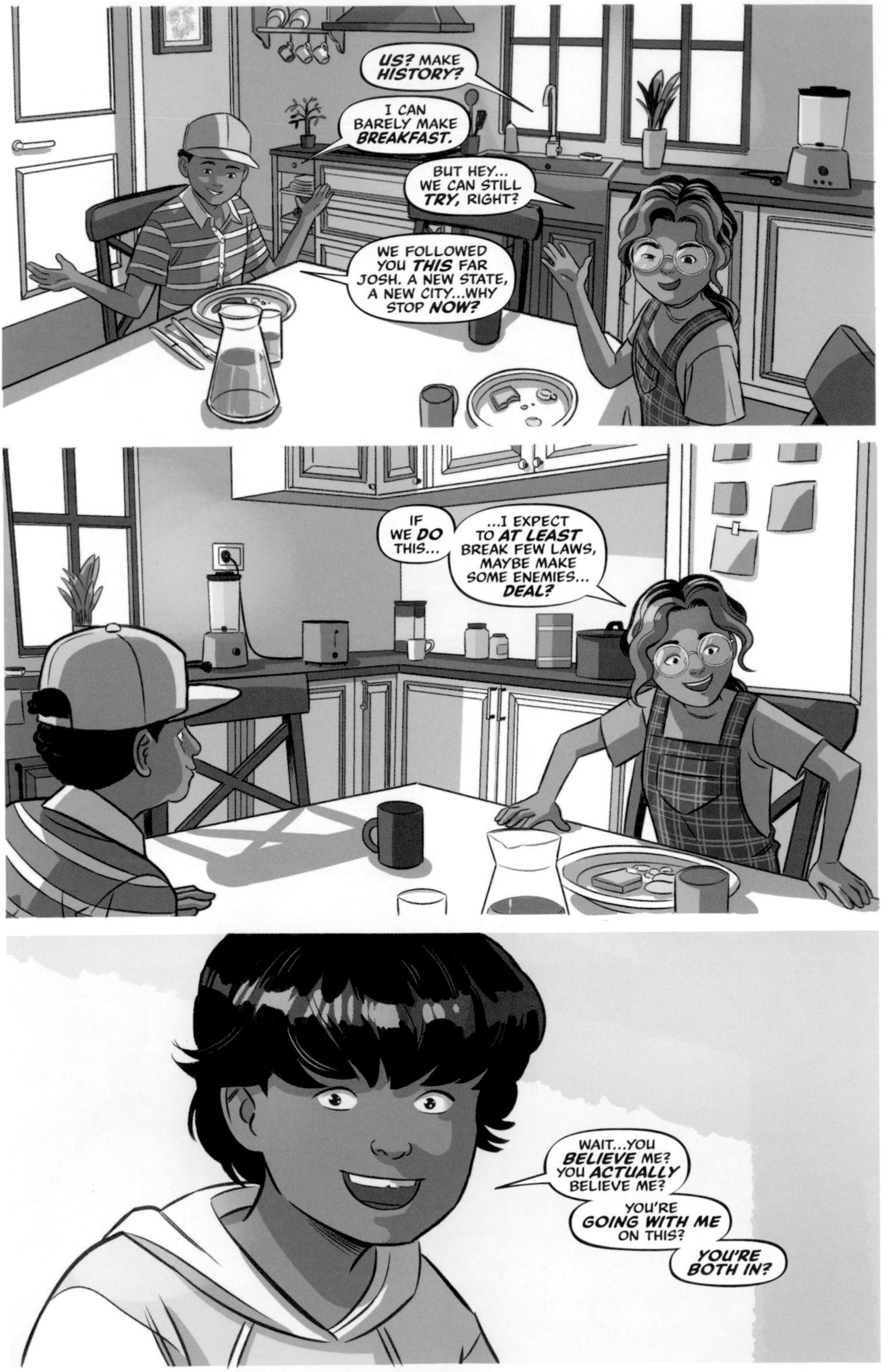
US? MAKE HISTORY?
I CAN BARELY MAKE BREAKFAST.
BUT HEY... WE CAN STILL TRY, RIGHT?
WE FOLLOWED YOU THIS FAR JOSH. A NEW STATE, A NEW CITY...WHY STOP NOW?
IF WE DO THIS...
...I EXPECT TO AT LEAST BREAK FEW LAWS, MAYBE MAKE SOME ENEMIES... DEAL?
WAIT...YOU BELIEVE ME? YOU ACTUALLY BELIEVE ME?
YOU'RE GOING WITH ME ON THIS?
YOU'RE BOTH IN?

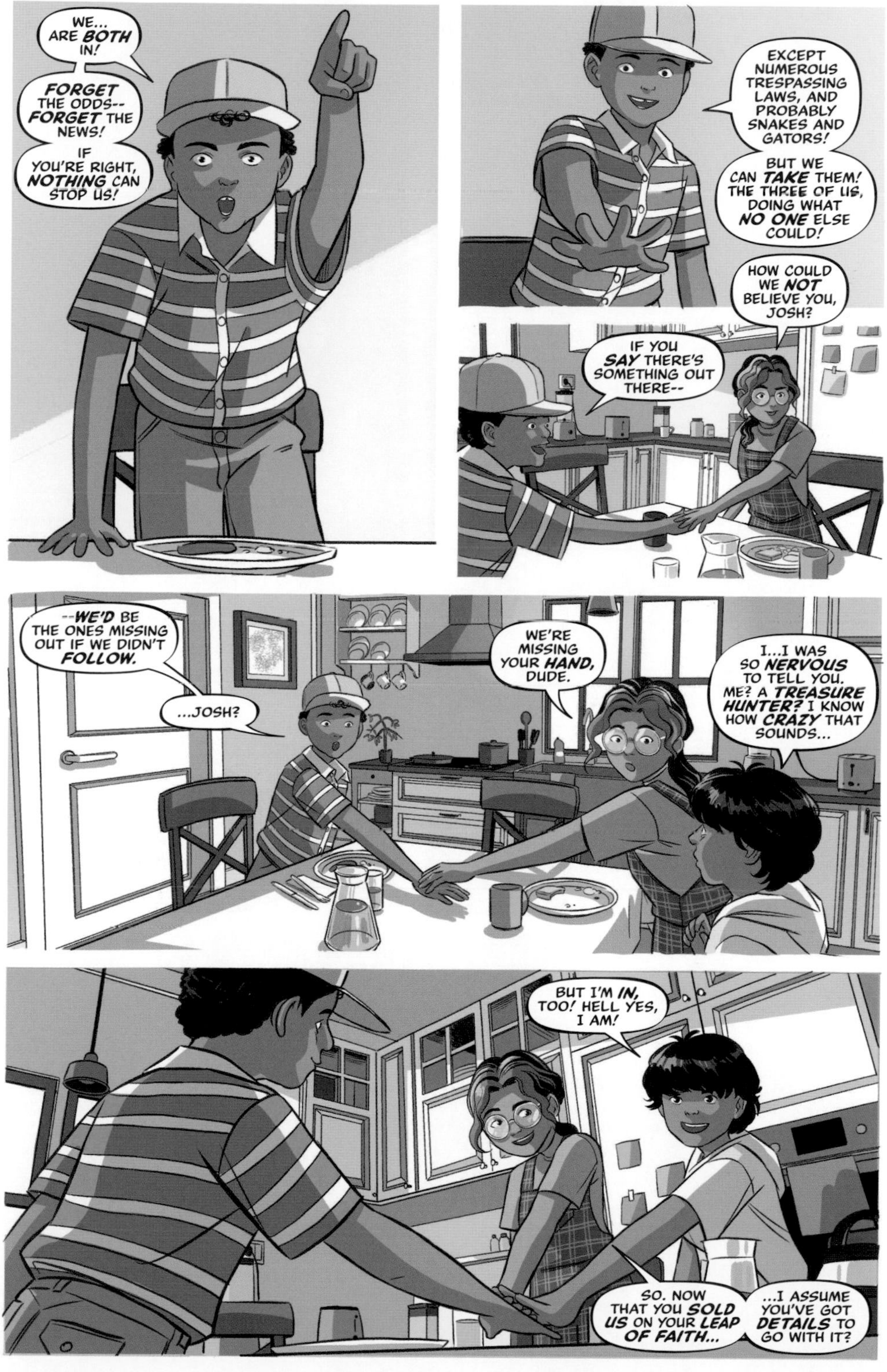
WE... ARE BOTH IN!
FORGET THE ODDS-- FORGET THE NEWS!
IF YOU'RE RIGHT, NOTHING CAN STOP US!
EXCEPT NUMEROUS TRESPASSING LAWS, AND PROBABLY SNAKES AND GATORS!
BUT WE CAN TAKE THEM! THE THREE OF US, DOING WHAT NO ONE ELSE COULD!
HOW COULD WE NOT BELIEVE YOU, JOSH?
IF YOU SAY THERE'S SOMETHING OUT THERE--
--WE'D BE THE ONES MISSING OUT IF WE DIDN'T FOLLOW.
...JOSH?
WE'RE MISSING YOUR HAND, DUDE.
I...I WAS SO NERVOUS TO TELL YOU. ME? A TREASURE HUNTER? I KNOW HOW CRAZY THAT SOUNDS...
BUT I'M IN, TOO! HELL YES, I AM!
SO. NOW THAT YOU SOLD US ON YOUR LEAP OF FAITH...
...I ASSUME YOU'VE GOT DETAILS TO GO WITH IT?

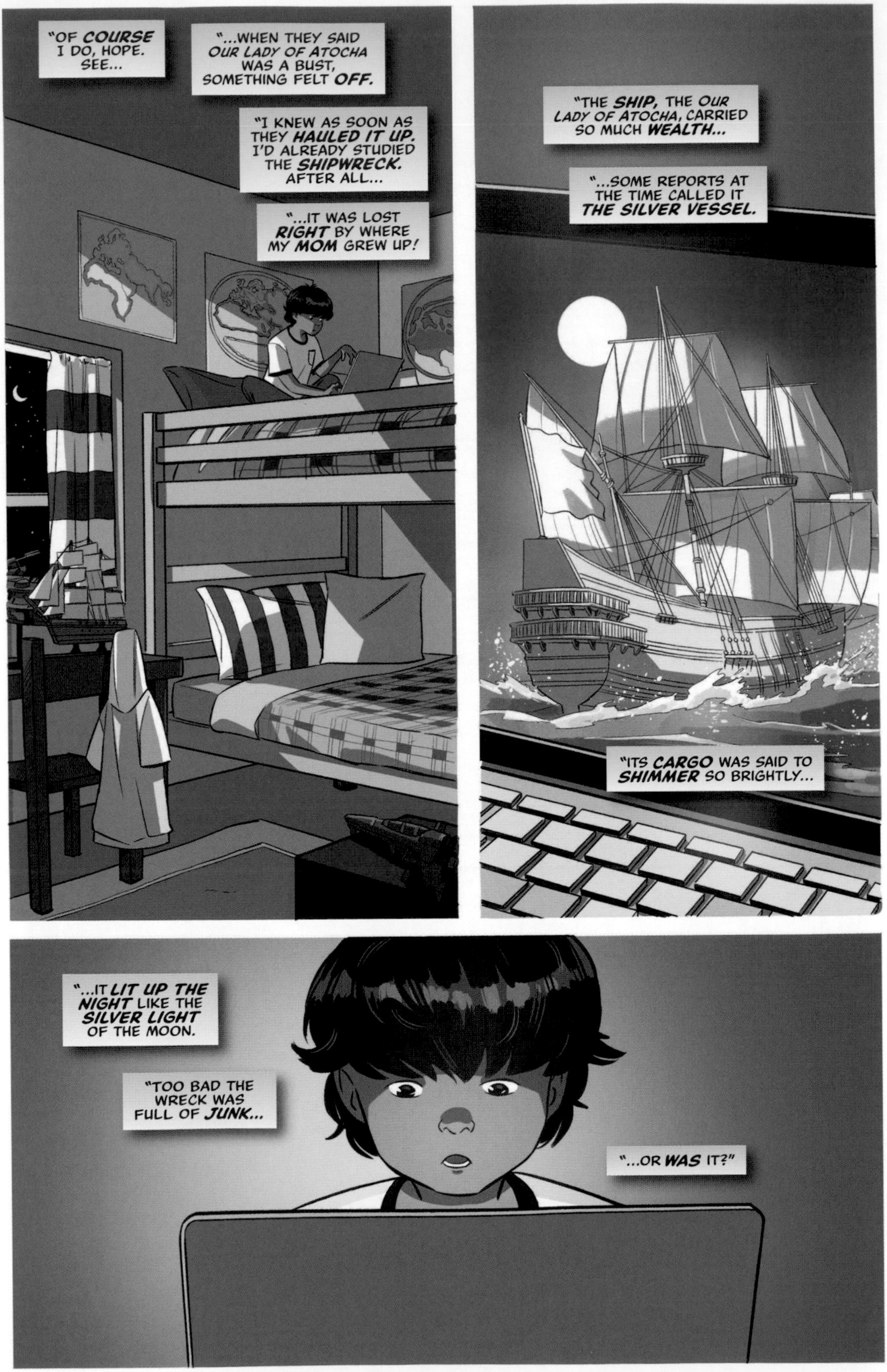
"OF COURSE I DO, HOPE. SEE...
"...WHEN THEY SAID OUR LADY OF ATOCHA WAS A BUST, SOMETHING FELT OFF.
"I KNEW AS SOON AS THEY HAULED IT UP. I'D ALREADY STUDIED THE SHIPWRECK. AFTER ALL...
"...IT WAS LOST RIGHT BY WHERE MY MOM GREW UP!
"THE SHIP, THE OUR LADY OF ATOCHA, CARRIED SO MUCH WEALTH...
"...SOME REPORTS AT THE TIME CALLED IT THE SILVER VESSEL.
"ITS CARGO WAS SAID TO SHIMMER SO BRIGHTLY...
"...IT LIT UP THE NIGHT LIKE THE SILVER LIGHT OF THE MOON.
"TOO BAD THE WRECK WAS FULL OF JUNK...
"...OR WAS IT?"

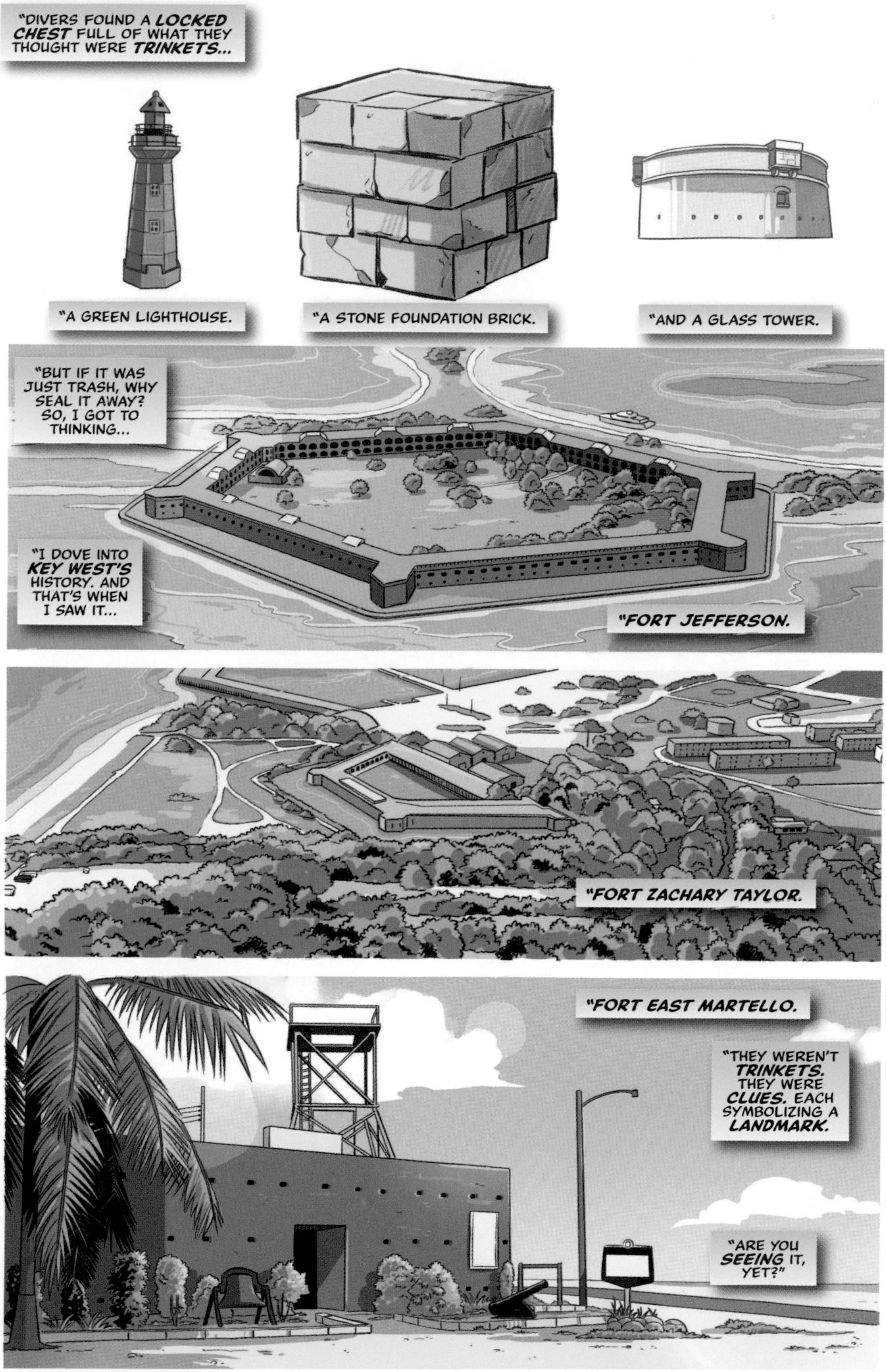

"DIVERS FOUND A **LOCKED CHEST** FULL OF WHAT THEY THOUGHT WERE **TRINKETS...**
"A GREEN LIGHTHOUSE.
"A STONE FOUNDATION BRICK.
"AND A GLASS TOWER.
"BUT IF IT WAS JUST TRASH, WHY SEAL IT AWAY? SO, I GOT TO THINKING...
"I DOVE INTO **KEY WEST'S** HISTORY. AND THAT'S WHEN I SAW IT...
"FORT JEFFERSON.
"FORT ZACHARY TAYLOR.
"FORT EAST MARTELLO.
"THEY WEREN'T **TRINKETS.** THEY WERE **CLUES.** EACH SYMBOLIZING A **LANDMARK.**
"ARE YOU **SEEING** IT, YET?"

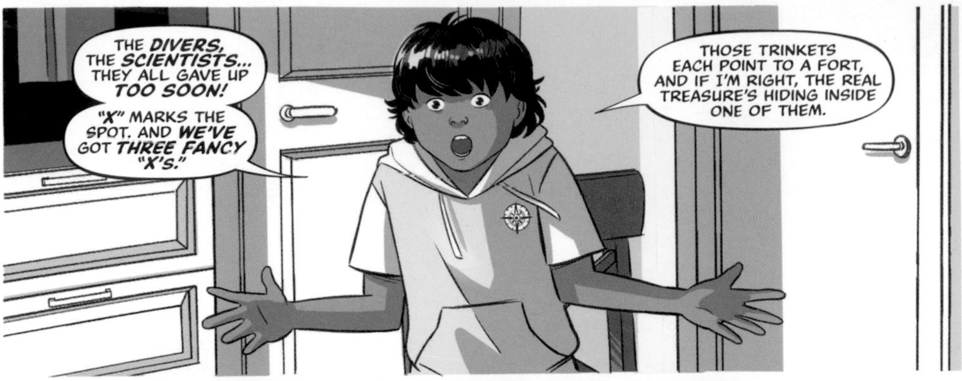
THE DIVERS, THE SCIENTISTS... THEY ALL GAVE UP TOO SOON!
"X" MARKS THE SPOT. AND WE'VE GOT THREE FANCY "X'S."
THOSE TRINKETS EACH POINT TO A FORT, AND IF I'M RIGHT, THE REAL TREASURE'S HIDING INSIDE ONE OF THEM.

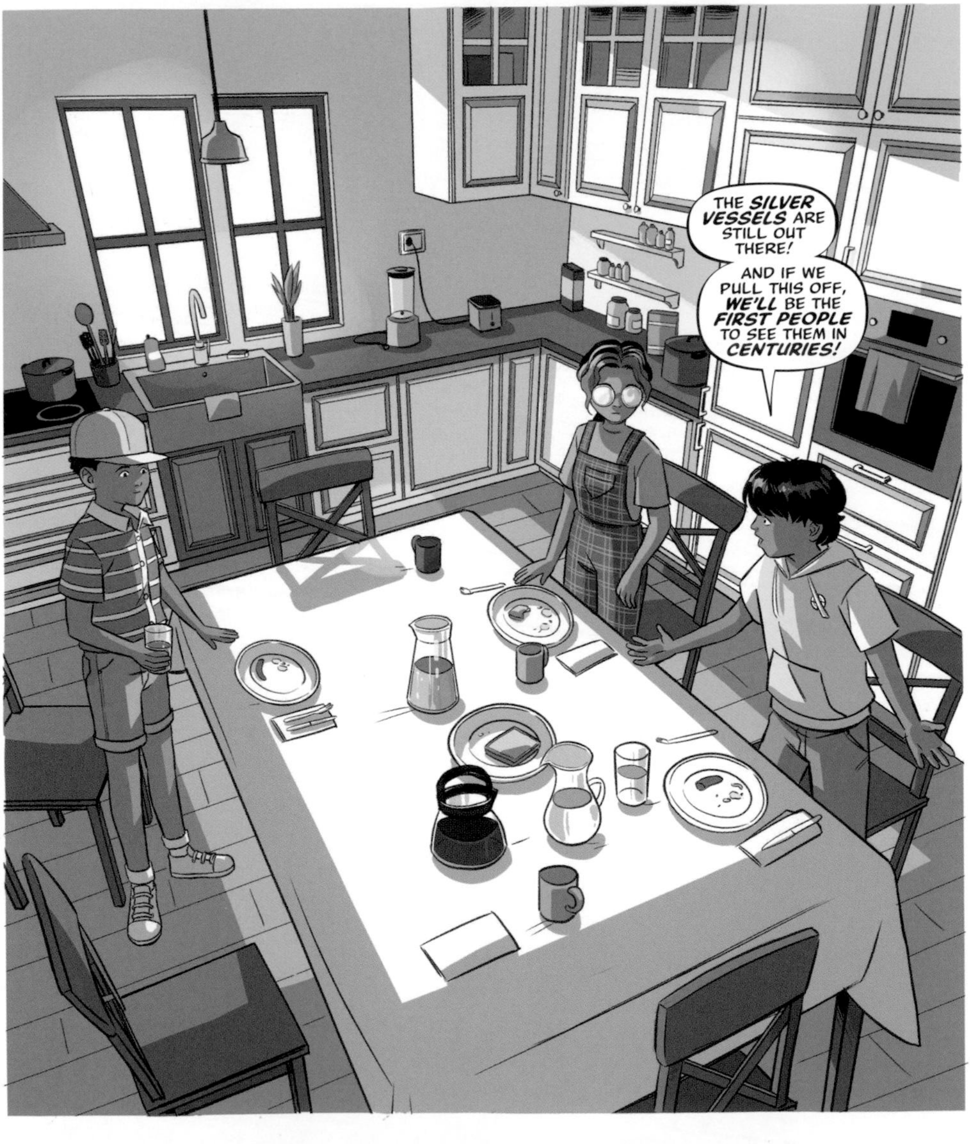
THE SILVER VESSELS ARE STILL OUT THERE!
AND IF WE PULL THIS OFF, WE'LL BE THE FIRST PEOPLE TO SEE THEM IN CENTURIES!

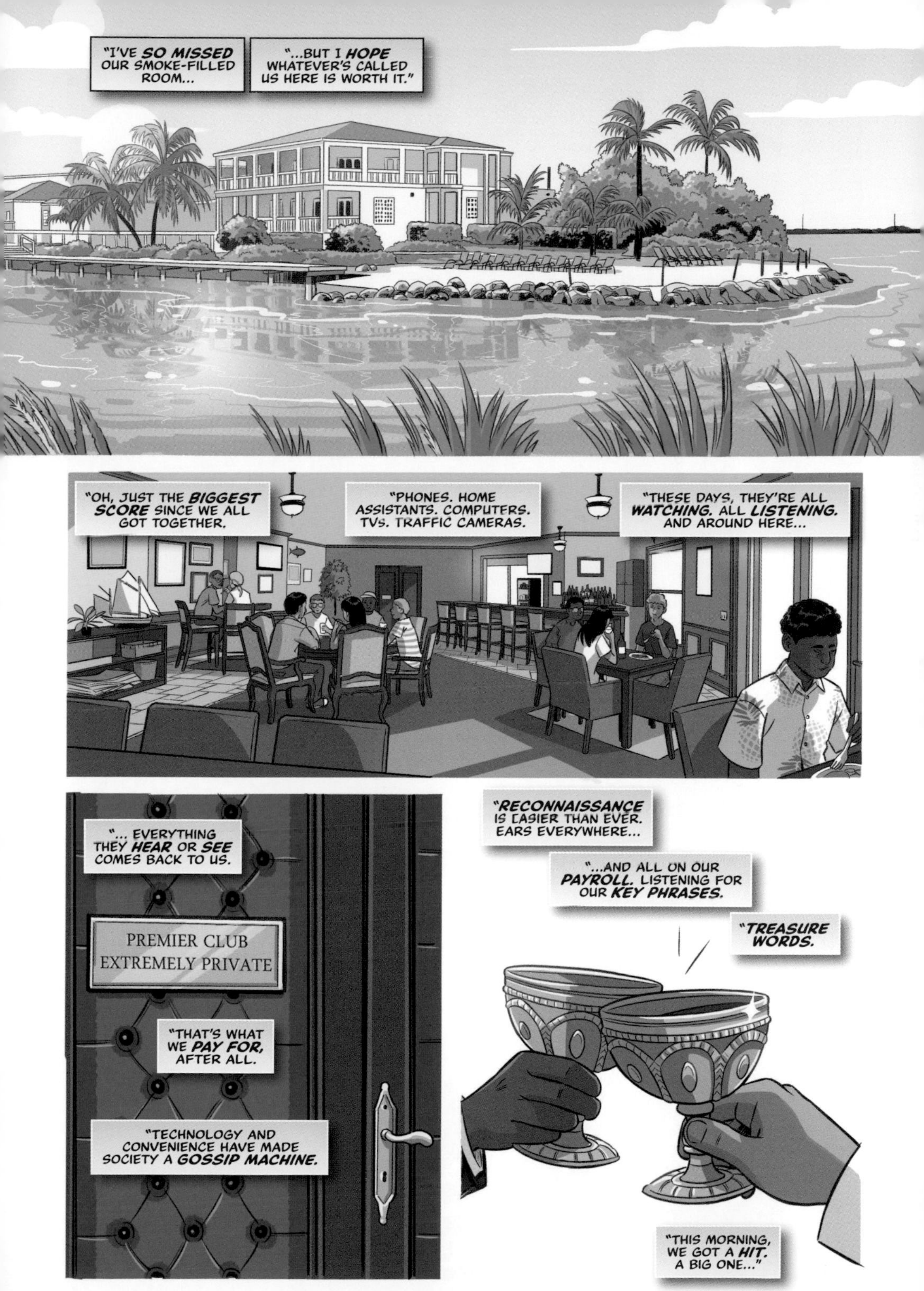
"I'VE SO MISSED OUR SMOKE-FILLED ROOM...
"...BUT I HOPE WHATEVER'S CALLED US HERE IS WORTH IT."
"OH, JUST THE BIGGEST SCORE SINCE WE ALL GOT TOGETHER.
"PHONES. HOME ASSISTANTS. COMPUTERS. TVS. TRAFFIC CAMERAS.
"THESE DAYS, THEY'RE ALL WATCHING. ALL LISTENING. AND AROUND HERE...
"... EVERYTHING THEY HEAR OR SEE COMES BACK TO US.
PREMIER CLUB EXTREMELY PRIVATE
"THAT'S WHAT WE PAY FOR, AFTER ALL.
"TECHNOLOGY AND CONVENIENCE HAVE MADE SOCIETY A GOSSIP MACHINE.
"RECONNAISSANCE IS EASIER THAN EVER. EARS EVERYWHERE...
"...AND ALL ON OUR PAYROLL. LISTENING FOR OUR KEY PHRASES.
"TREASURE WORDS.
"THIS MORNING, WE GOT A HIT. A BIG ONE..."

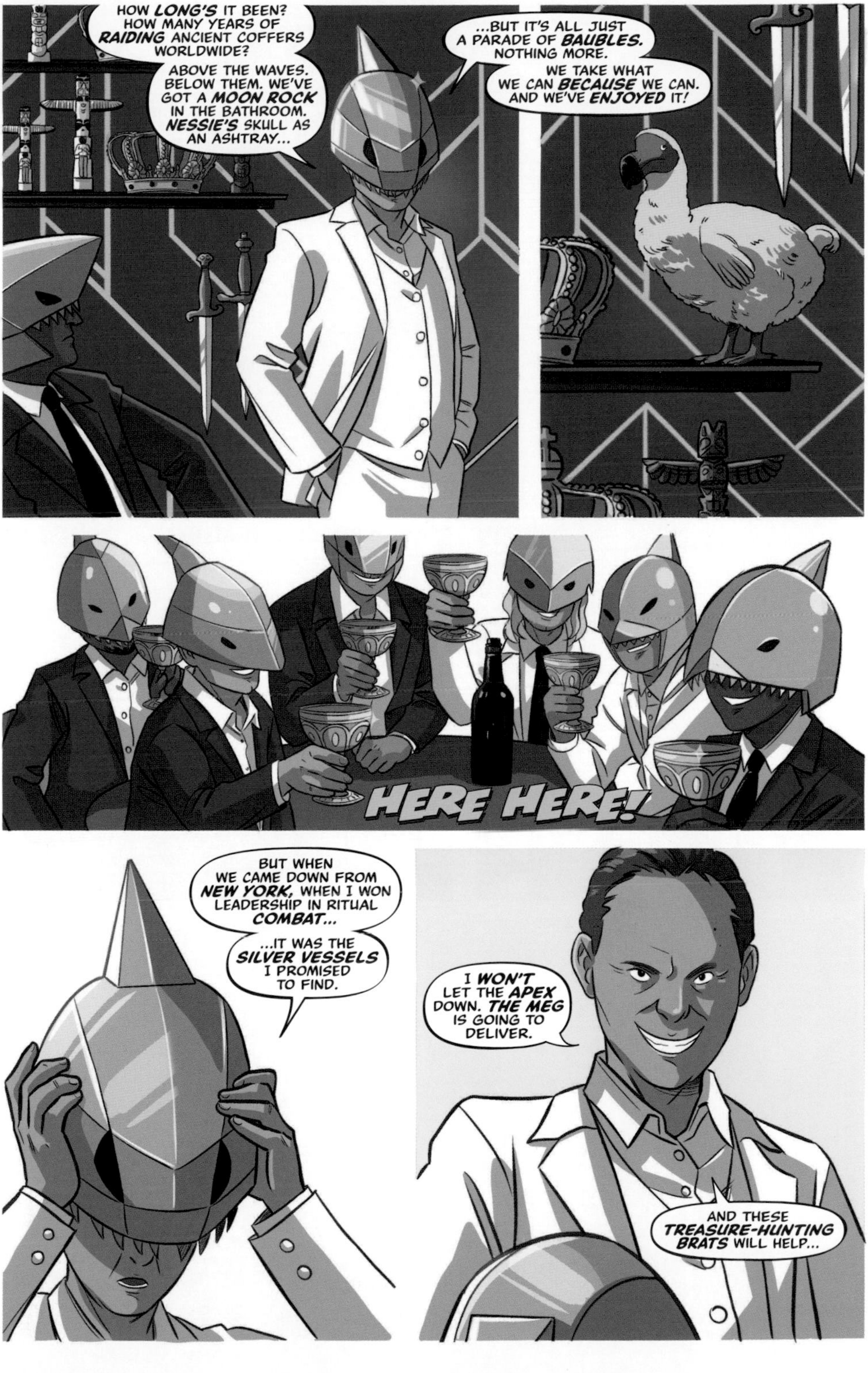

HOW LONG'S IT BEEN? HOW MANY YEARS OF RAIDING ANCIENT COFFERS WORLDWIDE?
ABOVE THE WAVES. BELOW THEM. WE'VE GOT A MOON ROCK IN THE BATHROOM. NESSIE'S SKULL AS AN ASHTRAY...
...BUT IT'S ALL JUST A PARADE OF BAUBLES. NOTHING MORE.
WE TAKE WHAT WE CAN BECAUSE WE CAN. AND WE'VE ENJOYED IT!
HERE HERE!
BUT WHEN WE CAME DOWN FROM NEW YORK, WHEN I WON LEADERSHIP IN RITUAL COMBAT...
...IT WAS THE SILVER VESSELS I PROMISED TO FIND.
I WON'T LET THE APEX DOWN. THE MEG IS GOING TO DELIVER.
AND THESE TREASURE-HUNTING BRATS WILL HELP...

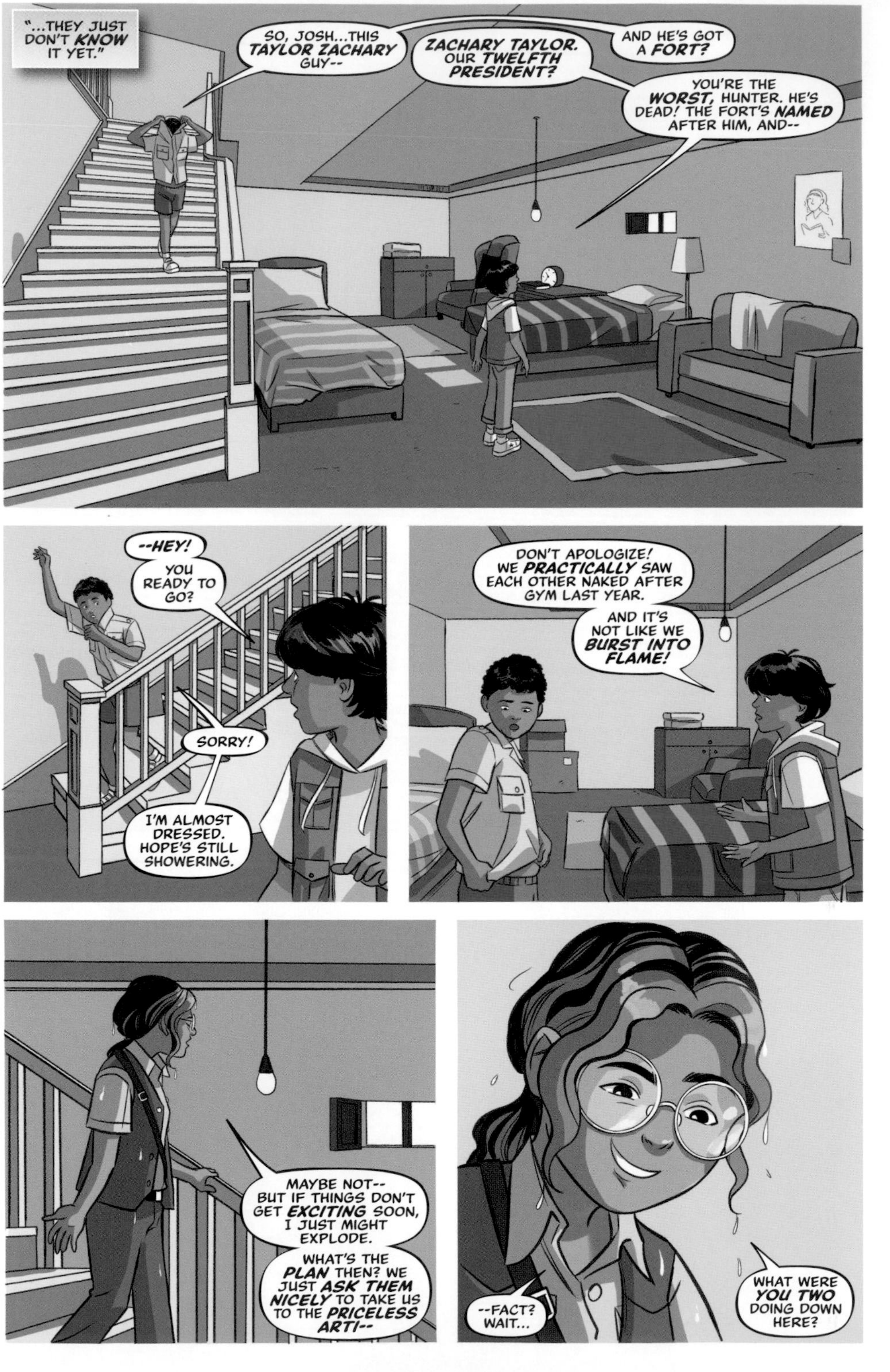
"...THEY JUST DON'T KNOW IT YET."
SO, JOSH...THIS TAYLOR ZACHARY GUY--
ZACHARY TAYLOR. OUR TWELFTH PRESIDENT?
AND HE'S GOT A FORT?
YOU'RE THE WORST, HUNTER. HE'S DEAD! THE FORT'S NAMED AFTER HIM, AND--
--HEY!
YOU READY TO GO?
SORRY!
I'M ALMOST DRESSED. HOPE'S STILL SHOWERING.
DON'T APOLOGIZE! WE PRACTICALLY SAW EACH OTHER NAKED AFTER GYM LAST YEAR.
AND IT'S NOT LIKE WE BURST INTO FLAME!
MAYBE NOT-- BUT IF THINGS DON'T GET EXCITING SOON, I JUST MIGHT EXPLODE.
WHAT'S THE PLAN THEN? WE JUST ASK THEM NICELY TO TAKE US TO THE PRICELESS ARTI--
--FACT? WAIT...
WHAT WERE YOU TWO DOING DOWN HERE?

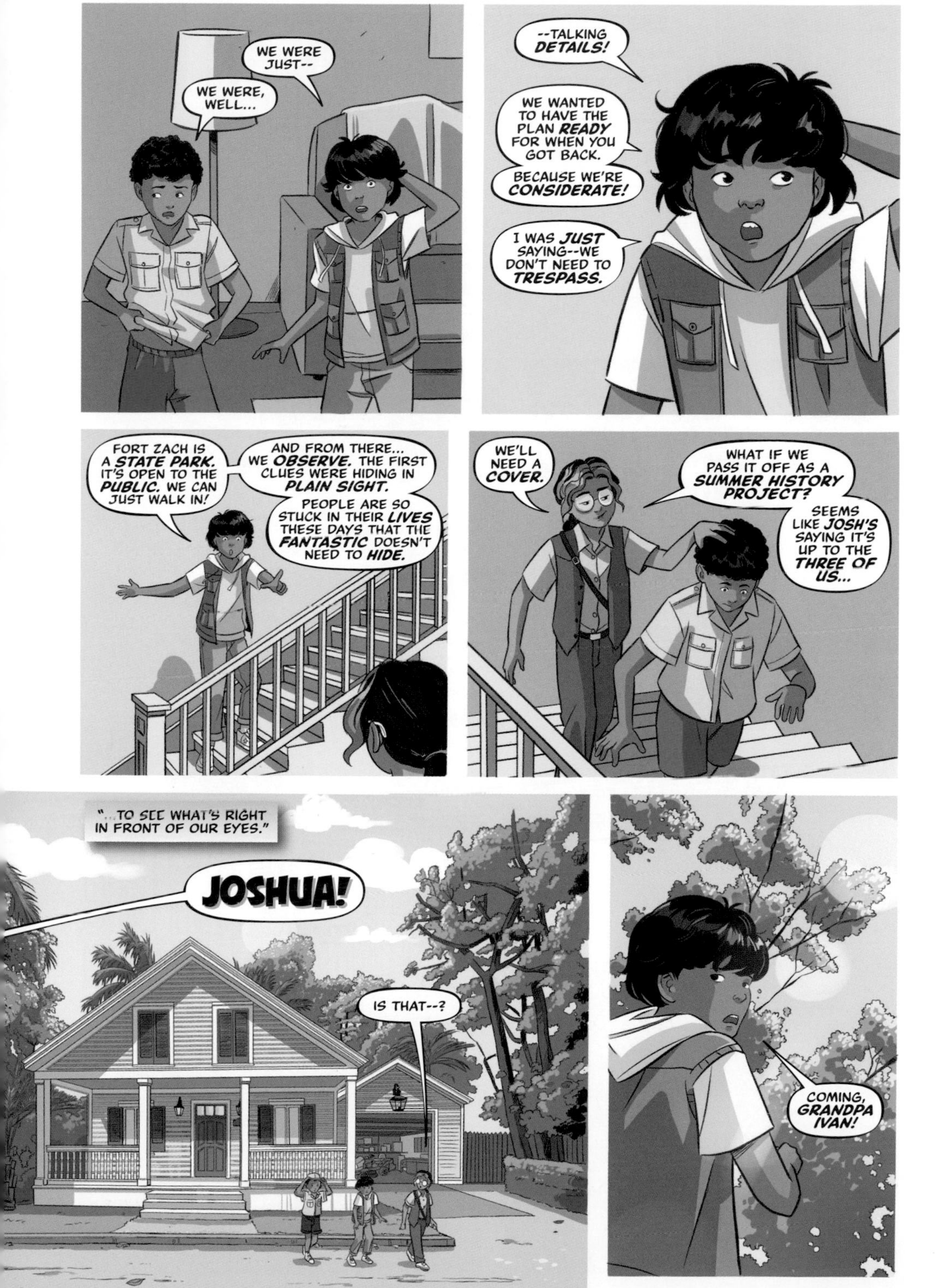
WE WERE JUST--
WE WERE, WELL...
--TALKING DETAILS!
WE WANTED TO HAVE THE PLAN READY FOR WHEN YOU GOT BACK.
BECAUSE WE'RE CONSIDERATE!
I WAS JUST SAYING--WE DON'T NEED TO TRESPASS.
FORT ZACH IS A STATE PARK. IT'S OPEN TO THE PUBLIC. WE CAN JUST WALK IN!
AND FROM THERE... WE OBSERVE. THE FIRST CLUES WERE HIDING IN PLAIN SIGHT.
PEOPLE ARE SO STUCK IN THEIR LIVES THESE DAYS THAT THE FANTASTIC DOESN'T NEED TO HIDE.
WE'LL NEED A COVER.
WHAT IF WE PASS IT OFF AS A SUMMER HISTORY PROJECT?
SEEMS LIKE JOSH'S SAYING IT'S UP TO THE THREE OF US...
"...TO SEE WHAT'S RIGHT IN FRONT OF OUR EYES."
JOSHUA!
IS THAT--?
COMING, GRANDPA IVAN!

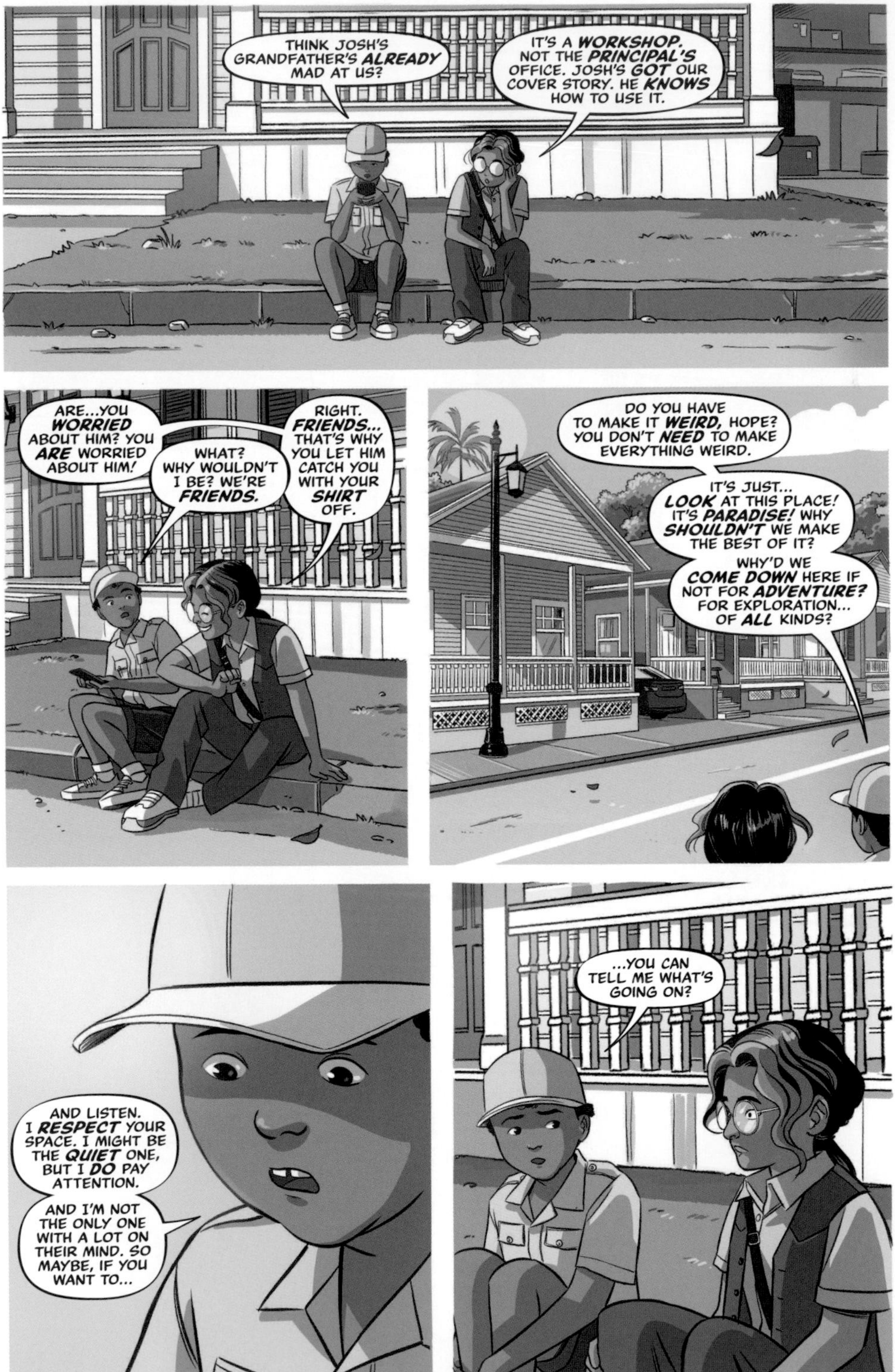
THINK JOSH'S GRANDFATHER'S ALREADY MAD AT US?
IT'S A WORKSHOP. NOT THE PRINCIPAL'S OFFICE. JOSH'S GOT OUR COVER STORY. HE KNOWS HOW TO USE IT.
ARE...YOU WORRIED ABOUT HIM? YOU ARE WORRIED ABOUT HIM!
WHAT? WHY WOULDN'T I BE? WE'RE FRIENDS.
RIGHT. FRIENDS... THAT'S WHY YOU LET HIM CATCH YOU WITH YOUR SHIRT OFF.
DO YOU HAVE TO MAKE IT WEIRD, HOPE? YOU DON'T NEED TO MAKE EVERYTHING WEIRD.
IT'S JUST... LOOK AT THIS PLACE! IT'S PARADISE! WHY SHOULDN'T WE MAKE THE BEST OF IT?
WHY'D WE COME DOWN HERE IF NOT FOR ADVENTURE? FOR EXPLORATION... OF ALL KINDS?
AND LISTEN. I RESPECT YOUR SPACE. I MIGHT BE THE QUIET ONE, BUT I DO PAY ATTENTION.
AND I'M NOT THE ONLY ONE WITH A LOT ON THEIR MIND. SO MAYBE, IF YOU WANT TO...
...YOU CAN TELL ME WHAT'S GOING ON?

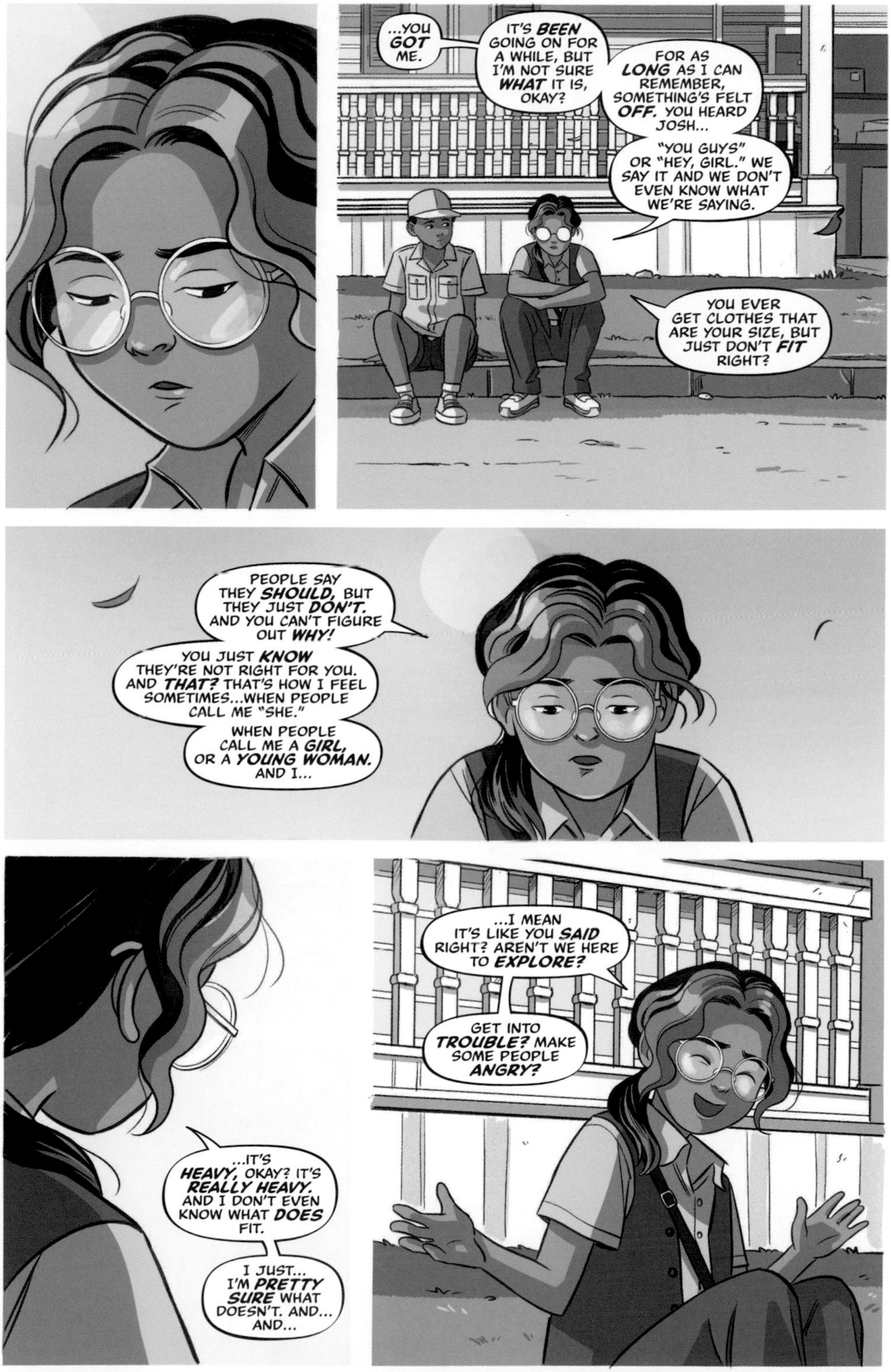
...YOU GOT ME.
IT'S BEEN GOING ON FOR A WHILE, BUT I'M NOT SURE WHAT IT IS, OKAY?
FOR AS LONG AS I CAN REMEMBER, SOMETHING'S FELT OFF. YOU HEARD JOSH...
"YOU GUYS" OR "HEY, GIRL." WE SAY IT AND WE DON'T EVEN KNOW WHAT WE'RE SAYING.
YOU EVER GET CLOTHES THAT ARE YOUR SIZE, BUT JUST DON'T FIT RIGHT?
PEOPLE SAY THEY SHOULD, BUT THEY JUST DON'T. AND YOU CAN'T FIGURE OUT WHY!
YOU JUST KNOW THEY'RE NOT RIGHT FOR YOU. AND THAT? THAT'S HOW I FEEL SOMETIMES...WHEN PEOPLE CALL ME "SHE."
WHEN PEOPLE CALL ME A GIRL, OR A YOUNG WOMAN. AND I...
...IT'S HEAVY, OKAY? IT'S REALLY HEAVY. AND I DON'T EVEN KNOW WHAT DOES FIT.
I JUST... I'M PRETTY SURE WHAT DOESN'T. AND... AND...
...I MEAN IT'S LIKE YOU SAID RIGHT? AREN'T WE HERE TO EXPLORE?
GET INTO TROUBLE? MAKE SOME PEOPLE ANGRY?

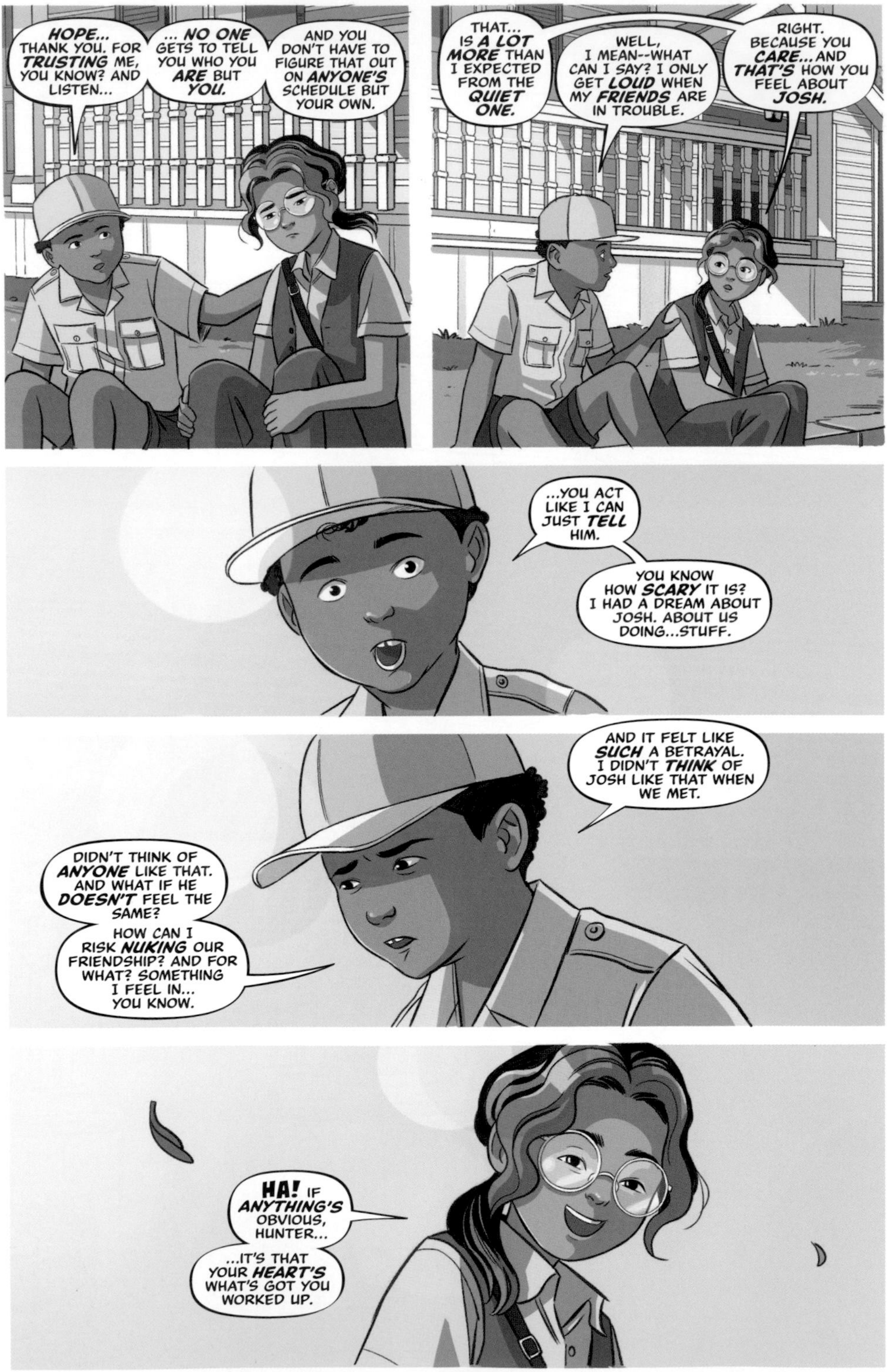
HOPE... THANK YOU. FOR TRUSTING ME, YOU KNOW? AND LISTEN...
... NO ONE GETS TO TELL YOU WHO YOU ARE BUT YOU.
AND YOU DON'T HAVE TO FIGURE THAT OUT ON ANYONE'S SCHEDULE BUT YOUR OWN.
THAT... IS A LOT MORE THAN I EXPECTED FROM THE QUIET ONE.
WELL, I MEAN--WHAT CAN I SAY? I ONLY GET LOUD WHEN MY FRIENDS ARE IN TROUBLE.
RIGHT. BECAUSE YOU CARE... AND THAT'S HOW YOU FEEL ABOUT JOSH.
...YOU ACT LIKE I CAN JUST TELL HIM.
YOU KNOW HOW SCARY IT IS? I HAD A DREAM ABOUT JOSH. ABOUT US DOING...STUFF.
AND IT FELT LIKE SUCH A BETRAYAL. I DIDN'T THINK OF JOSH LIKE THAT WHEN WE MET.
DIDN'T THINK OF ANYONE LIKE THAT. AND WHAT IF HE DOESN'T FEEL THE SAME?
HOW CAN I RISK NUKING OUR FRIENDSHIP? AND FOR WHAT? SOMETHING I FEEL IN... YOU KNOW.
HA! IF ANYTHING'S OBVIOUS, HUNTER...
...IT'S THAT YOUR HEART'S WHAT'S GOT YOU WORKED UP.

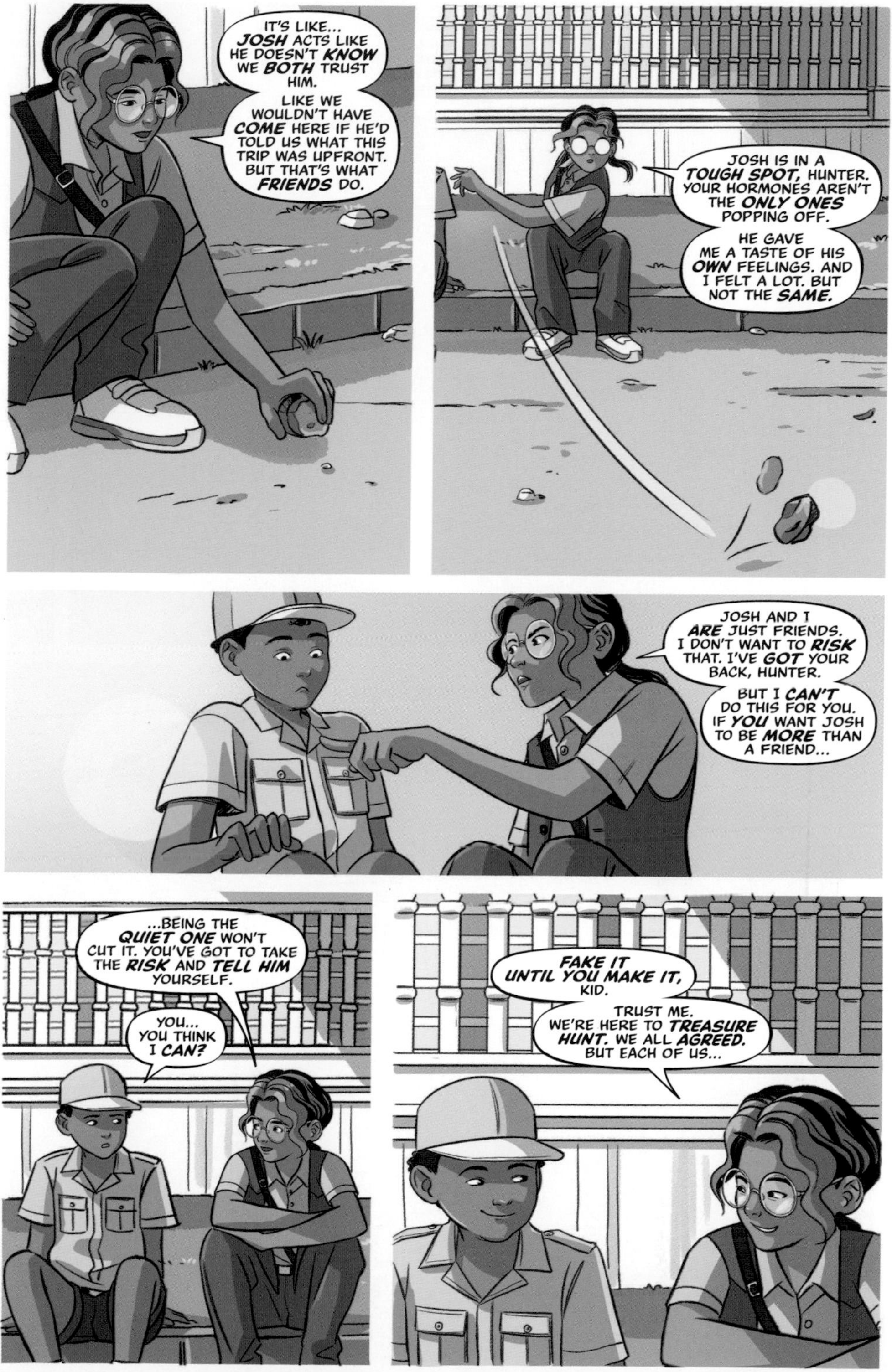
IT'S LIKE... JOSH ACTS LIKE HE DOESN'T KNOW WE BOTH TRUST HIM.
LIKE WE WOULDN'T HAVE COME HERE IF HE'D TOLD US WHAT THIS TRIP WAS UPFRONT. BUT THAT'S WHAT FRIENDS DO.
JOSH IS IN A TOUGH SPOT, HUNTER. YOUR HORMONES AREN'T THE ONLY ONES POPPING OFF.
HE GAVE ME A TASTE OF HIS OWN FEELINGS. AND I FELT A LOT. BUT NOT THE SAME.
JOSH AND I ARE JUST FRIENDS. I DON'T WANT TO RISK THAT. I'VE GOT YOUR BACK, HUNTER.
BUT I CAN'T DO THIS FOR YOU. IF YOU WANT JOSH TO BE MORE THAN A FRIEND...
...BEING THE QUIET ONE WON'T CUT IT. YOU'VE GOT TO TAKE THE RISK AND TELL HIM YOURSELF.
YOU... YOU THINK I CAN?
FAKE IT UNTIL YOU MAKE IT, KID.
TRUST ME. WE'RE HERE TO TREASURE HUNT. WE ALL AGREED. BUT EACH OF US...

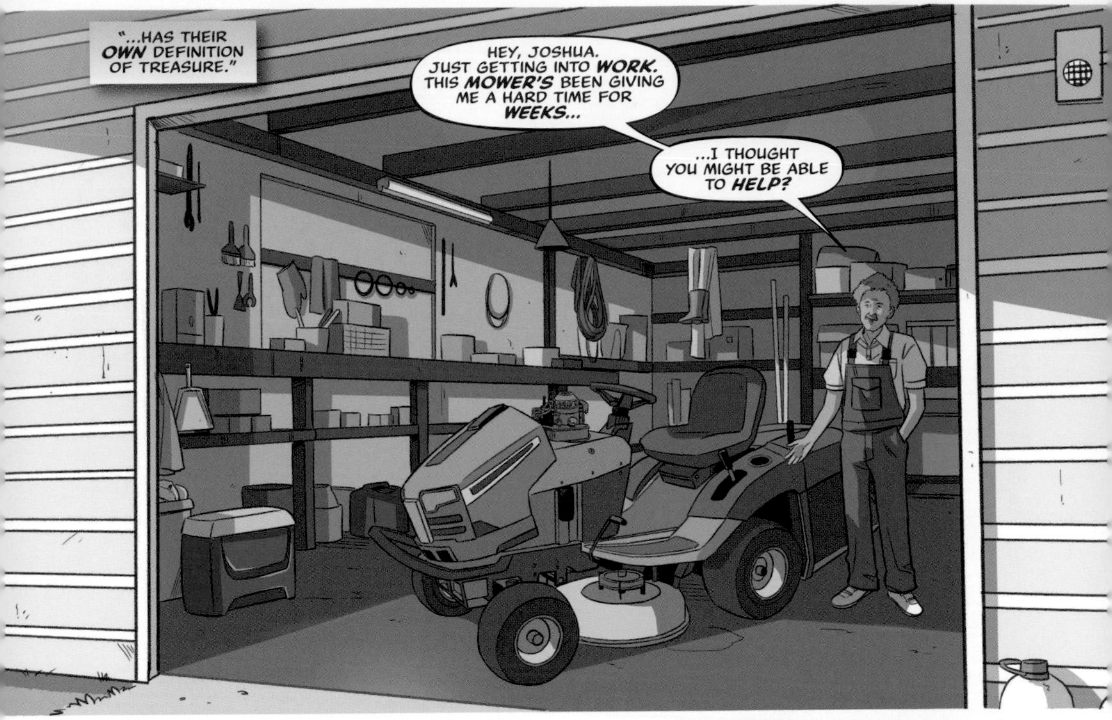
"...HAS THEIR OWN DEFINITION OF TREASURE."
HEY, JOSHUA. JUST GETTING INTO WORK. THIS MOWER'S BEEN GIVING ME A HARD TIME FOR WEEKS...
...I THOUGHT YOU MIGHT BE ABLE TO HELP?

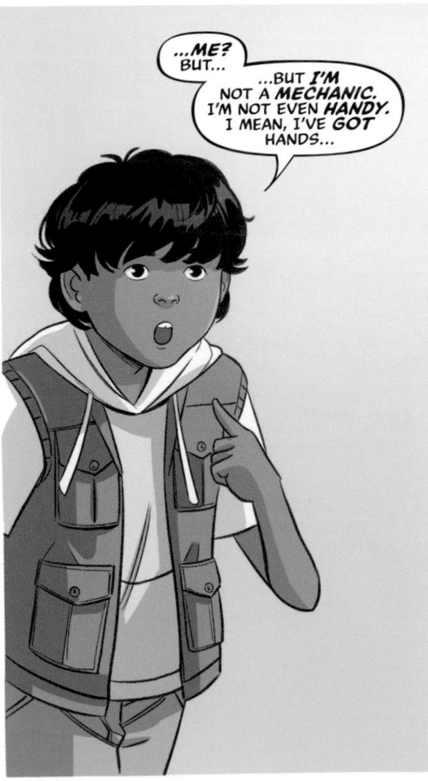
...ME? BUT...
...BUT I'M NOT A MECHANIC. I'M NOT EVEN HANDY. I MEAN, I'VE GOT HANDS...

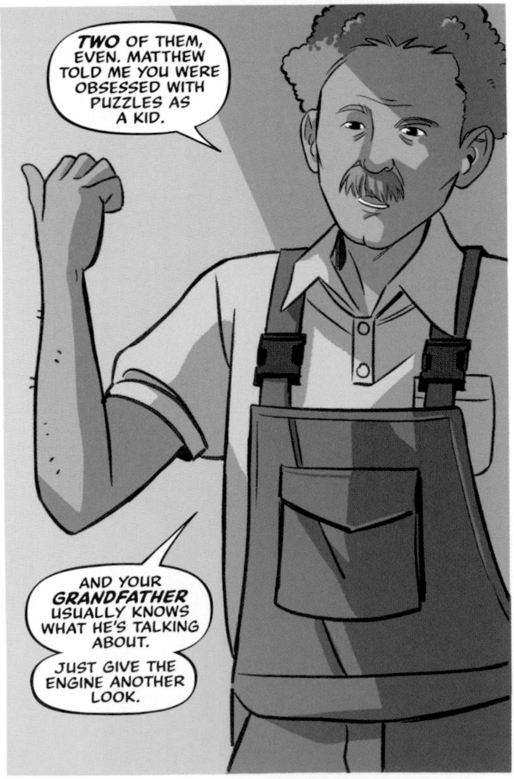
TWO OF THEM, EVEN. MATTHEW TOLD ME YOU WERE OBSESSED WITH PUZZLES AS A KID.
AND YOUR GRANDFATHER USUALLY KNOWS WHAT HE'S TALKING ABOUT.
JUST GIVE THE ENGINE ANOTHER LOOK.

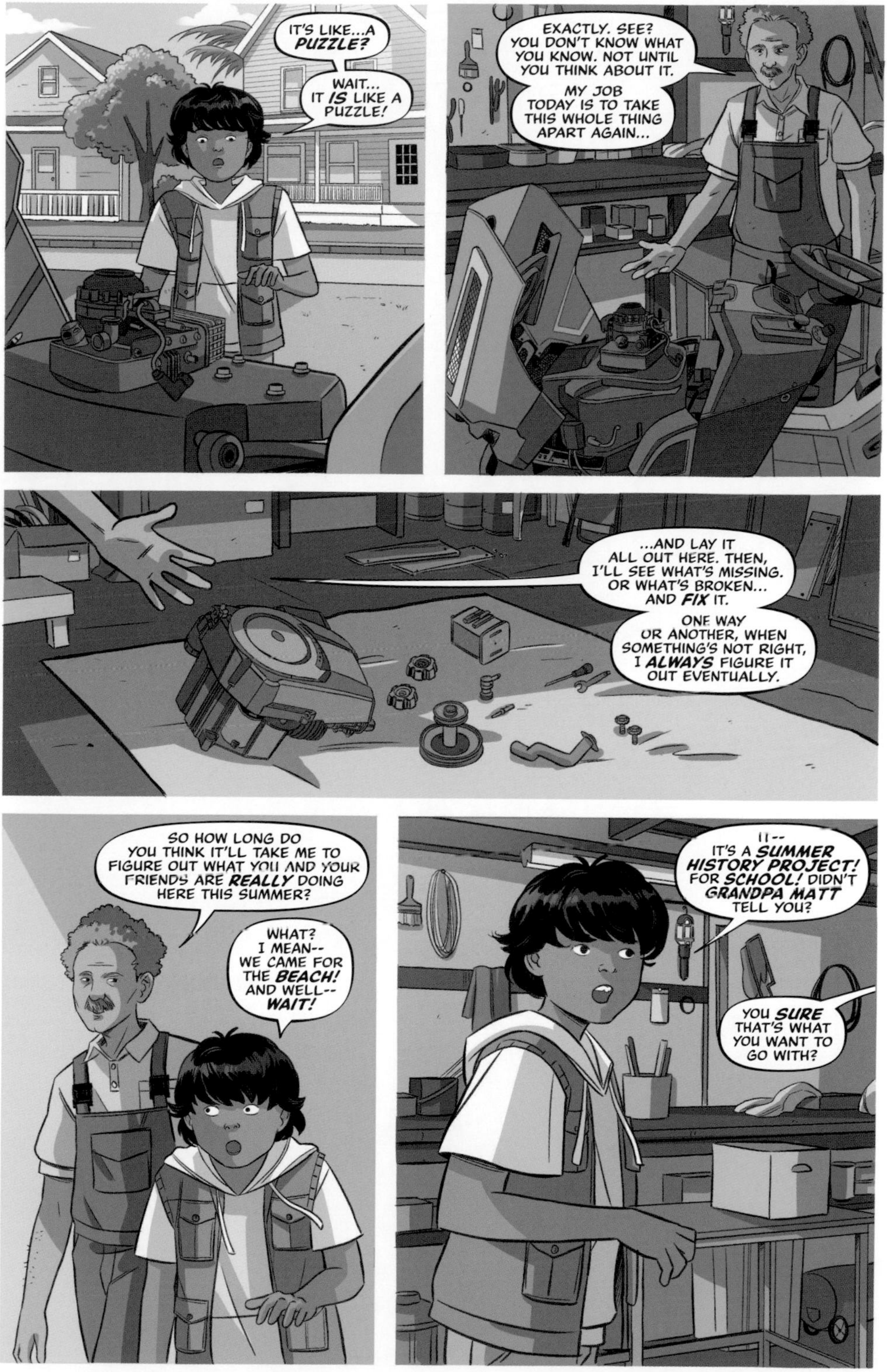
IT'S LIKE...A PUZZLE?
WAIT... IT IS LIKE A PUZZLE!
EXACTLY. SEE? YOU DON'T KNOW WHAT YOU KNOW. NOT UNTIL YOU THINK ABOUT IT.
MY JOB TODAY IS TO TAKE THIS WHOLE THING APART AGAIN...
...AND LAY IT ALL OUT HERE. THEN, I'LL SEE WHAT'S MISSING. OR WHAT'S BROKEN... AND FIX IT.
ONE WAY OR ANOTHER, WHEN SOMETHING'S NOT RIGHT, I ALWAYS FIGURE IT OUT EVENTUALLY.
SO HOW LONG DO YOU THINK IT'LL TAKE ME TO FIGURE OUT WHAT YOU AND YOUR FRIENDS ARE REALLY DOING HERE THIS SUMMER?
WHAT? I MEAN-- WE CAME FOR THE BEACH! AND WELL-- WAIT!
I! -- IT'S A SUMMER HISTORY PROJECT! FOR SCHOOL! DIDN'T GRANDPA MATT TELL YOU?
YOU SURE THAT'S WHAT YOU WANT TO GO WITH?

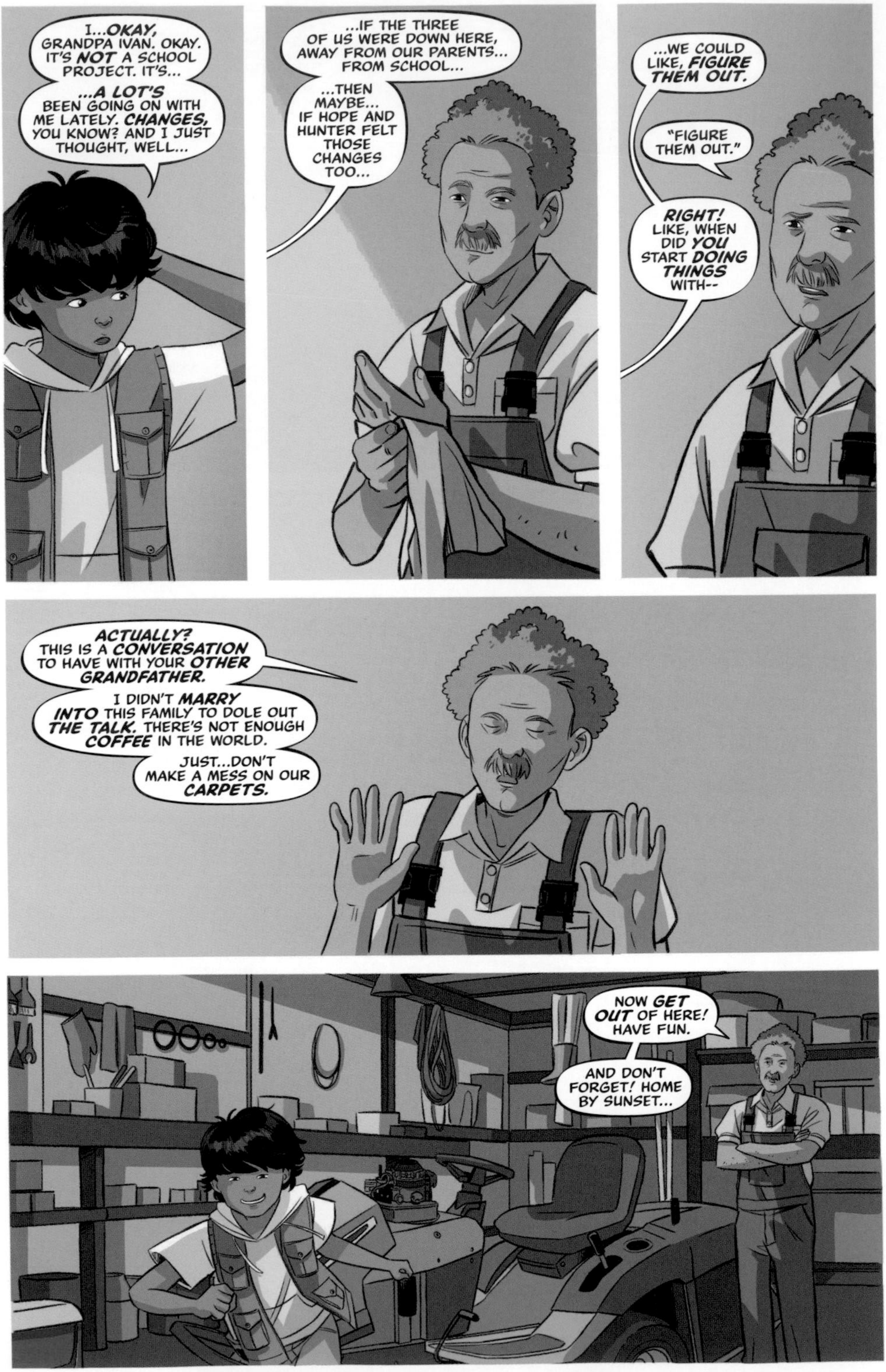
I...OKAY, GRANDPA IVAN. OKAY. IT'S NOT A SCHOOL PROJECT. IT'S...
...A LOT'S BEEN GOING ON WITH ME LATELY. CHANGES, YOU KNOW? AND I JUST THOUGHT, WELL...
...IF THE THREE OF US WERE DOWN HERE, AWAY FROM OUR PARENTS... FROM SCHOOL...
...THEN MAYBE... IF HOPE AND HUNTER FELT THOSE CHANGES TOO...
...WE COULD LIKE, FIGURE THEM OUT.
"FIGURE THEM OUT."
RIGHT! LIKE, WHEN DID YOU START DOING THINGS WITH--
ACTUALLY? THIS IS A CONVERSATION TO HAVE WITH YOUR OTHER GRANDFATHER.
I DIDN'T MARRY INTO THIS FAMILY TO DOLE OUT THE TALK. THERE'S NOT ENOUGH COFFEE IN THE WORLD.
JUST...DON'T MAKE A MESS ON OUR CARPETS.
NOW GET OUT OF HERE! HAVE FUN.
AND DON'T FORGET! HOME BY SUNSET...

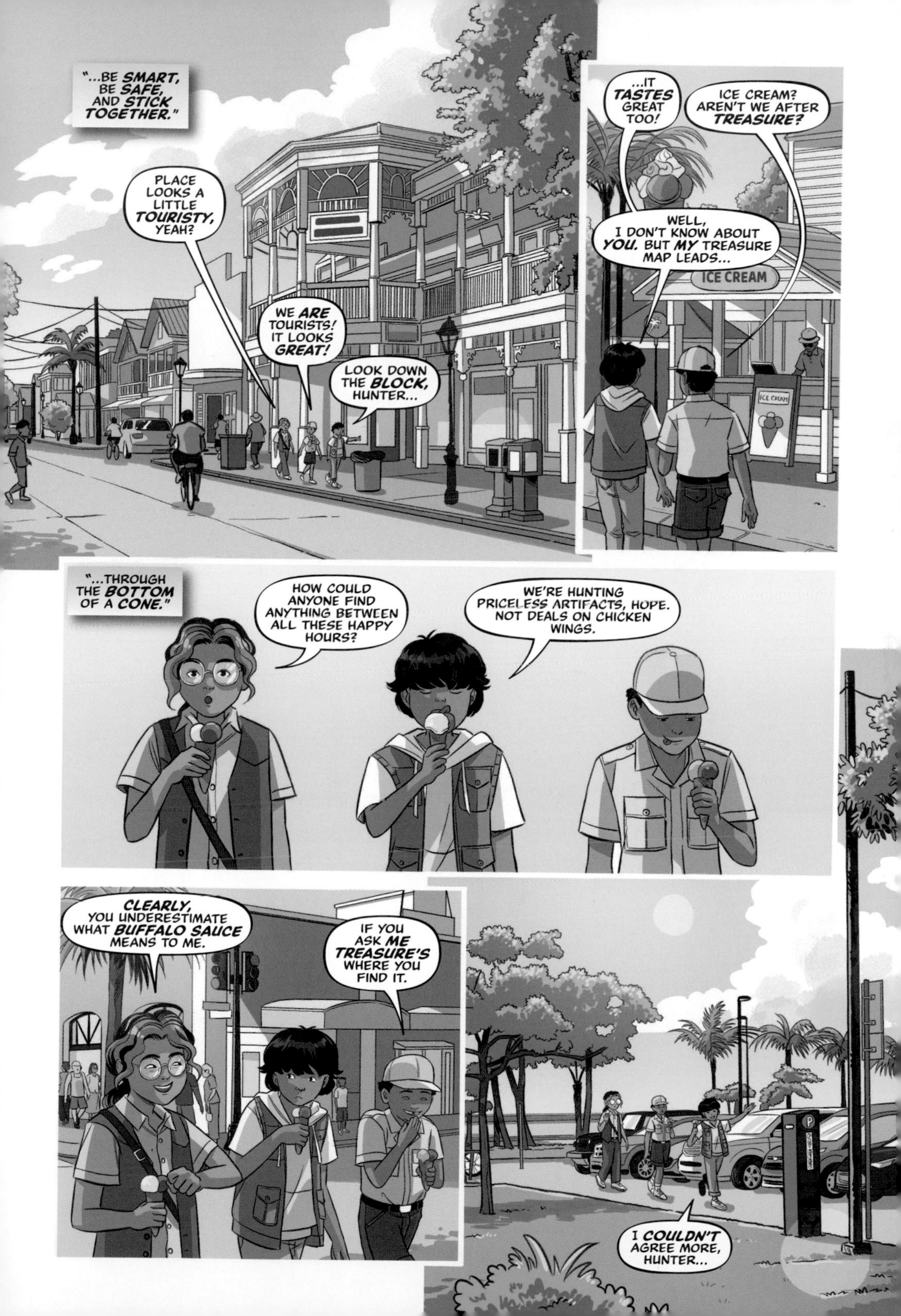
"...BE SMART, BE SAFE, AND STICK TOGETHER."
PLACE LOOKS A LITTLE TOURISTY, YEAH?
WE ARE TOURISTS! IT LOOKS GREAT!
LOOK DOWN THE BLOCK, HUNTER...
...IT TASTES GREAT TOO!
ICE CREAM? AREN'T WE AFTER TREASURE?
WELL, I DON'T KNOW ABOUT YOU. BUT MY TREASURE MAP LEADS...
ICE CREAM
ICE CREAM
"...THROUGH THE BOTTOM OF A CONE."
HOW COULD ANYONE FIND ANYTHING BETWEEN ALL THESE HAPPY HOURS?
WE'RE HUNTING PRICELESS ARTIFACTS, HOPE. NOT DEALS ON CHICKEN WINGS.
CLEARLY, YOU UNDERESTIMATE WHAT BUFFALO SAUCE MEANS TO ME.
IF YOU ASK ME TREASURE'S WHERE YOU FIND IT.
I COULDN'T AGREE MORE, HUNTER...

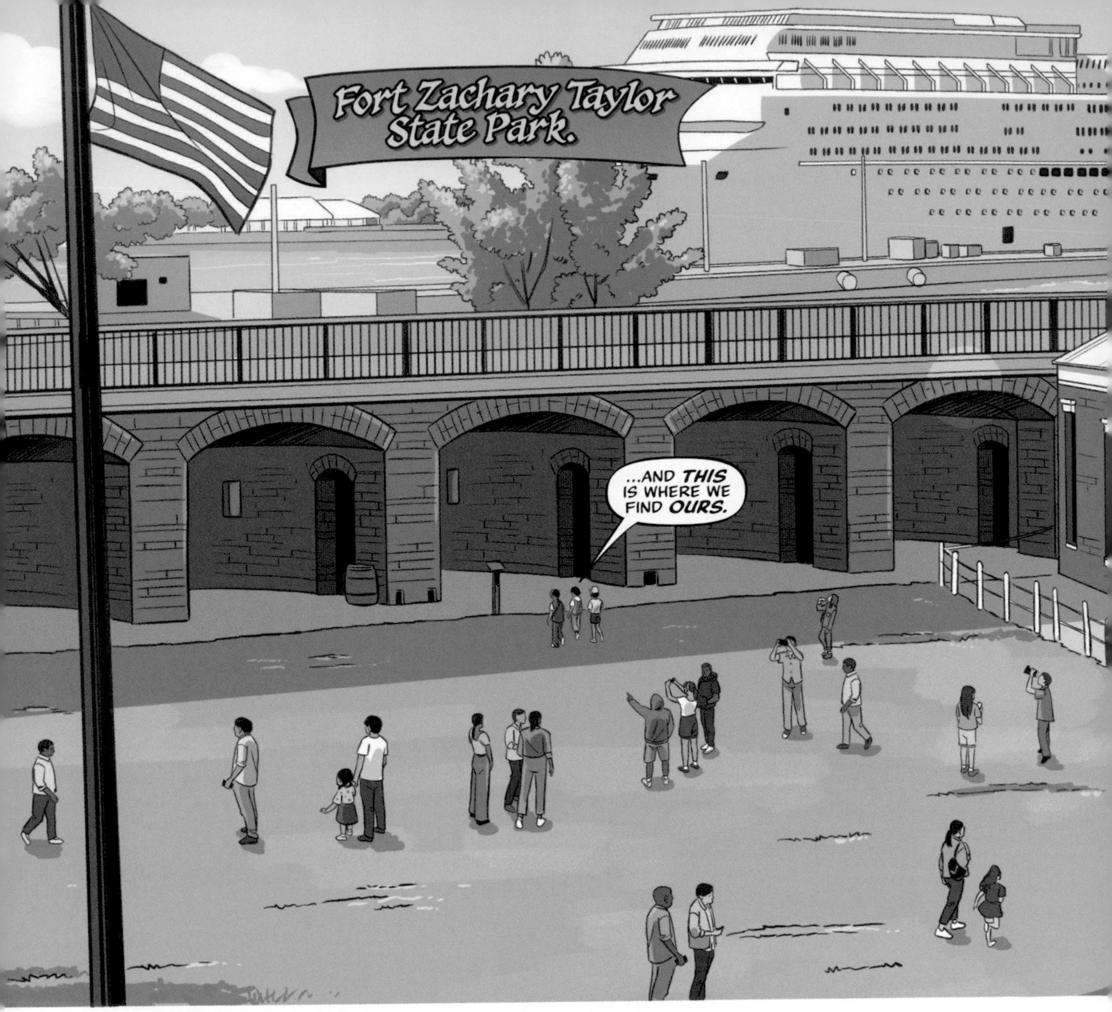
Fort Zachary Taylor State Park.
...AND THIS IS WHERE WE FIND OURS.

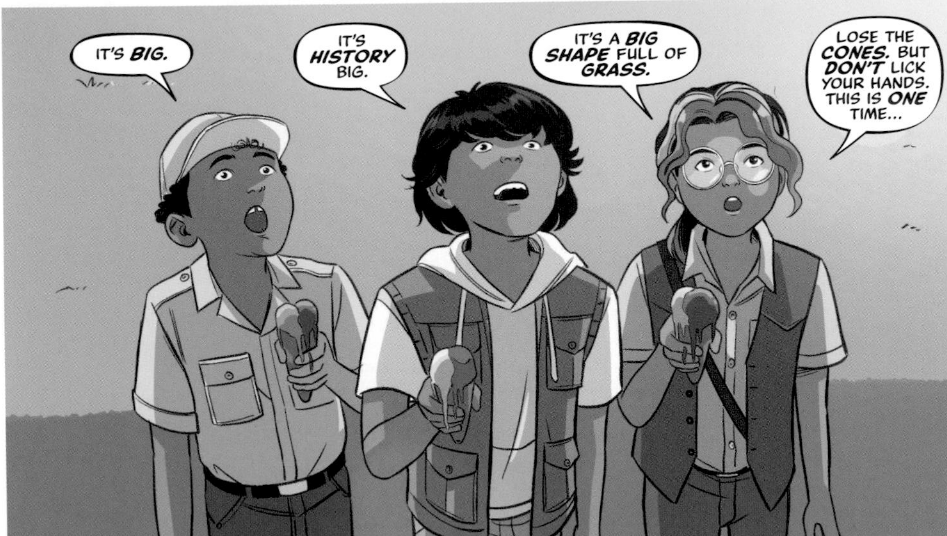
IT'S BIG.
IT'S HISTORY BIG.
IT'S A BIG SHAPE FULL OF GRASS.
LOSE THE CONES. BUT DON'T LICK YOUR HANDS. THIS IS ONE TIME...

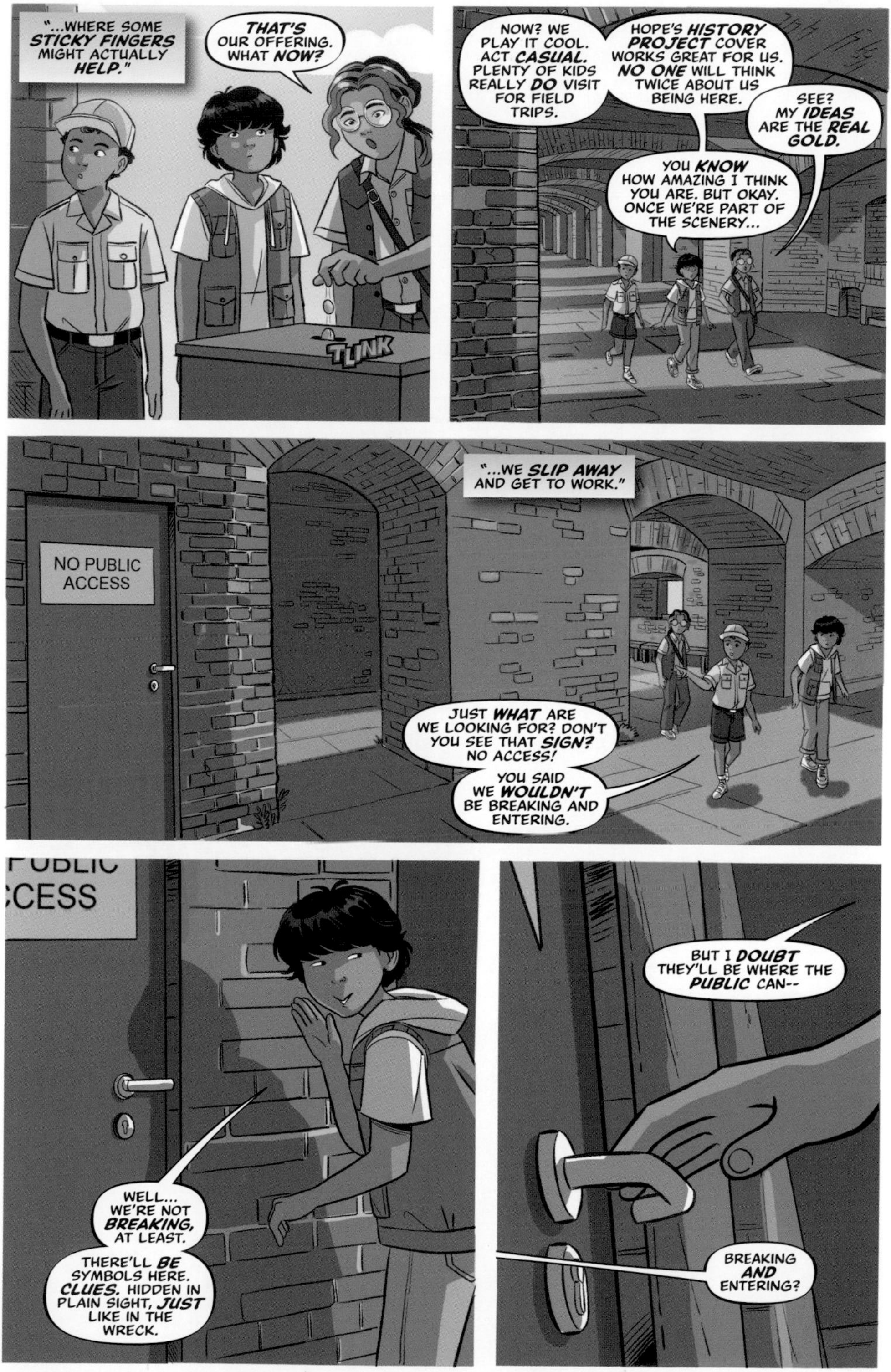
"...WHERE SOME STICKY FINGERS MIGHT ACTUALLY HELP."
THAT'S OUR OFFERING. WHAT NOW?
TLINK
NOW? WE PLAY IT COOL. ACT CASUAL. PLENTY OF KIDS REALLY DO VISIT FOR FIELD TRIPS.
HOPE'S HISTORY PROJECT COVER WORKS GREAT FOR US. NO ONE WILL THINK TWICE ABOUT US BEING HERE.
SEE? MY IDEAS ARE THE REAL GOLD.
YOU KNOW HOW AMAZING I THINK YOU ARE. BUT OKAY. ONCE WE'RE PART OF THE SCENERY...
"...WE SLIP AWAY AND GET TO WORK."
NO PUBLIC ACCESS
JUST WHAT ARE WE LOOKING FOR? DON'T YOU SEE THAT SIGN? NO ACCESS!
YOU SAID WE WOULDN'T BE BREAKING AND ENTERING.
PUBLIC CCESS
WELL... WE'RE NOT BREAKING, AT LEAST.
THERE'LL BE SYMBOLS HERE. CLUES. HIDDEN IN PLAIN SIGHT, JUST LIKE IN THE WRECK.
BUT I DOUBT THEY'LL BE WHERE THE PUBLIC CAN--
BREAKING AND ENTERING?

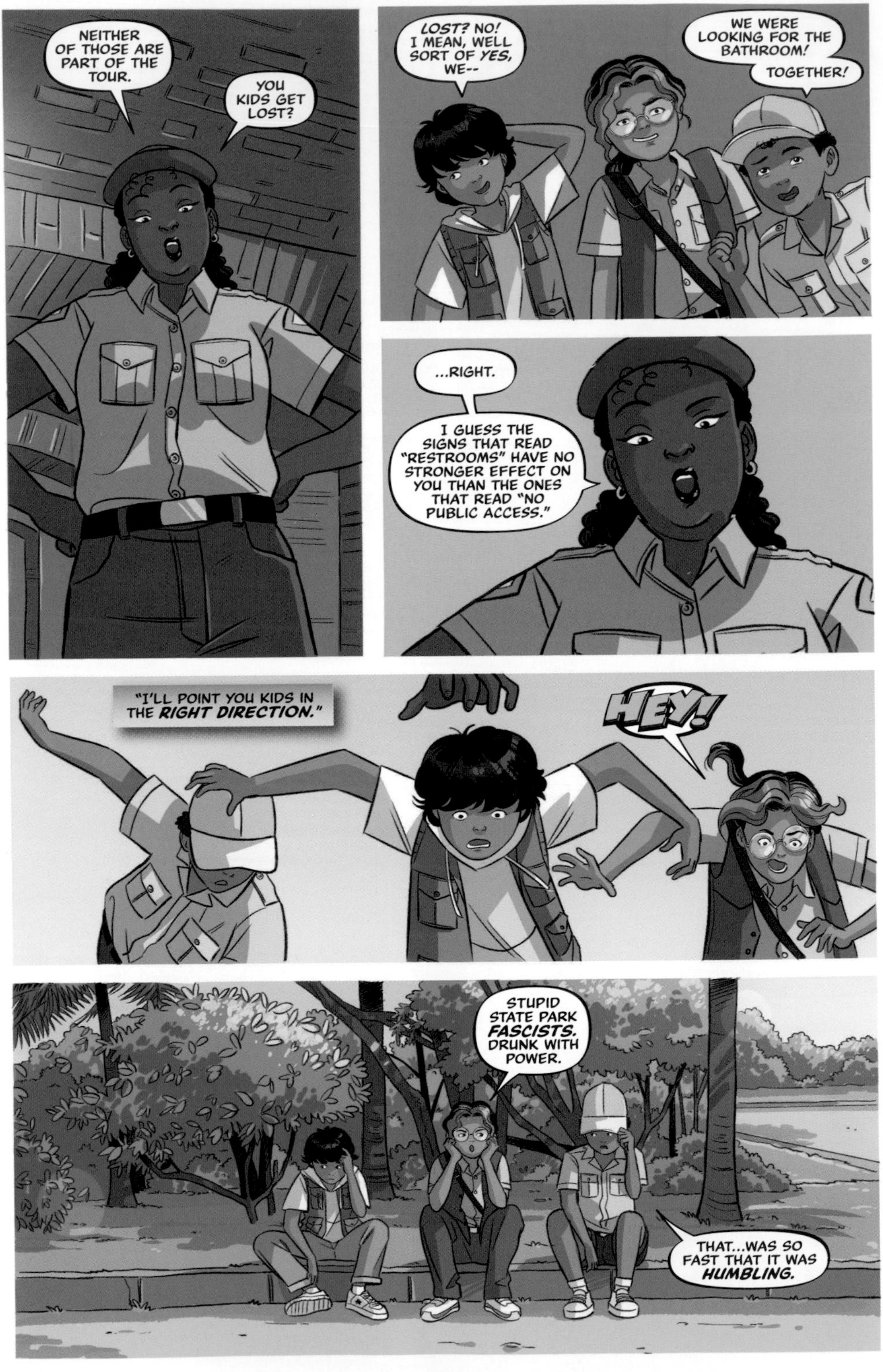
NEITHER OF THOSE ARE PART OF THE TOUR.
YOU KIDS GET LOST?
LOST? NO! I MEAN, WELL SORT OF YES, WE--
WE WERE LOOKING FOR THE BATHROOM!
TOGETHER!
...RIGHT.
I GUESS THE SIGNS THAT READ "RESTROOMS" HAVE NO STRONGER EFFECT ON YOU THAN THE ONES THAT READ "NO PUBLIC ACCESS."
"I'LL POINT YOU KIDS IN THE RIGHT DIRECTION."
HEY!
STUPID STATE PARK FASCISTS. DRUNK WITH POWER.
THAT...WAS SO FAST THAT IT WAS HUMBLING.

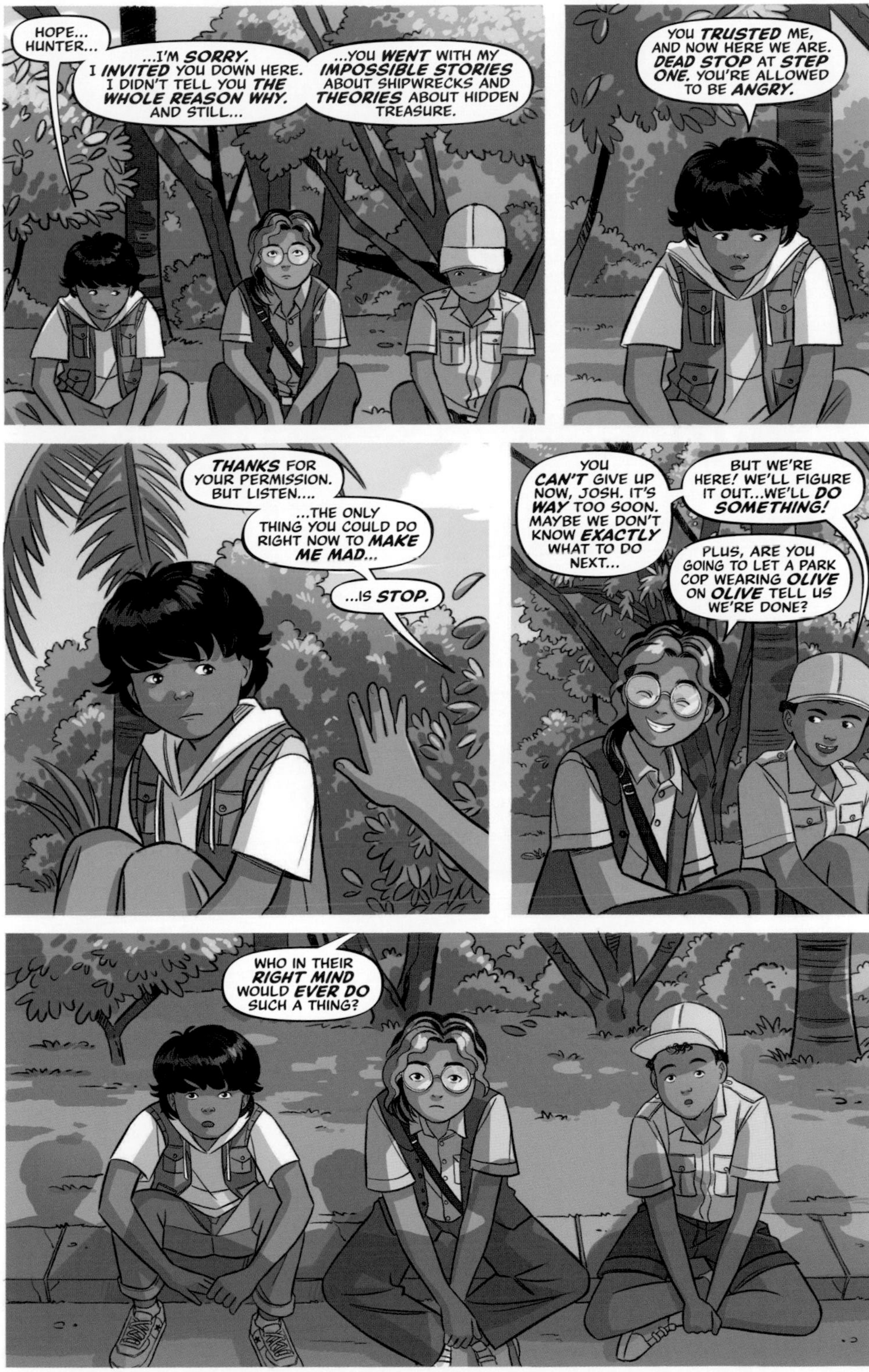
HOPE... HUNTER...
...I'M SORRY. I INVITED YOU DOWN HERE. I DIDN'T TELL YOU THE WHOLE REASON WHY. AND STILL...
...YOU WENT WITH MY IMPOSSIBLE STORIES ABOUT SHIPWRECKS AND THEORIES ABOUT HIDDEN TREASURE.
YOU TRUSTED ME, AND NOW HERE WE ARE. DEAD STOP AT STEP ONE. YOU'RE ALLOWED TO BE ANGRY.
THANKS FOR YOUR PERMISSION. BUT LISTEN....
...THE ONLY THING YOU COULD DO RIGHT NOW TO MAKE ME MAD...
...IS STOP.
YOU CAN'T GIVE UP NOW, JOSH. IT'S WAY TOO SOON. MAYBE WE DON'T KNOW EXACTLY WHAT TO DO NEXT...
BUT WE'RE HERE! WE'LL FIGURE IT OUT...WE'LL DO SOMETHING!
PLUS, ARE YOU GOING TO LET A PARK COP WEARING OLIVE ON OLIVE TELL US WE'RE DONE?
WHO IN THEIR RIGHT MIND WOULD EVER DO SUCH A THING?

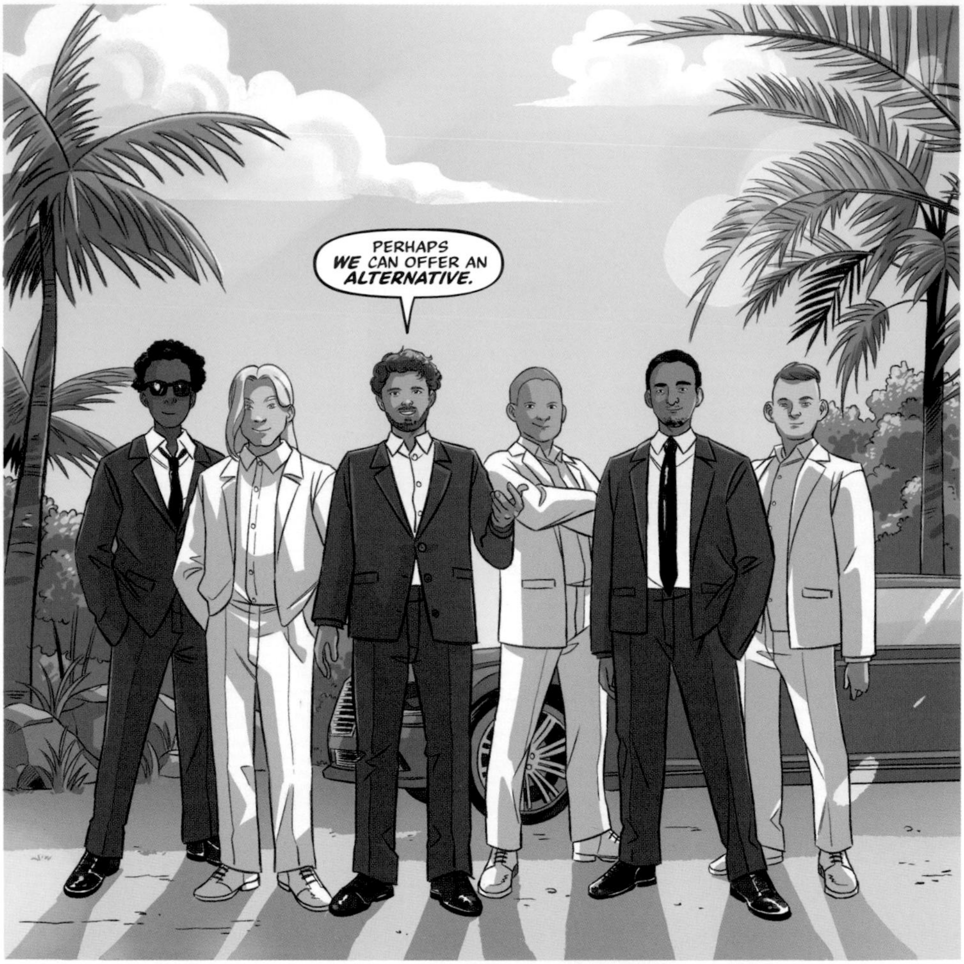
PERHAPS **WE** CAN OFFER AN **ALTERNATIVE.**

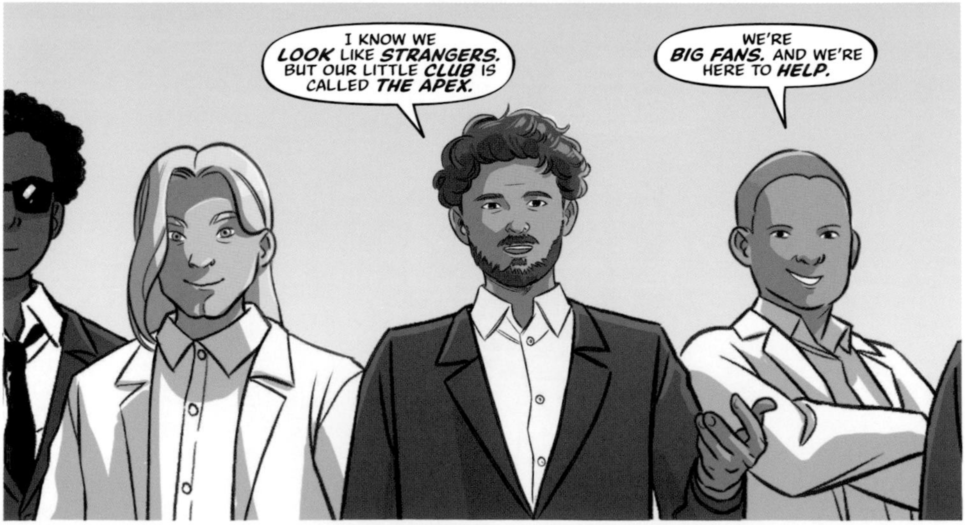
I KNOW WE **LOOK** LIKE **STRANGERS.** BUT OUR LITTLE **CLUB** IS CALLED **THE APEX.**
WE'RE **BIG FANS.** AND WE'RE HERE TO **HELP.**

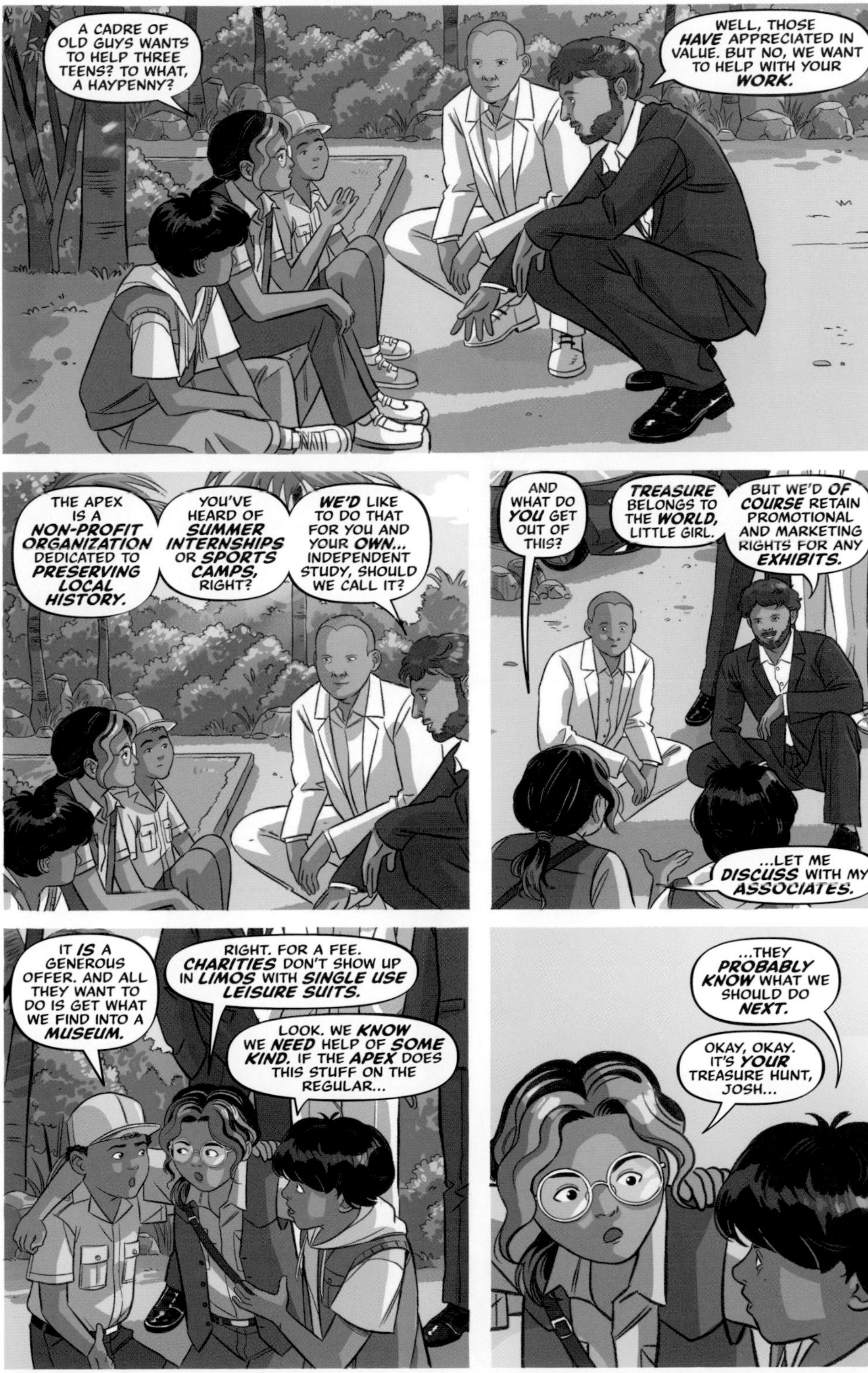
A CADRE OF OLD GUYS WANTS TO HELP THREE TEENS? TO WHAT, A HAYPENNY?
WELL, THOSE HAVE APPRECIATED IN VALUE. BUT NO, WE WANT TO HELP WITH YOUR WORK.
THE APEX IS A NON-PROFIT ORGANIZATION DEDICATED TO PRESERVING LOCAL HISTORY.
YOU'VE HEARD OF SUMMER INTERNSHIPS OR SPORTS CAMPS, RIGHT?
WE'D LIKE TO DO THAT FOR YOU AND YOUR OWN... INDEPENDENT STUDY, SHOULD WE CALL IT?
AND WHAT DO YOU GET OUT OF THIS?
TREASURE BELONGS TO THE WORLD, LITTLE GIRL.
BUT WE'D OF COURSE RETAIN PROMOTIONAL AND MARKETING RIGHTS FOR ANY EXHIBITS.
...LET ME DISCUSS WITH MY ASSOCIATES.
IT IS A GENEROUS OFFER. AND ALL THEY WANT TO DO IS GET WHAT WE FIND INTO A MUSEUM.
RIGHT. FOR A FEE. CHARITIES DON'T SHOW UP IN LIMOS WITH SINGLE USE LEISURE SUITS.
LOOK. WE KNOW WE NEED HELP OF SOME KIND. IF THE APEX DOES THIS STUFF ON THE REGULAR...
...THEY PROBABLY KNOW WHAT WE SHOULD DO NEXT.
OKAY, OKAY. IT'S YOUR TREASURE HUNT, JOSH...

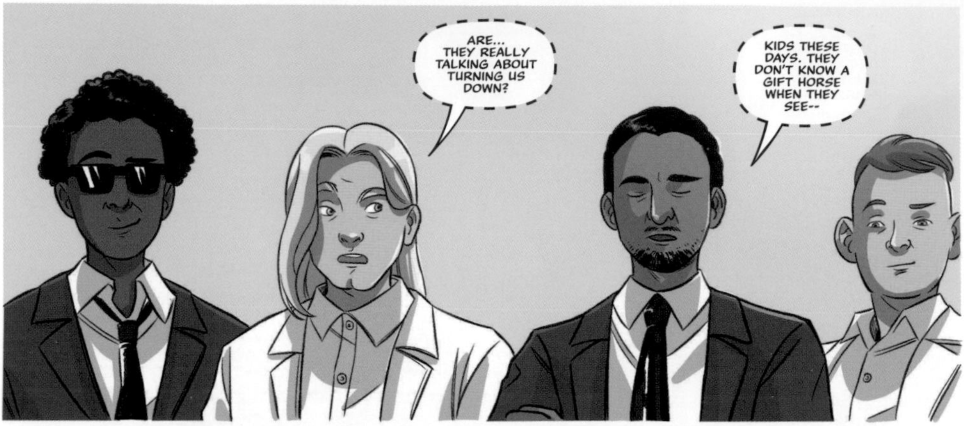
ARE... THEY REALLY TALKING ABOUT TURNING US DOWN?
KIDS THESE DAYS. THEY DON'T KNOW A GIFT HORSE WHEN THEY SEE--

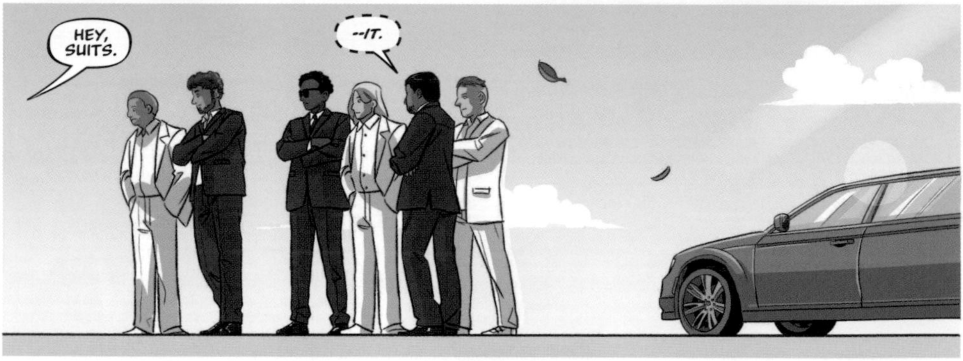
HEY, SUITS.
--IT.

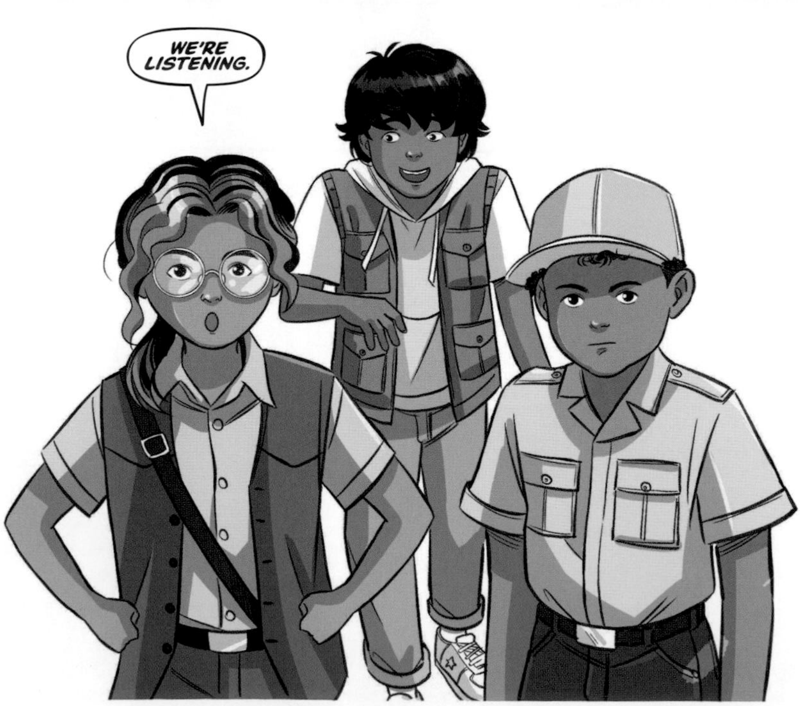
WE'RE LISTENING.

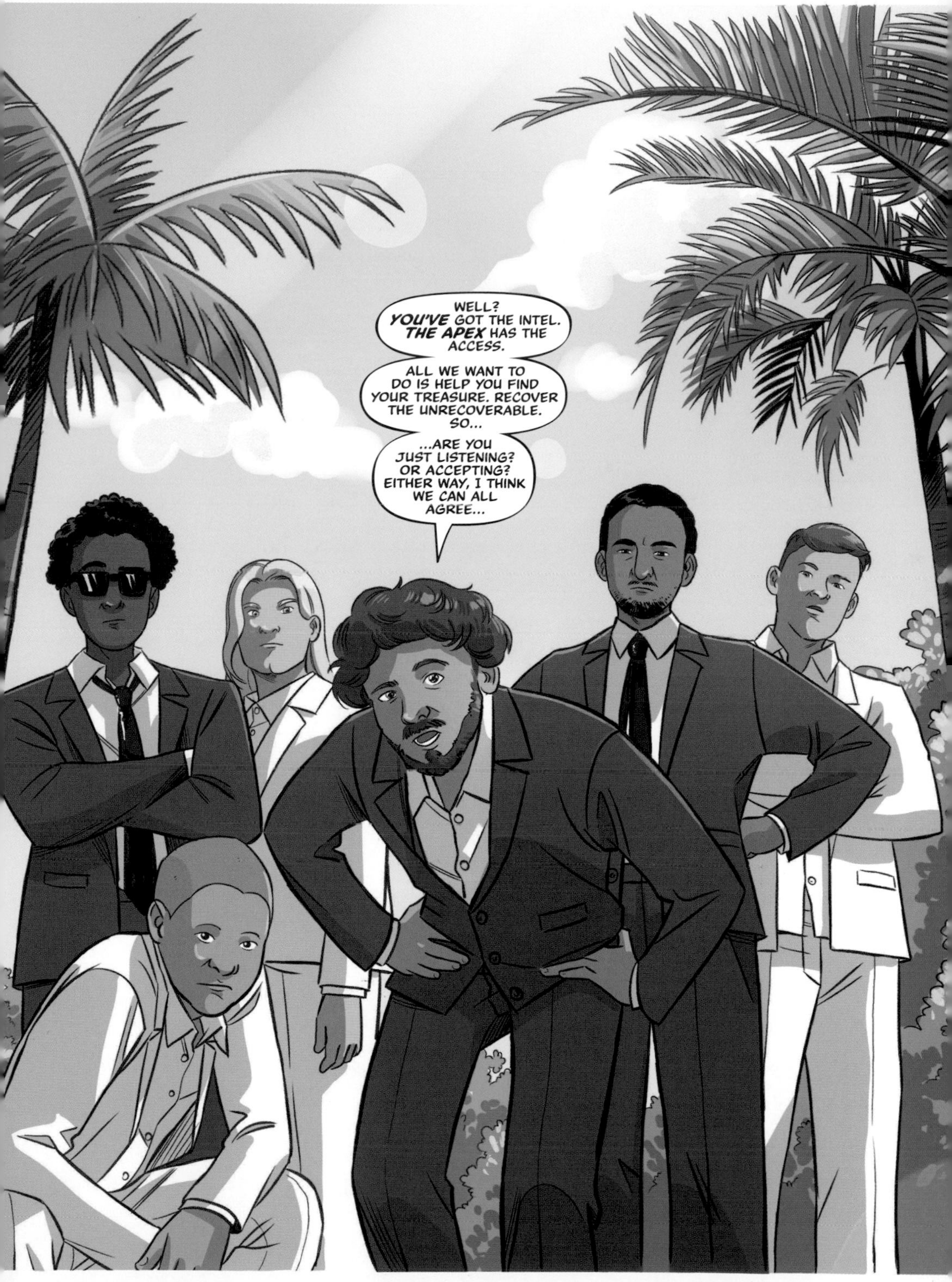
WELL? *YOU'VE* GOT THE INTEL. *THE APEX* HAS THE ACCESS.
ALL WE WANT TO DO IS HELP YOU FIND YOUR TREASURE. RECOVER THE UNRECOVERABLE. SO...
...ARE YOU JUST LISTENING? OR ACCEPTING? EITHER WAY, I THINK WE CAN ALL AGREE...

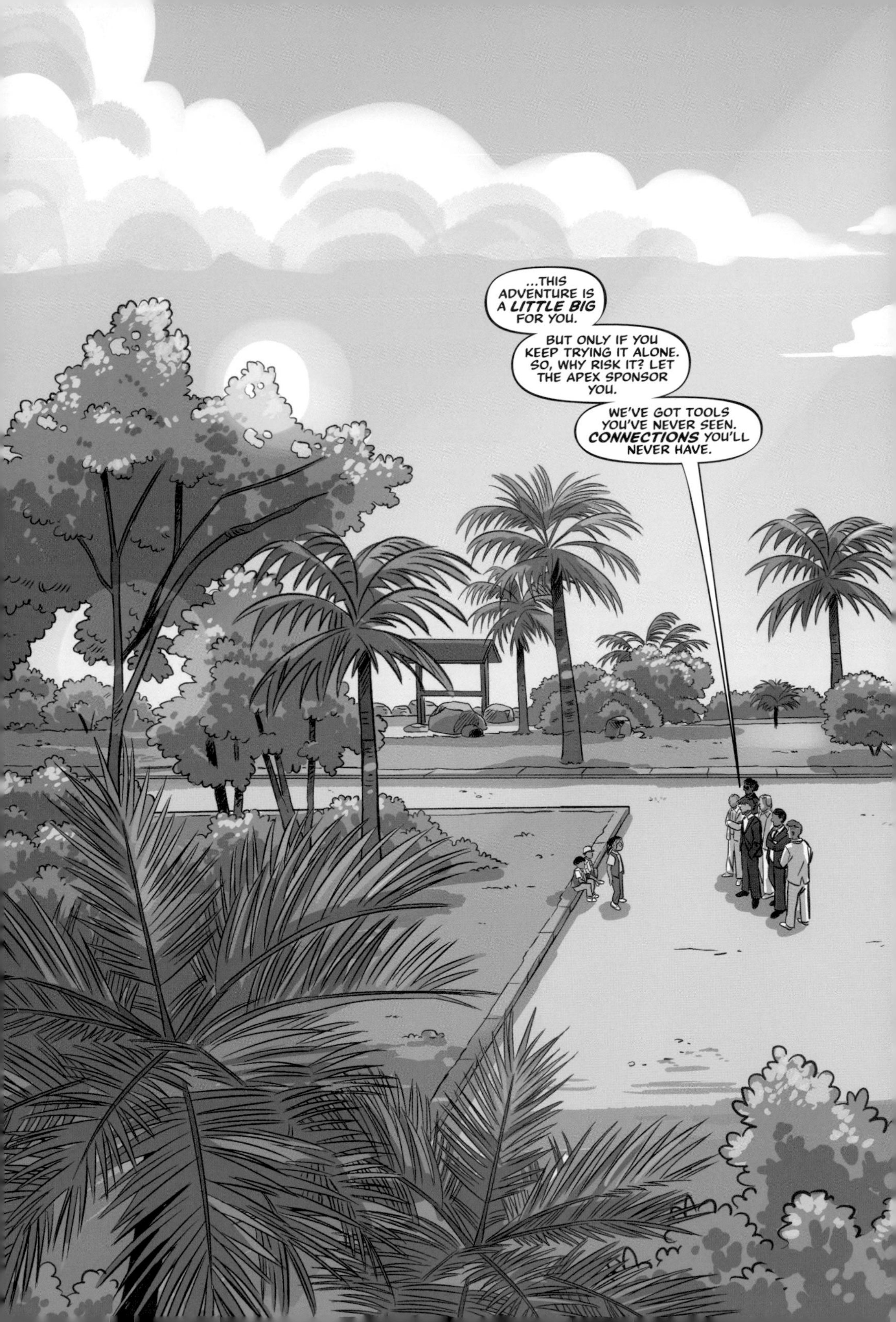
...THIS ADVENTURE IS A LITTLE BIG FOR YOU.
BUT ONLY IF YOU KEEP TRYING IT ALONE. SO, WHY RISK IT? LET THE APEX SPONSOR YOU.
WE'VE GOT TOOLS YOU'VE NEVER SEEN. CONNECTIONS YOU'LL NEVER HAVE.

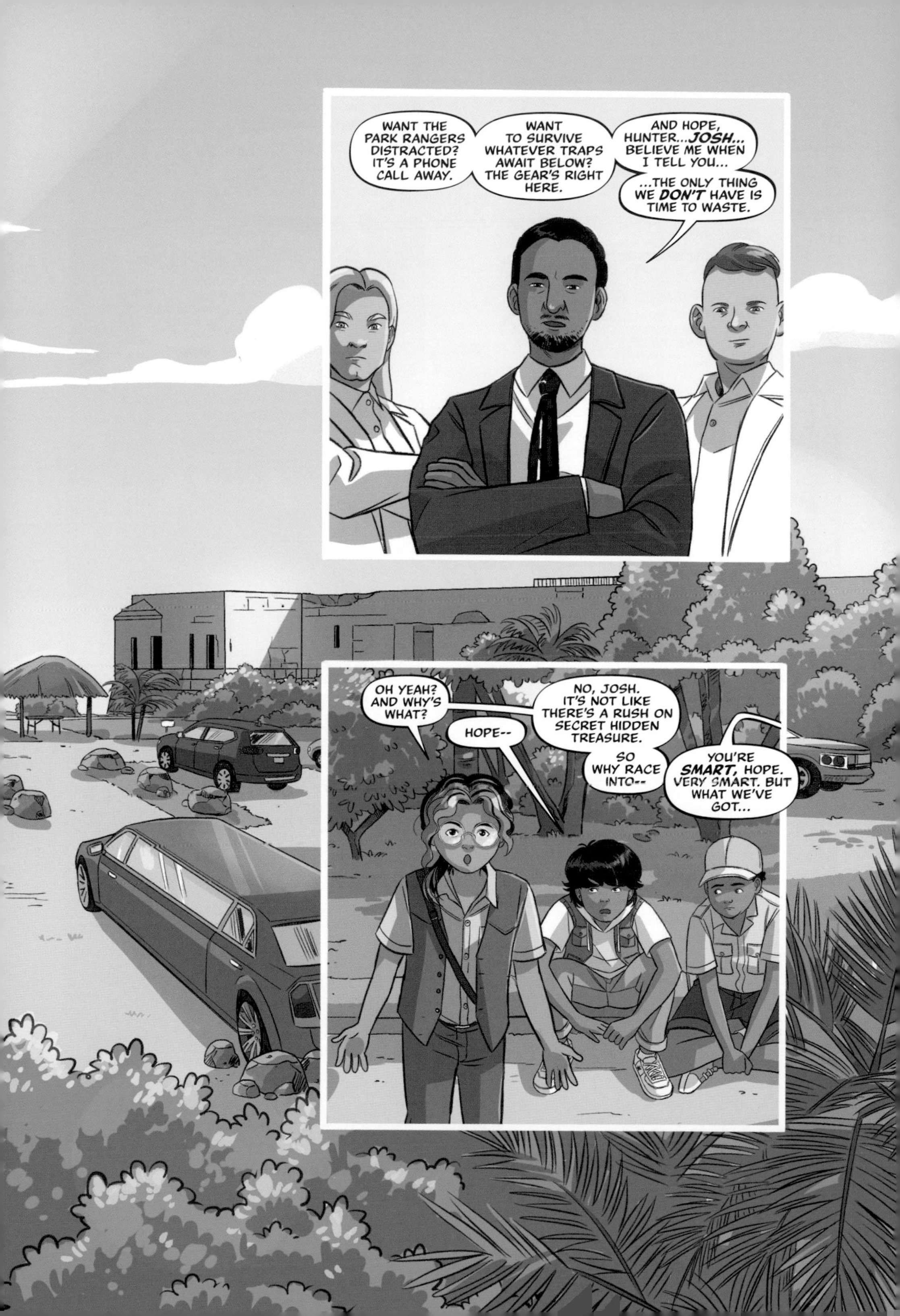
WANT THE PARK RANGERS DISTRACTED? IT'S A PHONE CALL AWAY.
WANT TO SURVIVE WHATEVER TRAPS AWAIT BELOW? THE GEAR'S RIGHT HERE.
AND HOPE, HUNTER...JOSH... BELIEVE ME WHEN I TELL YOU...
...THE ONLY THING WE DON'T HAVE IS TIME TO WASTE.
OH YEAH? AND WHY'S WHAT?
HOPE--
NO, JOSH. IT'S NOT LIKE THERE'S A RUSH ON SECRET HIDDEN TREASURE.
SO WHY RACE INTO--
YOU'RE SMART, HOPE. VERY SMART. BUT WHAT WE'VE GOT...

...IS *PERSPECTIVE.*

YOU HAVEN'T HEARD OF THE APEX BECAUSE IT'S NOT ABOUT US. ARE WE OLD MONEY? YES.

THAT HAPPENS WHEN YOU'VE DONE THIS FOR A *LONG TIME...* AND THE CLOCK IS ALWAYS TICKING.

YOU THINK *JOSH* IS REALLY THE ONLY ONE TO DECIPHER THE CLUES IN THAT SHIPWRECK?

WE'RE NOT *ALONE* IN WATCHING FOR LOST TREASURES.

PLENTY OF OTHERS WILL BE HERE SOON ENOUGH.

THEY MIGHT EVEN BE NAMES AND ORGANIZATIONS YOU RECOGNIZE. BUT ALL THEY WANT IS PROFIT.

OUR SECRECY IS A *FEATURE* OF OUR MISSION, NOT A GLITCH. WE DON'T WANT FAME...

...WE WANT TO *PROTECT* LOST CULTURE FROM THE FAME-SEEKERS.

SO, WHAT? WE GET THE *SILVER VESSELS* FOR YOU, THEN THEY GO INTO YOUR VAULT? YOU THINK WE'RE STUPID, OR--

DON'T BE *RUDE*, HOPE. IT...KIND OF MAKES SENSE. MAYBE THE VESSELS WOULDN'T BE IN A MUSEUM...

...BUT THEY *DEFINITELY* WOULDN'T BE OUT ON SOME BLACK MARKET.

IF, I MEAN...

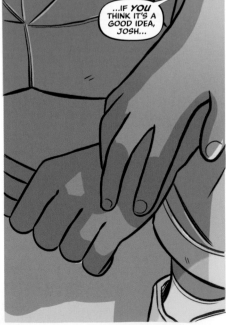

...IF *YOU* THINK IT'S A GOOD IDEA, JOSH...

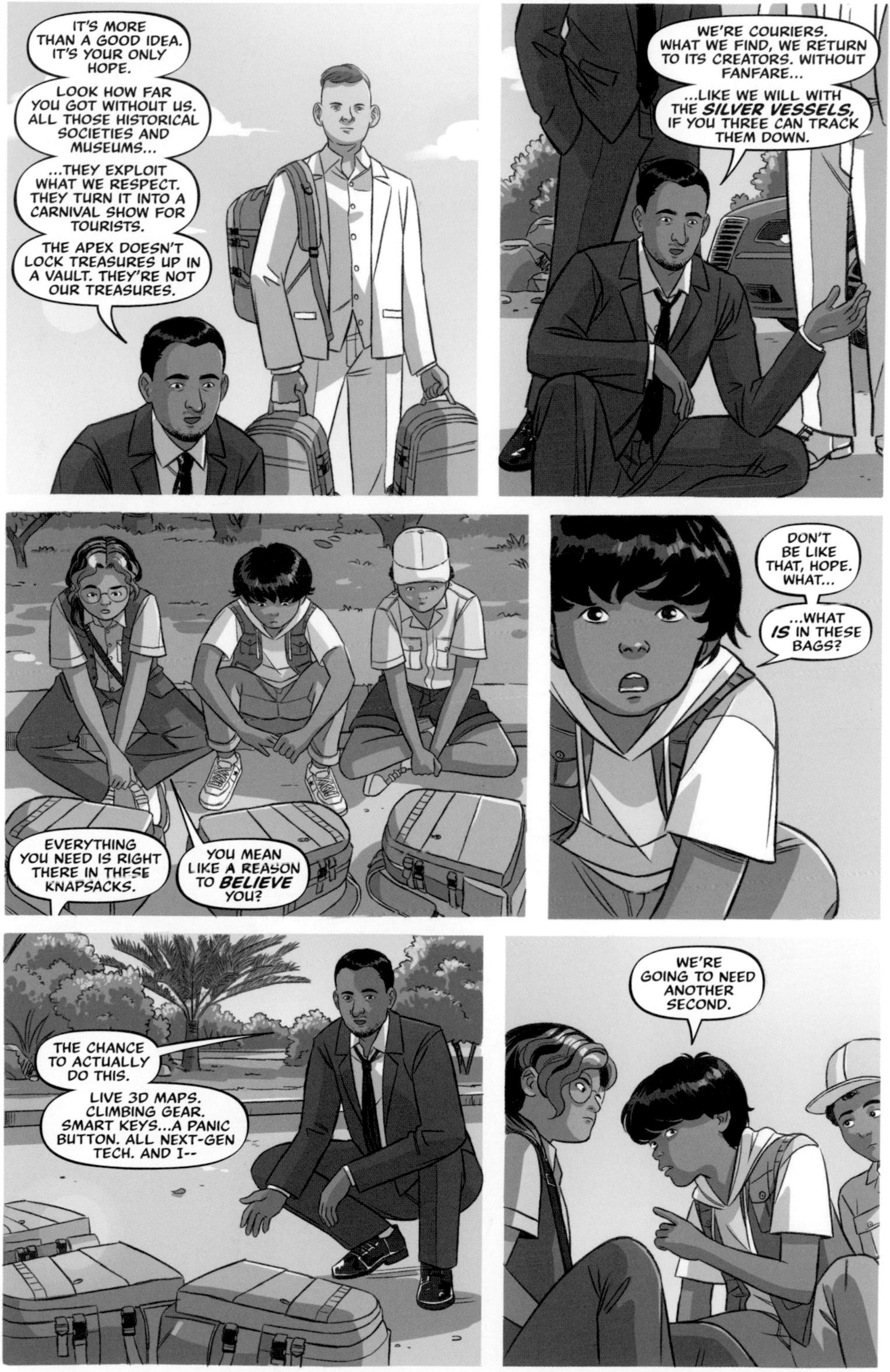
IT'S MORE THAN A GOOD IDEA. IT'S YOUR ONLY HOPE.
LOOK HOW FAR YOU GOT WITHOUT US. ALL THOSE HISTORICAL SOCIETIES AND MUSEUMS...
...THEY EXPLOIT WHAT WE RESPECT. THEY TURN IT INTO A CARNIVAL SHOW FOR TOURISTS.
THE APEX DOESN'T LOCK TREASURES UP IN A VAULT. THEY'RE NOT OUR TREASURES.
WE'RE COURIERS. WHAT WE FIND, WE RETURN TO ITS CREATORS. WITHOUT FANFARE...
...LIKE WE WILL WITH THE **SILVER VESSELS,** IF YOU THREE CAN TRACK THEM DOWN.
EVERYTHING YOU NEED IS RIGHT THERE IN THESE KNAPSACKS.
YOU MEAN LIKE A REASON TO **BELIEVE** YOU?
DON'T BE LIKE THAT, HOPE. WHAT...
...WHAT **IS** IN THESE BAGS?
THE CHANCE TO ACTUALLY DO THIS.
LIVE 3D MAPS. CLIMBING GEAR. SMART KEYS...A PANIC BUTTON. ALL NEXT-GEN TECH. AND I--
WE'RE GOING TO NEED ANOTHER SECOND.

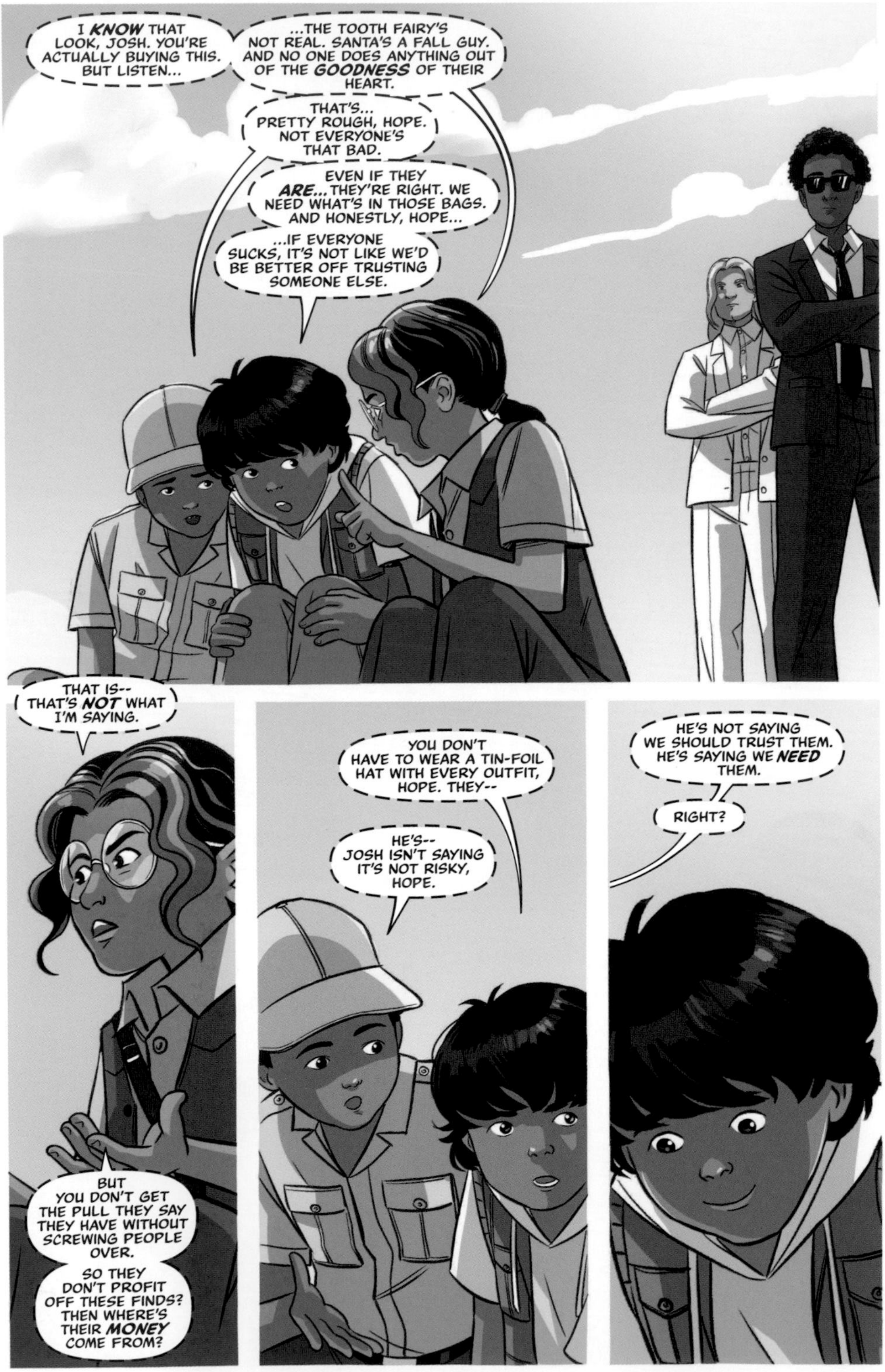
I KNOW THAT LOOK, JOSH. YOU'RE ACTUALLY BUYING THIS. BUT LISTEN...
...THE TOOTH FAIRY'S NOT REAL. SANTA'S A FALL GUY. AND NO ONE DOES ANYTHING OUT OF THE GOODNESS OF THEIR HEART.
THAT'S... PRETTY ROUGH, HOPE. NOT EVERYONE'S THAT BAD.
EVEN IF THEY ARE... THEY'RE RIGHT. WE NEED WHAT'S IN THOSE BAGS. AND HONESTLY, HOPE...
...IF EVERYONE SUCKS, IT'S NOT LIKE WE'D BE BETTER OFF TRUSTING SOMEONE ELSE.
THAT IS-- THAT'S NOT WHAT I'M SAYING.
BUT YOU DON'T GET THE PULL THEY SAY THEY HAVE WITHOUT SCREWING PEOPLE OVER.
SO THEY DON'T PROFIT OFF THESE FINDS? THEN WHERE'S THEIR MONEY COME FROM?
YOU DON'T HAVE TO WEAR A TIN-FOIL HAT WITH EVERY OUTFIT, HOPE. THEY--
HE'S-- JOSH ISN'T SAYING IT'S NOT RISKY, HOPE.
HE'S NOT SAYING WE SHOULD TRUST THEM. HE'S SAYING WE NEED THEM.
RIGHT?

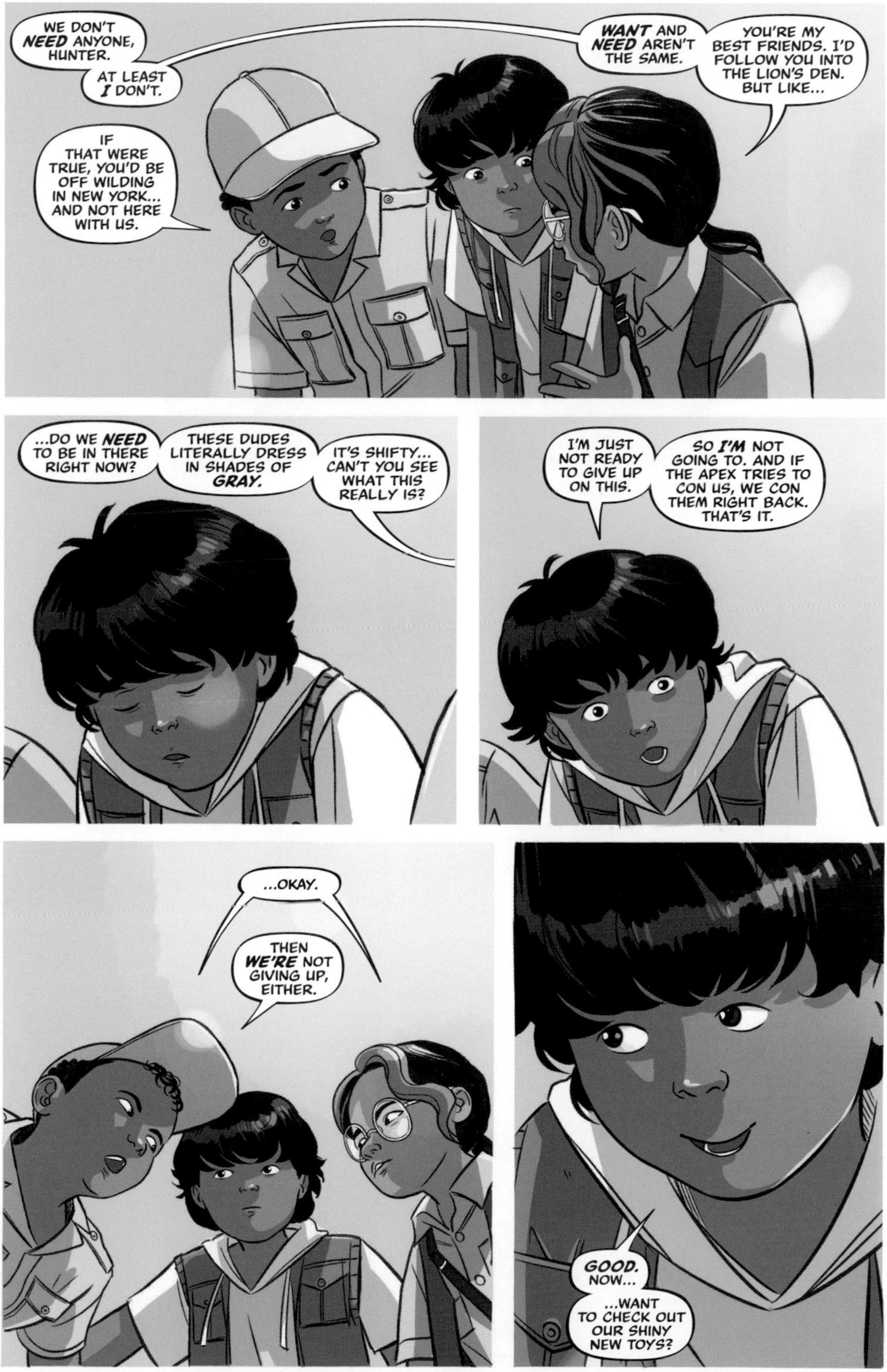
WE DON'T NEED ANYONE, HUNTER.
AT LEAST I DON'T.
WANT AND NEED AREN'T THE SAME.
IF THAT WERE TRUE, YOU'D BE OFF WILDING IN NEW YORK... AND NOT HERE WITH US.
YOU'RE MY BEST FRIENDS. I'D FOLLOW YOU INTO THE LION'S DEN. BUT LIKE...
...DO WE NEED TO BE IN THERE RIGHT NOW?
THESE DUDES LITERALLY DRESS IN SHADES OF GRAY.
IT'S SHIFTY... CAN'T YOU SEE WHAT THIS REALLY IS?
I'M JUST NOT READY TO GIVE UP ON THIS.
SO I'M NOT GOING TO. AND IF THE APEX TRIES TO CON US, WE CON THEM RIGHT BACK. THAT'S IT.
...OKAY.
THEN WE'RE NOT GIVING UP, EITHER.
GOOD. NOW...
...WANT TO CHECK OUT OUR SHINY NEW TOYS?

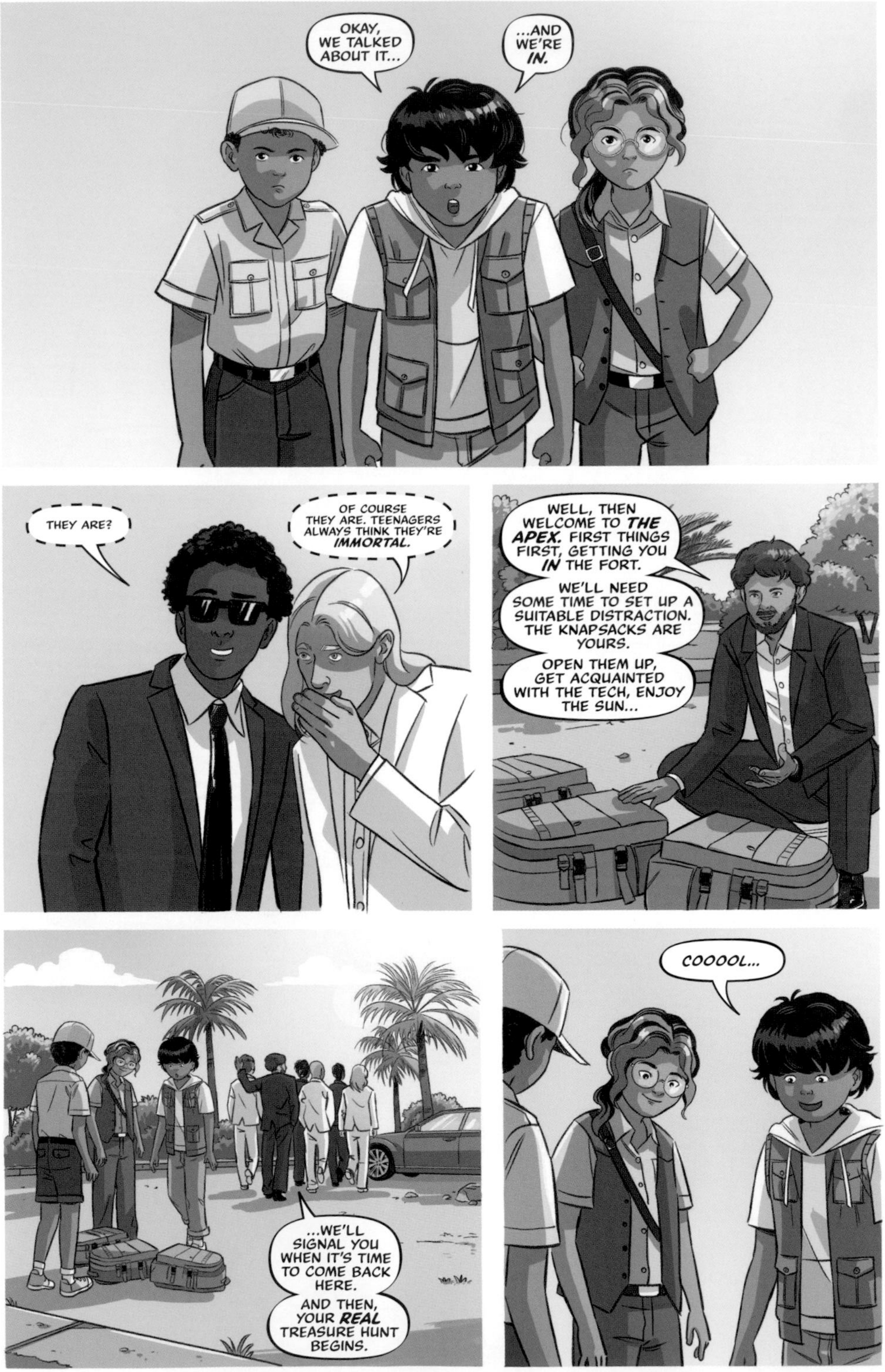
OKAY, WE TALKED ABOUT IT...
...AND WE'RE *IN.*
THEY ARE?
OF COURSE THEY ARE. TEENAGERS ALWAYS THINK THEY'RE *IMMORTAL.*
WELL, THEN WELCOME TO *THE APEX.* FIRST THINGS FIRST, GETTING YOU *IN* THE FORT.
WE'LL NEED SOME TIME TO SET UP A SUITABLE DISTRACTION. THE KNAPSACKS ARE YOURS.
OPEN THEM UP, GET ACQUAINTED WITH THE TECH, ENJOY THE SUN...
...WE'LL SIGNAL YOU WHEN IT'S TIME TO COME BACK HERE.
AND THEN, YOUR *REAL* TREASURE HUNT BEGINS.
COOOOL...

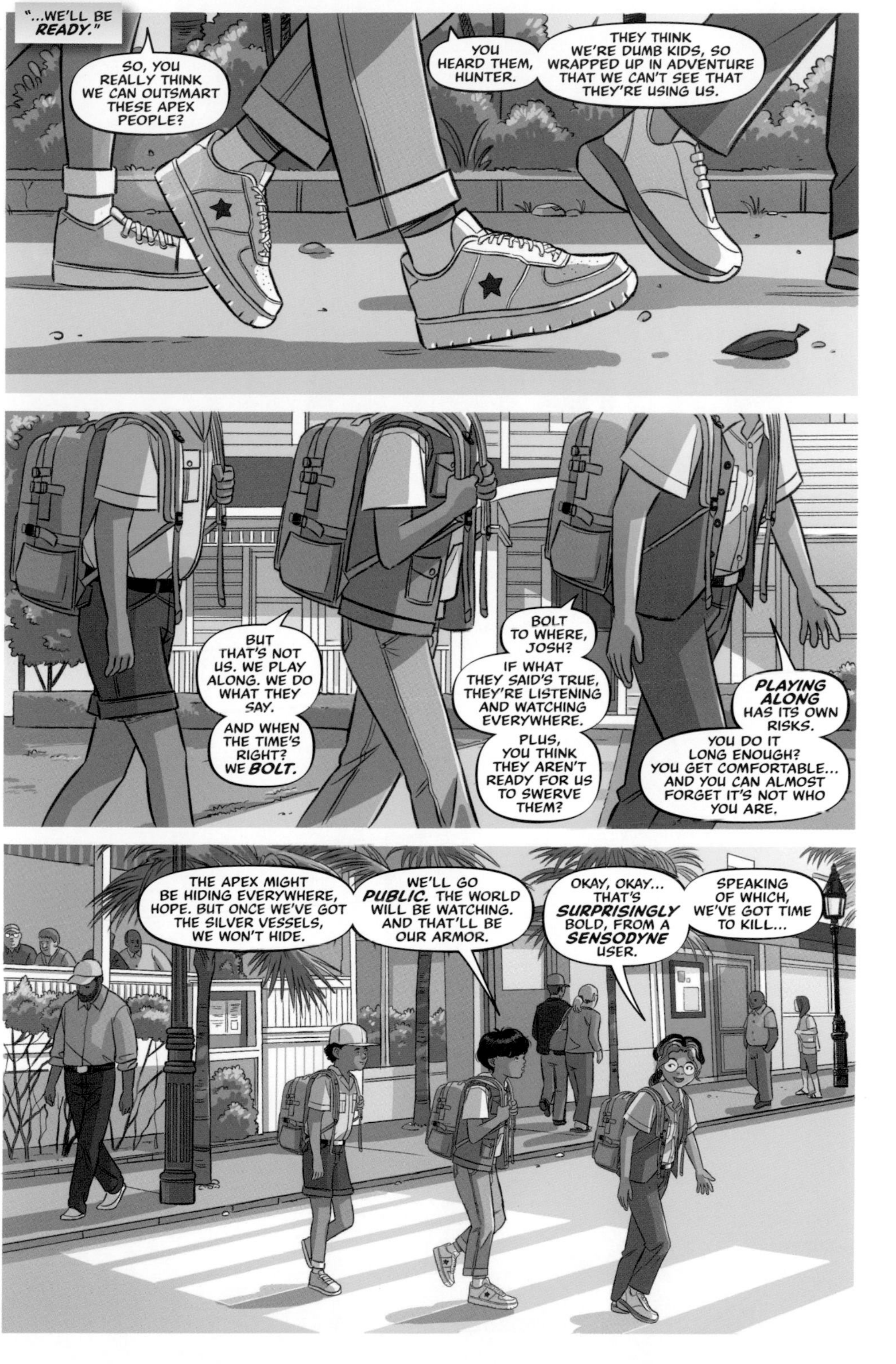
"...WE'LL BE *READY.*"
SO, YOU REALLY THINK WE CAN OUTSMART THESE APEX PEOPLE?
YOU HEARD THEM, HUNTER.
THEY THINK WE'RE DUMB KIDS, SO WRAPPED UP IN ADVENTURE THAT WE CAN'T SEE THAT THEY'RE USING US.
BUT THAT'S NOT US. WE PLAY ALONG. WE DO WHAT THEY SAY.
AND WHEN THE TIME'S RIGHT? WE *BOLT.*
BOLT TO WHERE, JOSH?
IF WHAT THEY SAID'S TRUE, THEY'RE LISTENING AND WATCHING EVERYWHERE.
PLUS, YOU THINK THEY AREN'T READY FOR US TO SWERVE THEM?
PLAYING ALONG HAS ITS OWN RISKS.
YOU DO IT LONG ENOUGH? YOU GET COMFORTABLE... AND YOU CAN ALMOST FORGET IT'S NOT WHO YOU ARE.
THE APEX MIGHT BE HIDING EVERYWHERE, HOPE. BUT ONCE WE'VE GOT THE SILVER VESSELS, WE WON'T HIDE.
WE'LL GO *PUBLIC.* THE WORLD WILL BE WATCHING. AND THAT'LL BE OUR ARMOR.
OKAY, OKAY... THAT'S *SURPRISINGLY* BOLD, FROM A *SENSODYNE* USER.
SPEAKING OF WHICH, WE'VE GOT TIME TO KILL...

"...AND FILLINGS TO TEST."

I'M SO WIRED.

I'M SO NUMB. I *HAD* TO MAKE THAT JOKE. NOW I'M THE ONE WITH THE MOUTH FULL OF FROZEN SILVER.

I'VE NEVER HAD MORE THAN THREE ICED COFFEES IN A DAY. I FEEL LIKE A *GOD*.

ICE CREAM

WHO NEEDS GODHOOD WHEN THERE'S GADGETS?

LOOK AT THIS STUFF... THEY WEREN'T KIDDING.

IS THAT--

LIVE MAGNETIC IMAGING? YUP.

THAT *CAN'T* BE A--

LOCAL SURVEILLANCE SCRAMBLER? SURE CAN.

IT'S ALL IN THE NOTES THEY LEFT IN THE--

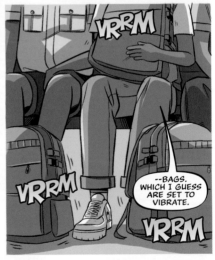

VRRM

VRRM

--BAGS. WHICH I GUESS ARE SET TO VIBRATE.

VRRM

THAT'S THE APEX'S SIGNAL...

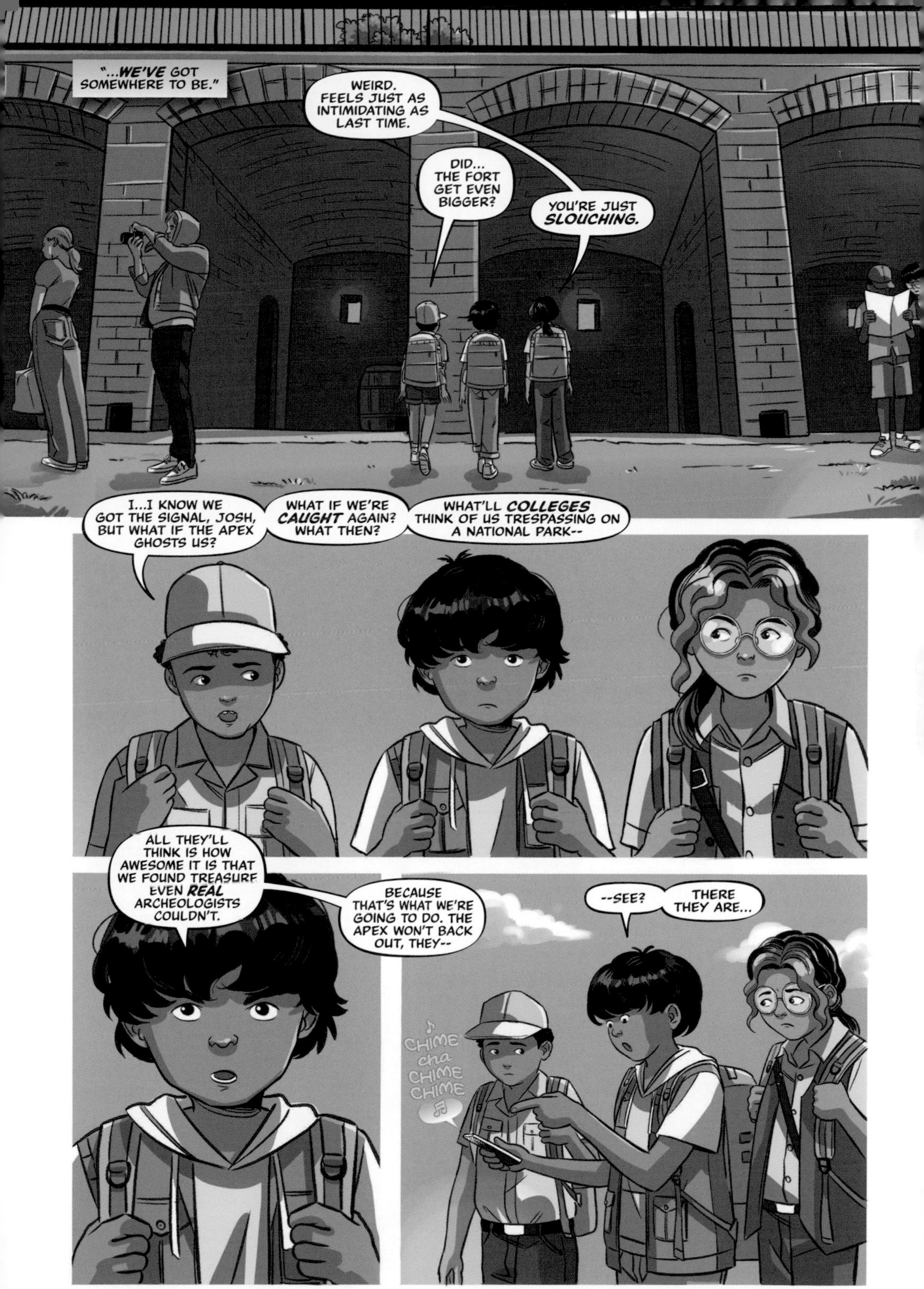
"...WE'VE GOT SOMEWHERE TO BE."
WEIRD. FEELS JUST AS INTIMIDATING AS LAST TIME.
DID... THE FORT GET EVEN BIGGER?
YOU'RE JUST SLOUCHING.
I...I KNOW WE GOT THE SIGNAL, JOSH, BUT WHAT IF THE APEX GHOSTS US?
WHAT IF WE'RE CAUGHT AGAIN? WHAT THEN?
WHAT'LL COLLEGES THINK OF US TRESPASSING ON A NATIONAL PARK--
ALL THEY'LL THINK IS HOW AWESOME IT IS THAT WE FOUND TREASURE EVEN REAL ARCHEOLOGISTS COULDN'T.
BECAUSE THAT'S WHAT WE'RE GOING TO DO. THE APEX WON'T BACK OUT, THEY--
CHIME cha CHIME CHIME
--SEE?
THERE THEY ARE...

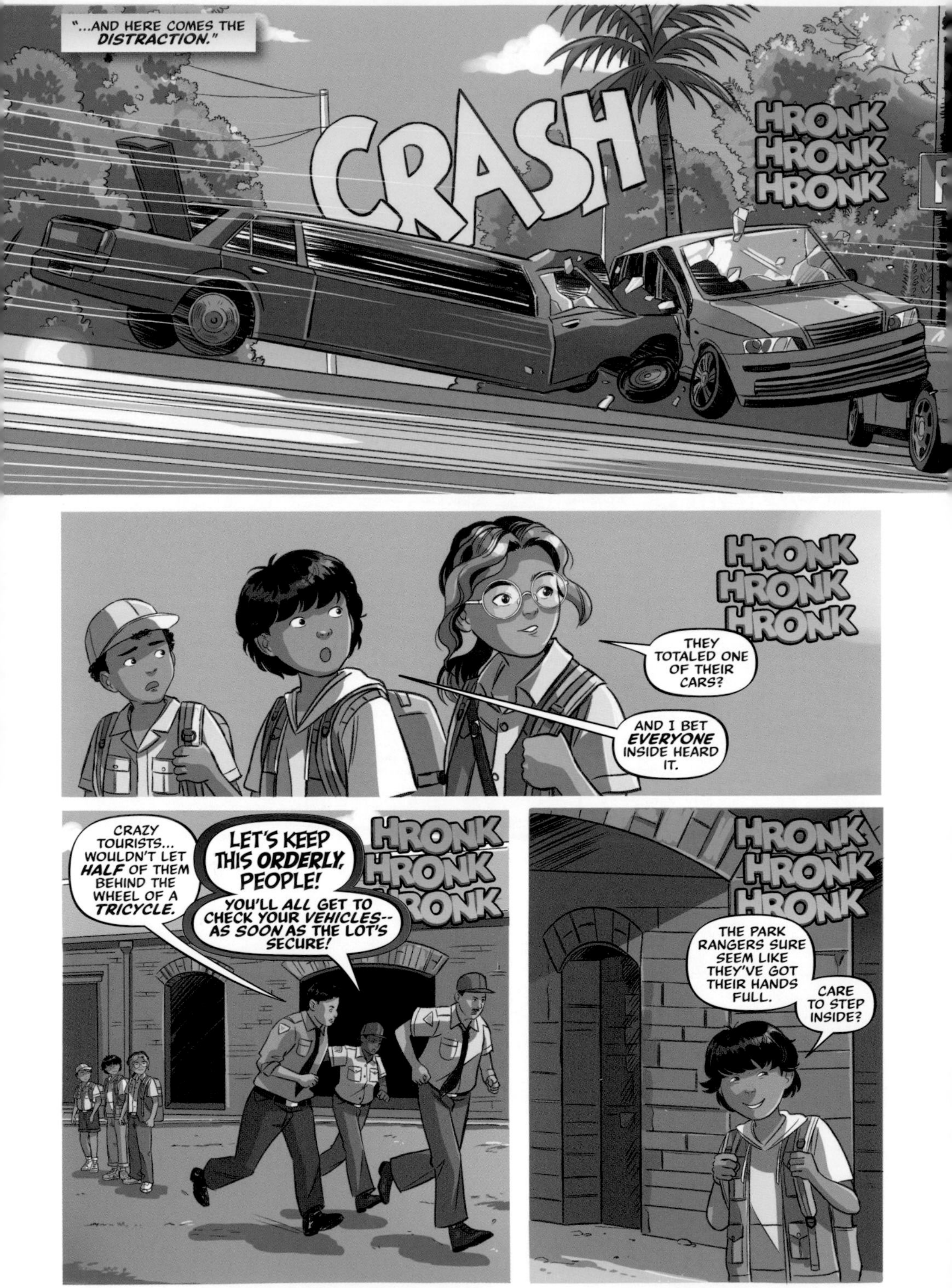
"...AND HERE COMES THE *DISTRACTION.*"
CRASH
HRONK HRONK HRONK
HRONK HRONK HRONK
THEY TOTALED ONE OF THEIR CARS?
AND I BET *EVERYONE* INSIDE HEARD IT.
CRAZY TOURISTS... WOULDN'T LET *HALF* OF THEM BEHIND THE WHEEL OF A *TRICYCLE.*
LET'S KEEP THIS *ORDERLY,* PEOPLE!
YOU'LL *ALL* GET TO CHECK YOUR *VEHICLES*-- AS *SOON* AS THE LOT'S SECURE!
HRONK HRONK HRONK
THE PARK RANGERS SURE SEEM LIKE THEY'VE GOT THEIR HANDS FULL.
CARE TO STEP INSIDE?

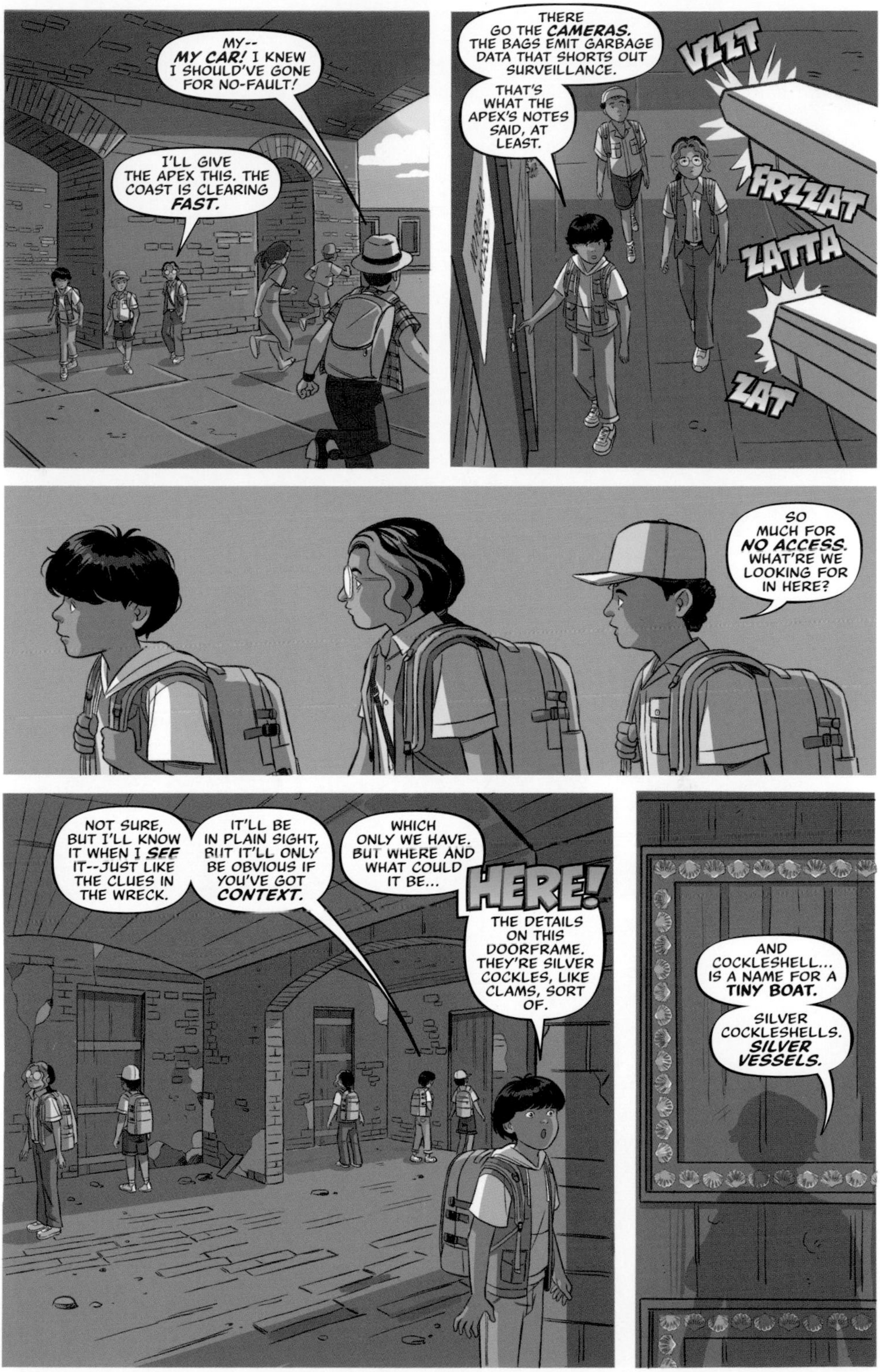
MY-- MY CAR! I KNEW I SHOULD'VE GONE FOR NO-FAULT!
I'LL GIVE THE APEX THIS. THE COAST IS CLEARING FAST.
THERE GO THE CAMERAS. THE BAGS EMIT GARBAGE DATA THAT SHORTS OUT SURVEILLANCE.
THAT'S WHAT THE APEX'S NOTES SAID, AT LEAST.
VZZT
FRZZAT
ZATTA
ZAT
SO MUCH FOR NO ACCESS. WHAT'RE WE LOOKING FOR IN HERE?
NOT SURE, BUT I'LL KNOW IT WHEN I SEE IT--JUST LIKE THE CLUES IN THE WRECK.
IT'LL BE IN PLAIN SIGHT, BUT IT'LL ONLY BE OBVIOUS IF YOU'VE GOT CONTEXT.
WHICH ONLY WE HAVE. BUT WHERE AND WHAT COULD IT BE...
HERE!
THE DETAILS ON THIS DOORFRAME. THEY'RE SILVER COCKLES, LIKE CLAMS, SORT OF.
AND COCKLESHELL... IS A NAME FOR A TINY BOAT.
SILVER COCKLESHELLS. SILVER VESSELS.

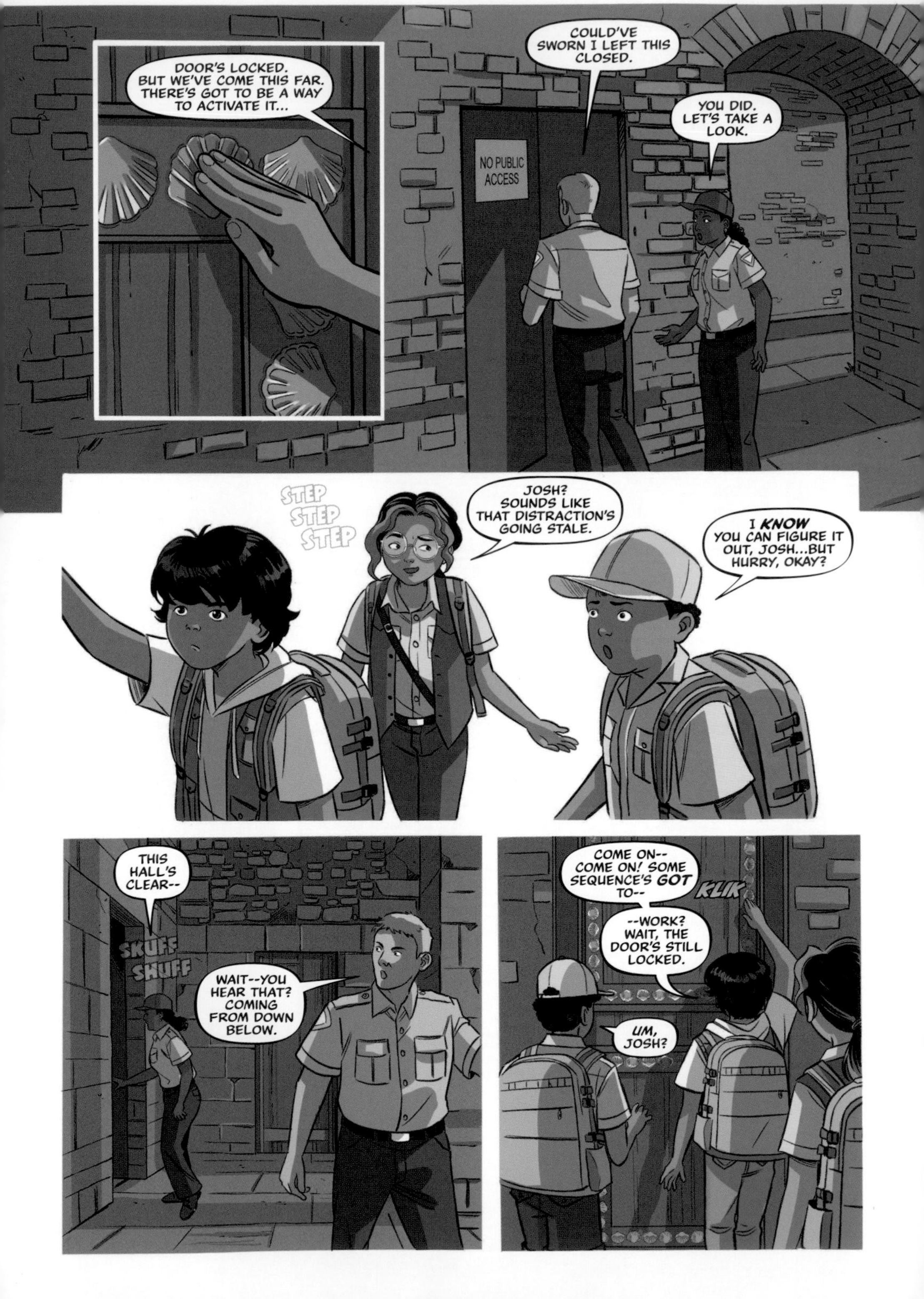
DOOR'S LOCKED. BUT WE'VE COME THIS FAR. THERE'S GOT TO BE A WAY TO ACTIVATE IT...
COULD'VE SWORN I LEFT THIS CLOSED.
NO PUBLIC ACCESS
YOU DID. LET'S TAKE A LOOK.
STEP STEP STEP
JOSH? SOUNDS LIKE THAT DISTRACTION'S GOING STALE.
I KNOW YOU CAN FIGURE IT OUT, JOSH...BUT HURRY, OKAY?
THIS HALL'S CLEAR--
SKUFF SHUFF
WAIT--YOU HEAR THAT? COMING FROM DOWN BELOW.
COME ON-- COME ON! SOME SEQUENCE'S GOT TO--
KLIK
--WORK? WAIT, THE DOOR'S STILL LOCKED.
UM, JOSH?

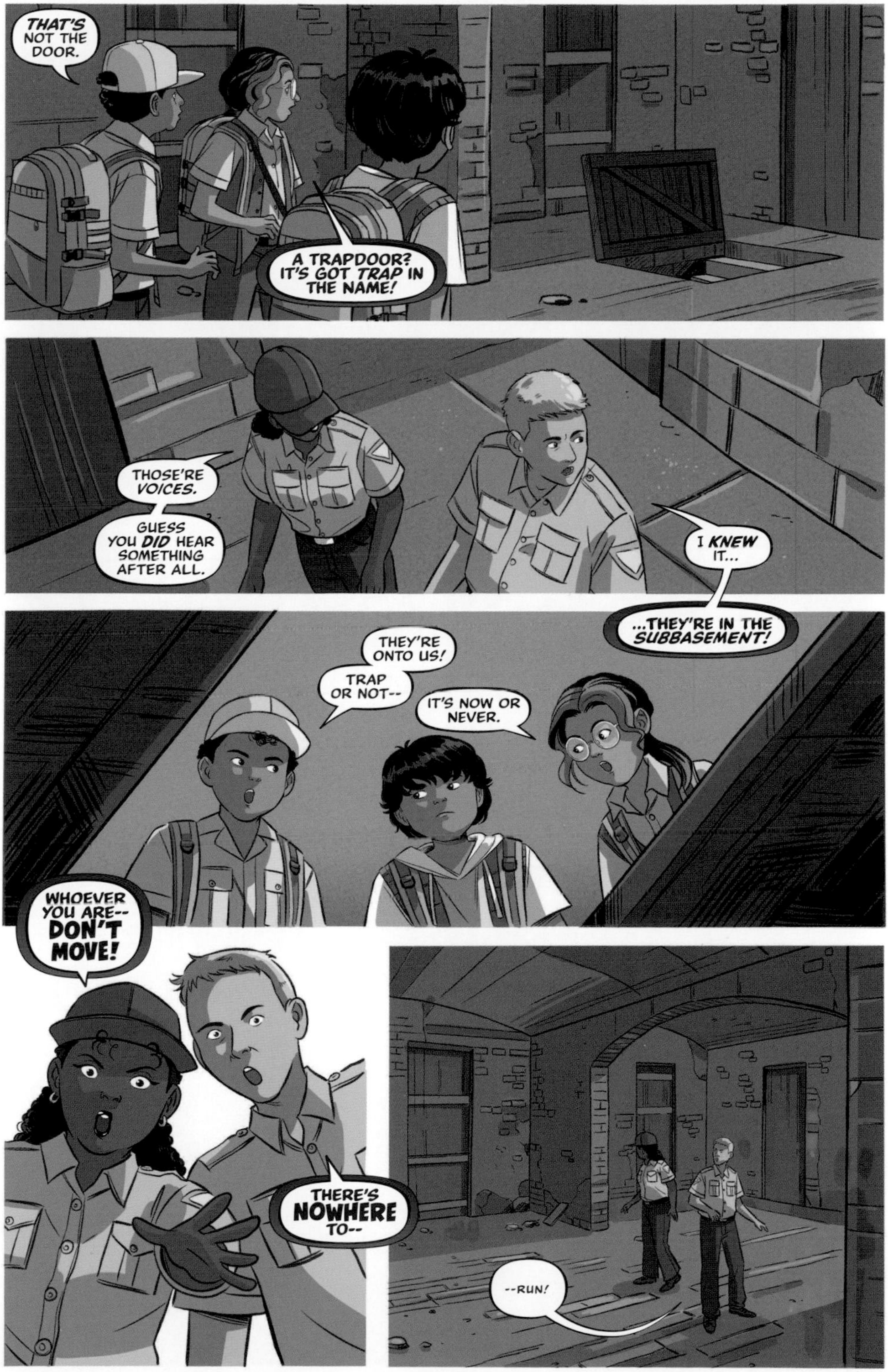
THAT'S NOT THE DOOR.
A TRAPDOOR? IT'S GOT TRAP IN THE NAME!
THOSE'RE VOICES.
GUESS YOU DID HEAR SOMETHING AFTER ALL.
I KNEW IT...
...THEY'RE IN THE SUBBASEMENT!
THEY'RE ONTO US!
TRAP OR NOT--
IT'S NOW OR NEVER.
WHOEVER YOU ARE-- DON'T MOVE!
THERE'S NOWHERE TO--
--RUN!

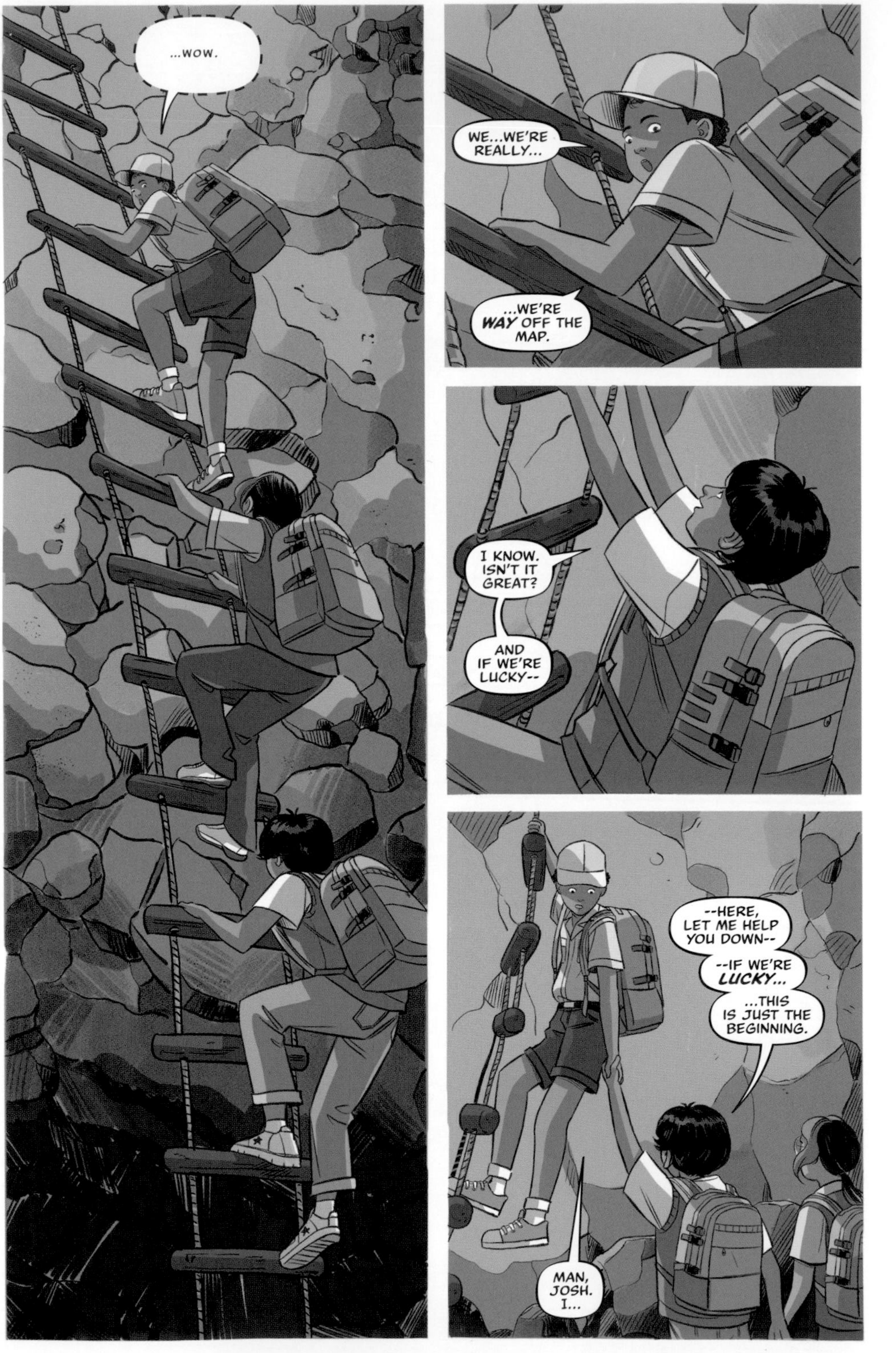
...WOW.
WE...WE'RE REALLY...
...WE'RE **WAY** OFF THE MAP.
I KNOW. ISN'T IT GREAT?
AND IF WE'RE LUCKY--
--HERE, LET ME HELP YOU DOWN--
--IF WE'RE **LUCKY...**
...THIS IS JUST THE BEGINNING.
MAN, JOSH. I...

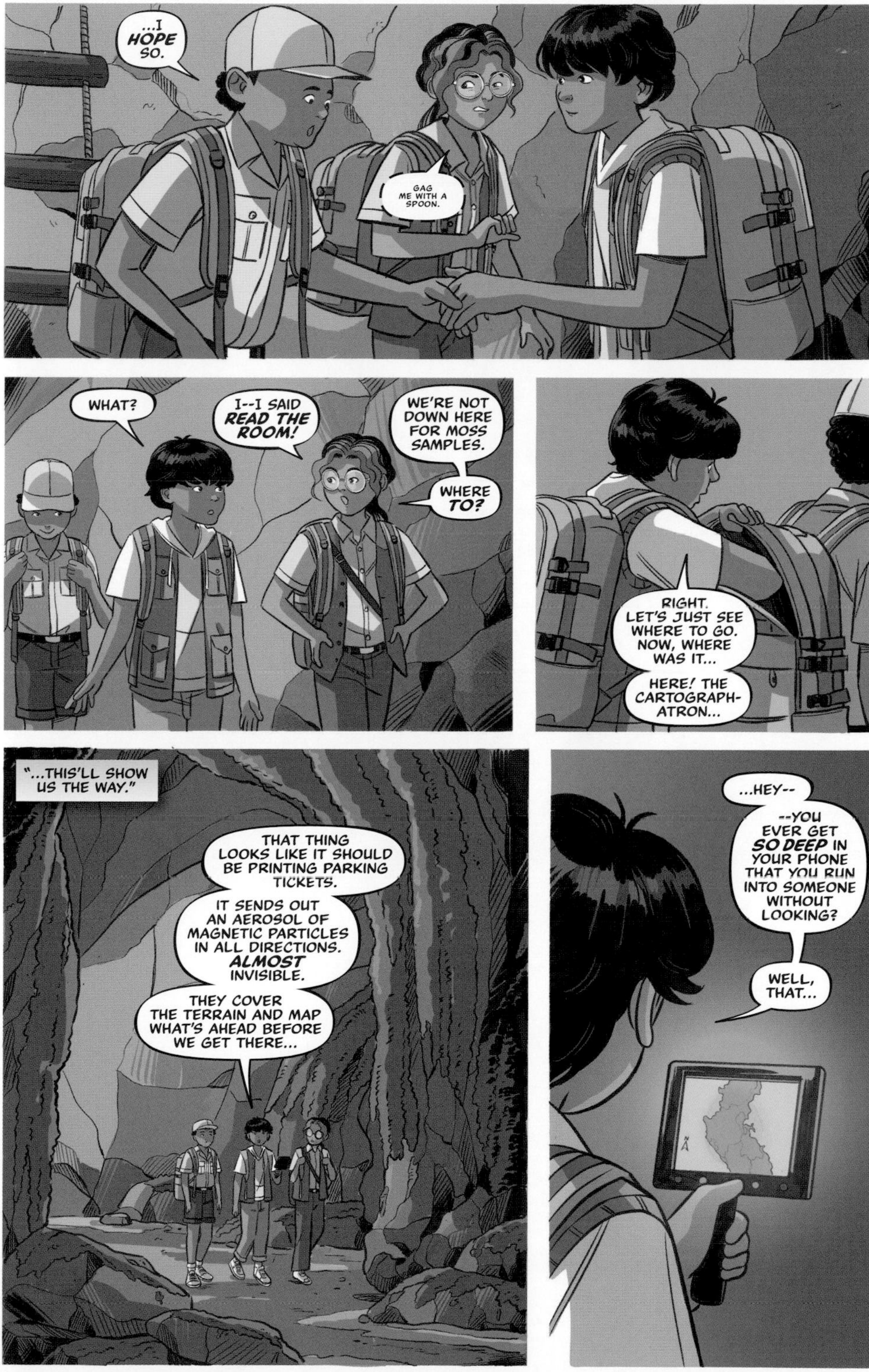
...I HOPE SO.
GAG ME WITH A SPOON.
WHAT?
I--I SAID READ THE ROOM!
WE'RE NOT DOWN HERE FOR MOSS SAMPLES.
WHERE TO?
RIGHT. LET'S JUST SEE WHERE TO GO. NOW, WHERE WAS IT...
HERE! THE CARTOGRAPH-ATRON...
"...THIS'LL SHOW US THE WAY."
THAT THING LOOKS LIKE IT SHOULD BE PRINTING PARKING TICKETS.
IT SENDS OUT AN AEROSOL OF MAGNETIC PARTICLES IN ALL DIRECTIONS. ALMOST INVISIBLE.
THEY COVER THE TERRAIN AND MAP WHAT'S AHEAD BEFORE WE GET THERE...
...HEY--
--YOU EVER GET SO DEEP IN YOUR PHONE THAT YOU RUN INTO SOMEONE WITHOUT LOOKING?
WELL, THAT...

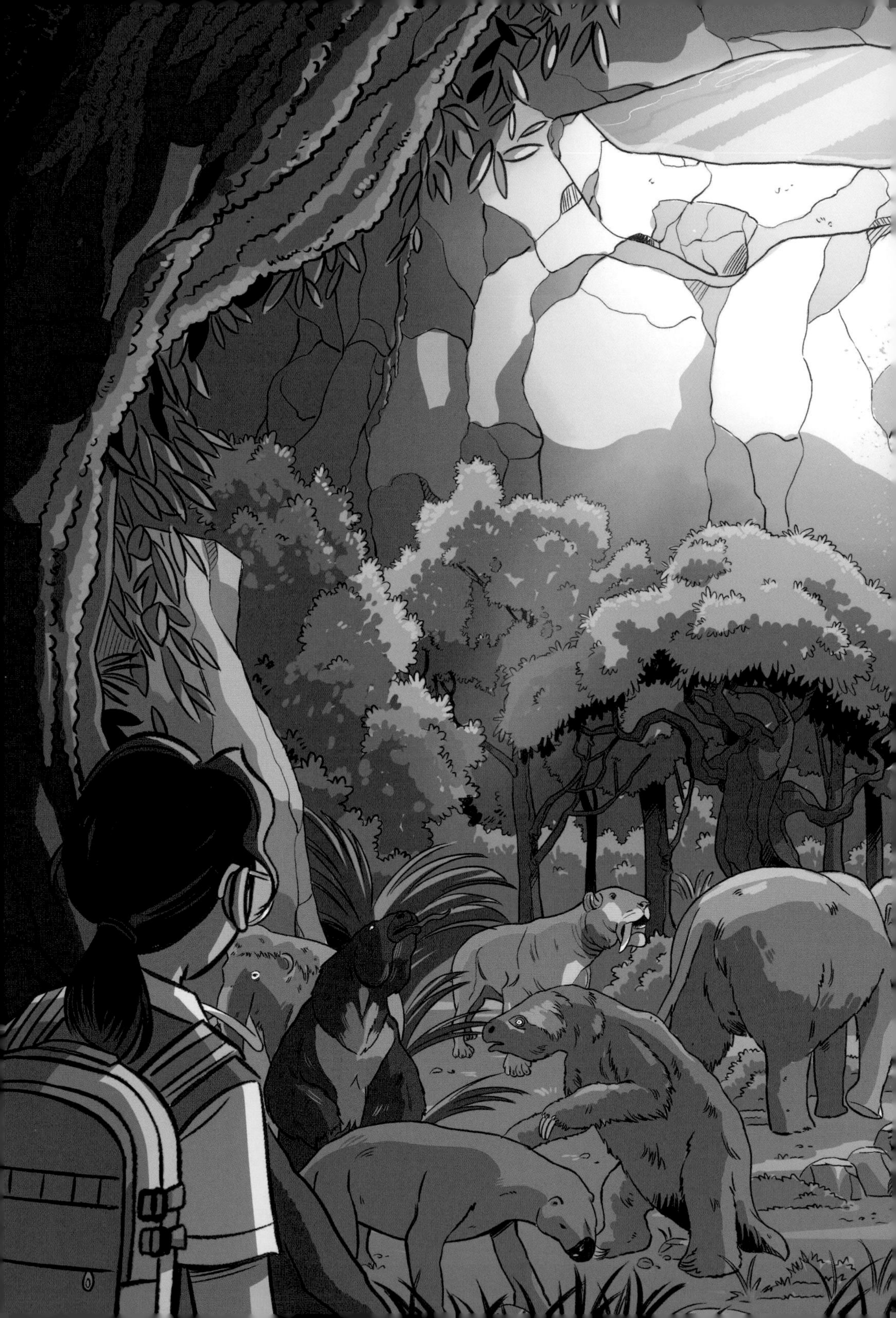

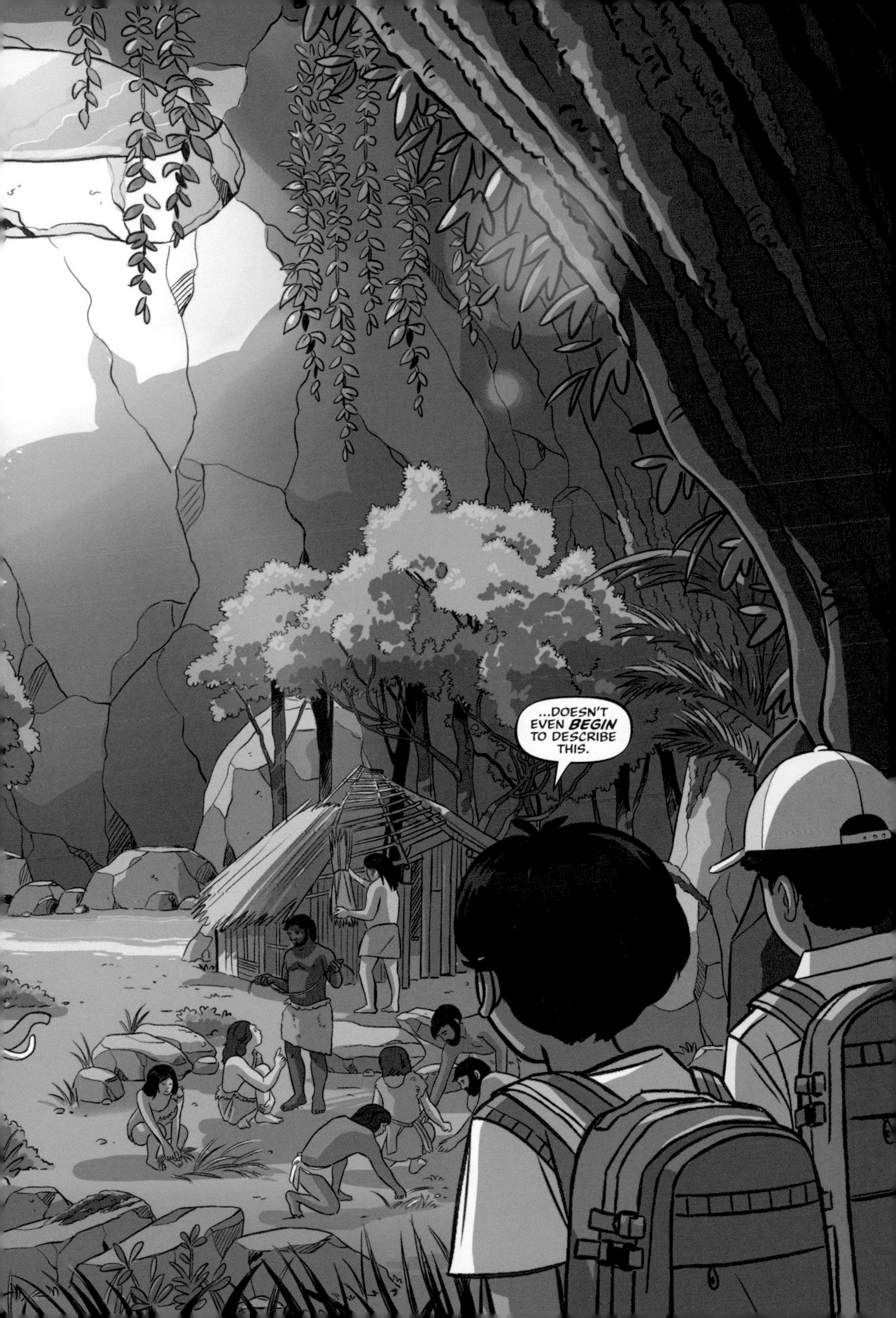
...DOESN'T EVEN BEGIN TO DESCRIBE THIS.

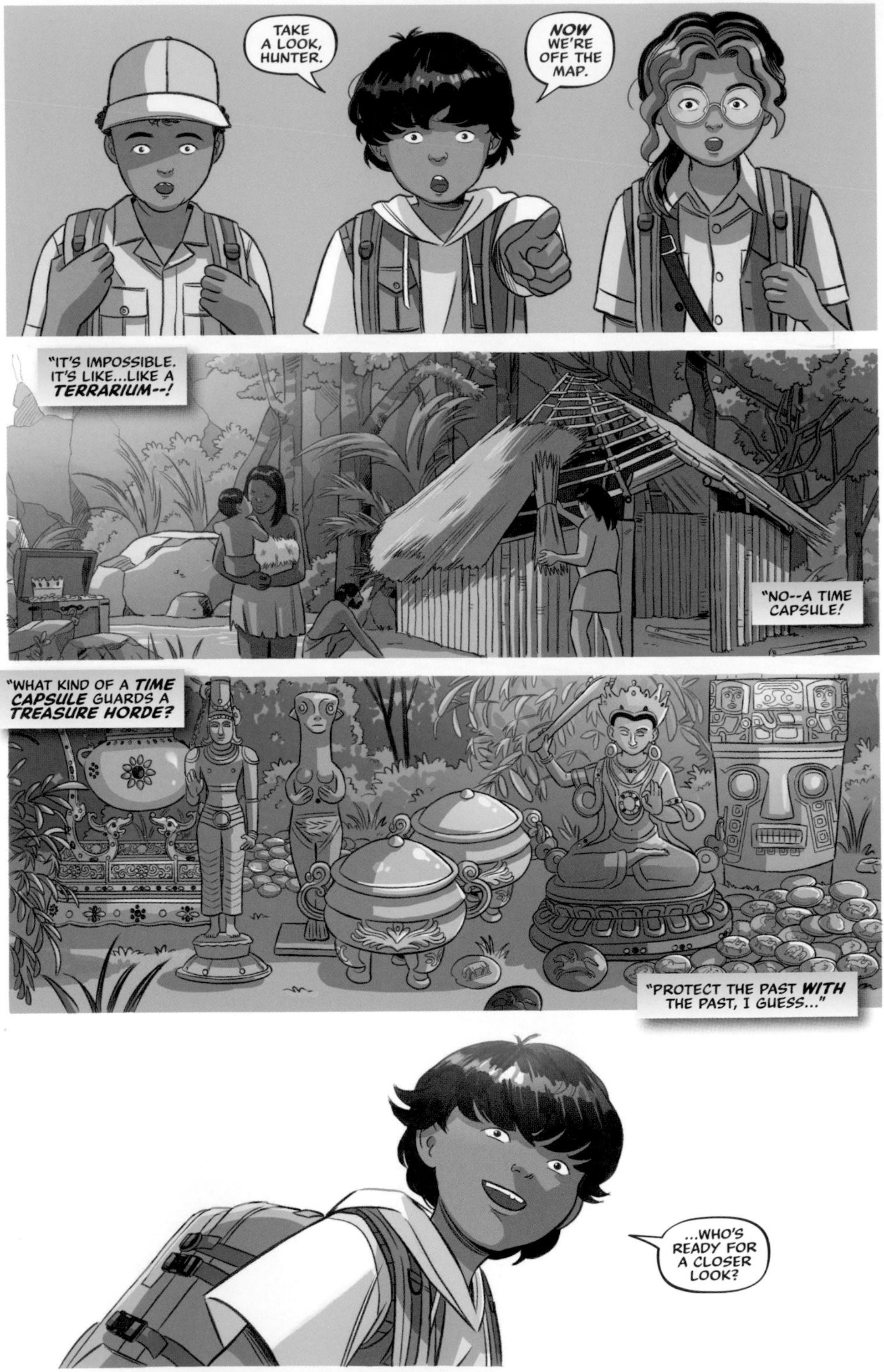
TAKE A LOOK, HUNTER.
NOW WE'RE OFF THE MAP.
"IT'S IMPOSSIBLE. IT'S LIKE...LIKE A TERRARIUM--!
"NO--A TIME CAPSULE!
"WHAT KIND OF A TIME CAPSULE GUARDS A TREASURE HORDE?
"PROTECT THE PAST WITH THE PAST, I GUESS..."
...WHO'S READY FOR A CLOSER LOOK?

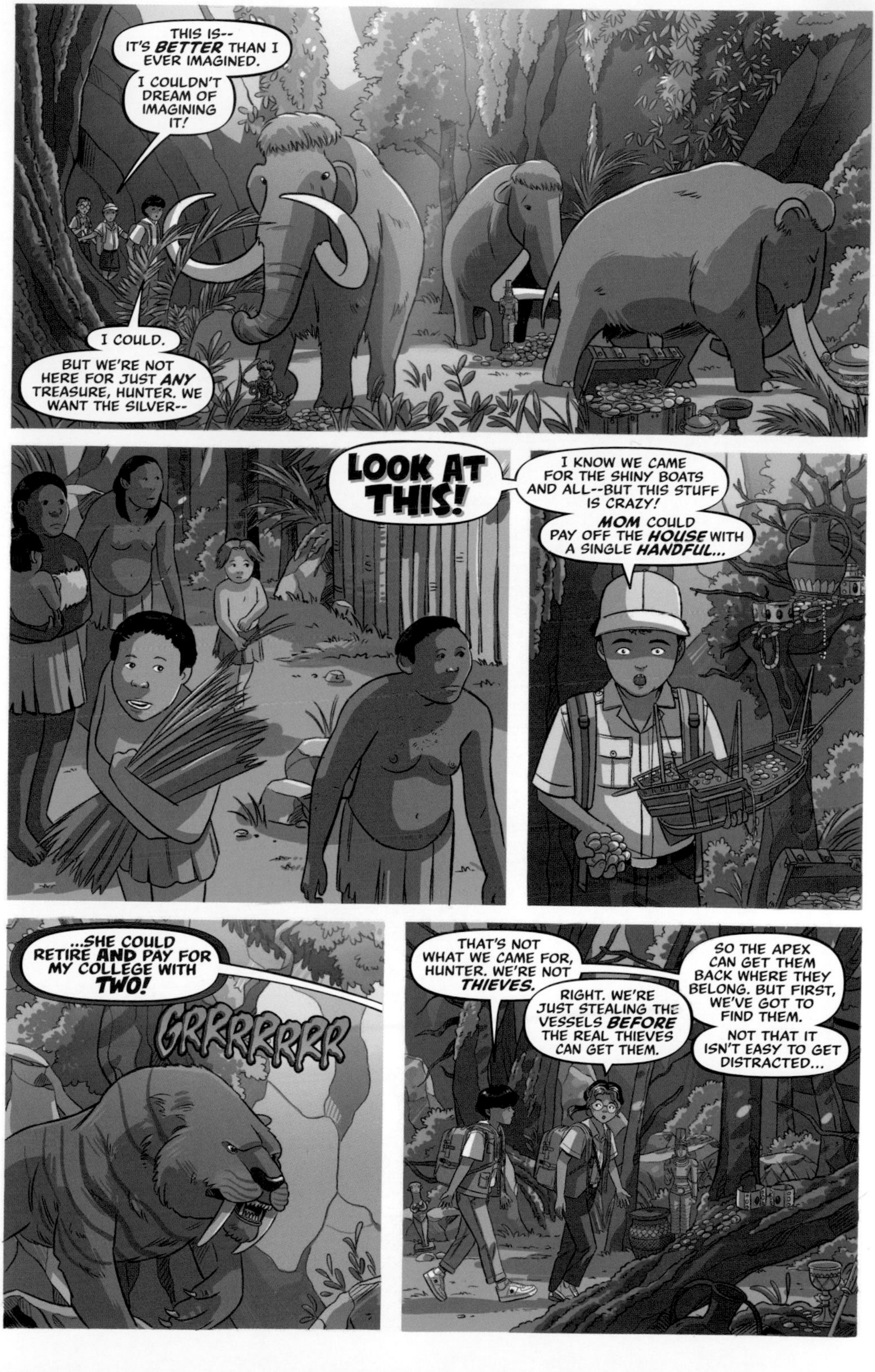
THIS IS-- IT'S BETTER THAN I EVER IMAGINED.
I COULDN'T DREAM OF IMAGINING IT!
I COULD.
BUT WE'RE NOT HERE FOR JUST ANY TREASURE, HUNTER. WE WANT THE SILVER--
LOOK AT THIS!
I KNOW WE CAME FOR THE SHINY BOATS AND ALL--BUT THIS STUFF IS CRAZY!
MOM COULD PAY OFF THE HOUSE WITH A SINGLE HANDFUL...
...SHE COULD RETIRE AND PAY FOR MY COLLEGE WITH TWO!
GRRRRRRR
THAT'S NOT WHAT WE CAME FOR, HUNTER. WE'RE NOT THIEVES.
RIGHT. WE'RE JUST STEALING THE VESSELS BEFORE THE REAL THIEVES CAN GET THEM.
SO THE APEX CAN GET THEM BACK WHERE THEY BELONG. BUT FIRST, WE'VE GOT TO FIND THEM.
NOT THAT IT ISN'T EASY TO GET DISTRACTED...

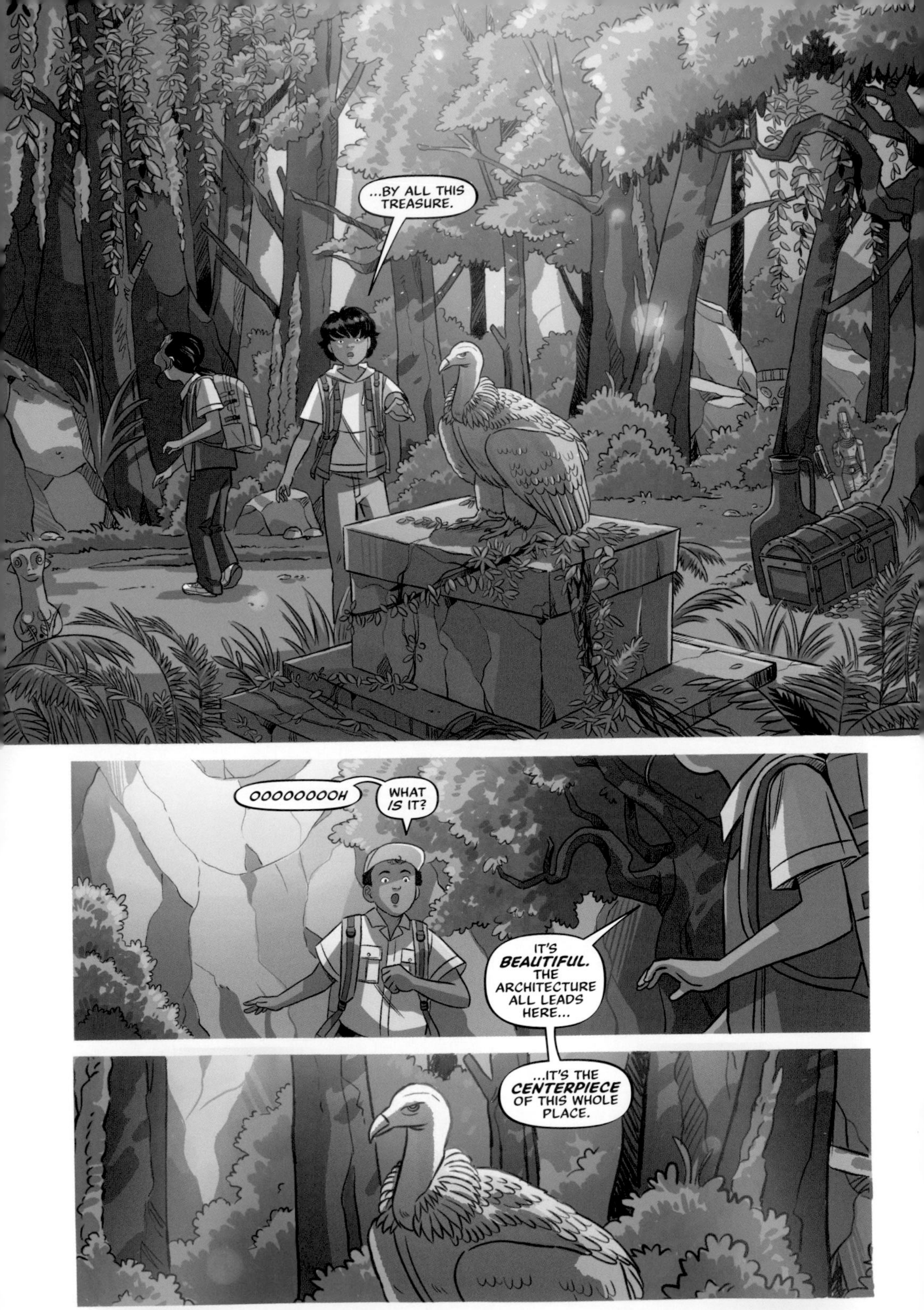
...BY ALL THIS TREASURE.
OOOOOOOOH
WHAT IS IT?
IT'S BEAUTIFUL. THE ARCHITECTURE ALL LEADS HERE...
...IT'S THE CENTERPIECE OF THIS WHOLE PLACE.

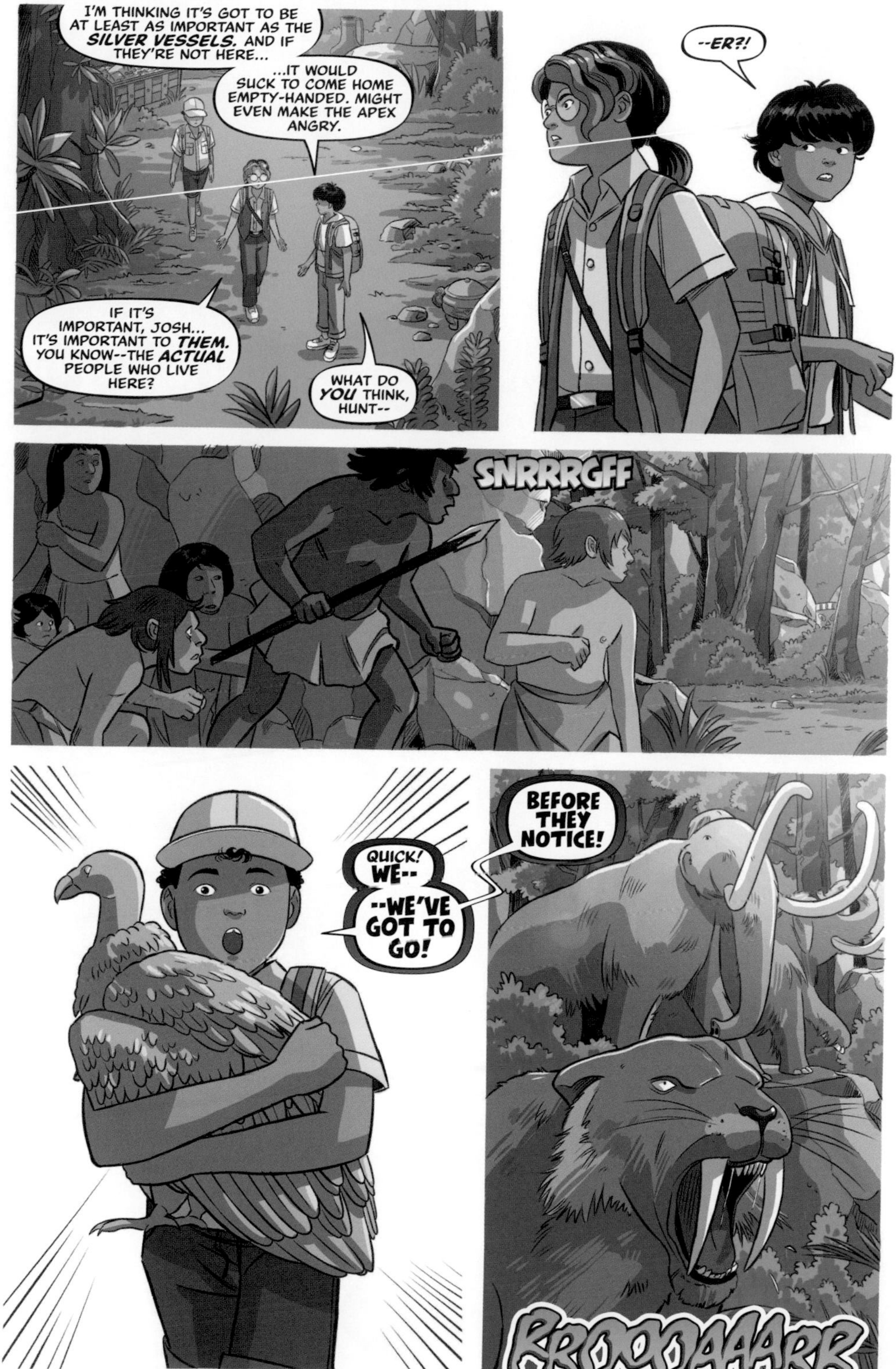
I'M THINKING IT'S GOT TO BE AT LEAST AS IMPORTANT AS THE SILVER VESSELS. AND IF THEY'RE NOT HERE...
...IT WOULD SUCK TO COME HOME EMPTY-HANDED. MIGHT EVEN MAKE THE APEX ANGRY.
IF IT'S IMPORTANT, JOSH... IT'S IMPORTANT TO THEM. YOU KNOW--THE ACTUAL PEOPLE WHO LIVE HERE?
WHAT DO YOU THINK, HUNT--
--ER?!
SNRRRGFF
QUICK! WE--
--WE'VE GOT TO GO!
BEFORE THEY NOTICE!
KROOOAAARR

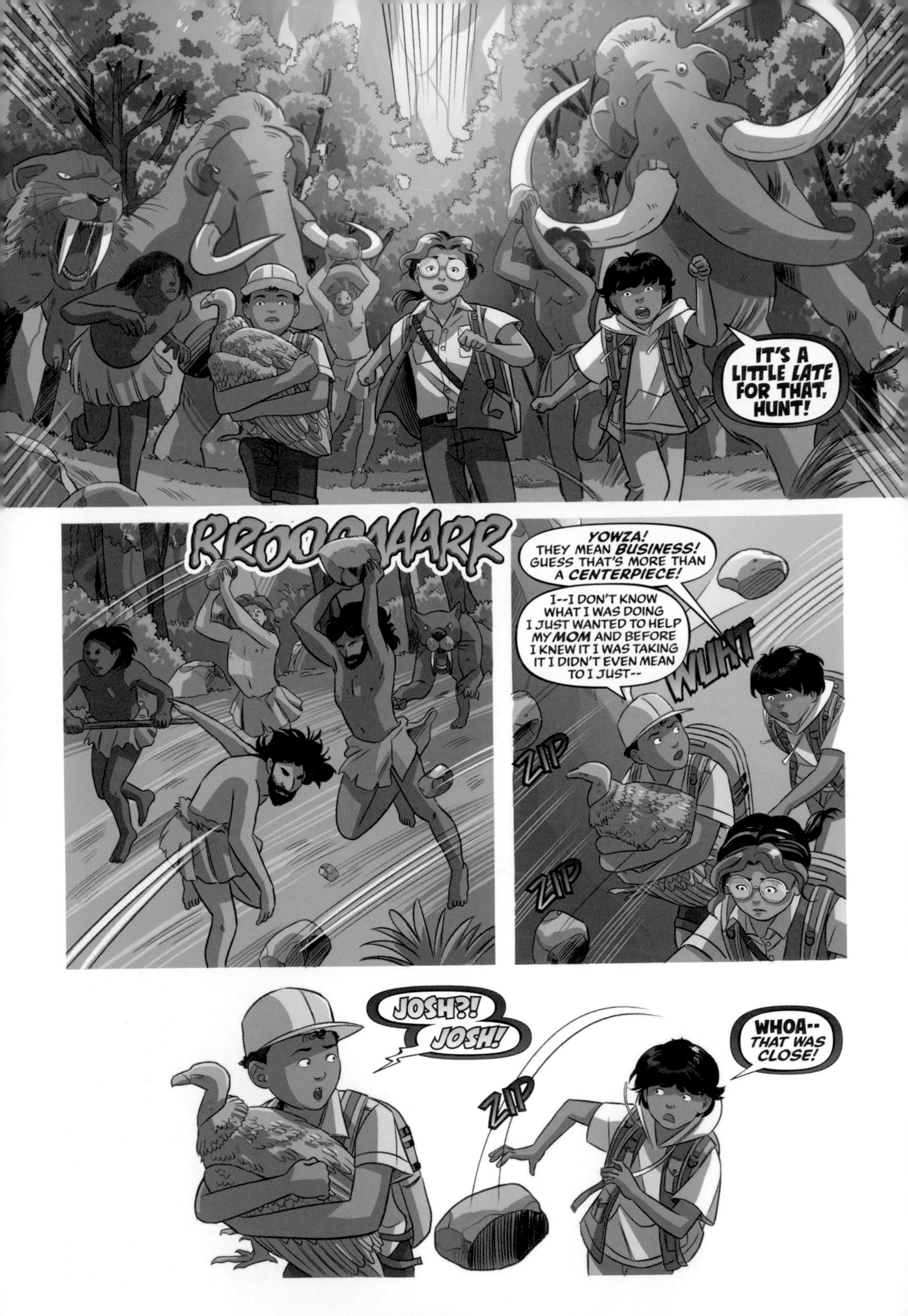

IT'S A LITTLE *LATE* FOR THAT, HUNT!
RROOOAARR
YOWZA! THEY MEAN ***BUSINESS!*** GUESS THAT'S MORE THAN A ***CENTERPIECE!***
I--I DON'T KNOW WHAT I WAS DOING I JUST WANTED TO HELP MY ***MOM*** AND BEFORE I KNEW IT I WAS TAKING IT I DIDN'T EVEN MEAN TO I JUST--
WUHT
ZIP
ZIP
JOSH?!
JOSH!
ZIP
WHOA-- *THAT WAS CLOSE!*

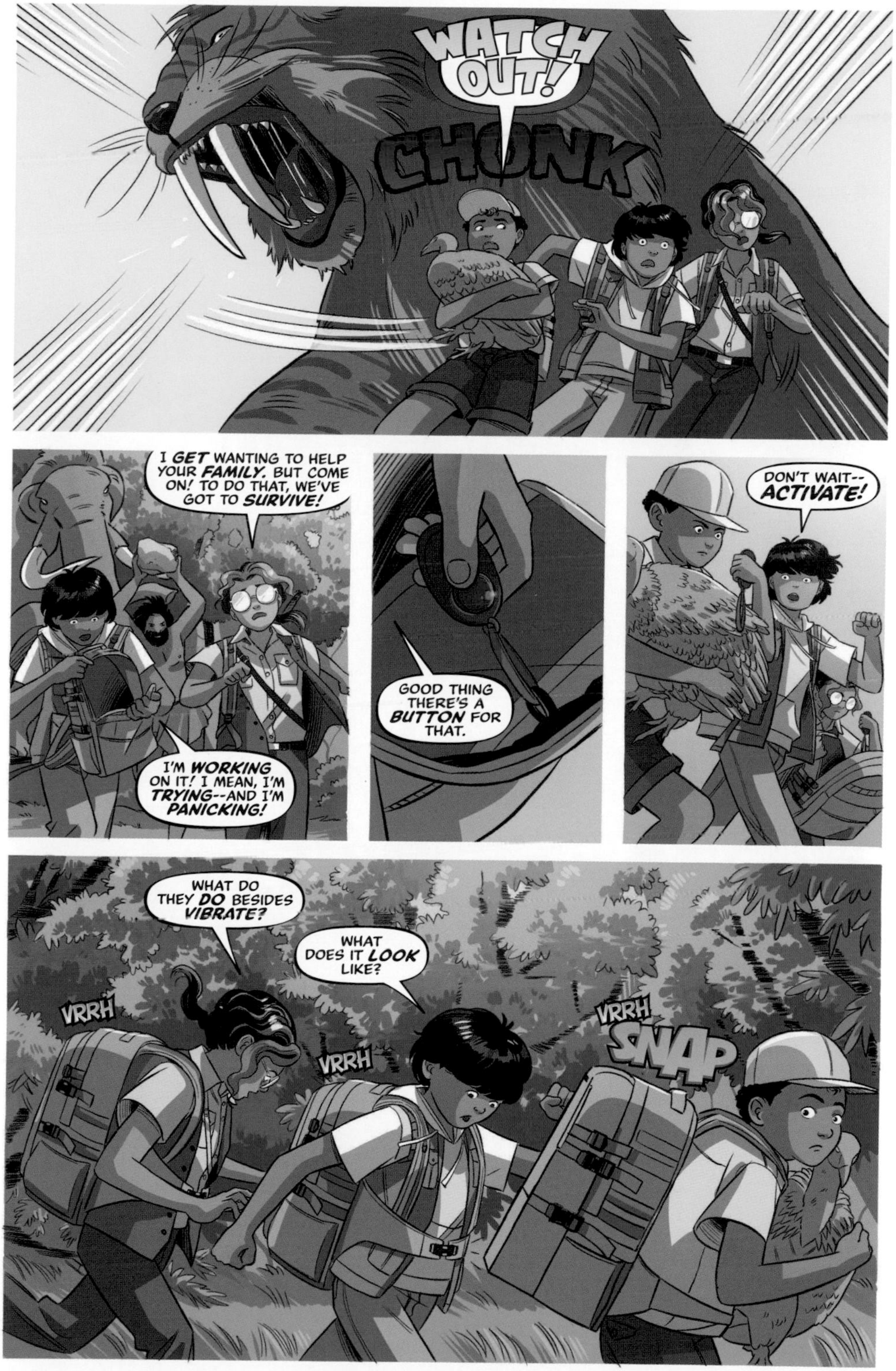
WATCH OUT!
CHONK
I GET WANTING TO HELP YOUR FAMILY. BUT COME ON! TO DO THAT, WE'VE GOT TO SURVIVE!
I'M WORKING ON IT! I MEAN, I'M TRYING--AND I'M PANICKING!
GOOD THING THERE'S A BUTTON FOR THAT.
DON'T WAIT-- ACTIVATE!
WHAT DO THEY DO BESIDES VIBRATE?
WHAT DOES IT LOOK LIKE?
VRRH
VRRH
VRRH
SNAP

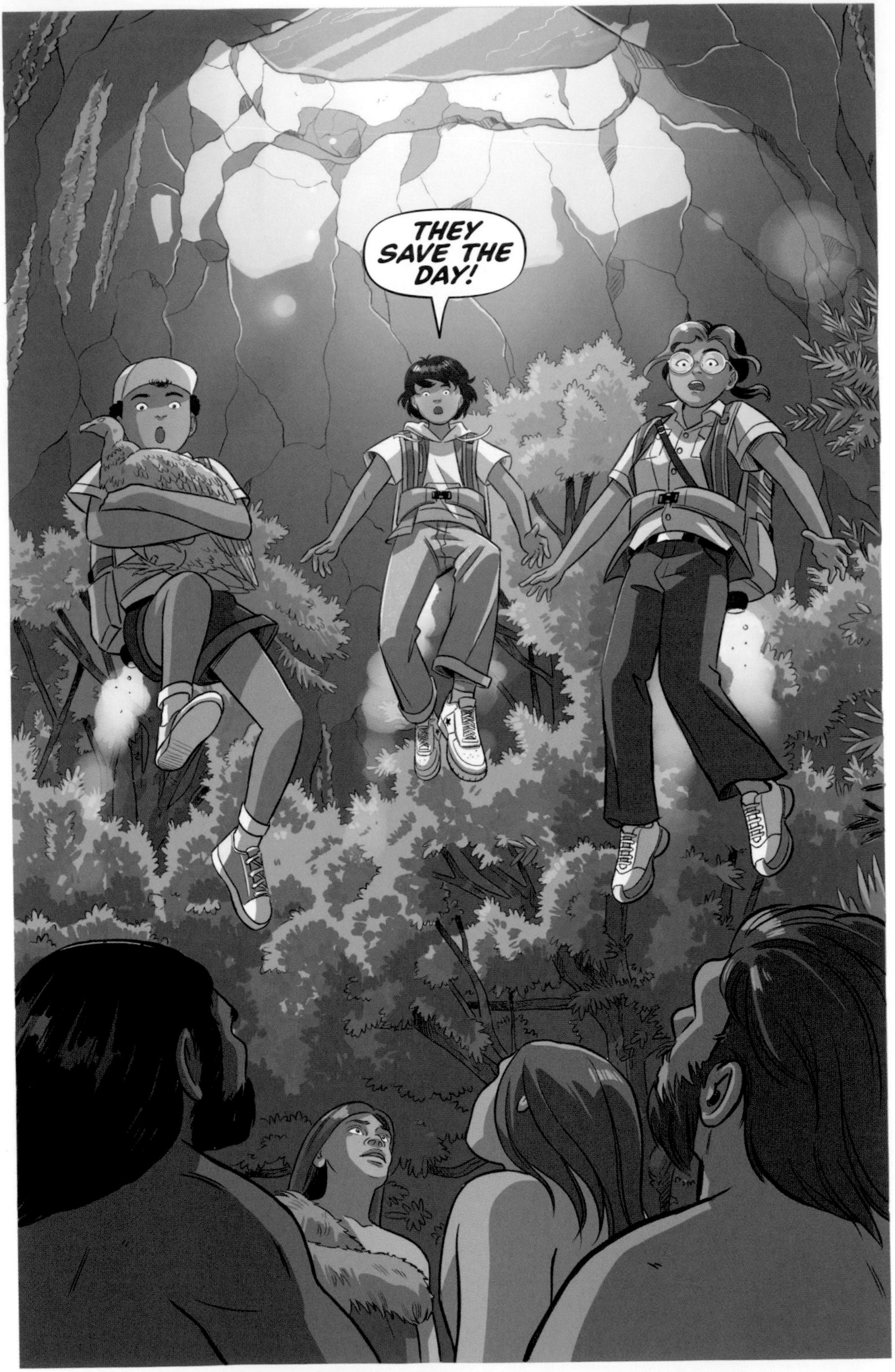
THEY SAVE THE DAY!

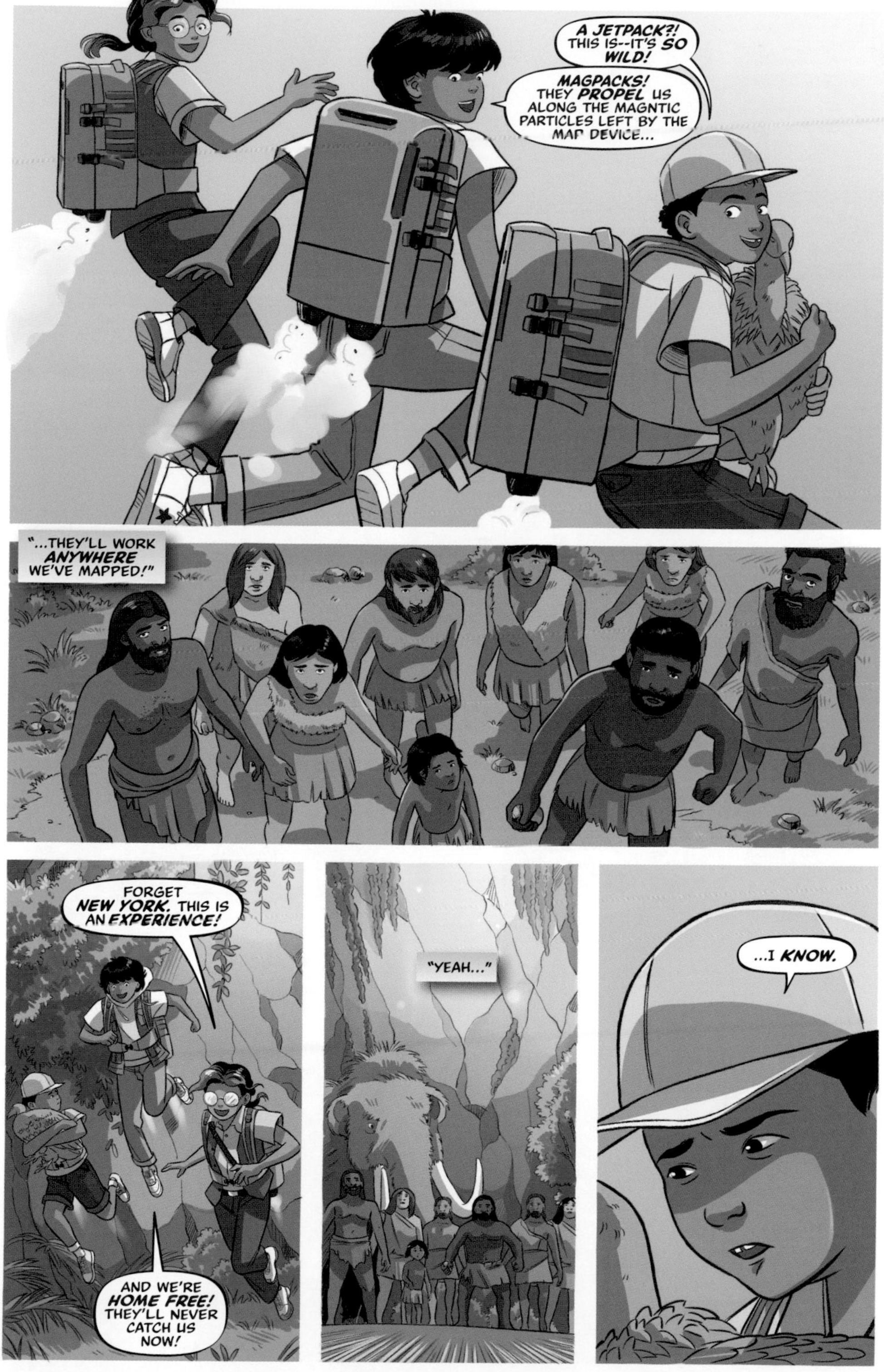

A JETPACK?! THIS IS--IT'S SO WILD!
MAGPACKS! THEY PROPEL US ALONG THE MAGNTIC PARTICLES LEFT BY THE MAP DEVICE...
"...THEY'LL WORK ANYWHERE WE'VE MAPPED!"
FORGET NEW YORK. THIS IS AN EXPERIENCE!
AND WE'RE HOME FREE! THEY'LL NEVER CATCH US NOW!
"YEAH..."
...I KNOW.

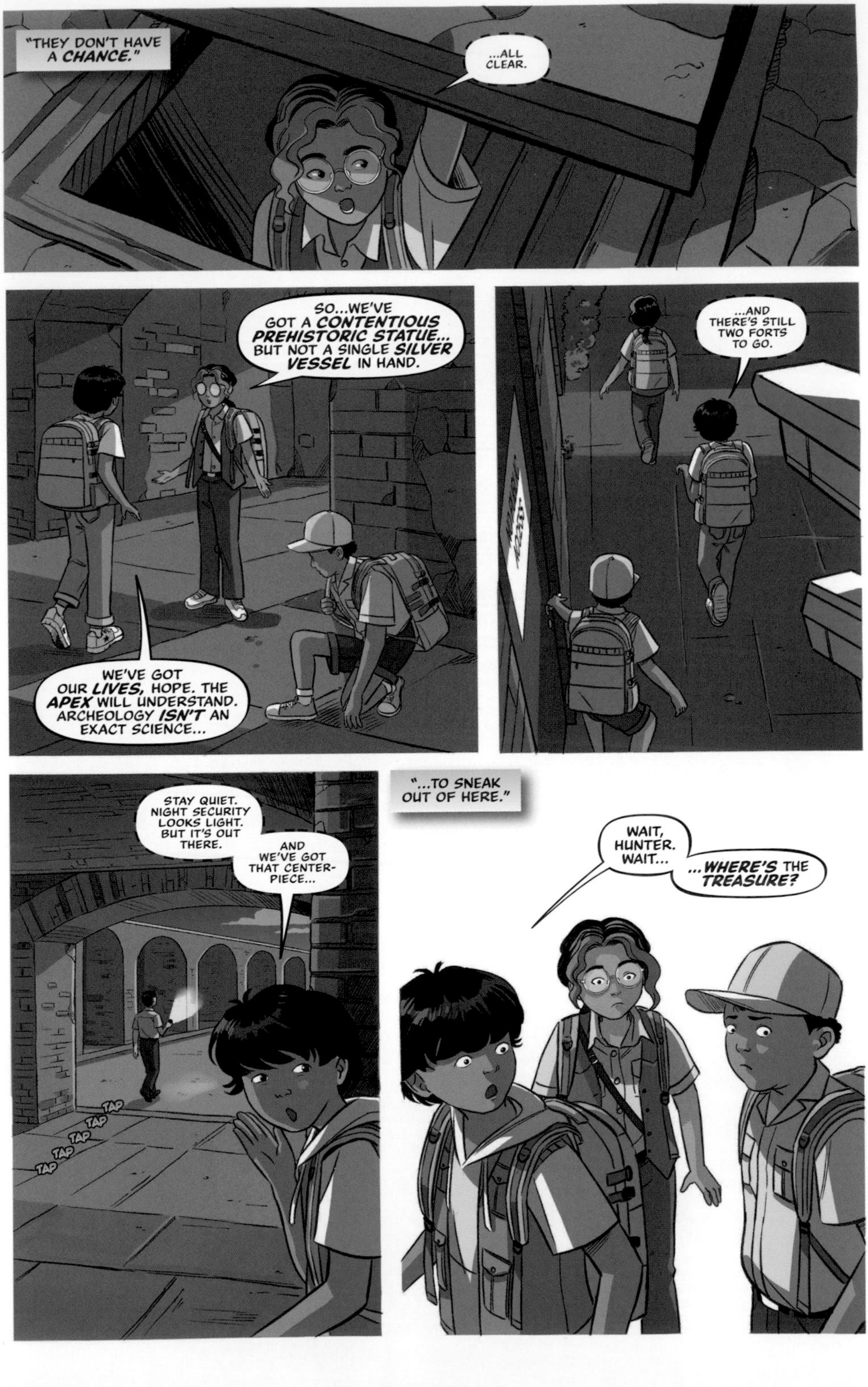
"THEY DON'T HAVE A CHANCE."
...ALL CLEAR.
SO...WE'VE GOT A CONTENTIOUS PREHISTORIC STATUE... BUT NOT A SINGLE SILVER VESSEL IN HAND.
WE'VE GOT OUR LIVES, HOPE. THE APEX WILL UNDERSTAND. ARCHEOLOGY ISN'T AN EXACT SCIENCE...
...AND THERE'S STILL TWO FORTS TO GO.
STAY QUIET. NIGHT SECURITY LOOKS LIGHT. BUT IT'S OUT THERE.
AND WE'VE GOT THAT CENTER-PIECE...
TAP TAP TAP TAP TAP
"...TO SNEAK OUT OF HERE."
WAIT, HUNTER. WAIT...
...WHERE'S THE TREASURE?

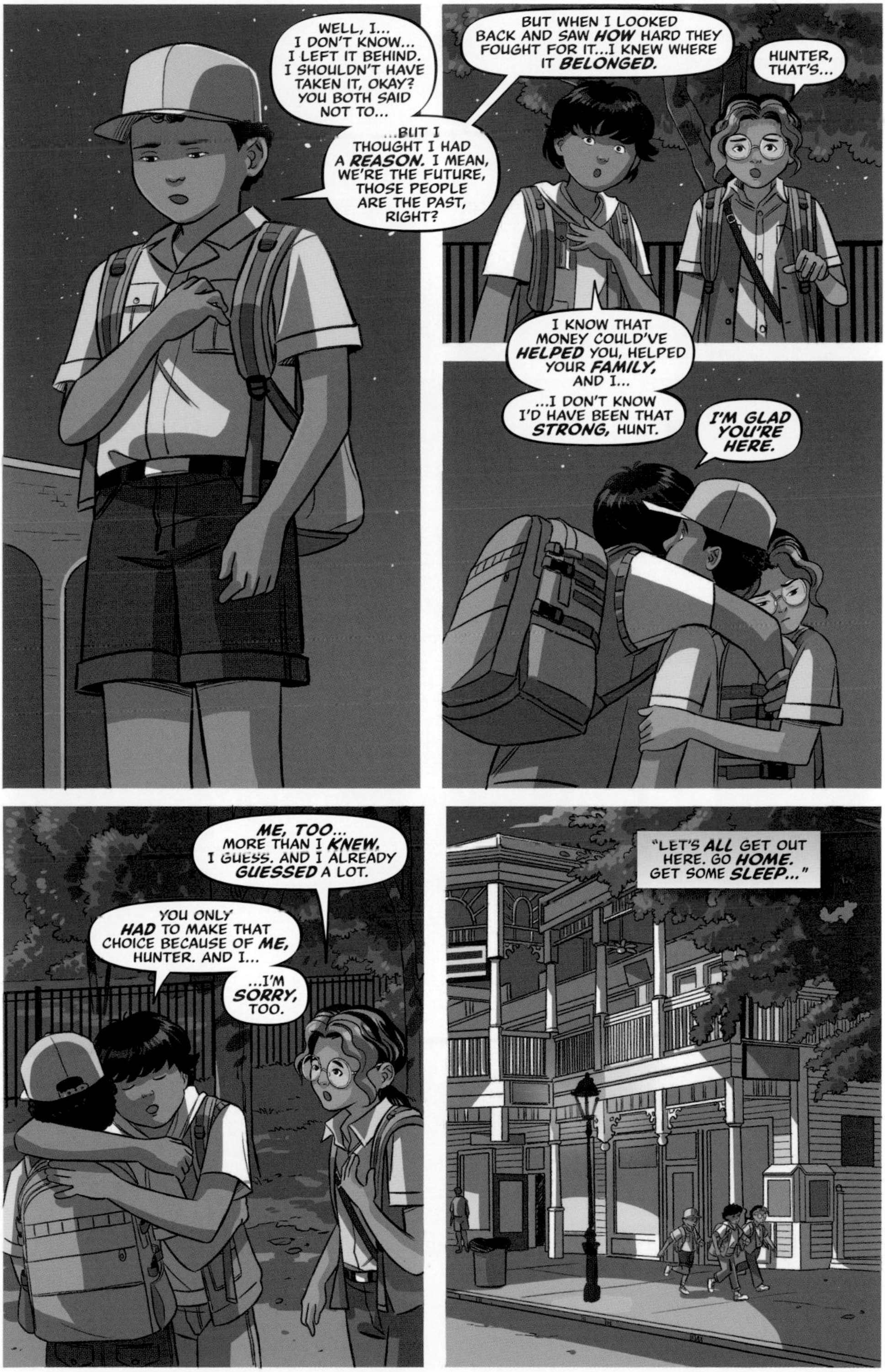

WELL, I... I DON'T KNOW... I LEFT IT BEHIND. I SHOULDN'T HAVE TAKEN IT, OKAY? YOU BOTH SAID NOT TO...
...BUT I THOUGHT I HAD A REASON. I MEAN, WE'RE THE FUTURE, THOSE PEOPLE ARE THE PAST, RIGHT?
BUT WHEN I LOOKED BACK AND SAW HOW HARD THEY FOUGHT FOR IT...I KNEW WHERE IT BELONGED.
HUNTER, THAT'S...
I KNOW THAT MONEY COULD'VE HELPED YOU, HELPED YOUR FAMILY, AND I...
...I DON'T KNOW I'D HAVE BEEN THAT STRONG, HUNT.
I'M GLAD YOU'RE HERE.
ME, TOO... MORE THAN I KNEW, I GUESS. AND I ALREADY GUESSED A LOT.
YOU ONLY HAD TO MAKE THAT CHOICE BECAUSE OF ME, HUNTER. AND I...
...I'M SORRY, TOO.
"LET'S ALL GET OUT HERE. GO HOME. GET SOME SLEEP..."

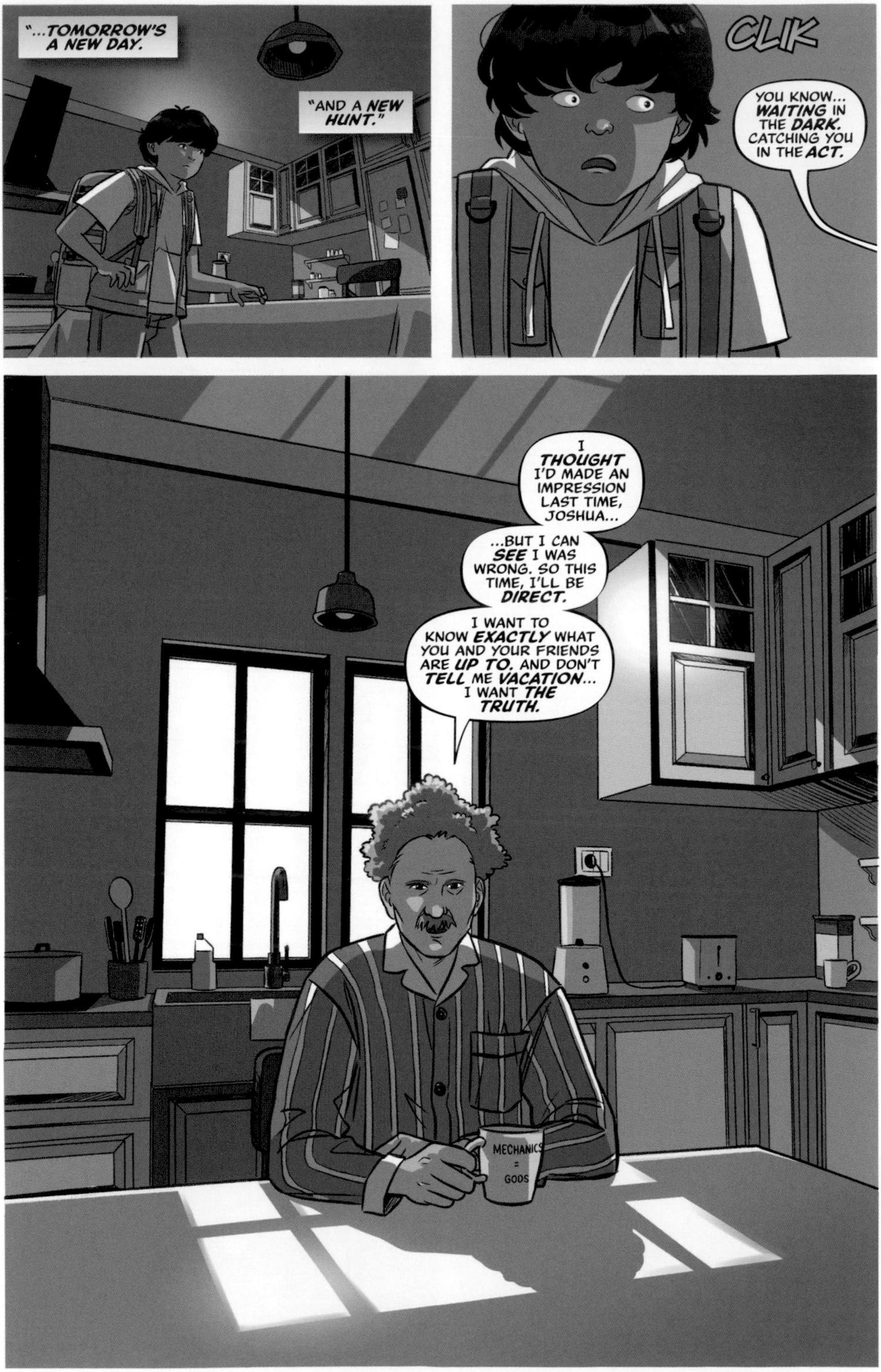
"...TOMORROW'S A NEW DAY.
"AND A NEW HUNT."
CLIK
YOU KNOW... WAITING IN THE DARK. CATCHING YOU IN THE ACT.
I THOUGHT I'D MADE AN IMPRESSION LAST TIME, JOSHUA...
...BUT I CAN SEE I WAS WRONG. SO THIS TIME, I'LL BE DIRECT.
I WANT TO KNOW EXACTLY WHAT YOU AND YOUR FRIENDS ARE UP TO. AND DON'T TELL ME VACATION... I WANT THE TRUTH.
MECHANICS = GODS

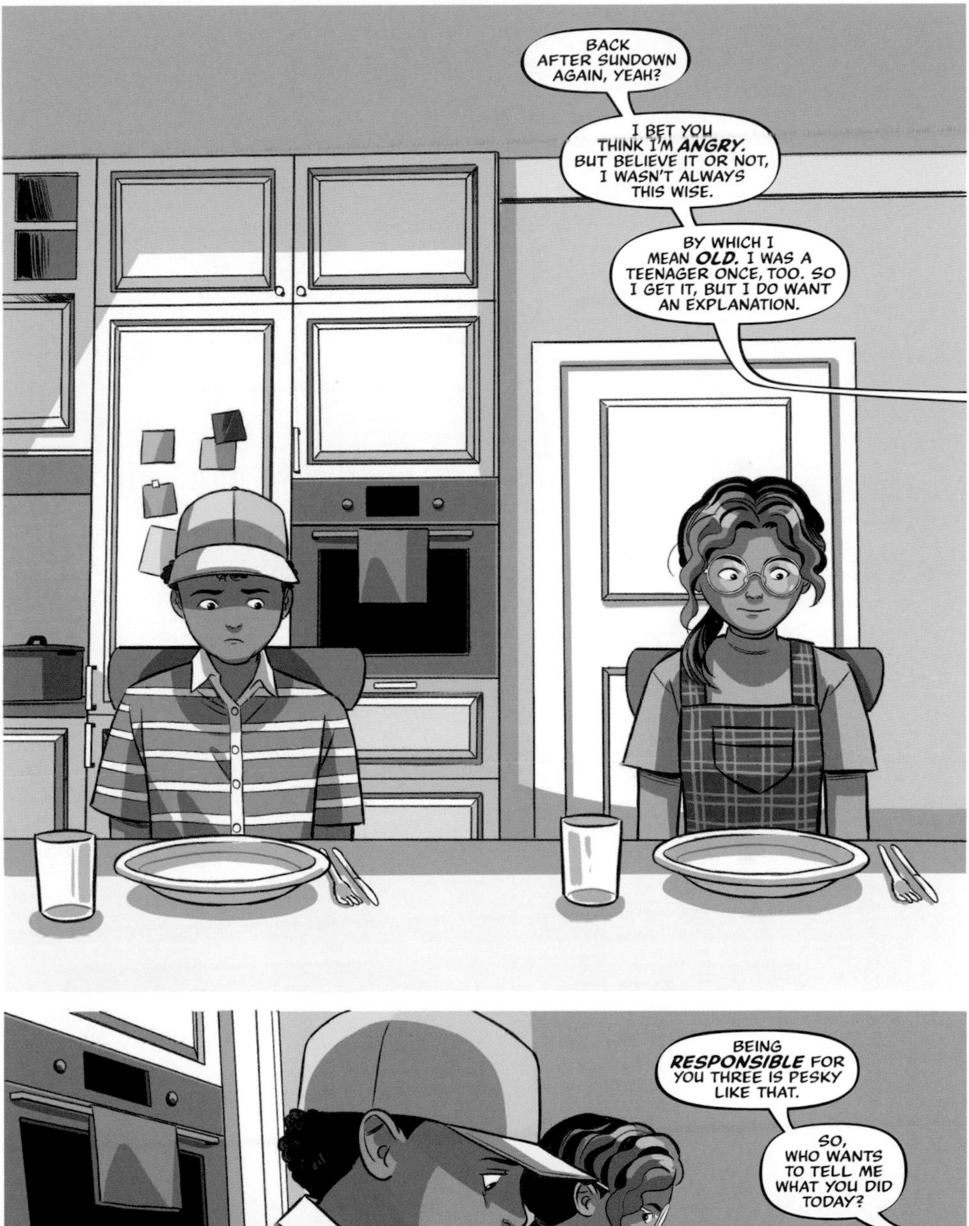
BACK AFTER SUNDOWN AGAIN, YEAH?
I BET YOU THINK I'M ANGRY. BUT BELIEVE IT OR NOT, I WASN'T ALWAYS THIS WISE.
BY WHICH I MEAN OLD. I WAS A TEENAGER ONCE, TOO. SO I GET IT, BUT I DO WANT AN EXPLANATION.

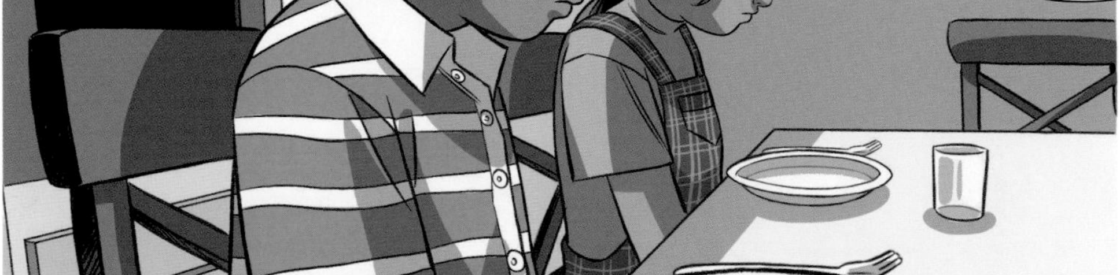
BEING RESPONSIBLE FOR YOU THREE IS PESKY LIKE THAT.
SO, WHO WANTS TO TELL ME WHAT YOU DID TODAY?

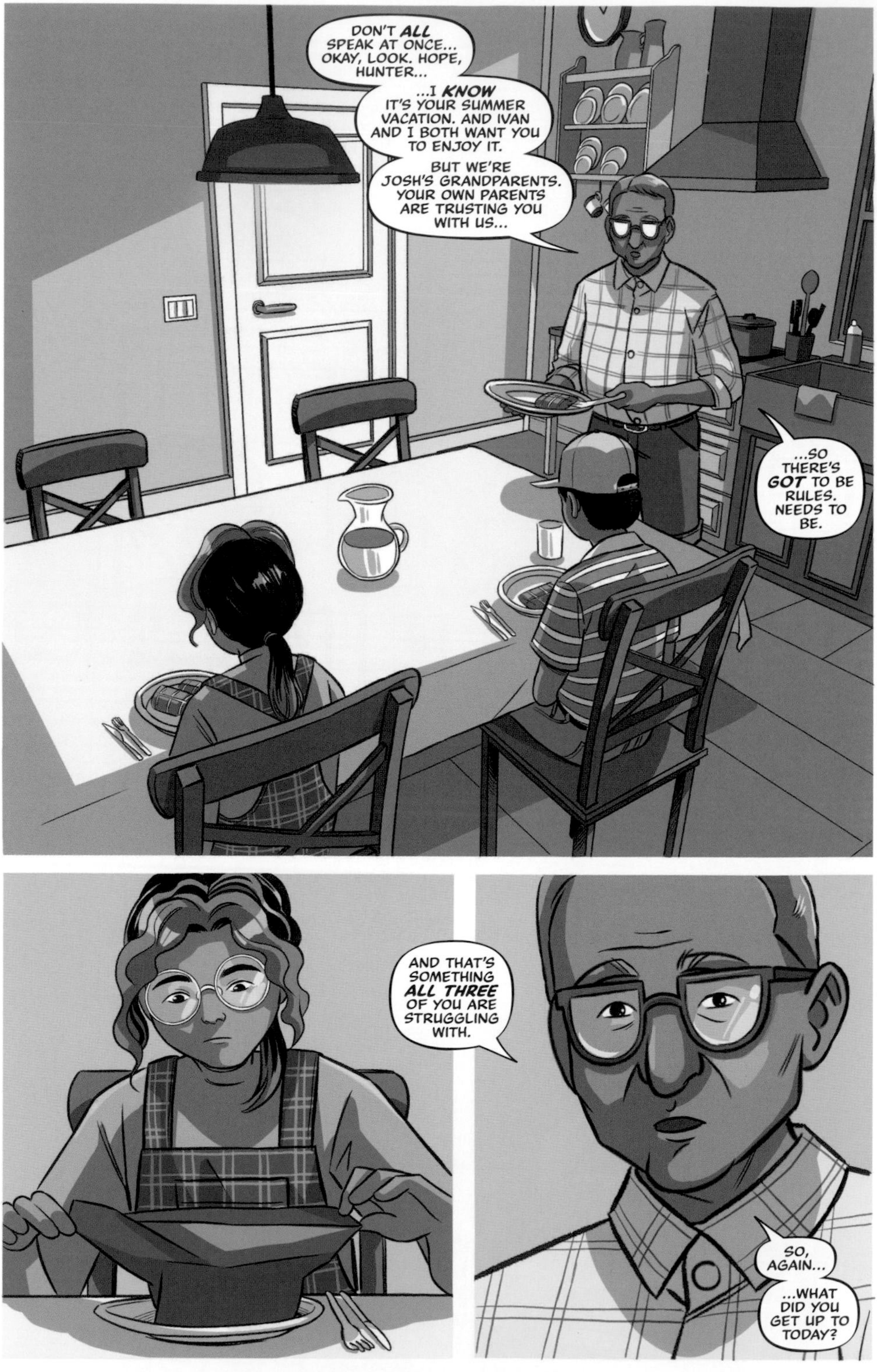
DON'T ALL SPEAK AT ONCE... OKAY, LOOK. HOPE, HUNTER...
...I KNOW IT'S YOUR SUMMER VACATION. AND IVAN AND I BOTH WANT YOU TO ENJOY IT.
BUT WE'RE JOSH'S GRANDPARENTS. YOUR OWN PARENTS ARE TRUSTING YOU WITH US...
...SO THERE'S GOT TO BE RULES. NEEDS TO BE.
AND THAT'S SOMETHING ALL THREE OF YOU ARE STRUGGLING WITH.
SO, AGAIN...
...WHAT DID YOU GET UP TO TODAY?

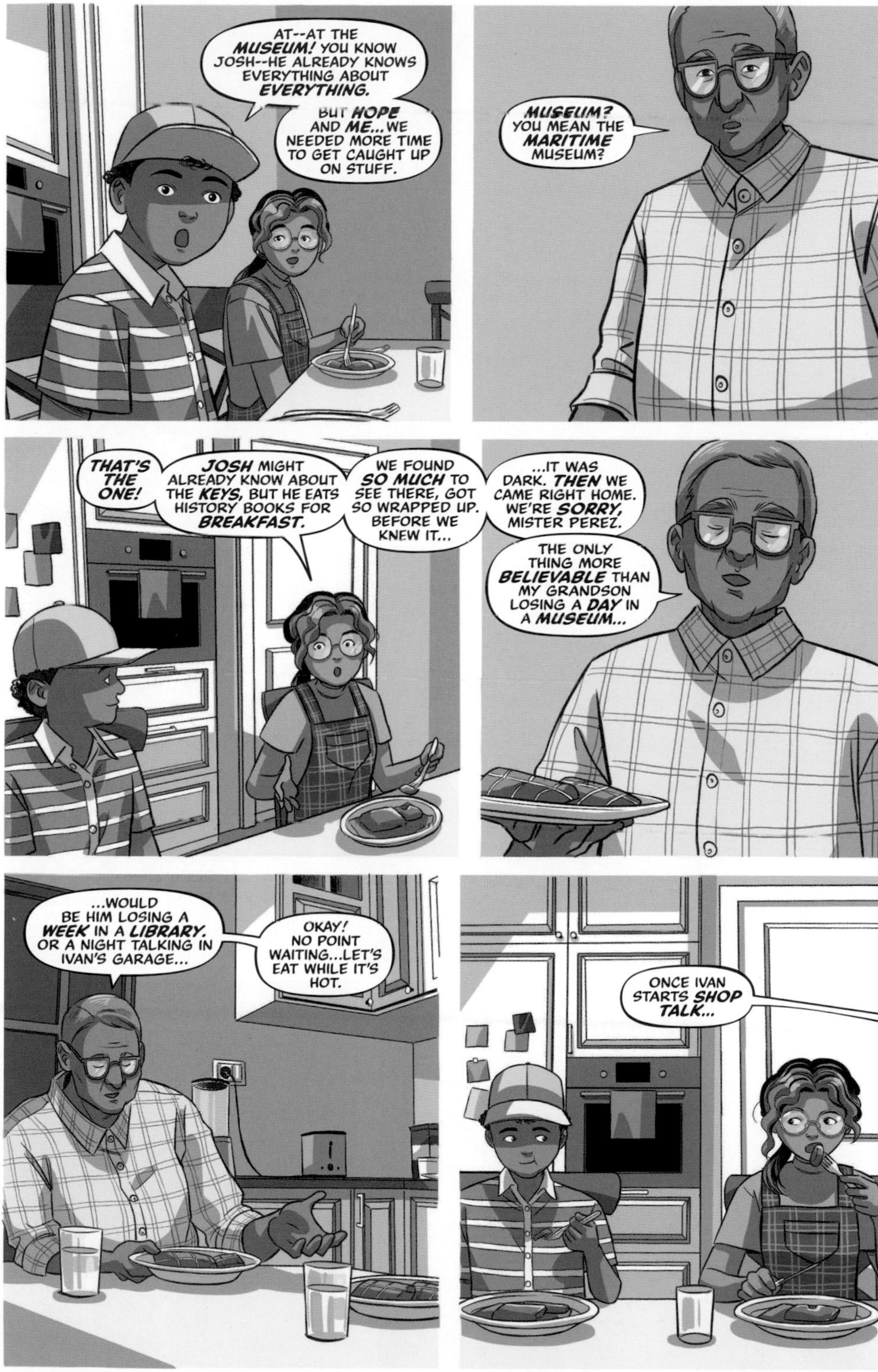
AT--AT THE MUSEUM! YOU KNOW JOSH--HE ALREADY KNOWS EVERYTHING ABOUT EVERYTHING.
BUT HOPE AND ME...WE NEEDED MORE TIME TO GET CAUGHT UP ON STUFF.
MUSEUM? YOU MEAN THE MARITIME MUSEUM?
THAT'S THE ONE!
JOSH MIGHT ALREADY KNOW ABOUT THE KEYS, BUT HE EATS HISTORY BOOKS FOR BREAKFAST.
WE FOUND SO MUCH TO SEE THERE, GOT SO WRAPPED UP. BEFORE WE KNEW IT...
...IT WAS DARK. THEN WE CAME RIGHT HOME. WE'RE SORRY, MISTER PEREZ.
THE ONLY THING MORE BELIEVABLE THAN MY GRANDSON LOSING A DAY IN A MUSEUM...
...WOULD BE HIM LOSING A WEEK IN A LIBRARY. OR A NIGHT TALKING IN IVAN'S GARAGE...
OKAY! NO POINT WAITING...LET'S EAT WHILE IT'S HOT.
ONCE IVAN STARTS SHOP TALK...

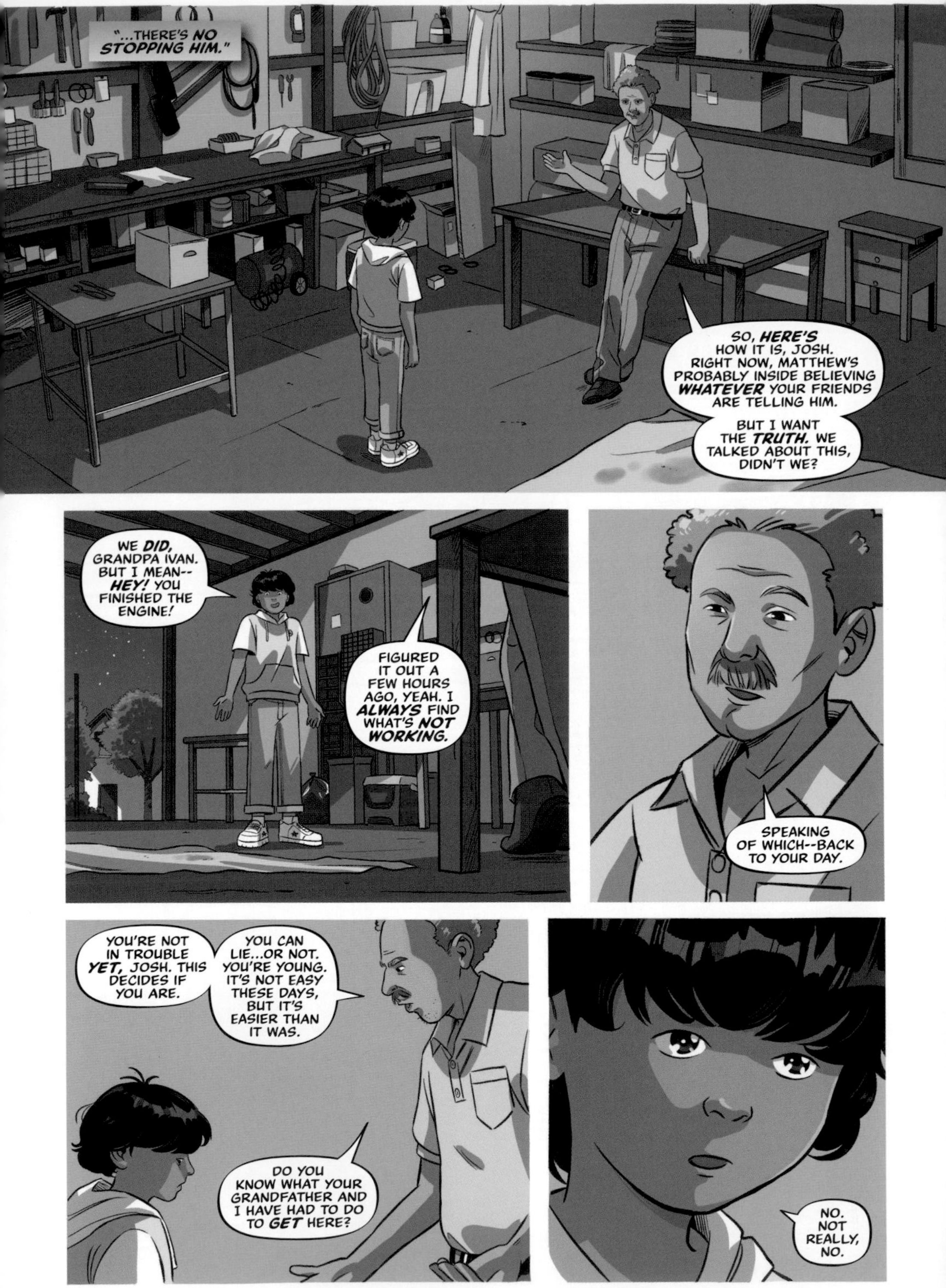
"...THERE'S NO STOPPING HIM."
SO, HERE'S HOW IT IS, JOSH. RIGHT NOW, MATTHEW'S PROBABLY INSIDE BELIEVING WHATEVER YOUR FRIENDS ARE TELLING HIM.
BUT I WANT THE TRUTH. WE TALKED ABOUT THIS, DIDN'T WE?
WE DID, GRANDPA IVAN. BUT I MEAN-- HEY! YOU FINISHED THE ENGINE!
FIGURED IT OUT A FEW HOURS AGO, YEAH. I ALWAYS FIND WHAT'S NOT WORKING.
SPEAKING OF WHICH--BACK TO YOUR DAY.
YOU'RE NOT IN TROUBLE YET, JOSH. THIS DECIDES IF YOU ARE.
YOU CAN LIE...OR NOT. YOU'RE YOUNG. IT'S NOT EASY THESE DAYS, BUT IT'S EASIER THAN IT WAS.
DO YOU KNOW WHAT YOUR GRANDFATHER AND I HAVE HAD TO DO TO GET HERE?
NO. NOT REALLY, NO.

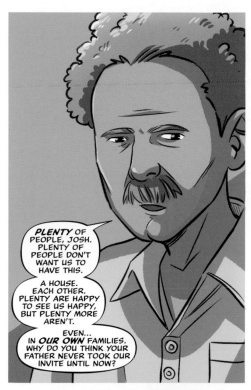

PLENTY OF PEOPLE, JOSH. PLENTY OF PEOPLE DON'T WANT US TO HAVE THIS.

A HOUSE. EACH OTHER. PLENTY ARE HAPPY TO SEE US HAPPY, BUT PLENTY MORE AREN'T.

EVEN... IN *OUR OWN* FAMILIES. WHY DO YOU THINK YOUR FATHER NEVER TOOK OUR INVITE UNTIL NOW?

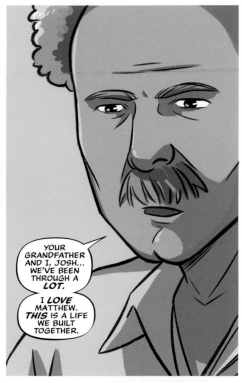

YOUR GRANDFATHER AND I, JOSH... WE'VE BEEN THROUGH A *LOT.*

I *LOVE* MATTHEW. *THIS* IS A LIFE WE BUILT TOGETHER.

YOU MIGHT THINK IT'S NO BIG DEAL TO SKIP OUT ON US. TELL SOME HARMLESS LIES.

BUT YOUR GRANDFATHER AND I LOVE YOU. WE WORRY ABOUT YOU. AND NO MATTER THE SIZE...

...LYING TO US JUST WON'T CUT IT.

SO, WHERE'D YOU GO TODAY?

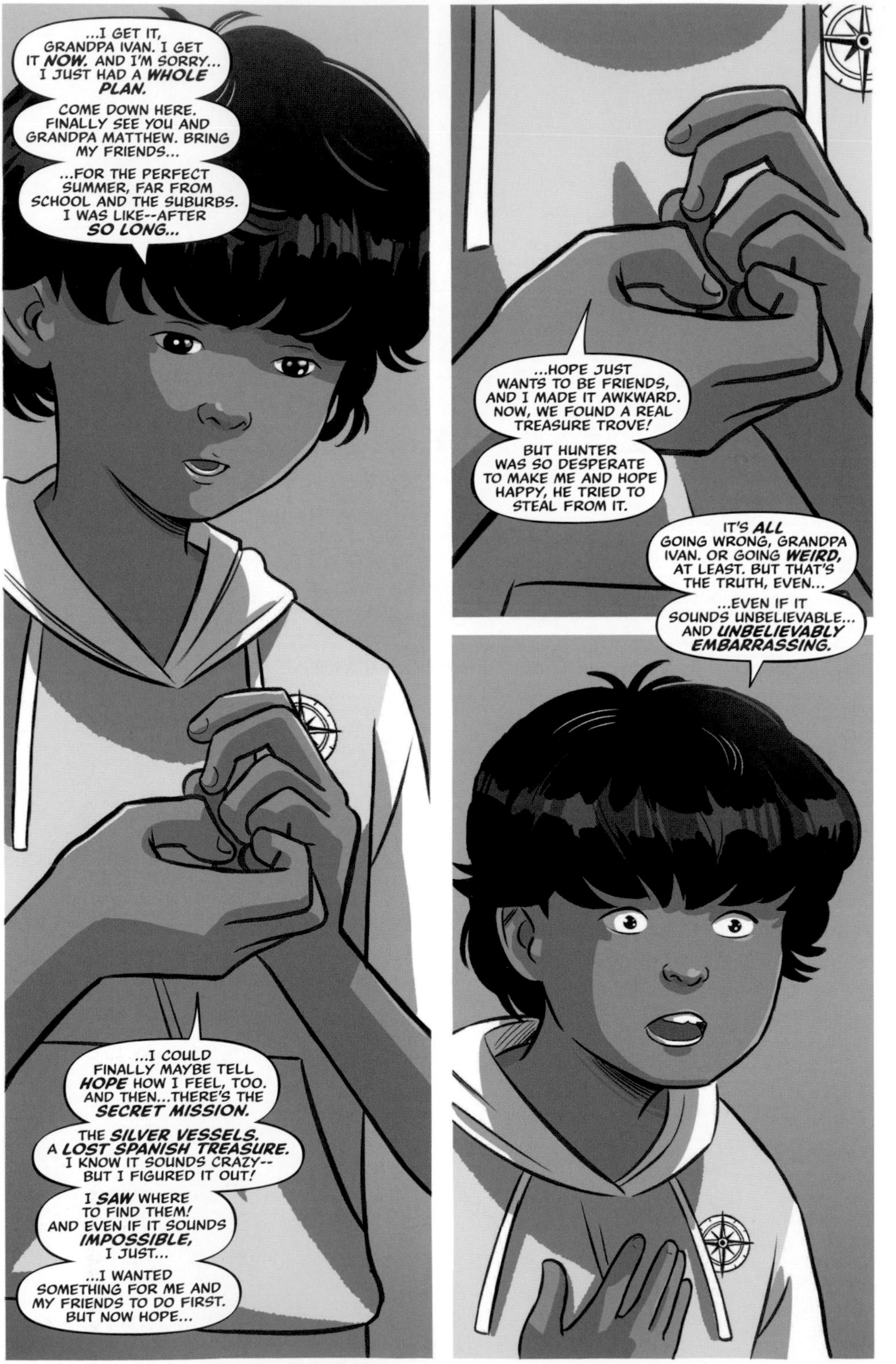

...I GET IT, GRANDPA IVAN. I GET IT NOW. AND I'M SORRY... I JUST HAD A WHOLE PLAN.
COME DOWN HERE. FINALLY SEE YOU AND GRANDPA MATTHEW. BRING MY FRIENDS...
...FOR THE PERFECT SUMMER, FAR FROM SCHOOL AND THE SUBURBS. I WAS LIKE--AFTER SO LONG...
...I COULD FINALLY MAYBE TELL HOPE HOW I FEEL, TOO. AND THEN...THERE'S THE SECRET MISSION.
THE SILVER VESSELS. A LOST SPANISH TREASURE. I KNOW IT SOUNDS CRAZY-- BUT I FIGURED IT OUT!
I SAW WHERE TO FIND THEM! AND EVEN IF IT SOUNDS IMPOSSIBLE, I JUST...
...I WANTED SOMETHING FOR ME AND MY FRIENDS TO DO FIRST. BUT NOW HOPE...
...HOPE JUST WANTS TO BE FRIENDS, AND I MADE IT AWKWARD. NOW, WE FOUND A REAL TREASURE TROVE!
BUT HUNTER WAS SO DESPERATE TO MAKE ME AND HOPE HAPPY, HE TRIED TO STEAL FROM IT.
IT'S ALL GOING WRONG, GRANDPA IVAN. OR GOING WEIRD, AT LEAST. BUT THAT'S THE TRUTH, EVEN...
...EVEN IF IT SOUNDS UNBELIEVABLE... AND UNBELIEVABLY EMBARRASSING.

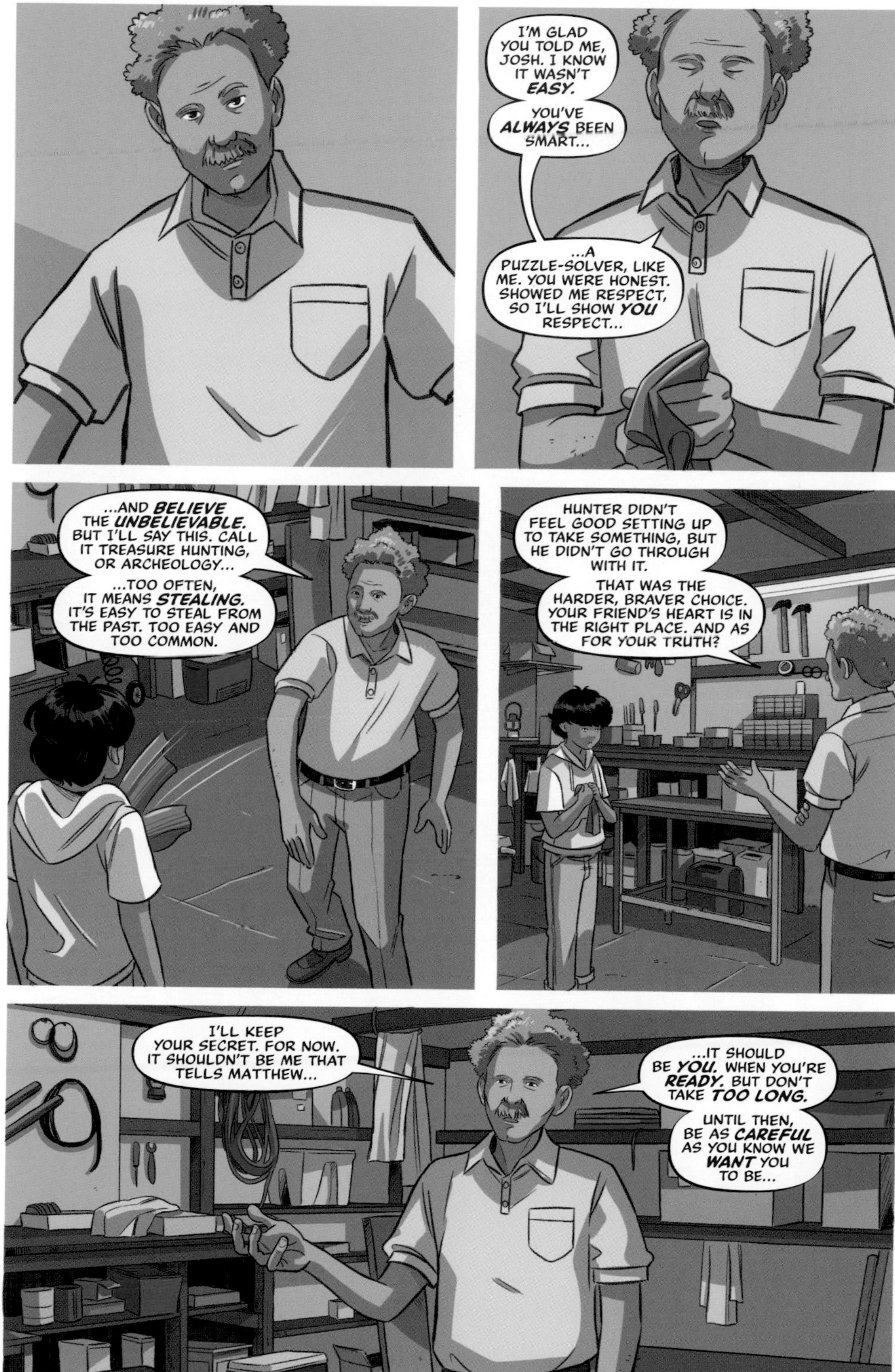
I'M GLAD YOU TOLD ME, JOSH. I KNOW IT WASN'T EASY.
YOU'VE ALWAYS BEEN SMART...
...A PUZZLE-SOLVER, LIKE ME. YOU WERE HONEST. SHOWED ME RESPECT, SO I'LL SHOW YOU RESPECT...
...AND BELIEVE THE UNBELIEVABLE. BUT I'LL SAY THIS. CALL IT TREASURE HUNTING, OR ARCHEOLOGY...
...TOO OFTEN, IT MEANS STEALING. IT'S EASY TO STEAL FROM THE PAST. TOO EASY AND TOO COMMON.
HUNTER DIDN'T FEEL GOOD SETTING UP TO TAKE SOMETHING, BUT HE DIDN'T GO THROUGH WITH IT.
THAT WAS THE HARDER, BRAVER CHOICE. YOUR FRIEND'S HEART IS IN THE RIGHT PLACE. AND AS FOR YOUR TRUTH?
I'LL KEEP YOUR SECRET. FOR NOW. IT SHOULDN'T BE ME THAT TELLS MATTHEW...
...IT SHOULD BE YOU. WHEN YOU'RE READY. BUT DON'T TAKE TOO LONG.
UNTIL THEN, BE AS CAREFUL AS YOU KNOW WE WANT YOU TO BE...

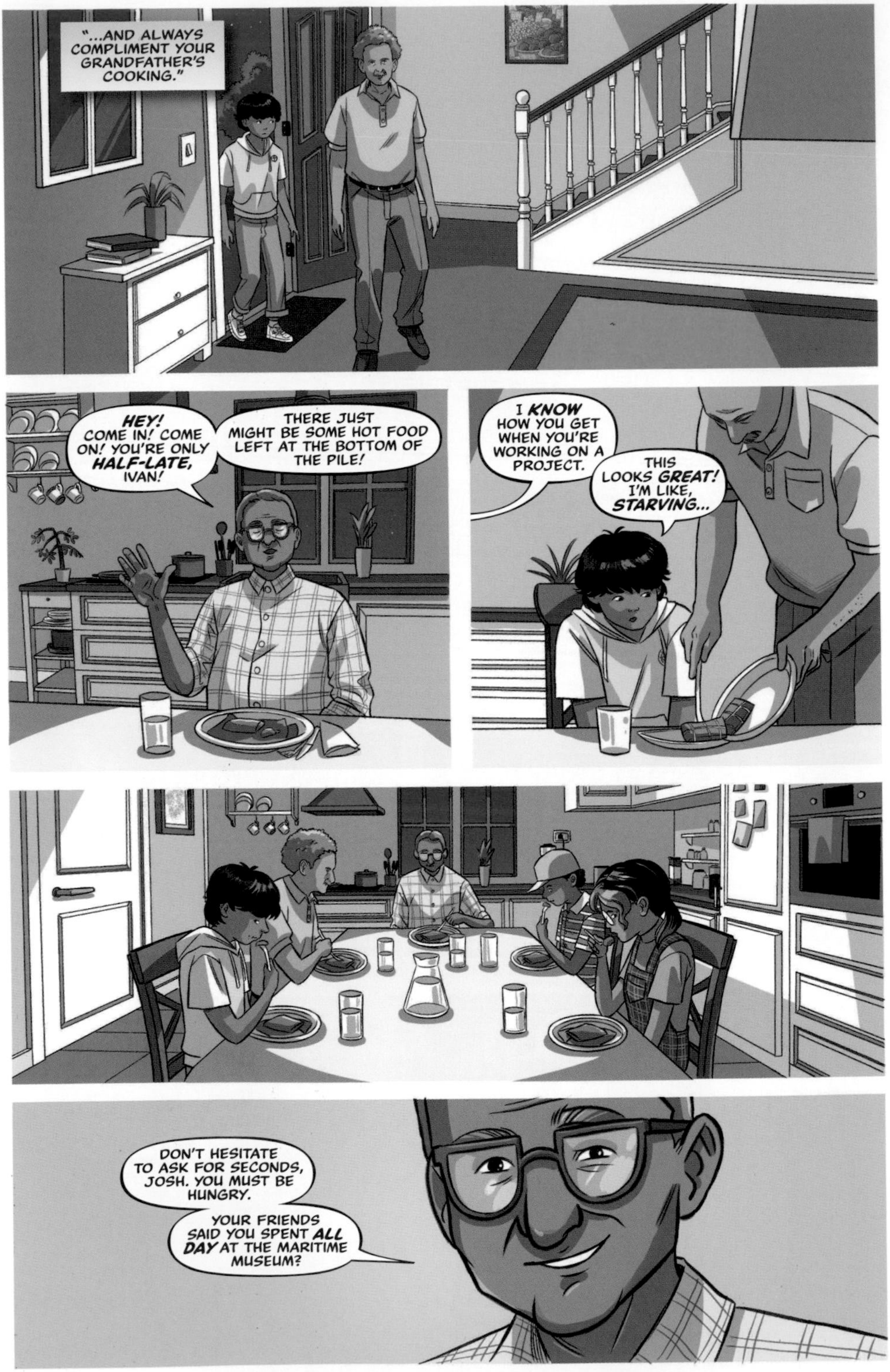
"...AND ALWAYS COMPLIMENT YOUR GRANDFATHER'S COOKING."
HEY! COME IN! COME ON! YOU'RE ONLY HALF-LATE, IVAN!
THERE JUST MIGHT BE SOME HOT FOOD LEFT AT THE BOTTOM OF THE PILE!
I KNOW HOW YOU GET WHEN YOU'RE WORKING ON A PROJECT.
THIS LOOKS GREAT! I'M LIKE, STARVING...
DON'T HESITATE TO ASK FOR SECONDS, JOSH. YOU MUST BE HUNGRY.
YOUR FRIENDS SAID YOU SPENT ALL DAY AT THE MARITIME MUSEUM?

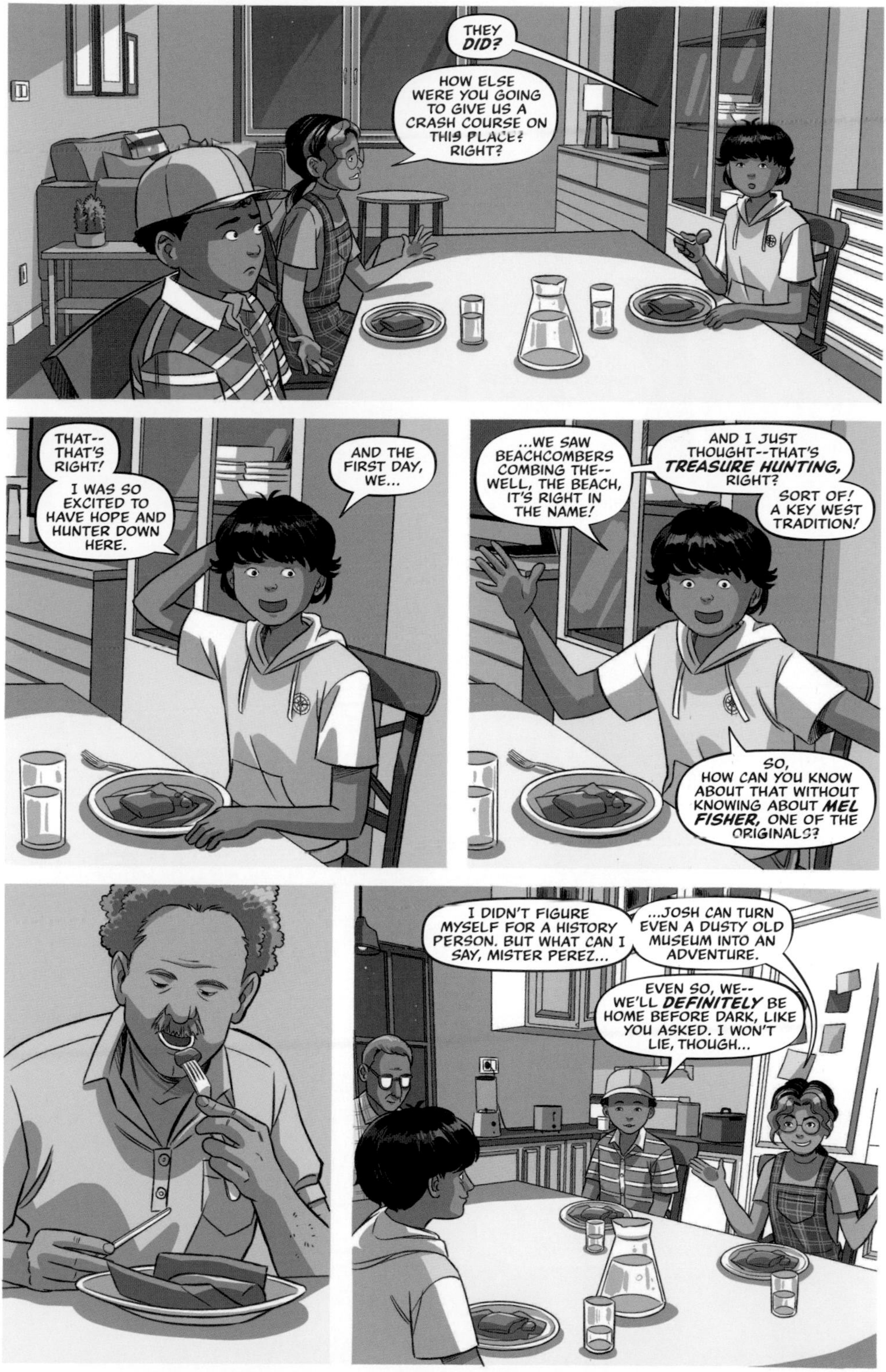
THEY DID?
HOW ELSE WERE YOU GOING TO GIVE US A CRASH COURSE ON THIS PLACE? RIGHT?
THAT--THAT'S RIGHT!
I WAS SO EXCITED TO HAVE HOPE AND HUNTER DOWN HERE.
AND THE FIRST DAY, WE...
...WE SAW BEACHCOMBERS COMBING THE--WELL, THE BEACH, IT'S RIGHT IN THE NAME!
AND I JUST THOUGHT--THAT'S TREASURE HUNTING, RIGHT?
SORT OF! A KEY WEST TRADITION!
SO, HOW CAN YOU KNOW ABOUT THAT WITHOUT KNOWING ABOUT MEL FISHER, ONE OF THE ORIGINALS?
I DIDN'T FIGURE MYSELF FOR A HISTORY PERSON. BUT WHAT CAN I SAY, MISTER PEREZ...
...JOSH CAN TURN EVEN A DUSTY OLD MUSEUM INTO AN ADVENTURE.
EVEN SO, WE--WE'LL DEFINITELY BE HOME BEFORE DARK, LIKE YOU ASKED. I WON'T LIE, THOUGH...

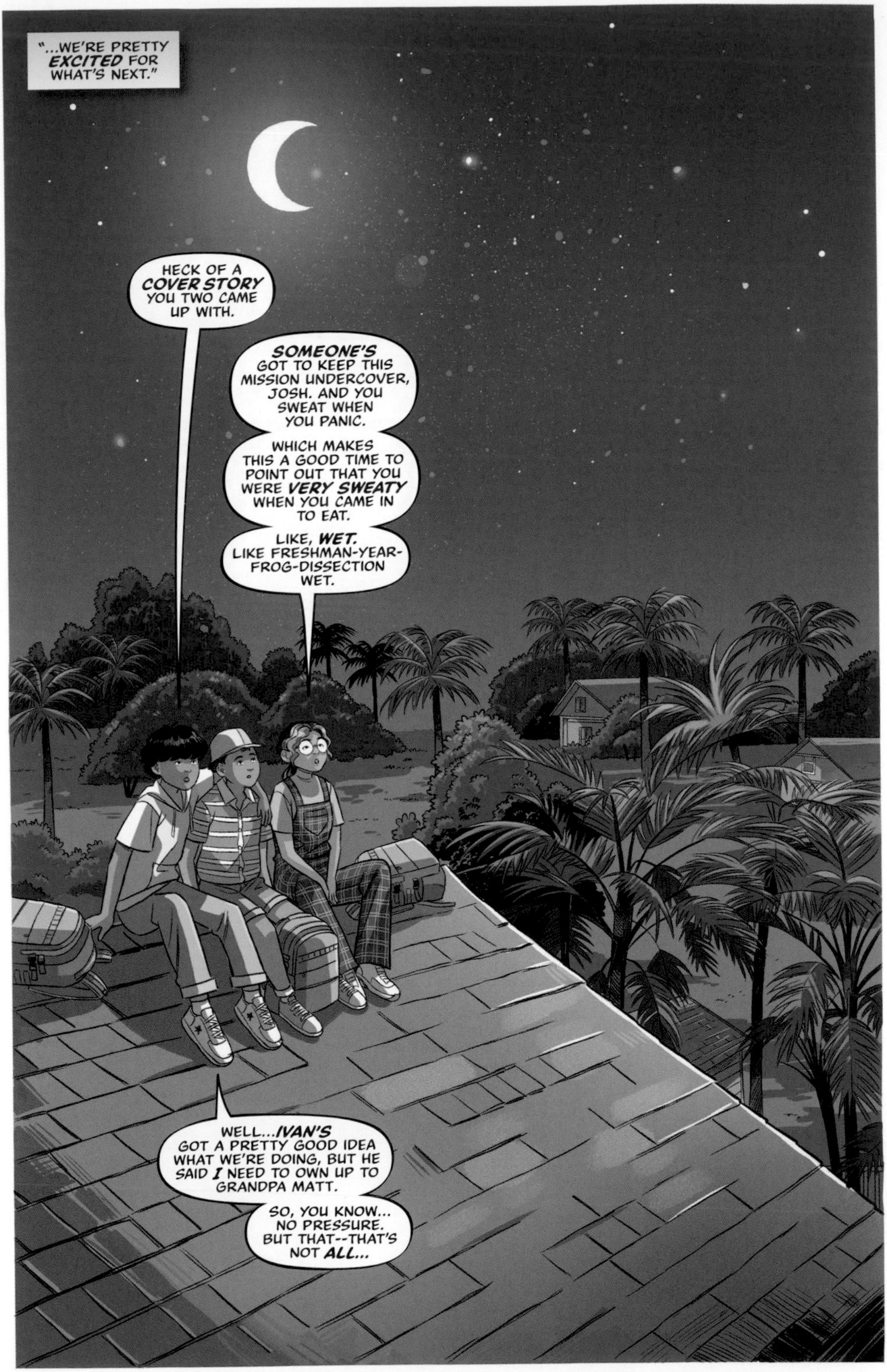
"...WE'RE PRETTY EXCITED FOR WHAT'S NEXT."
HECK OF A COVER STORY YOU TWO CAME UP WITH.
SOMEONE'S GOT TO KEEP THIS MISSION UNDERCOVER, JOSH. AND YOU SWEAT WHEN YOU PANIC.
WHICH MAKES THIS A GOOD TIME TO POINT OUT THAT YOU WERE VERY SWEATY WHEN YOU CAME IN TO EAT.
LIKE, WET. LIKE FRESHMAN-YEAR-FROG-DISSECTION WET.
WELL...IVAN'S GOT A PRETTY GOOD IDEA WHAT WE'RE DOING, BUT HE SAID I NEED TO OWN UP TO GRANDPA MATT.
SO, YOU KNOW... NO PRESSURE. BUT THAT--THAT'S NOT ALL...

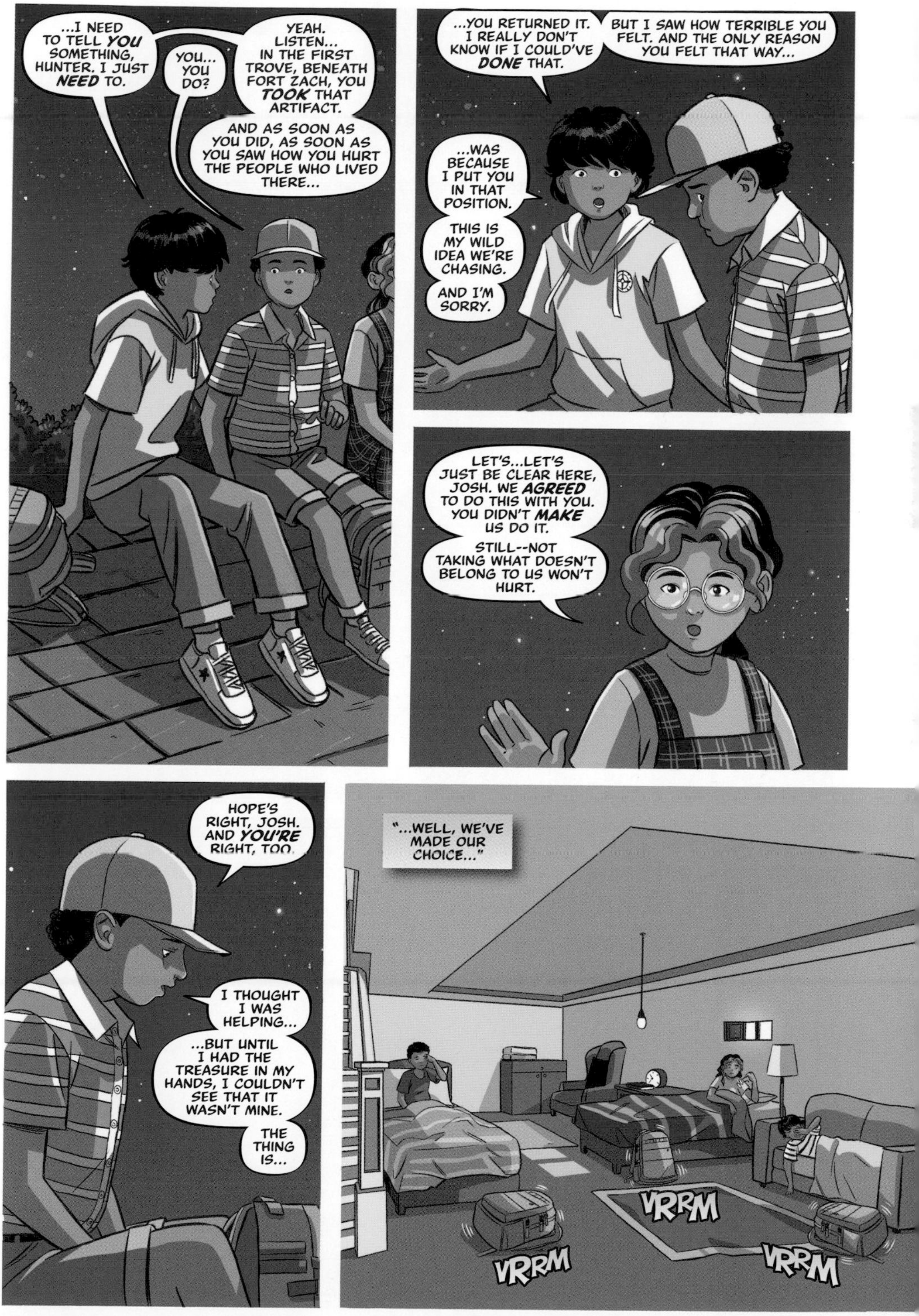
...I NEED TO TELL *YOU* SOMETHING, HUNTER. I JUST *NEED* TO.
YOU... YOU DO?
YEAH. LISTEN... IN THE FIRST TROVE, BENEATH FORT ZACH, YOU *TOOK* THAT ARTIFACT.
AND AS SOON AS YOU DID, AS SOON AS YOU SAW HOW YOU HURT THE PEOPLE WHO LIVED THERE...
...YOU RETURNED IT. I REALLY DON'T KNOW IF I COULD'VE *DONE* THAT.
BUT I SAW HOW TERRIBLE YOU FELT. AND THE ONLY REASON YOU FELT THAT WAY...
...WAS BECAUSE I PUT YOU IN THAT POSITION.
THIS IS MY WILD IDEA WE'RE CHASING.
AND I'M SORRY.
LET'S...LET'S JUST BE CLEAR HERE, JOSH. WE *AGREED* TO DO THIS WITH YOU. YOU DIDN'T *MAKE* US DO IT.
STILL--NOT TAKING WHAT DOESN'T BELONG TO US WON'T HURT.
HOPE'S RIGHT, JOSH. AND *YOU'RE* RIGHT, TOO.
I THOUGHT I WAS HELPING...
...BUT UNTIL I HAD THE TREASURE IN MY HANDS, I COULDN'T SEE THAT IT WASN'T MINE.
THE THING IS...
"...WELL, WE'VE MADE OUR CHOICE..."
VRRM
VRRM
VRRM

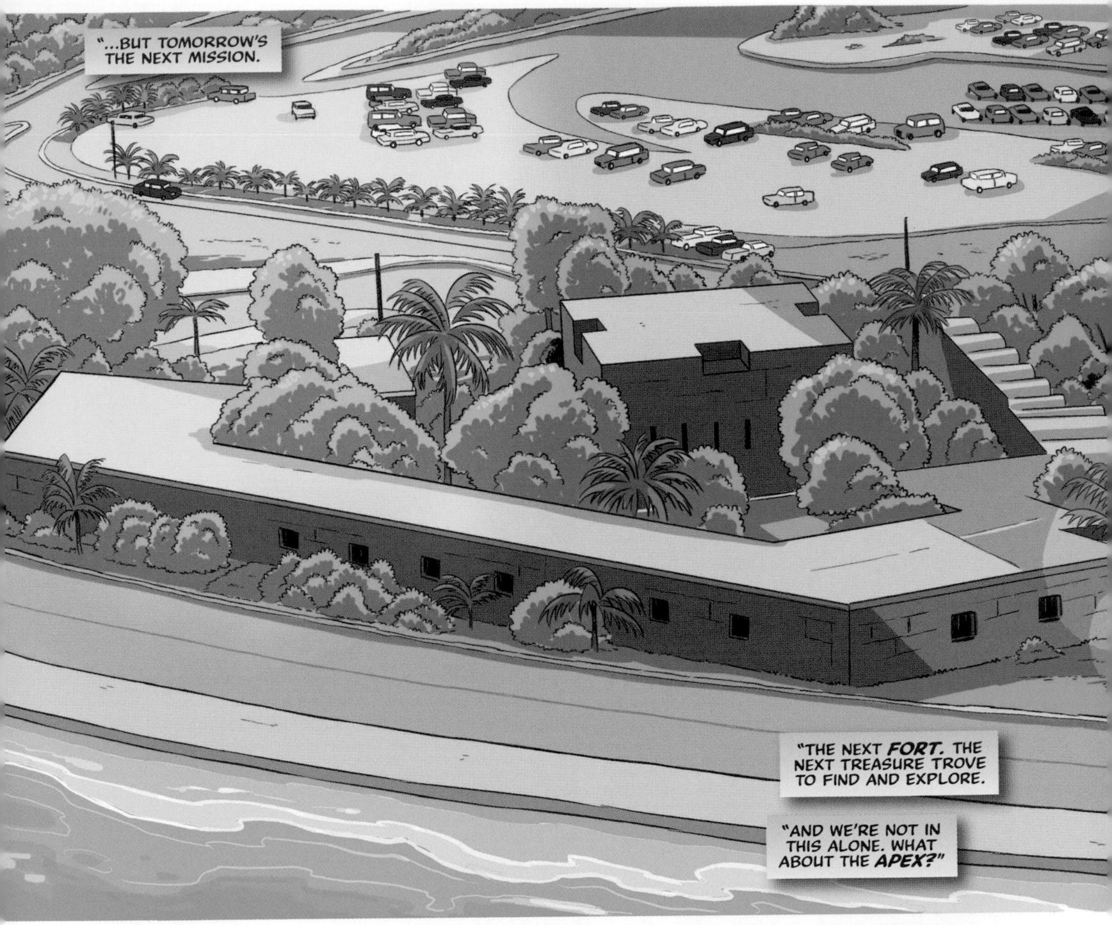
"...BUT TOMORROW'S THE NEXT MISSION.
"THE NEXT FORT. THE NEXT TREASURE TROVE TO FIND AND EXPLORE.
"AND WE'RE NOT IN THIS ALONE. WHAT ABOUT THE APEX?"

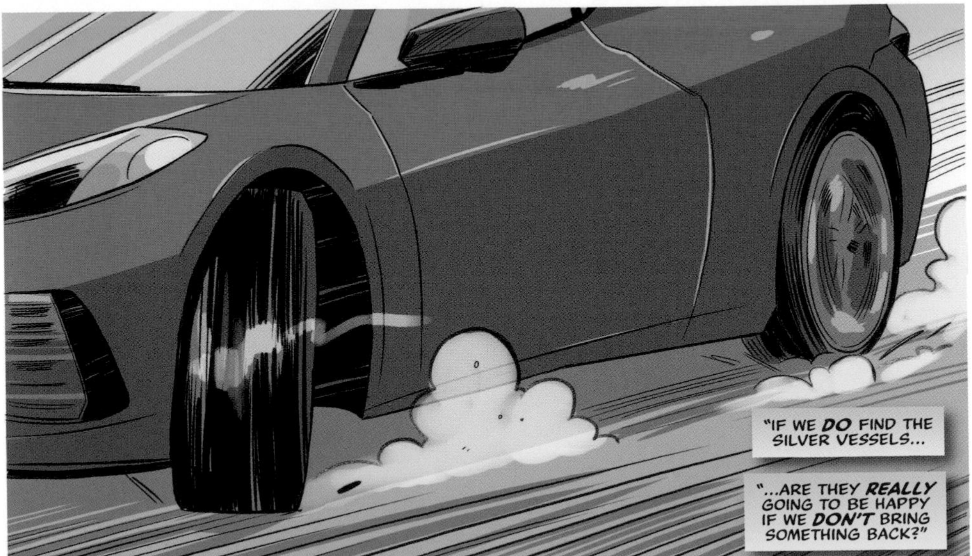
"IF WE DO FIND THE SILVER VESSELS...
"...ARE THEY REALLY GOING TO BE HAPPY IF WE DON'T BRING SOMETHING BACK?"

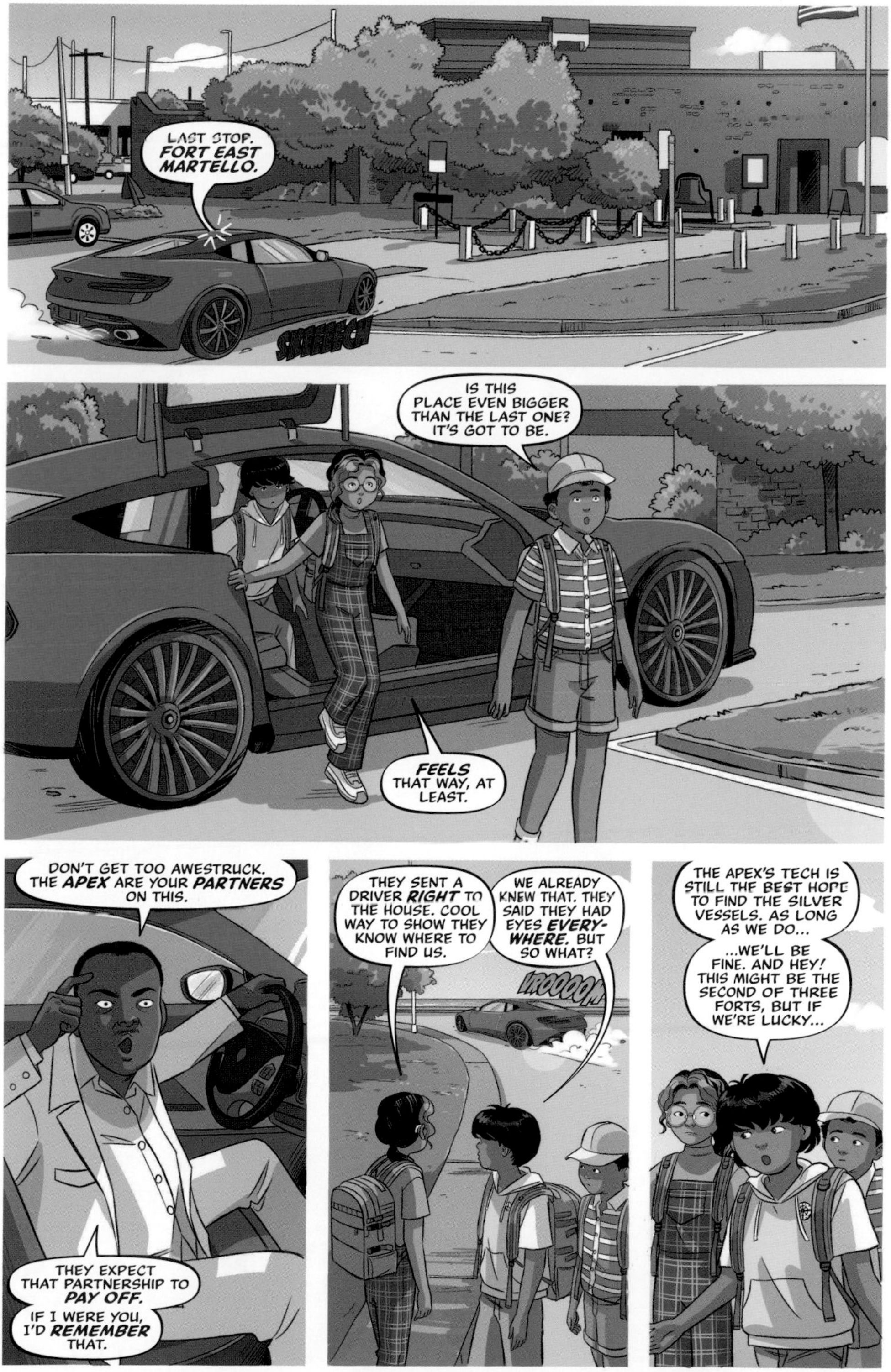

LAST STOP. FORT EAST MARTELLO.
SKREEECH
IS THIS PLACE EVEN BIGGER THAN THE LAST ONE? IT'S GOT TO BE.
FEELS THAT WAY, AT LEAST.
DON'T GET TOO AWESTRUCK. THE APEX ARE YOUR PARTNERS ON THIS.
THEY EXPECT THAT PARTNERSHIP TO PAY OFF.
IF I WERE YOU, I'D REMEMBER THAT.
THEY SENT A DRIVER RIGHT TO THE HOUSE. COOL WAY TO SHOW THEY KNOW WHERE TO FIND US.
WE ALREADY KNEW THAT. THEY SAID THEY HAD EYES EVERY-WHERE. BUT SO WHAT?
VROOOOM
THE APEX'S TECH IS STILL THE BEST HOPE TO FIND THE SILVER VESSELS. AS LONG AS WE DO...
...WE'LL BE FINE. AND HEY! THIS MIGHT BE THE SECOND OF THREE FORTS, BUT IF WE'RE LUCKY...

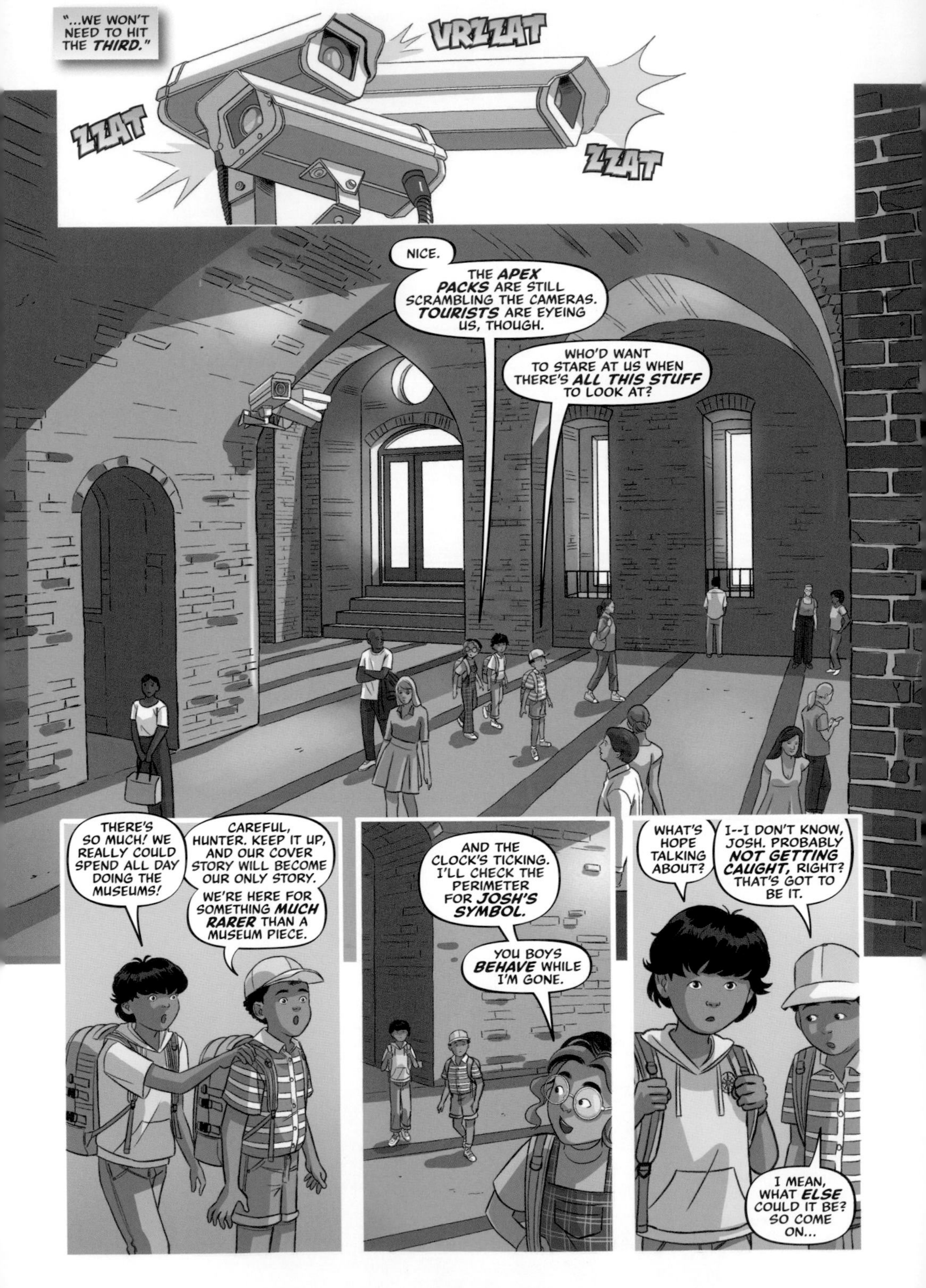
"...WE WON'T NEED TO HIT THE THIRD."
VRZZAT
ZZAT
ZZAT
NICE.
THE APEX PACKS ARE STILL SCRAMBLING THE CAMERAS. TOURISTS ARE EYEING US, THOUGH.
WHO'D WANT TO STARE AT US WHEN THERE'S ALL THIS STUFF TO LOOK AT?
THERE'S SO MUCH! WE REALLY COULD SPEND ALL DAY DOING THE MUSEUMS!
CAREFUL, HUNTER. KEEP IT UP, AND OUR COVER STORY WILL BECOME OUR ONLY STORY.
WE'RE HERE FOR SOMETHING MUCH RARER THAN A MUSEUM PIECE.
AND THE CLOCK'S TICKING. I'LL CHECK THE PERIMETER FOR JOSH'S SYMBOL.
YOU BOYS BEHAVE WHILE I'M GONE.
WHAT'S HOPE TALKING ABOUT?
I--I DON'T KNOW, JOSH. PROBABLY NOT GETTING CAUGHT, RIGHT? THAT'S GOT TO BE IT.
I MEAN, WHAT ELSE COULD IT BE? SO COME ON...

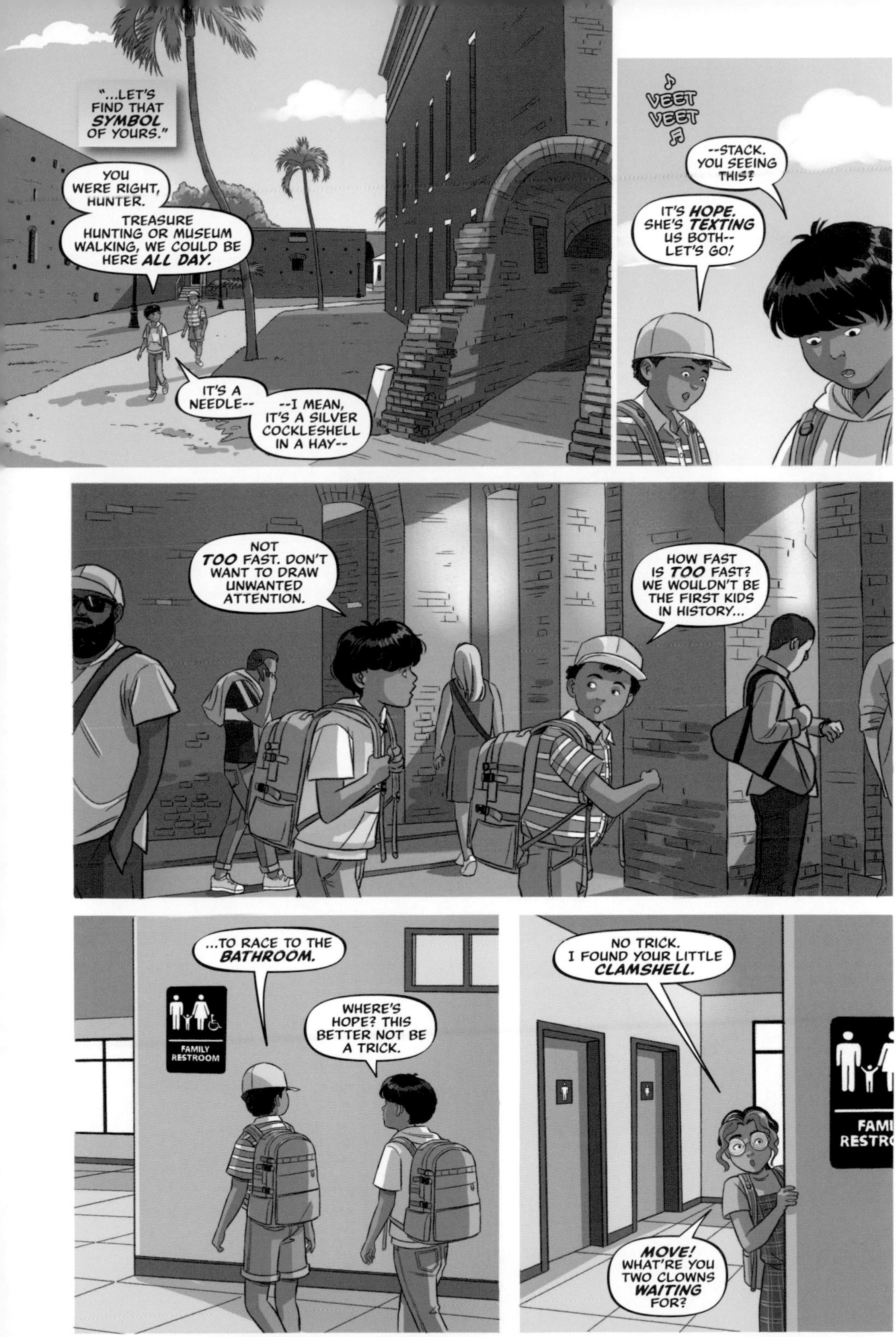
"...LET'S FIND THAT SYMBOL OF YOURS."
YOU WERE RIGHT, HUNTER.
TREASURE HUNTING OR MUSEUM WALKING, WE COULD BE HERE ALL DAY.
IT'S A NEEDLE--
--I MEAN, IT'S A SILVER COCKLESHELL IN A HAY--
VEET VEET
--STACK. YOU SEEING THIS?
IT'S HOPE. SHE'S TEXTING US BOTH-- LET'S GO!
NOT TOO FAST. DON'T WANT TO DRAW UNWANTED ATTENTION.
HOW FAST IS TOO FAST? WE WOULDN'T BE THE FIRST KIDS IN HISTORY...
...TO RACE TO THE BATHROOM.
FAMILY RESTROOM
WHERE'S HOPE? THIS BETTER NOT BE A TRICK.
NO TRICK. I FOUND YOUR LITTLE CLAMSHELL.
MOVE! WHAT'RE YOU TWO CLOWNS WAITING FOR?

YOU FOUND THE COCKLESHELL... HIDDEN IN THE *FAMILY BATHROOM?*

WELL, YOU KNOW ME. I *LOVE* A GOOD CHANGING TABLE.

NO-- THAT'S A JOKE. *A JOKE.* THE TRUTH IS, I WAS IN HERE...

...BECAUSE THE *OTHERS* DIDN'T FEEL RIGHT. SO HERE I WAS, DOING MY THING...

...AND THAT'S WHEN I SAW IT! COME LOOK!

BEHIND THE TOILET? YOU FOUND JOSH'S SYMBOL?

WHERE NO ONE BUT SOMEONE LOOKING WOULD SEE!

ETCHED INTO THE METAL!

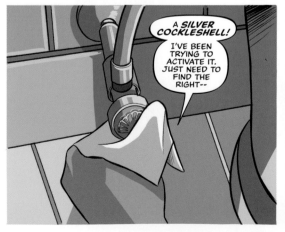

A *SILVER COCKLESHELL!*

I'VE BEEN TRYING TO ACTIVATE IT. JUST NEED TO FIND THE RIGHT--

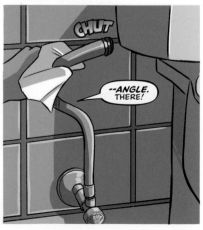

CHUT

--ANGLE. THERE!

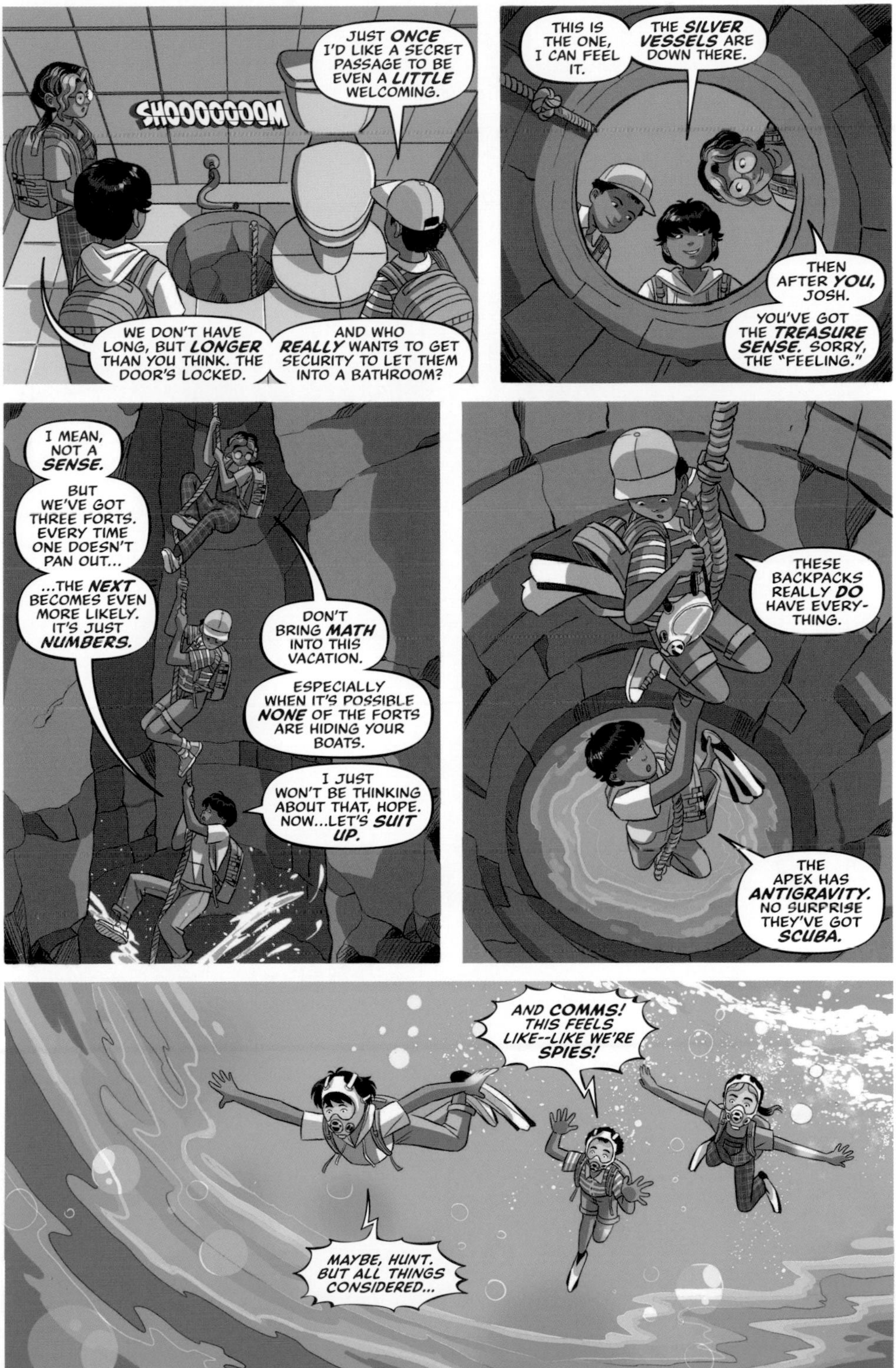
SHOOOOOOOM
JUST ONCE I'D LIKE A SECRET PASSAGE TO BE EVEN A LITTLE WELCOMING.
WE DON'T HAVE LONG, BUT LONGER THAN YOU THINK. THE DOOR'S LOCKED.
AND WHO REALLY WANTS TO GET SECURITY TO LET THEM INTO A BATHROOM?
THIS IS THE ONE, I CAN FEEL IT.
THE SILVER VESSELS ARE DOWN THERE.
THEN AFTER YOU, JOSH.
YOU'VE GOT THE TREASURE SENSE. SORRY, THE "FEELING."
I MEAN, NOT A SENSE.
BUT WE'VE GOT THREE FORTS. EVERY TIME ONE DOESN'T PAN OUT...
...THE NEXT BECOMES EVEN MORE LIKELY. IT'S JUST NUMBERS.
DON'T BRING MATH INTO THIS VACATION.
ESPECIALLY WHEN IT'S POSSIBLE NONE OF THE FORTS ARE HIDING YOUR BOATS.
I JUST WON'T BE THINKING ABOUT THAT, HOPE. NOW...LET'S SUIT UP.
THESE BACKPACKS REALLY DO HAVE EVERY-THING.
THE APEX HAS ANTIGRAVITY. NO SURPRISE THEY'VE GOT SCUBA.
AND COMMS! THIS FEELS LIKE--LIKE WE'RE SPIES!
MAYBE, HUNT. BUT ALL THINGS CONSIDERED...

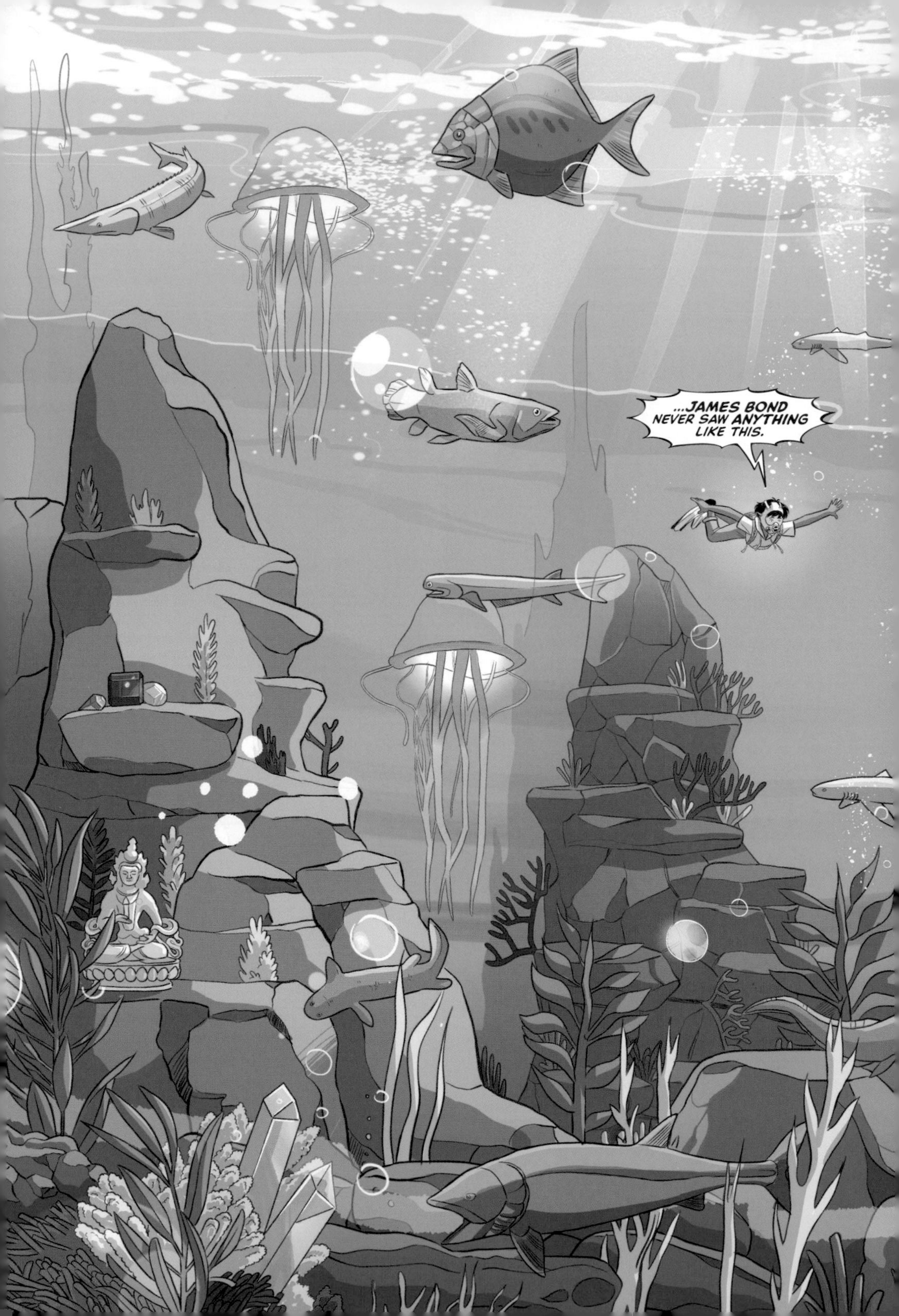
...JAMES BOND NEVER SAW ANYTHING LIKE THIS.

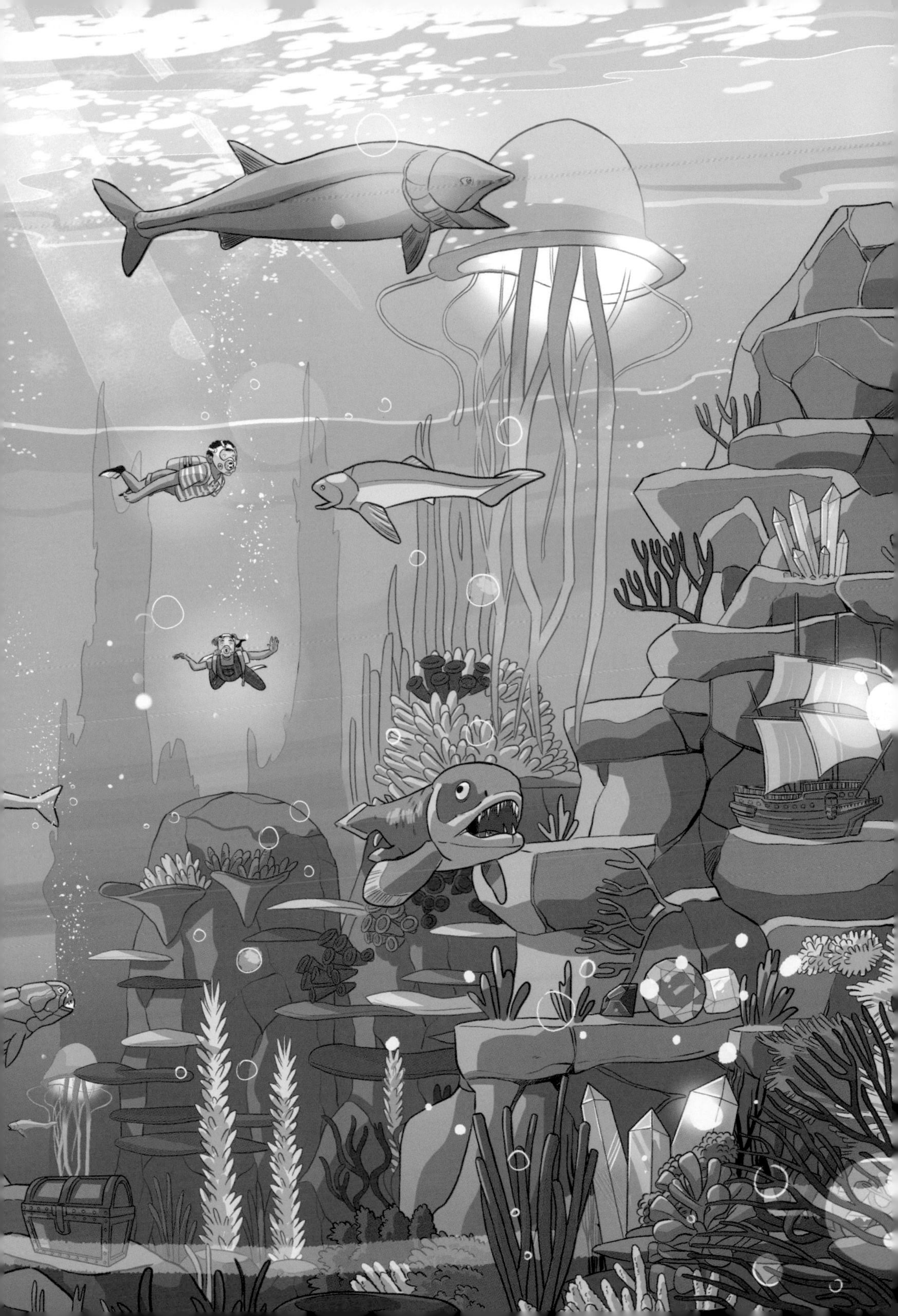

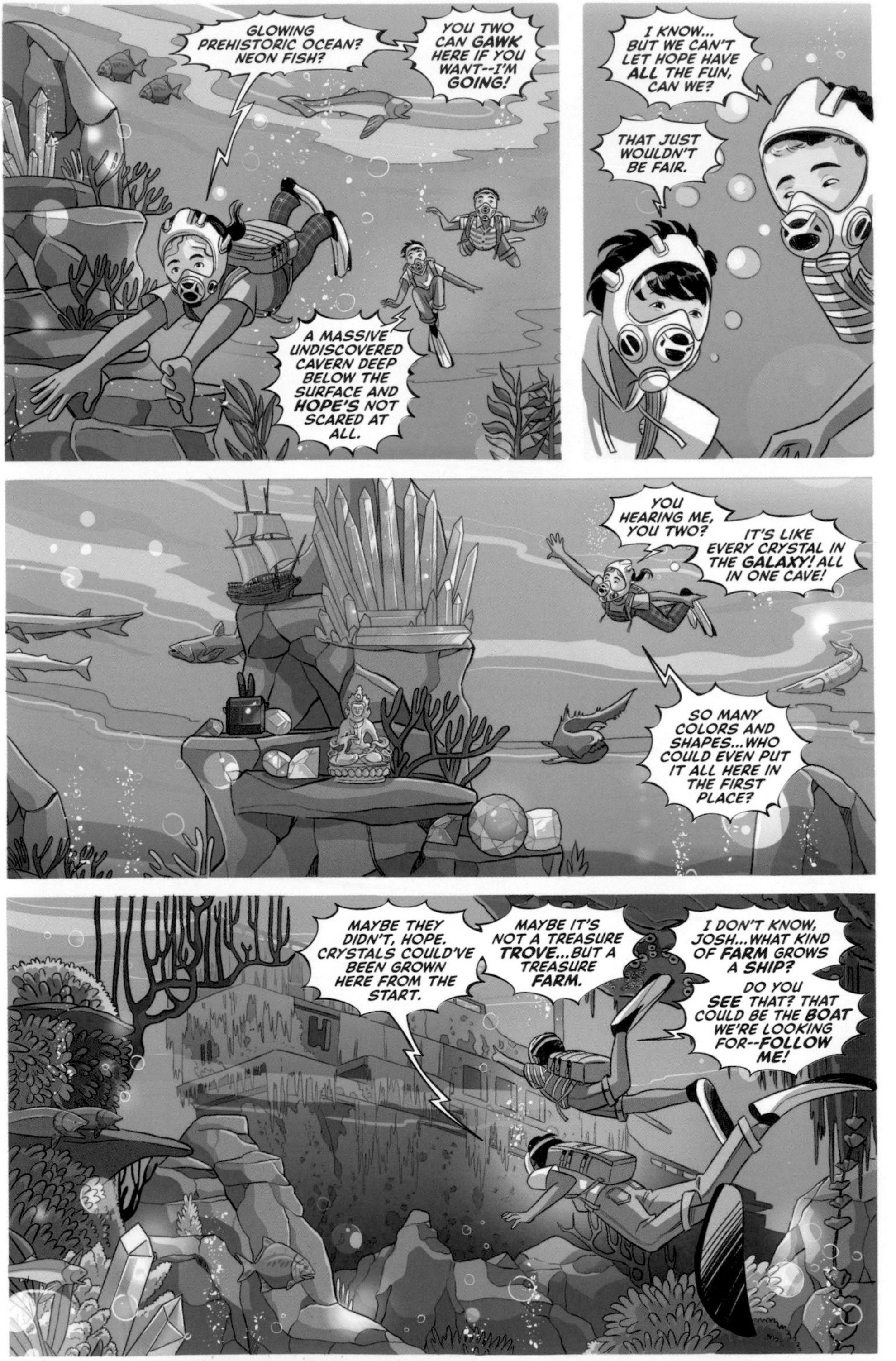

GLOWING PREHISTORIC OCEAN? NEON FISH?
YOU TWO CAN **GAWK** HERE IF YOU WANT--I'M **GOING!**
A MASSIVE UNDISCOVERED CAVERN DEEP BELOW THE SURFACE AND **HOPE'S** NOT SCARED AT ALL.
I KNOW... BUT WE CAN'T LET HOPE HAVE **ALL** THE FUN, CAN WE?
THAT JUST WOULDN'T BE FAIR.
YOU HEARING ME, YOU TWO?
IT'S LIKE EVERY CRYSTAL IN THE **GALAXY!** ALL IN ONE CAVE!
SO MANY COLORS AND SHAPES...WHO COULD EVEN PUT IT ALL HERE IN THE FIRST PLACE?
MAYBE THEY DIDN'T, HOPE. CRYSTALS COULD'VE BEEN GROWN HERE FROM THE START.
MAYBE IT'S NOT A TREASURE **TROVE**...BUT A TREASURE **FARM.**
I DON'T KNOW, JOSH...WHAT KIND OF **FARM** GROWS A **SHIP?**
DO YOU **SEE** THAT? THAT COULD BE THE **BOAT** WE'RE LOOKING FOR--**FOLLOW ME!**

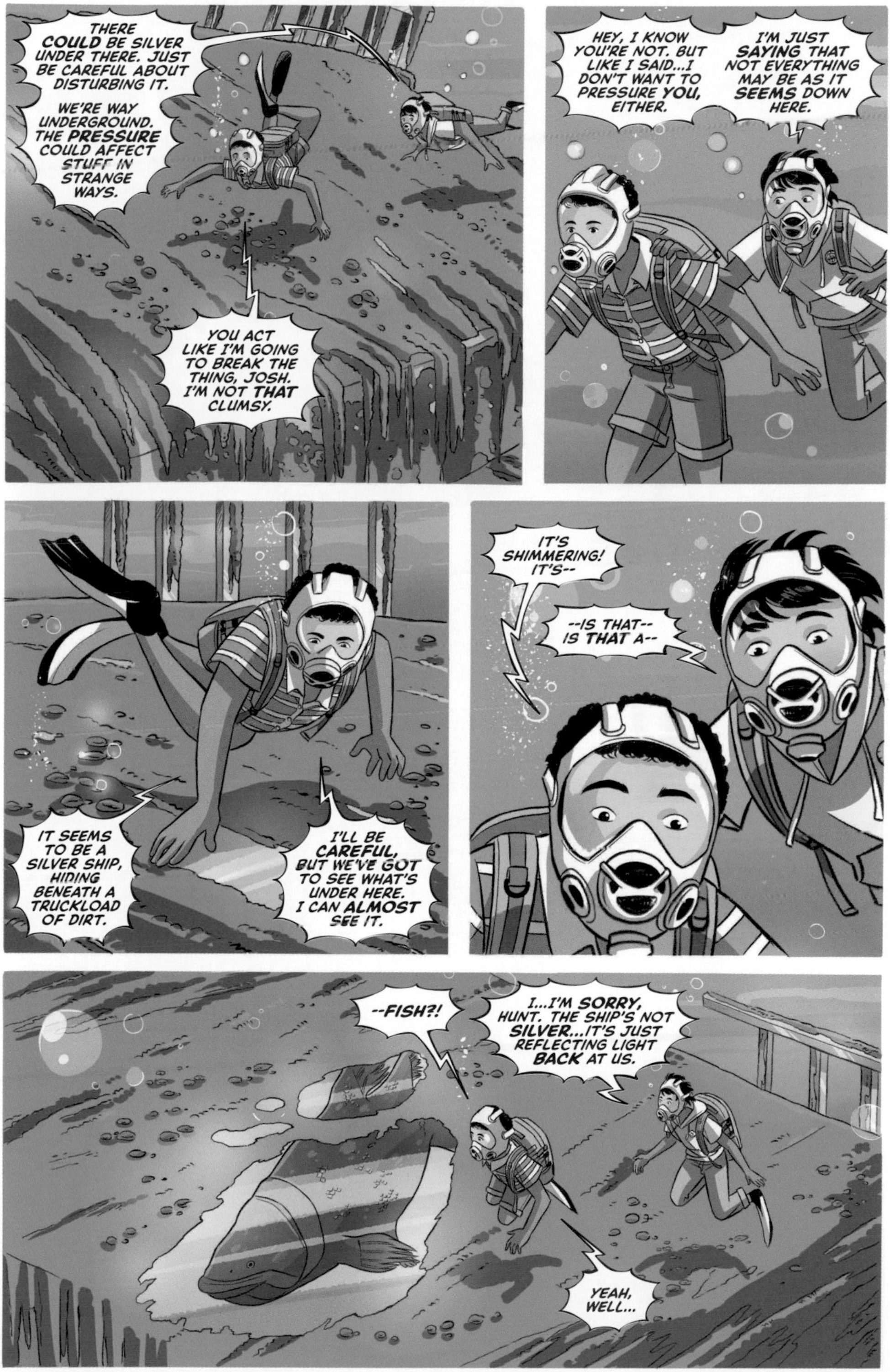
THERE COULD BE SILVER UNDER THERE. JUST BE CAREFUL ABOUT DISTURBING IT.
WE'RE WAY UNDERGROUND. THE PRESSURE COULD AFFECT STUFF IN STRANGE WAYS.
YOU ACT LIKE I'M GOING TO BREAK THE THING, JOSH. I'M NOT THAT CLUMSY.
HEY, I KNOW YOU'RE NOT. BUT LIKE I SAID...I DON'T WANT TO PRESSURE YOU, EITHER.
I'M JUST SAYING THAT NOT EVERYTHING MAY BE AS IT SEEMS DOWN HERE.
IT SEEMS TO BE A SILVER SHIP, HIDING BENEATH A TRUCKLOAD OF DIRT.
I'LL BE CAREFUL, BUT WE'VE GOT TO SEE WHAT'S UNDER HERE. I CAN ALMOST SEE IT.
IT'S SHIMMERING! IT'S--
--IS THAT-- IS THAT A--
--FISH?!
I...I'M SORRY, HUNT. THE SHIP'S NOT SILVER...IT'S JUST REFLECTING LIGHT BACK AT US.
YEAH, WELL...

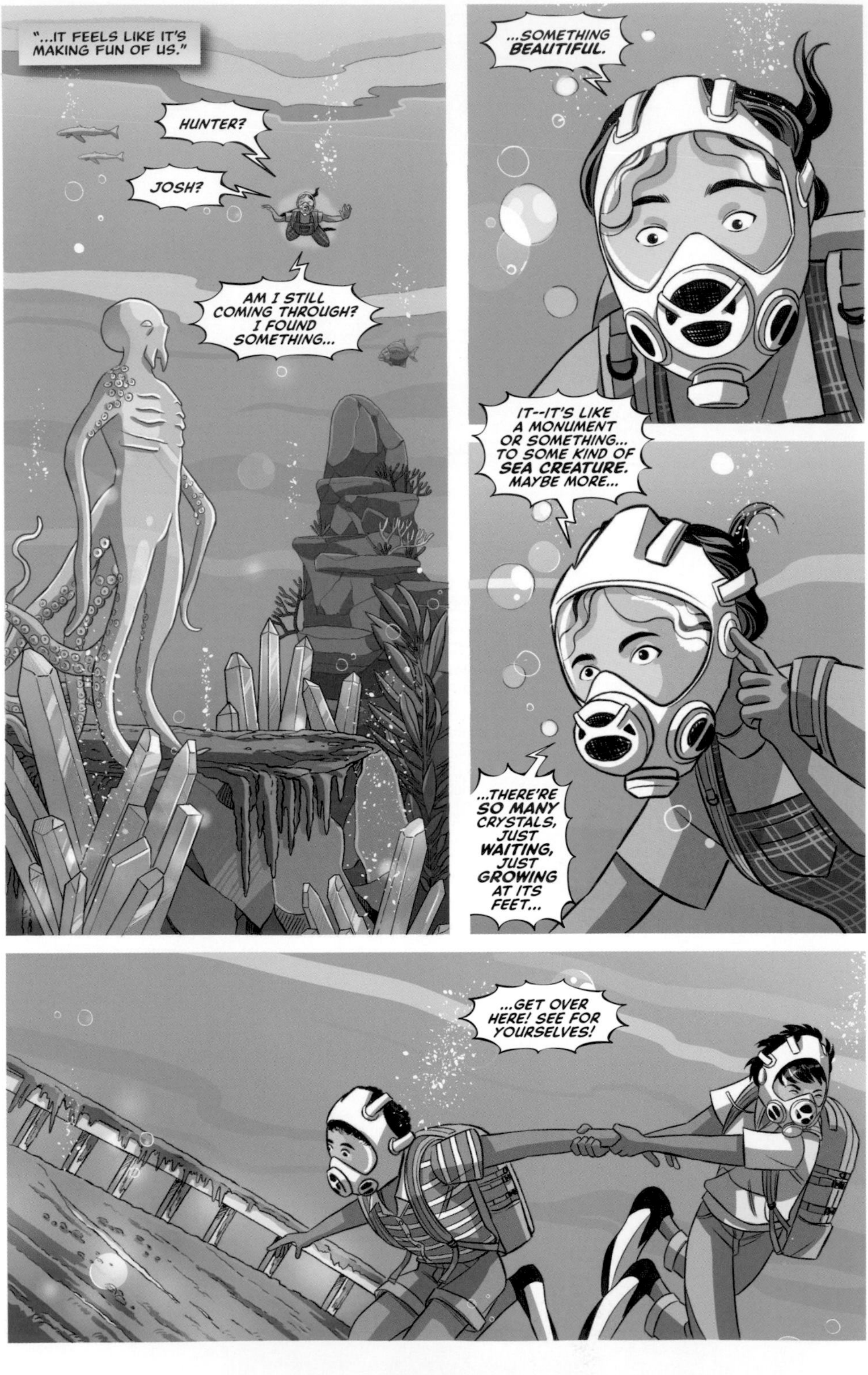
"...IT FEELS LIKE IT'S MAKING FUN OF US."
HUNTER?
JOSH?
AM I STILL COMING THROUGH? I FOUND SOMETHING...
...SOMETHING BEAUTIFUL.
IT--IT'S LIKE A MONUMENT OR SOMETHING... TO SOME KIND OF SEA CREATURE. MAYBE MORE...
...THERE'RE SO MANY CRYSTALS, JUST WAITING, JUST GROWING AT ITS FEET...
...GET OVER HERE! SEE FOR YOURSELVES!

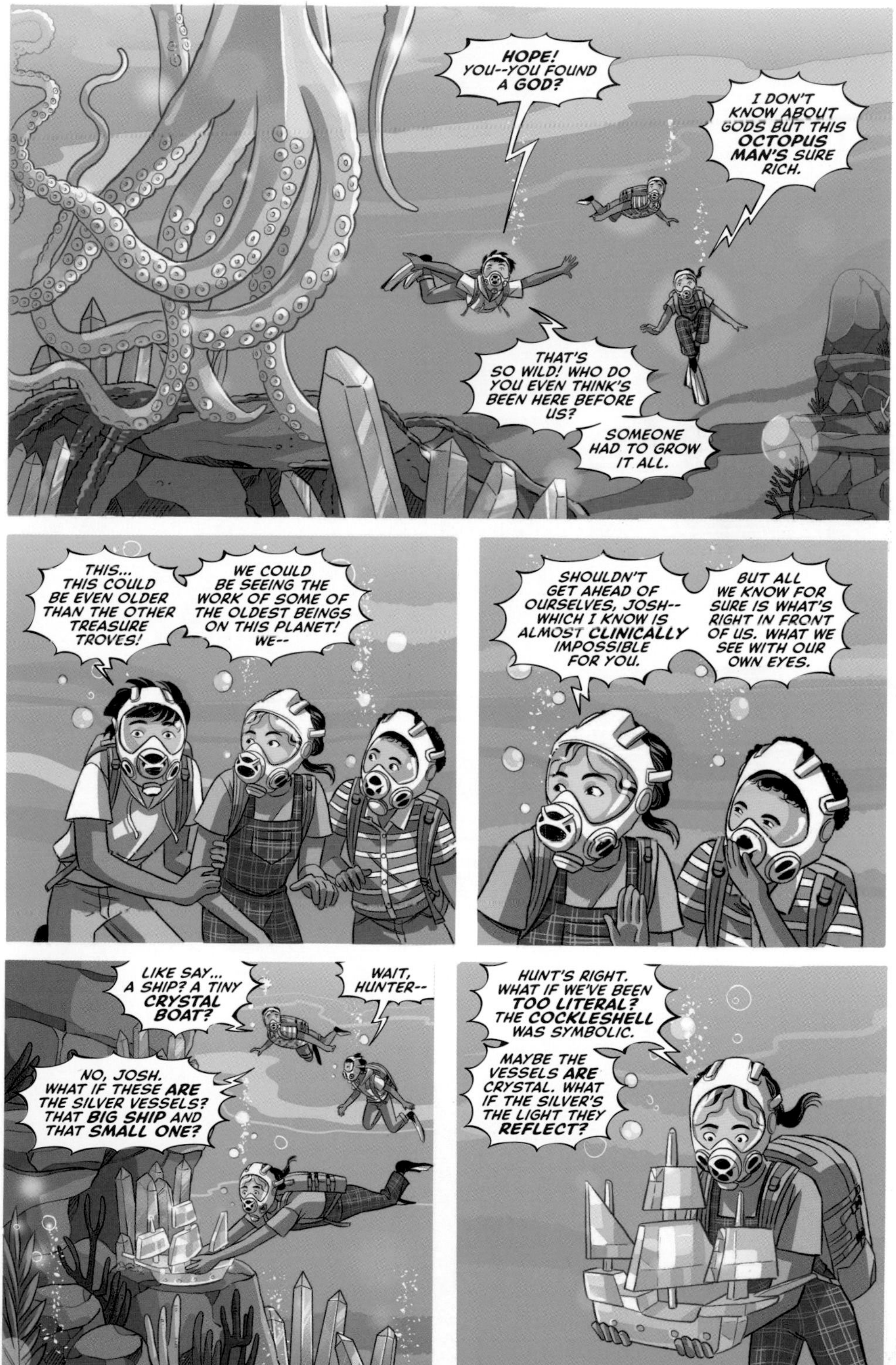
HOPE! YOU--YOU FOUND A GOD?
I DON'T KNOW ABOUT GODS BUT THIS OCTOPUS MAN'S SURE RICH.
THAT'S SO WILD! WHO DO YOU EVEN THINK'S BEEN HERE BEFORE US?
SOMEONE HAD TO GROW IT ALL.
THIS... THIS COULD BE EVEN OLDER THAN THE OTHER TREASURE TROVES!
WE COULD BE SEEING THE WORK OF SOME OF THE OLDEST BEINGS ON THIS PLANET! WE--
SHOULDN'T GET AHEAD OF OURSELVES, JOSH-- WHICH I KNOW IS ALMOST CLINICALLY IMPOSSIBLE FOR YOU.
BUT ALL WE KNOW FOR SURE IS WHAT'S RIGHT IN FRONT OF US. WHAT WE SEE WITH OUR OWN EYES.
LIKE SAY... A SHIP? A TINY CRYSTAL BOAT?
WAIT, HUNTER--
NO, JOSH. WHAT IF THESE ARE THE SILVER VESSELS? THAT BIG SHIP AND THAT SMALL ONE?
HUNT'S RIGHT. WHAT IF WE'VE BEEN TOO LITERAL? THE COCKLESHELL WAS SYMBOLIC.
MAYBE THE VESSELS ARE CRYSTAL. WHAT IF THE SILVER'S THE LIGHT THEY REFLECT?

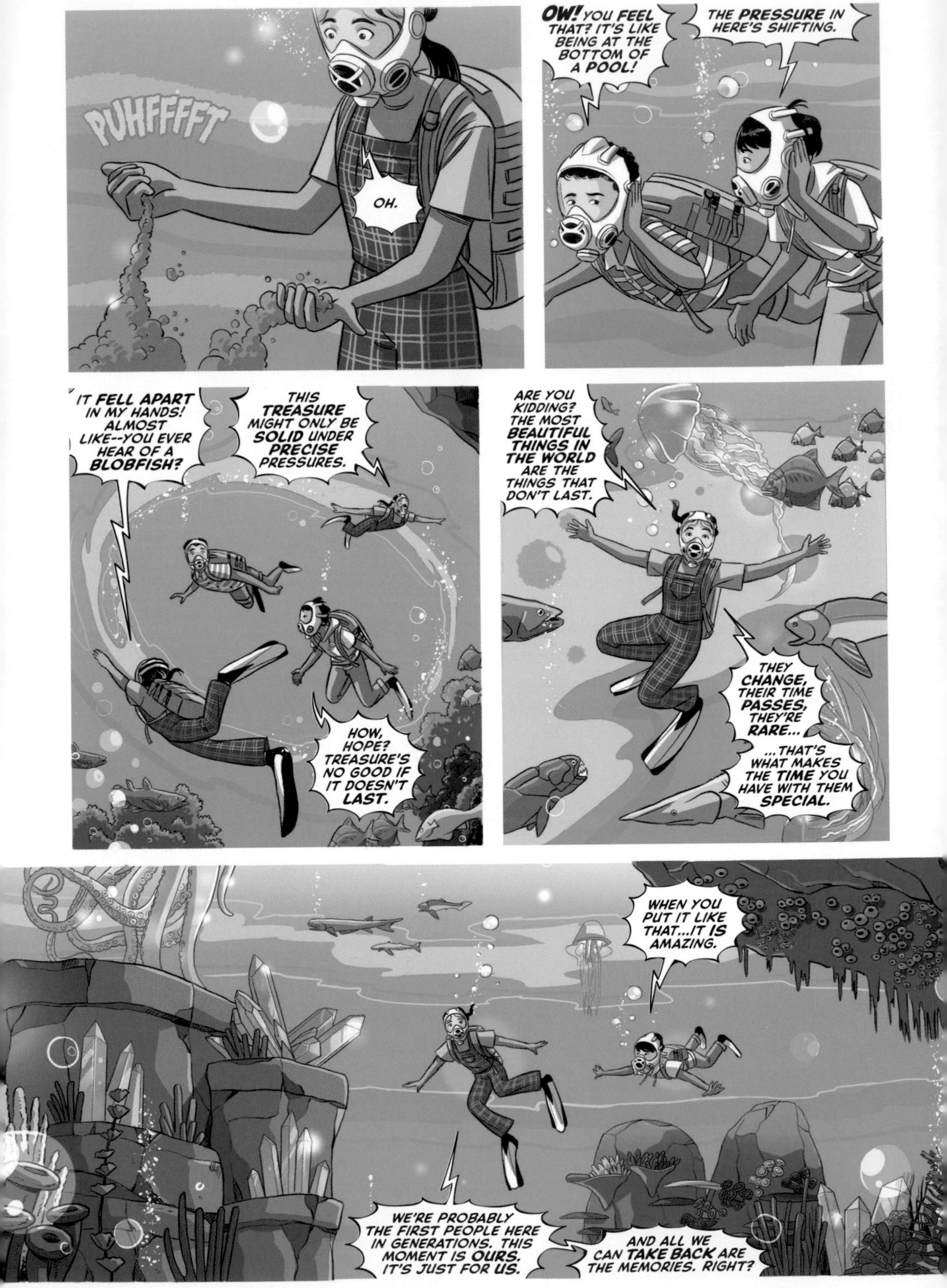
PUHFFFFT
OH.
OW! YOU FEEL THAT? IT'S LIKE BEING AT THE BOTTOM OF A POOL!
THE PRESSURE IN HERE'S SHIFTING.
IT FELL APART IN MY HANDS! ALMOST LIKE--YOU EVER HEAR OF A BLOBFISH?
THIS TREASURE MIGHT ONLY BE SOLID UNDER PRECISE PRESSURES.
HOW, HOPE? TREASURE'S NO GOOD IF IT DOESN'T LAST.
ARE YOU KIDDING? THE MOST BEAUTIFUL THINGS IN THE WORLD ARE THE THINGS THAT DON'T LAST.
THEY CHANGE, THEIR TIME PASSES, THEY'RE RARE...
...THAT'S WHAT MAKES THE TIME YOU HAVE WITH THEM SPECIAL.
WHEN YOU PUT IT LIKE THAT...IT IS AMAZING.
WE'RE PROBABLY THE FIRST PEOPLE HERE IN GENERATIONS. THIS MOMENT IS OURS. IT'S JUST FOR US.
AND ALL WE CAN TAKE BACK ARE THE MEMORIES. RIGHT?

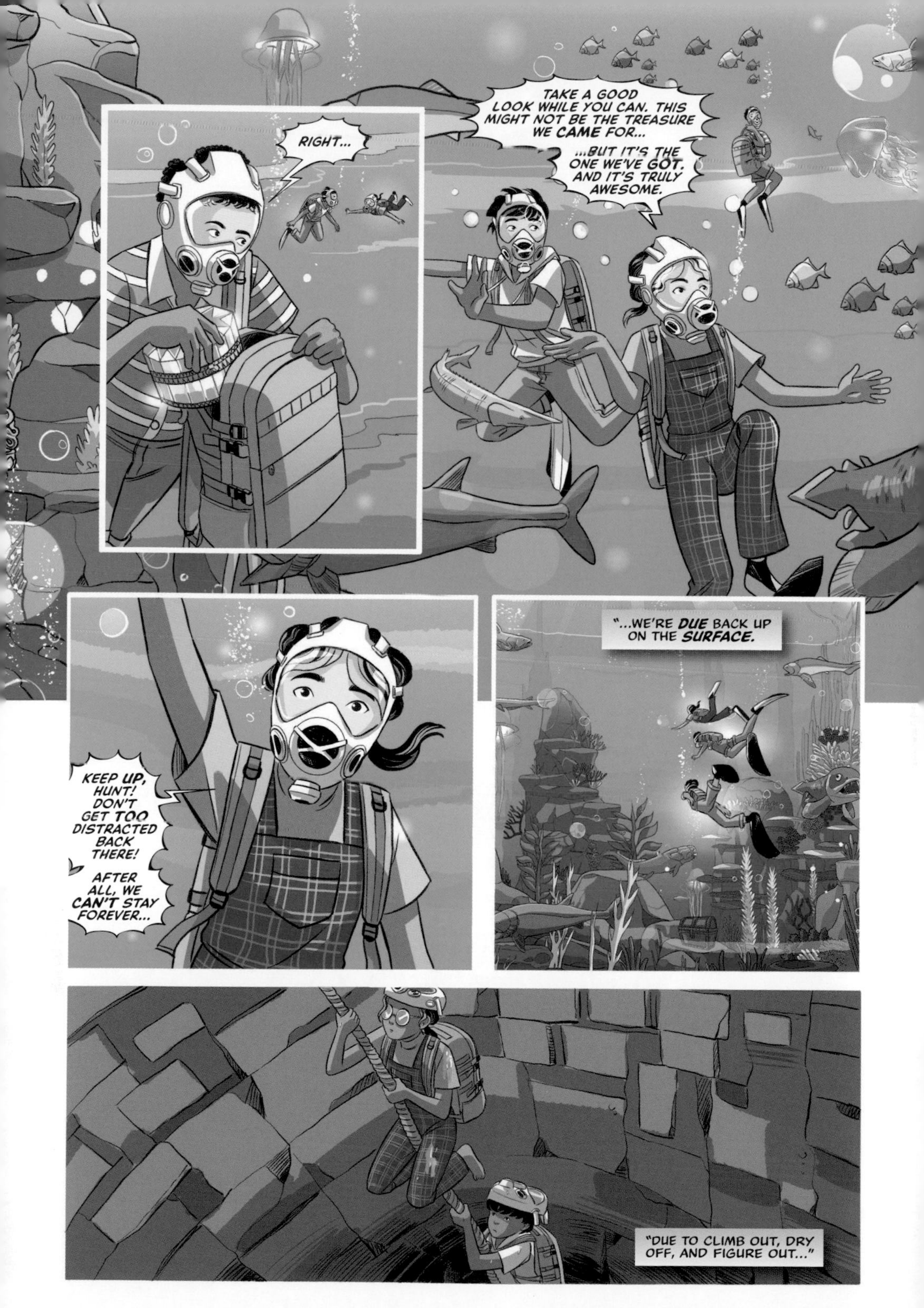
TAKE A GOOD LOOK WHILE YOU CAN. THIS MIGHT NOT BE THE TREASURE WE CAME FOR...
RIGHT...
...BUT IT'S THE ONE WE'VE GOT. AND IT'S TRULY AWESOME.
KEEP UP, HUNT! DON'T GET TOO DISTRACTED BACK THERE!
AFTER ALL, WE CAN'T STAY FOREVER...
"...WE'RE DUE BACK UP ON THE SURFACE.
"DUE TO CLIMB OUT, DRY OFF, AND FIGURE OUT..."

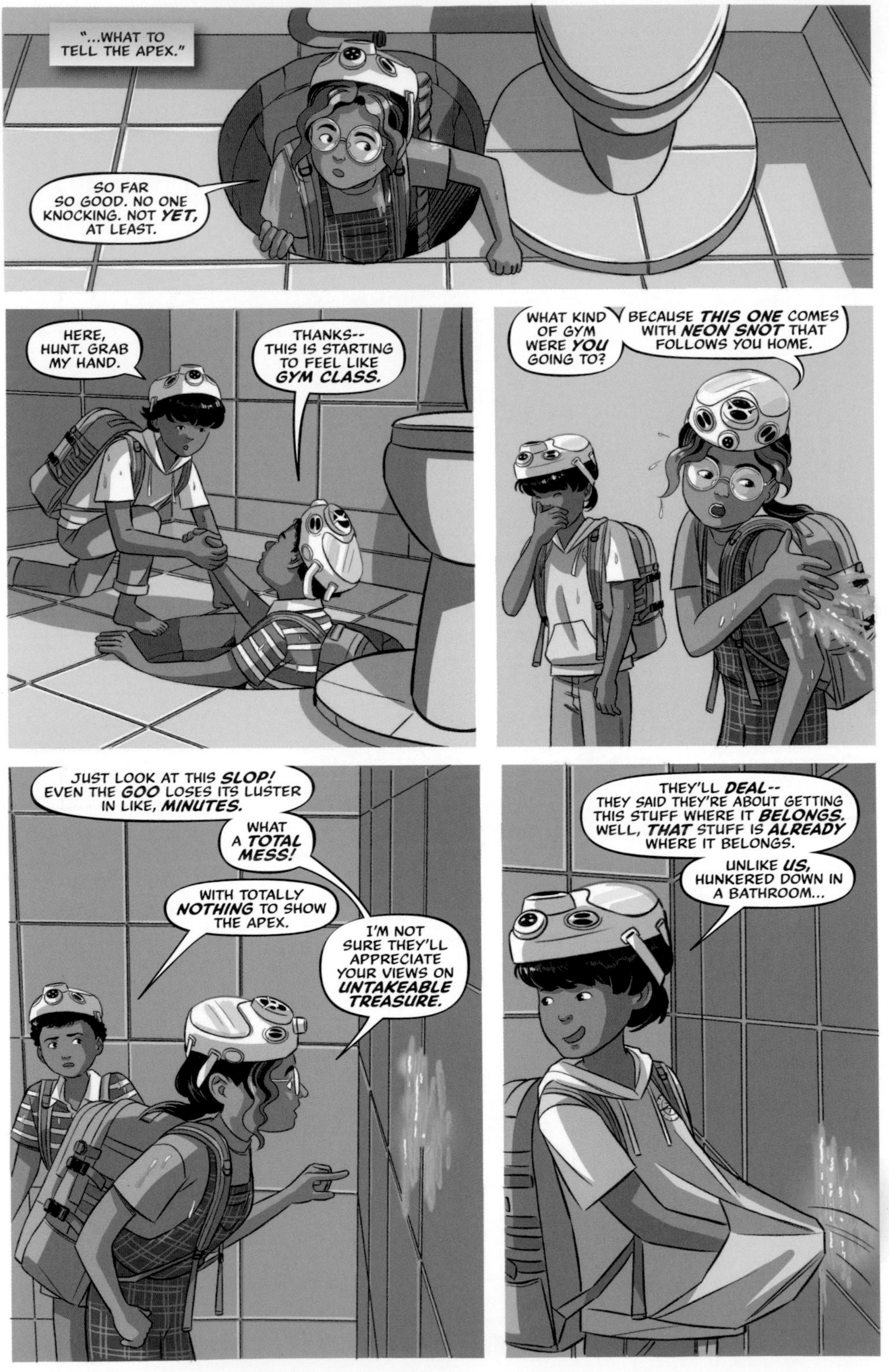
"...WHAT TO TELL THE APEX."
SO FAR SO GOOD. NO ONE KNOCKING. NOT YET, AT LEAST.
HERE, HUNT. GRAB MY HAND.
THANKS-- THIS IS STARTING TO FEEL LIKE GYM CLASS.
WHAT KIND OF GYM WERE YOU GOING TO?
BECAUSE THIS ONE COMES WITH NEON SNOT THAT FOLLOWS YOU HOME.
JUST LOOK AT THIS SLOP! EVEN THE GOO LOSES ITS LUSTER IN LIKE, MINUTES.
WHAT A TOTAL MESS!
WITH TOTALLY NOTHING TO SHOW THE APEX.
I'M NOT SURE THEY'LL APPRECIATE YOUR VIEWS ON UNTAKEABLE TREASURE.
THEY'LL DEAL-- THEY SAID THEY'RE ABOUT GETTING THIS STUFF WHERE IT BELONGS. WELL, THAT STUFF IS ALREADY WHERE IT BELONGS.
UNLIKE US, HUNKERED DOWN IN A BATHROOM...

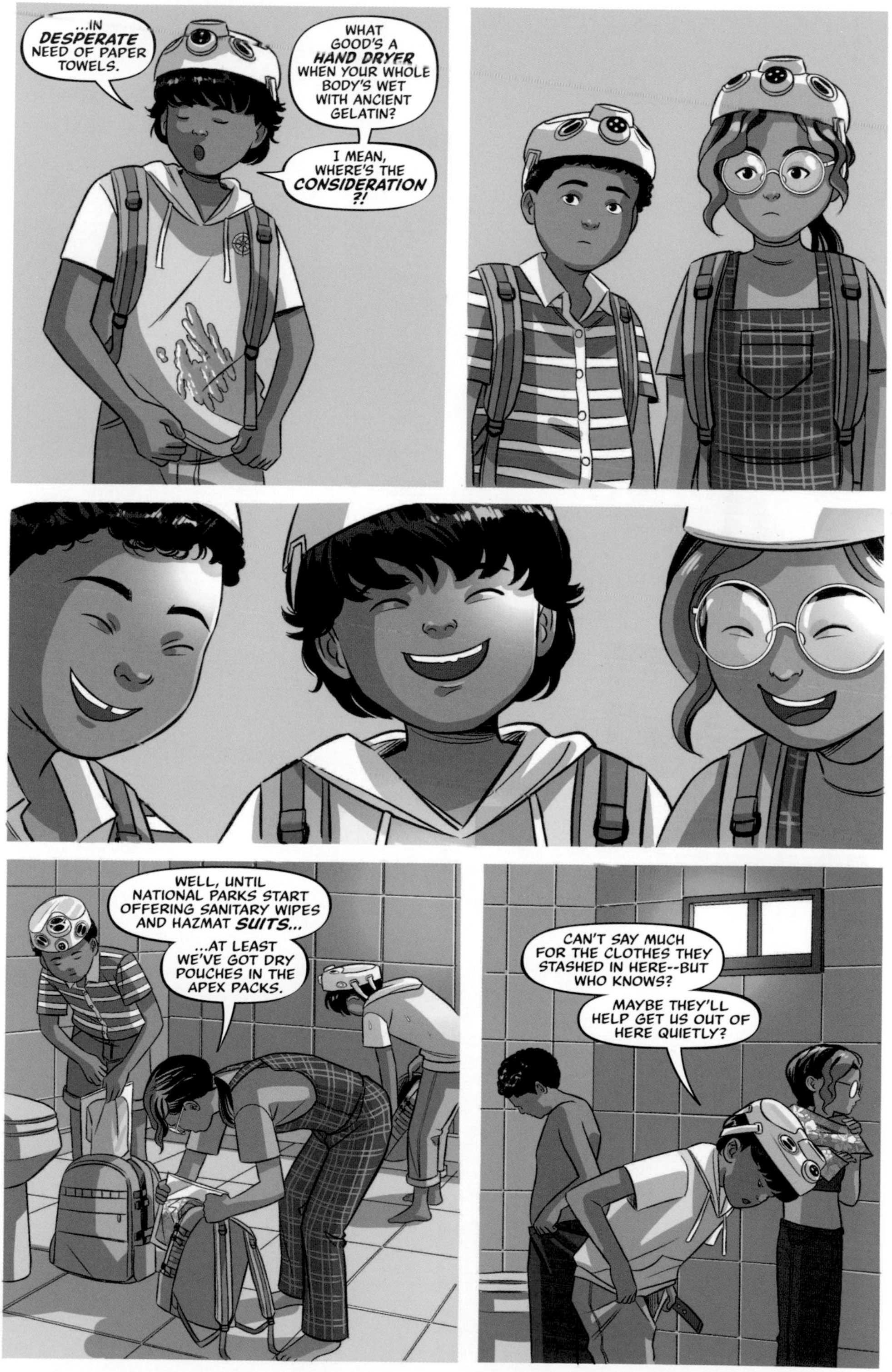
...IN DESPERATE NEED OF PAPER TOWELS.
WHAT GOOD'S A HAND DRYER WHEN YOUR WHOLE BODY'S WET WITH ANCIENT GELATIN?
I MEAN, WHERE'S THE CONSIDERATION ?!
WELL, UNTIL NATIONAL PARKS START OFFERING SANITARY WIPES AND HAZMAT SUITS...
...AT LEAST WE'VE GOT DRY POUCHES IN THE APEX PACKS.
CAN'T SAY MUCH FOR THE CLOTHES THEY STASHED IN HERE--BUT WHO KNOWS?
MAYBE THEY'LL HELP GET US OUT OF HERE QUIETLY?

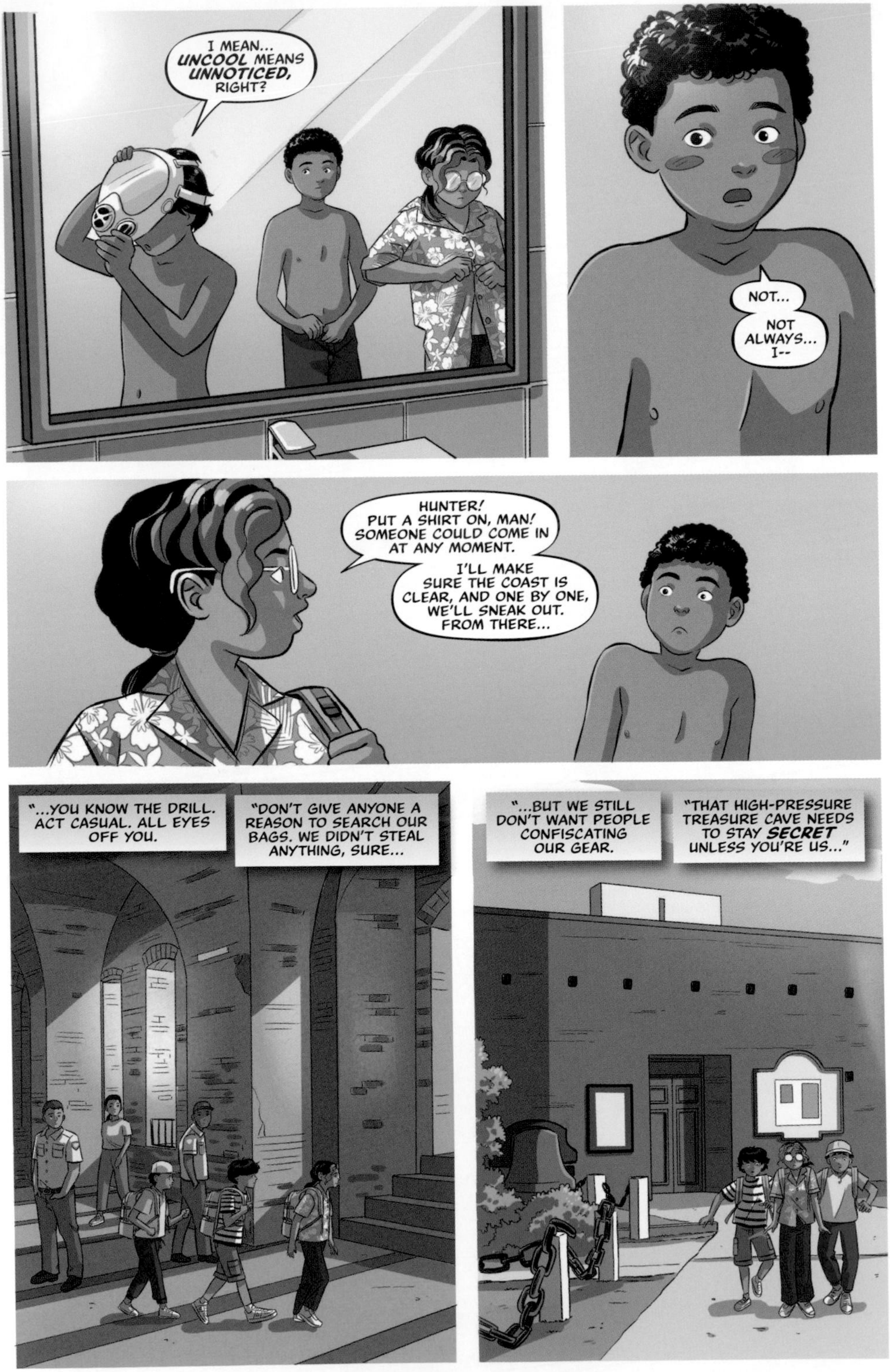
I MEAN... ***UNCOOL*** MEANS ***UNNOTICED,*** RIGHT?
NOT...
NOT ALWAYS... I--
HUNTER! PUT A SHIRT ON, MAN! SOMEONE COULD COME IN AT ANY MOMENT.
I'LL MAKE SURE THE COAST IS CLEAR, AND ONE BY ONE, WE'LL SNEAK OUT. FROM THERE...
"...YOU KNOW THE DRILL. ACT CASUAL. ALL EYES OFF YOU.
"DON'T GIVE ANYONE A REASON TO SEARCH OUR BAGS. WE DIDN'T STEAL ANYTHING, SURE...
"...BUT WE STILL DON'T WANT PEOPLE CONFISCATING OUR GEAR.
"THAT HIGH-PRESSURE TREASURE CAVE NEEDS TO STAY ***SECRET*** UNLESS YOU'RE US..."

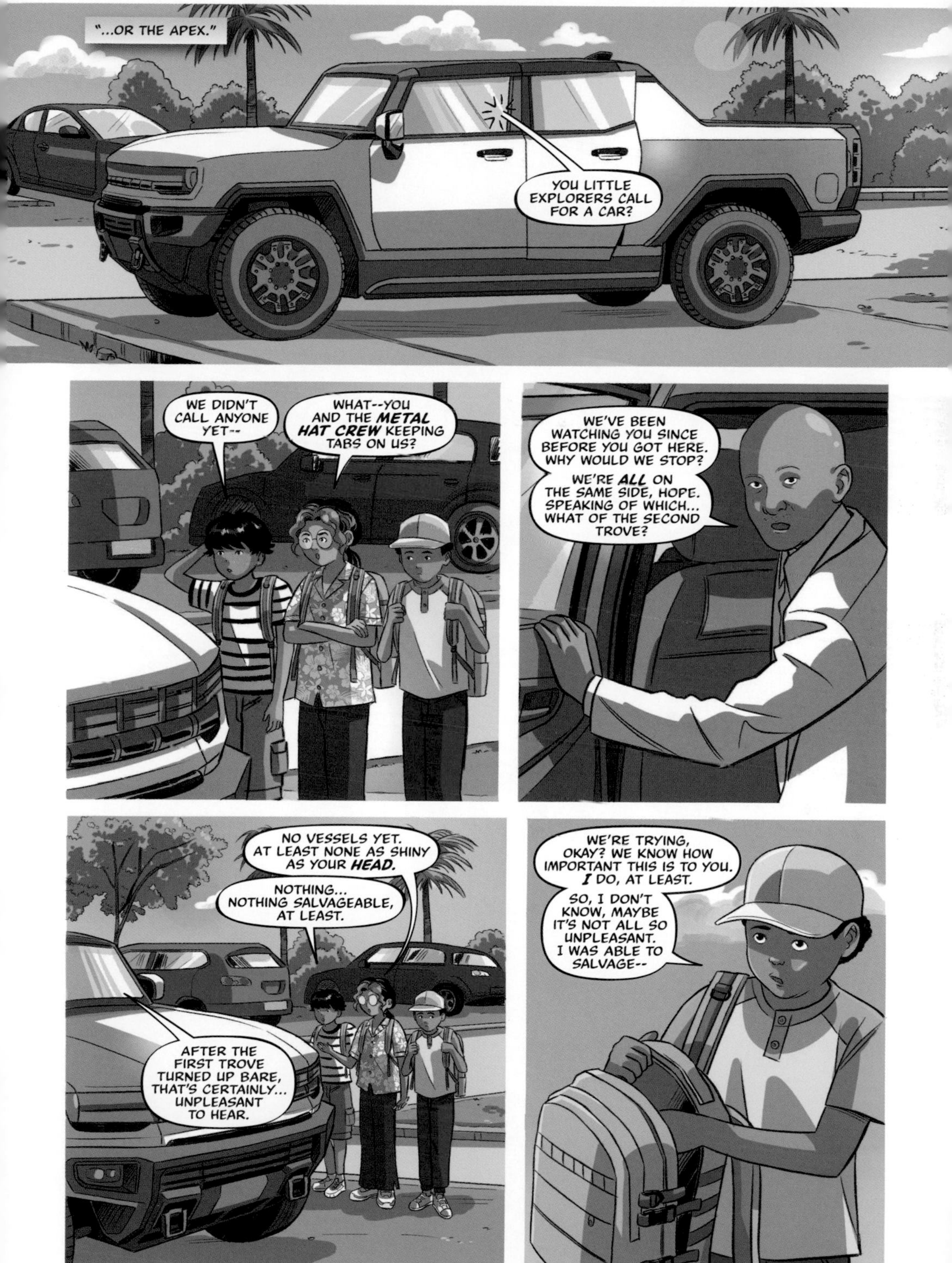

"...OR THE APEX."
YOU LITTLE EXPLORERS CALL FOR A CAR?
WE DIDN'T CALL ANYONE YET--
WHAT--YOU AND THE METAL HAT CREW KEEPING TABS ON US?
WE'VE BEEN WATCHING YOU SINCE BEFORE YOU GOT HERE. WHY WOULD WE STOP?
WE'RE ALL ON THE SAME SIDE, HOPE. SPEAKING OF WHICH... WHAT OF THE SECOND TROVE?
NO VESSELS YET. AT LEAST NONE AS SHINY AS YOUR HEAD.
NOTHING... NOTHING SALVAGEABLE, AT LEAST.
AFTER THE FIRST TROVE TURNED UP BARE, THAT'S CERTAINLY... UNPLEASANT TO HEAR.
WE'RE TRYING, OKAY? WE KNOW HOW IMPORTANT THIS IS TO YOU. I DO, AT LEAST.
SO, I DON'T KNOW, MAYBE IT'S NOT ALL SO UNPLEASANT. I WAS ABLE TO SALVAGE--

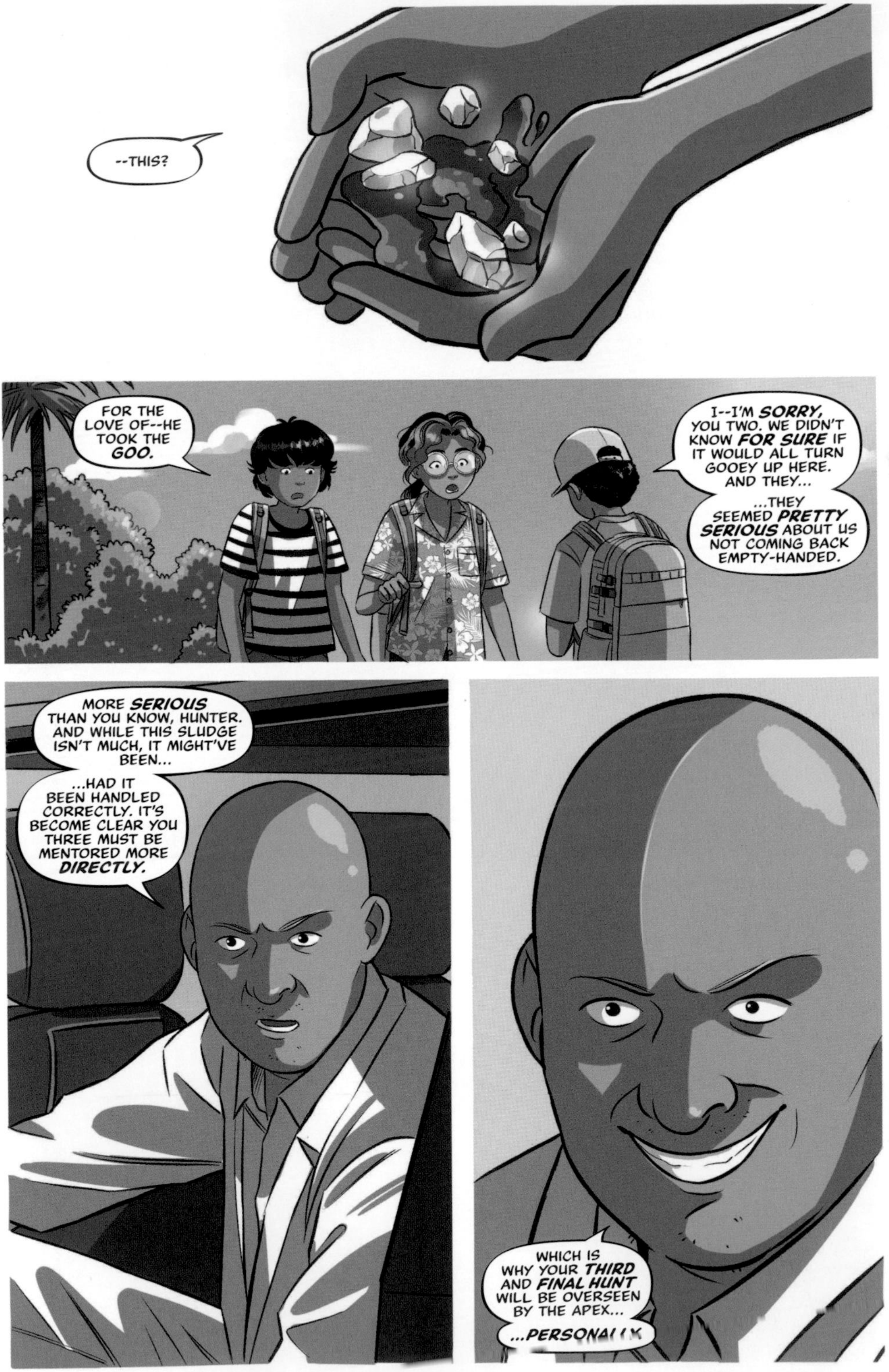
--THIS?
FOR THE LOVE OF--HE TOOK THE GOO.
I--I'M SORRY, YOU TWO. WE DIDN'T KNOW FOR SURE IF IT WOULD ALL TURN GOOEY UP HERE. AND THEY...
...THEY SEEMED PRETTY SERIOUS ABOUT US NOT COMING BACK EMPTY-HANDED.
MORE SERIOUS THAN YOU KNOW, HUNTER. AND WHILE THIS SLUDGE ISN'T MUCH, IT MIGHT'VE BEEN...
...HAD IT BEEN HANDLED CORRECTLY. IT'S BECOME CLEAR YOU THREE MUST BE MENTORED MORE DIRECTLY.
WHICH IS WHY YOUR THIRD AND FINAL HUNT WILL BE OVERSEEN BY THE APEX...
...PERSONALLY.

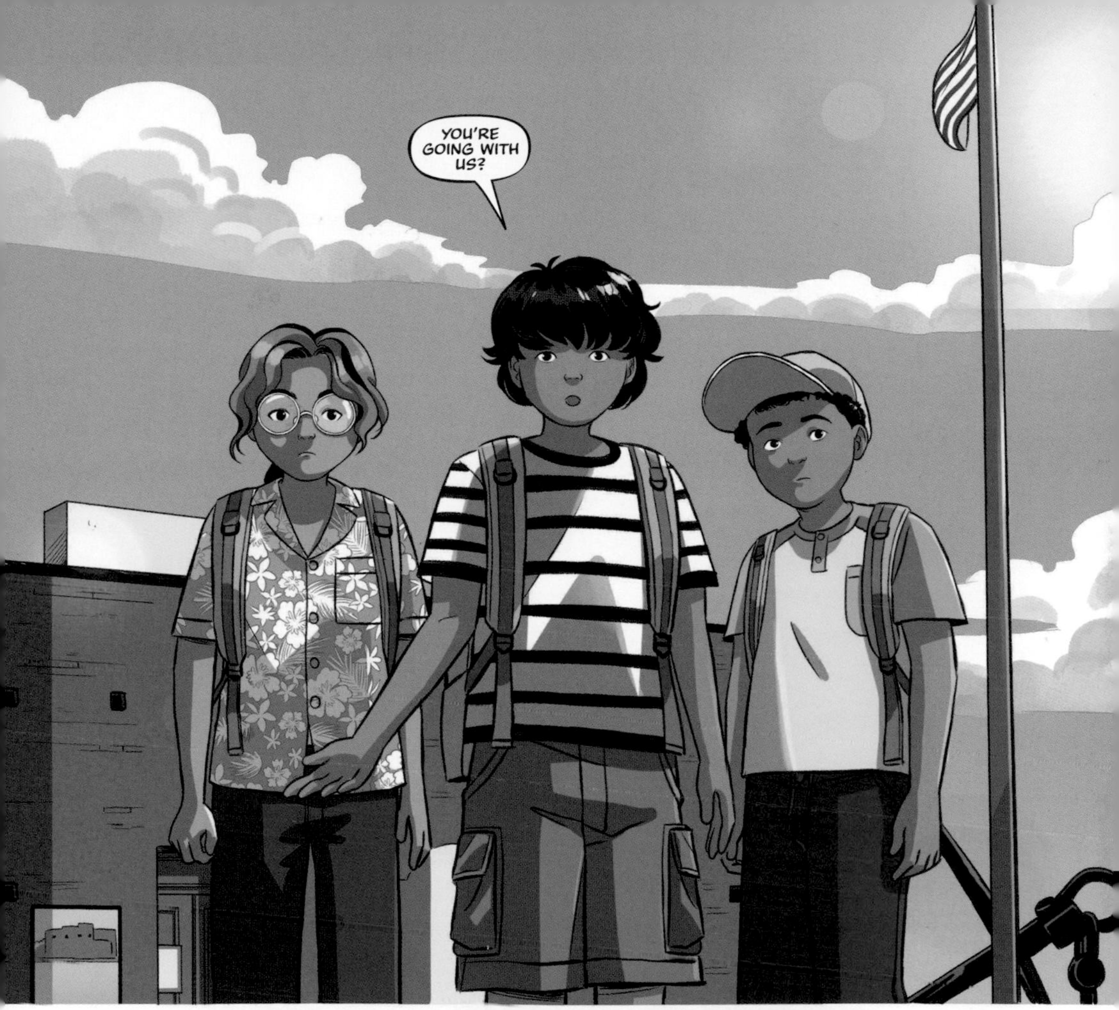
YOU'RE GOING WITH US?

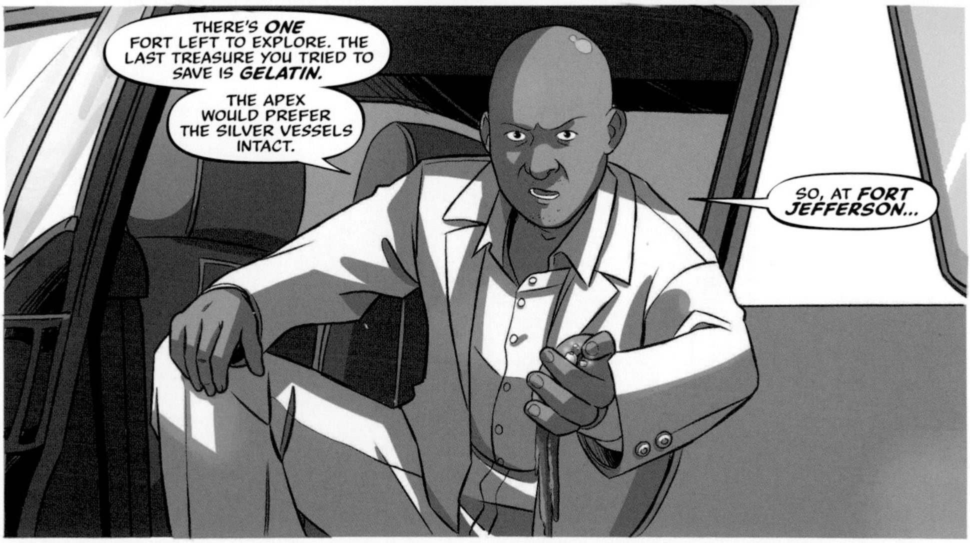
THERE'S ONE FORT LEFT TO EXPLORE. THE LAST TREASURE YOU TRIED TO SAVE IS GELATIN.
THE APEX WOULD PREFER THE SILVER VESSELS INTACT.
SO, AT FORT JEFFERSON...

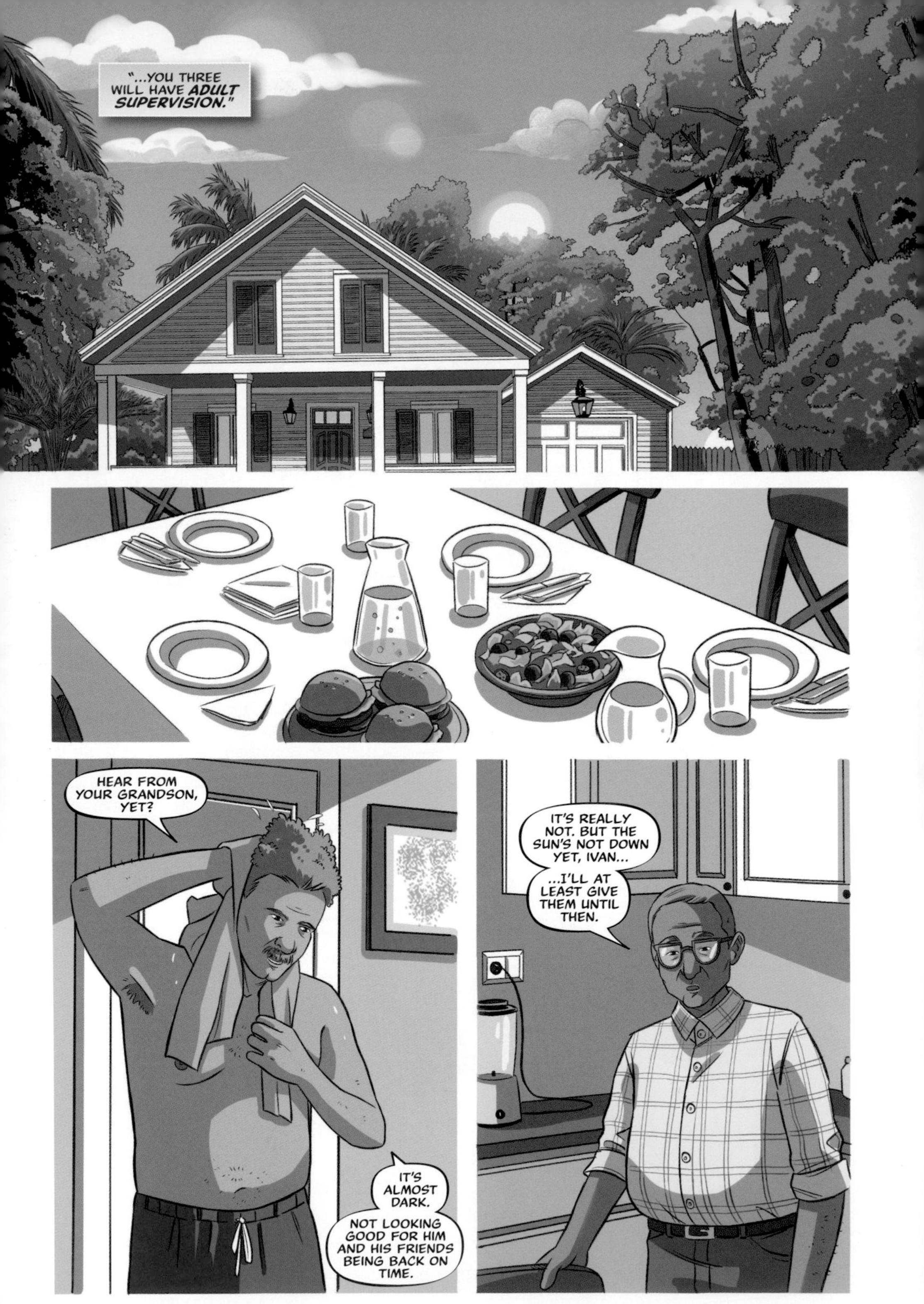
"...YOU THREE WILL HAVE ADULT SUPERVISION."
HEAR FROM YOUR GRANDSON, YET?
IT'S ALMOST DARK.
NOT LOOKING GOOD FOR HIM AND HIS FRIENDS BEING BACK ON TIME.
IT'S REALLY NOT. BUT THE SUN'S NOT DOWN YET, IVAN...
...I'LL AT LEAST GIVE THEM UNTIL THEN.

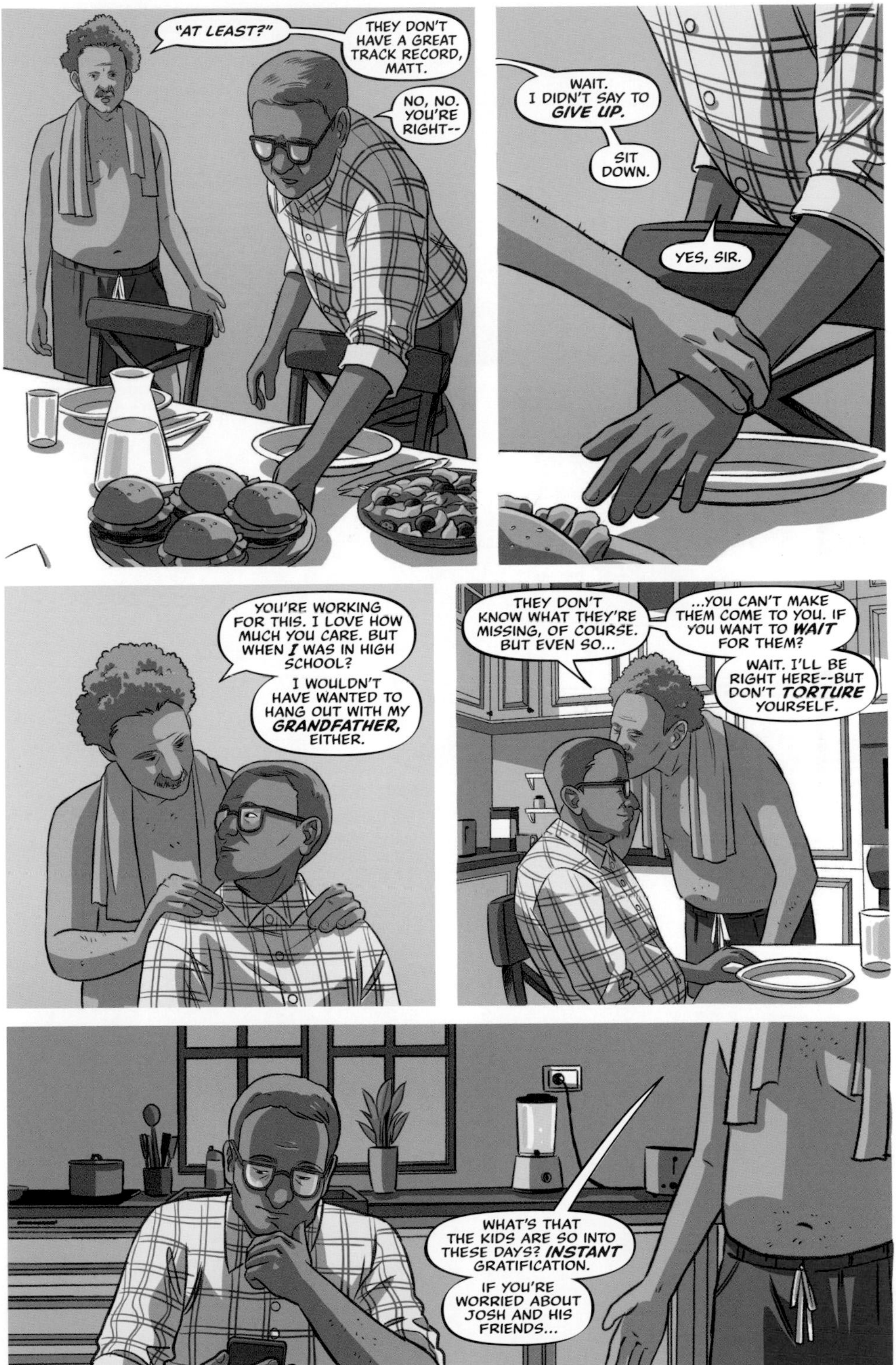
"AT LEAST?"
THEY DON'T HAVE A GREAT TRACK RECORD, MATT.
NO, NO. YOU'RE RIGHT--
WAIT. I DIDN'T SAY TO GIVE UP.
SIT DOWN.
YES, SIR.
YOU'RE WORKING FOR THIS. I LOVE HOW MUCH YOU CARE. BUT WHEN I WAS IN HIGH SCHOOL?
I WOULDN'T HAVE WANTED TO HANG OUT WITH MY GRANDFATHER, EITHER.
THEY DON'T KNOW WHAT THEY'RE MISSING, OF COURSE. BUT EVEN SO...
...YOU CAN'T MAKE THEM COME TO YOU. IF YOU WANT TO WAIT FOR THEM?
WAIT. I'LL BE RIGHT HERE--BUT DON'T TORTURE YOURSELF.
WHAT'S THAT THE KIDS ARE SO INTO THESE DAYS? INSTANT GRATIFICATION.
IF YOU'RE WORRIED ABOUT JOSH AND HIS FRIENDS...

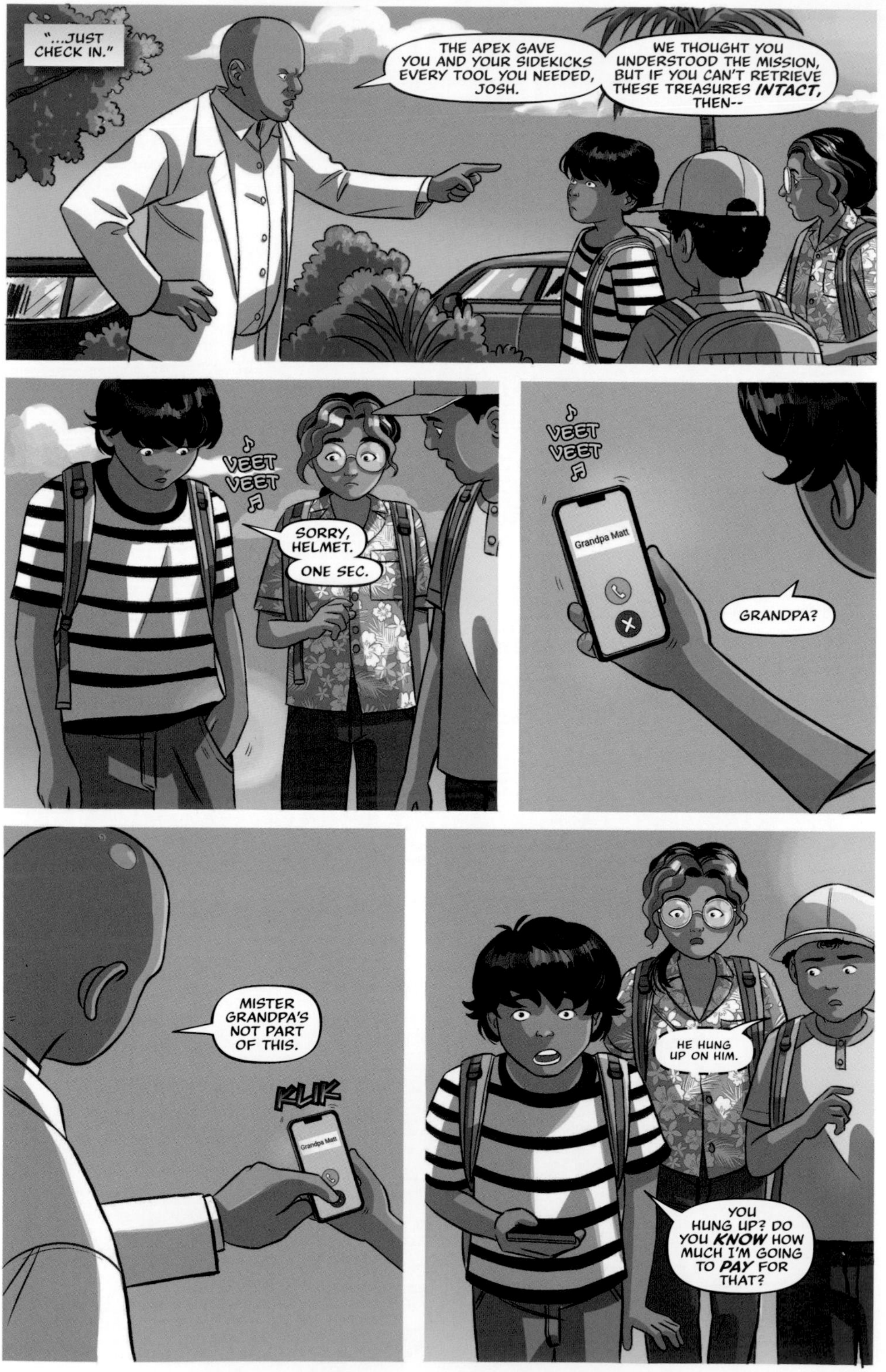
"...JUST CHECK IN."
THE APEX GAVE YOU AND YOUR SIDEKICKS EVERY TOOL YOU NEEDED, JOSH.
WE THOUGHT YOU UNDERSTOOD THE MISSION, BUT IF YOU CAN'T RETRIEVE THESE TREASURES *INTACT,* THEN--
VEET VEET
SORRY, HELMET.
ONE SEC.
VEET VEET
Grandpa Matt
GRANDPA?
MISTER GRANDPA'S NOT PART OF THIS.
KLIK
Grandpa Matt
HE HUNG UP ON HIM.
YOU HUNG UP? DO YOU *KNOW* HOW MUCH I'M GOING TO *PAY* FOR THAT?

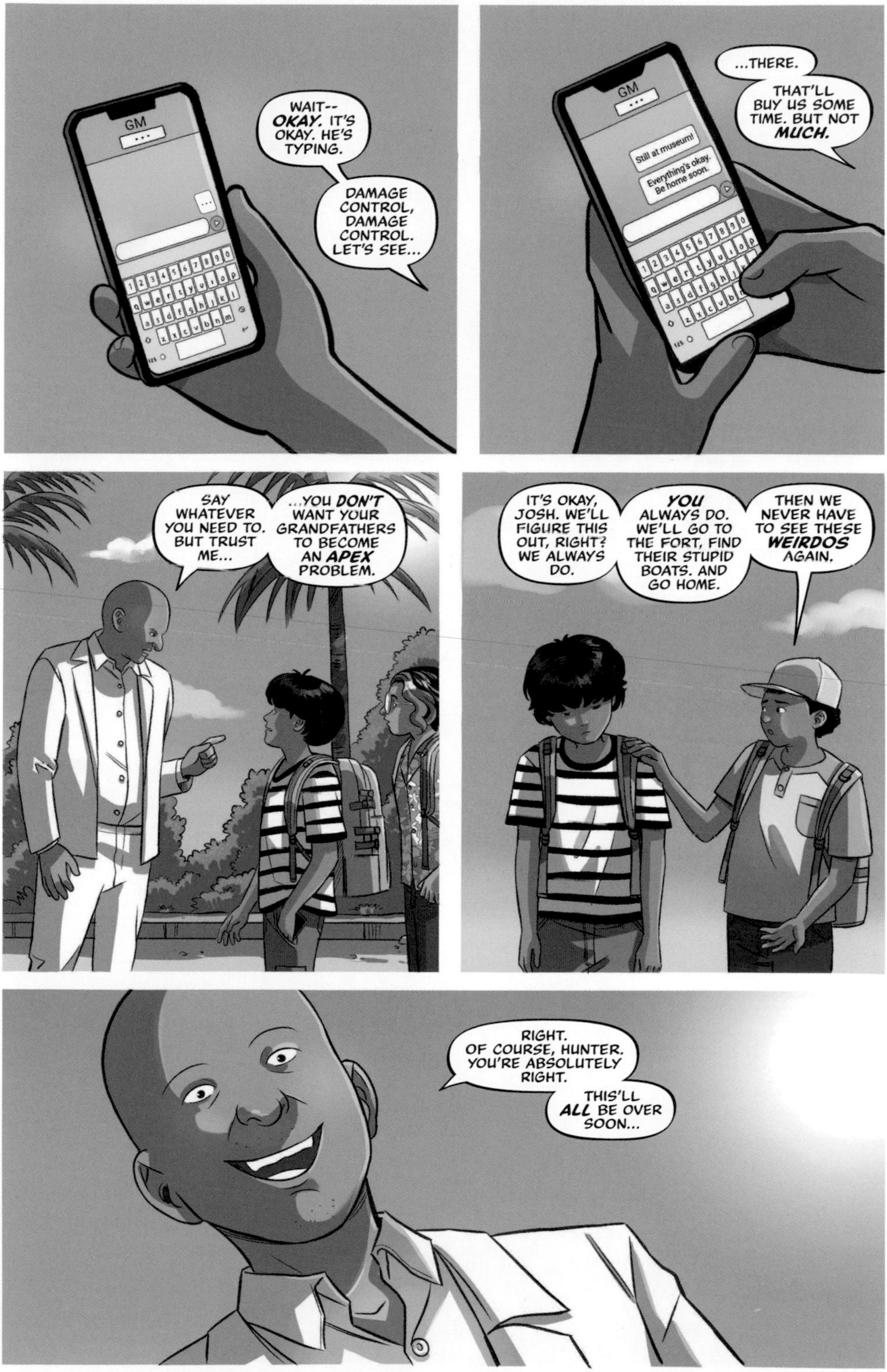
GM
WAIT-- OKAY. IT'S OKAY. HE'S TYPING.
DAMAGE CONTROL, DAMAGE CONTROL. LET'S SEE...
GM
Still at museum!
Everything's okay. Be home soon.
...THERE.
THAT'LL BUY US SOME TIME. BUT NOT MUCH.
SAY WHATEVER YOU NEED TO. BUT TRUST ME...
...YOU DON'T WANT YOUR GRANDFATHERS TO BECOME AN APEX PROBLEM.
IT'S OKAY, JOSH. WE'LL FIGURE THIS OUT, RIGHT? WE ALWAYS DO.
YOU ALWAYS DO. WE'LL GO TO THE FORT, FIND THEIR STUPID BOATS. AND GO HOME.
THEN WE NEVER HAVE TO SEE THESE WEIRDOS AGAIN.
RIGHT. OF COURSE, HUNTER. YOU'RE ABSOLUTELY RIGHT.
THIS'LL ALL BE OVER SOON...

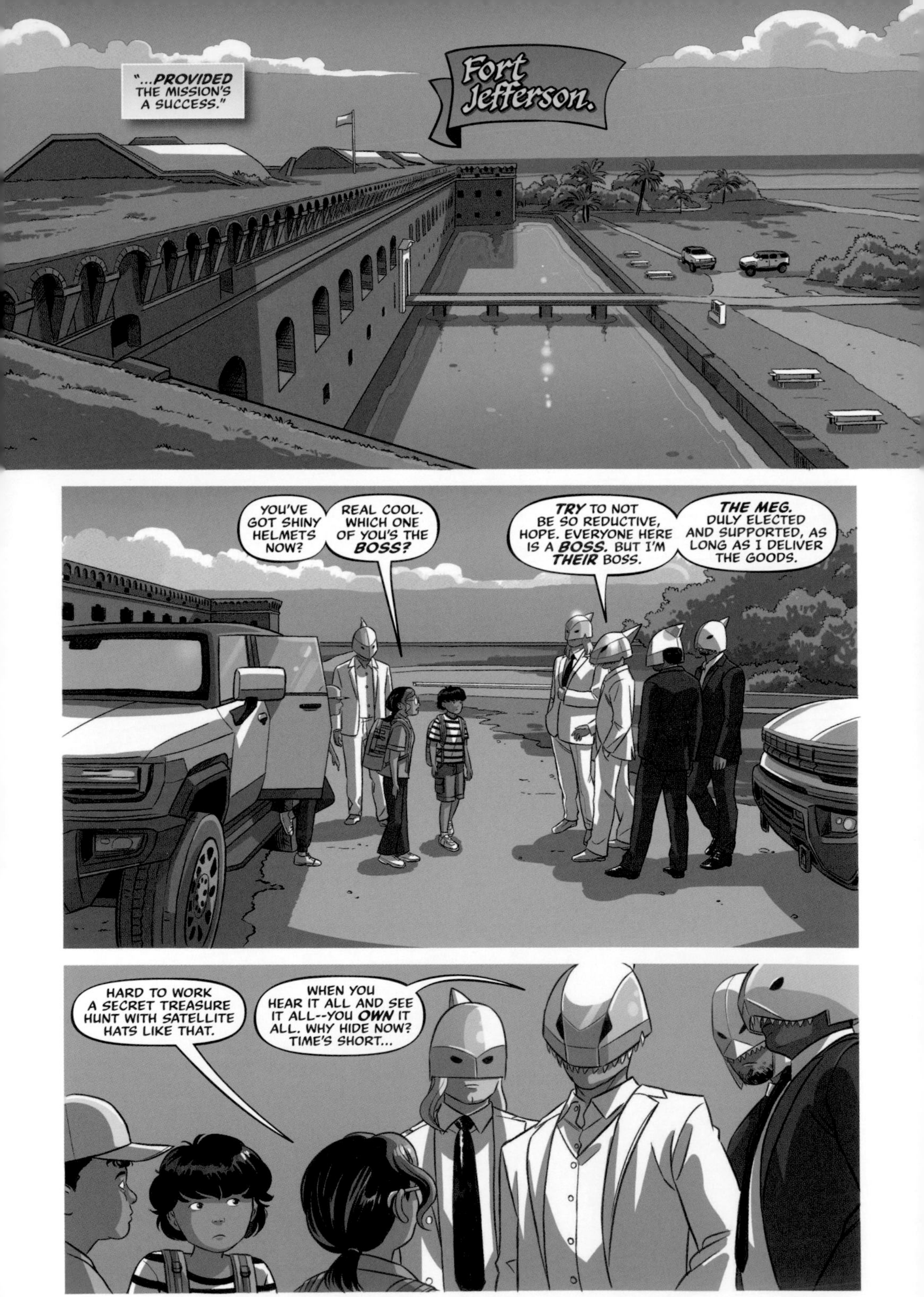
"...PROVIDED THE MISSION'S A SUCCESS."
Fort Jefferson.
YOU'VE GOT SHINY HELMETS NOW?
REAL COOL. WHICH ONE OF YOU'S THE BOSS?
TRY TO NOT BE SO REDUCTIVE, HOPE. EVERYONE HERE IS A BOSS. BUT I'M THEIR BOSS.
THE MEG. DULY ELECTED AND SUPPORTED, AS LONG AS I DELIVER THE GOODS.
HARD TO WORK A SECRET TREASURE HUNT WITH SATELLITE HATS LIKE THAT.
WHEN YOU HEAR IT ALL AND SEE IT ALL--YOU OWN IT ALL. WHY HIDE NOW? TIME'S SHORT...

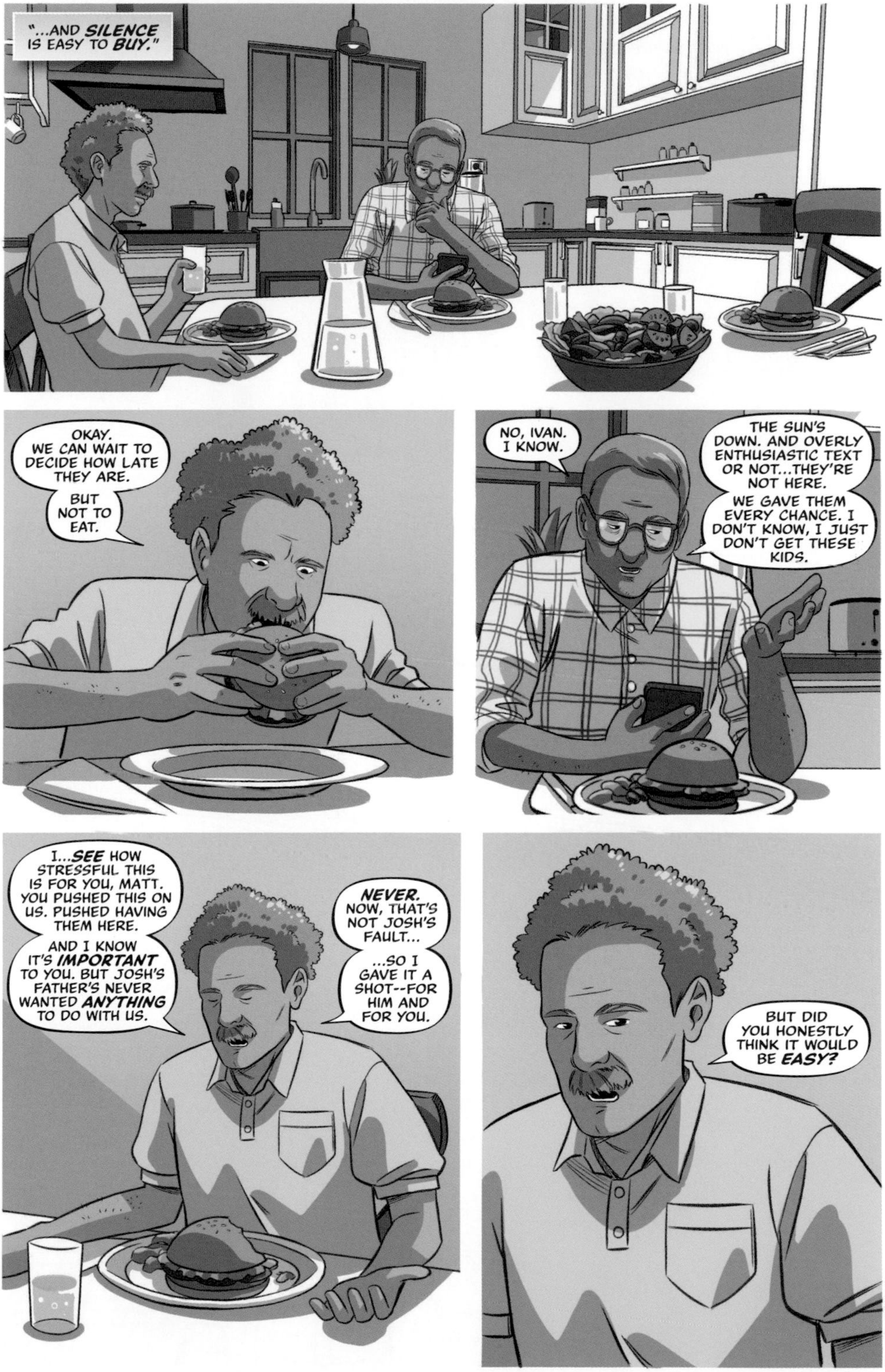
"...AND SILENCE IS EASY TO BUY."
OKAY. WE CAN WAIT TO DECIDE HOW LATE THEY ARE.
BUT NOT TO EAT.
NO, IVAN. I KNOW.
THE SUN'S DOWN. AND OVERLY ENTHUSIASTIC TEXT OR NOT...THEY'RE NOT HERE.
WE GAVE THEM EVERY CHANCE. I DON'T KNOW, I JUST DON'T GET THESE KIDS.
I...SEE HOW STRESSFUL THIS IS FOR YOU, MATT. YOU PUSHED THIS ON US. PUSHED HAVING THEM HERE.
AND I KNOW IT'S IMPORTANT TO YOU. BUT JOSH'S FATHER'S NEVER WANTED ANYTHING TO DO WITH US.
NEVER. NOW, THAT'S NOT JOSH'S FAULT...
...SO I GAVE IT A SHOT--FOR HIM AND FOR YOU.
BUT DID YOU HONESTLY THINK IT WOULD BE EASY?

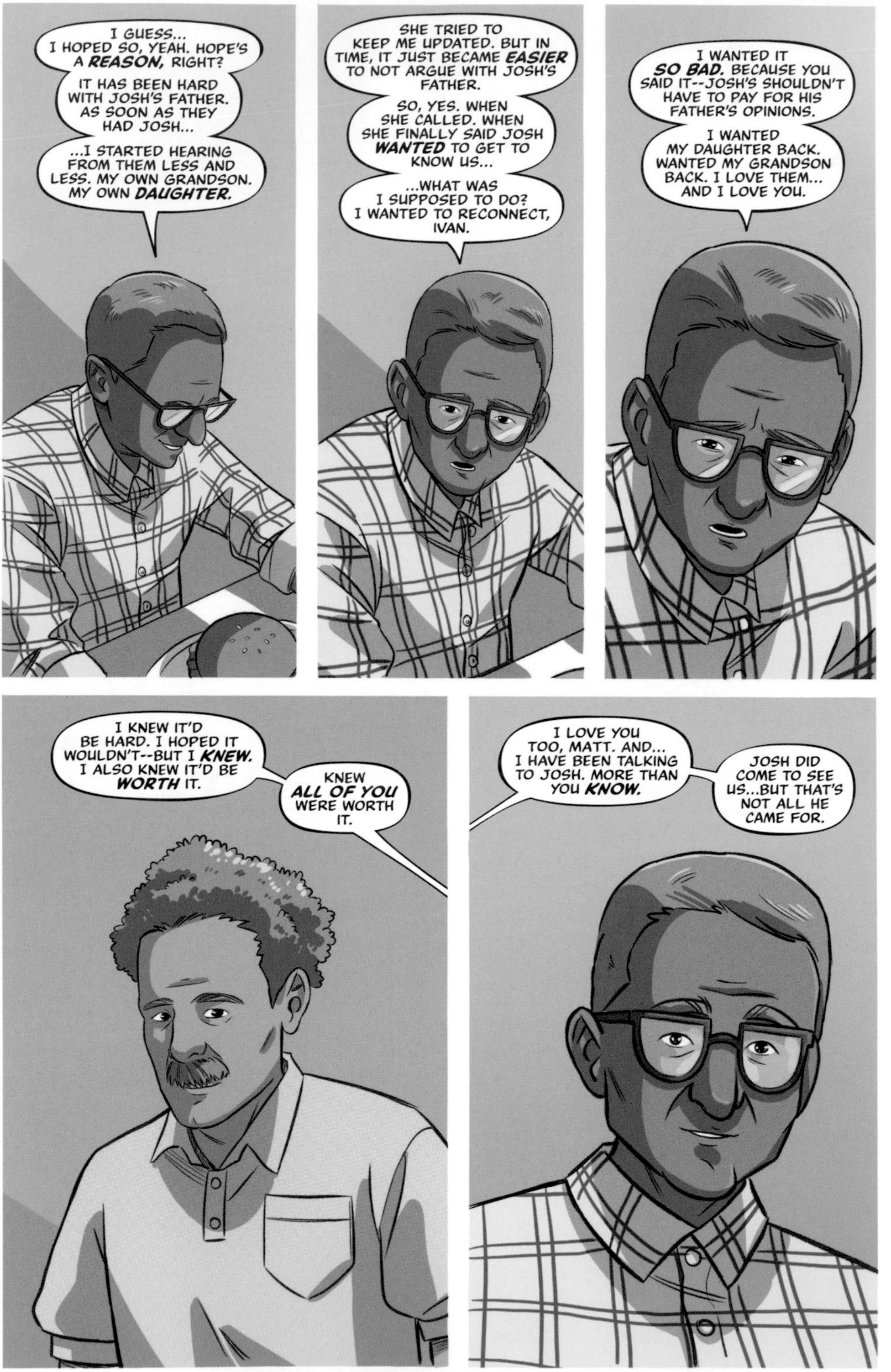
I GUESS... I HOPED SO, YEAH. HOPE'S A ***REASON,*** RIGHT?
IT HAS BEEN HARD WITH JOSH'S FATHER. AS SOON AS THEY HAD JOSH...
...I STARTED HEARING FROM THEM LESS AND LESS. MY OWN GRANDSON. MY OWN ***DAUGHTER.***
SHE TRIED TO KEEP ME UPDATED. BUT IN TIME, IT JUST BECAME ***EASIER*** TO NOT ARGUE WITH JOSH'S FATHER.
SO, YES. WHEN SHE CALLED. WHEN SHE FINALLY SAID JOSH ***WANTED*** TO GET TO KNOW US...
...WHAT WAS I SUPPOSED TO DO? I WANTED TO RECONNECT, IVAN.
I WANTED IT ***SO BAD.*** BECAUSE YOU SAID IT--JOSH'S SHOULDN'T HAVE TO PAY FOR HIS FATHER'S OPINIONS.
I WANTED MY DAUGHTER BACK. WANTED MY GRANDSON BACK. I LOVE THEM... AND I LOVE YOU.
I KNEW IT'D BE HARD. I HOPED IT WOULDN'T--BUT I ***KNEW.*** I ALSO KNEW IT'D BE ***WORTH*** IT.
KNEW ***ALL OF YOU*** WERE WORTH IT.
I LOVE YOU TOO, MATT. AND... I HAVE BEEN TALKING TO JOSH. MORE THAN YOU ***KNOW.***
JOSH DID COME TO SEE US...BUT THAT'S NOT ALL HE CAME FOR.

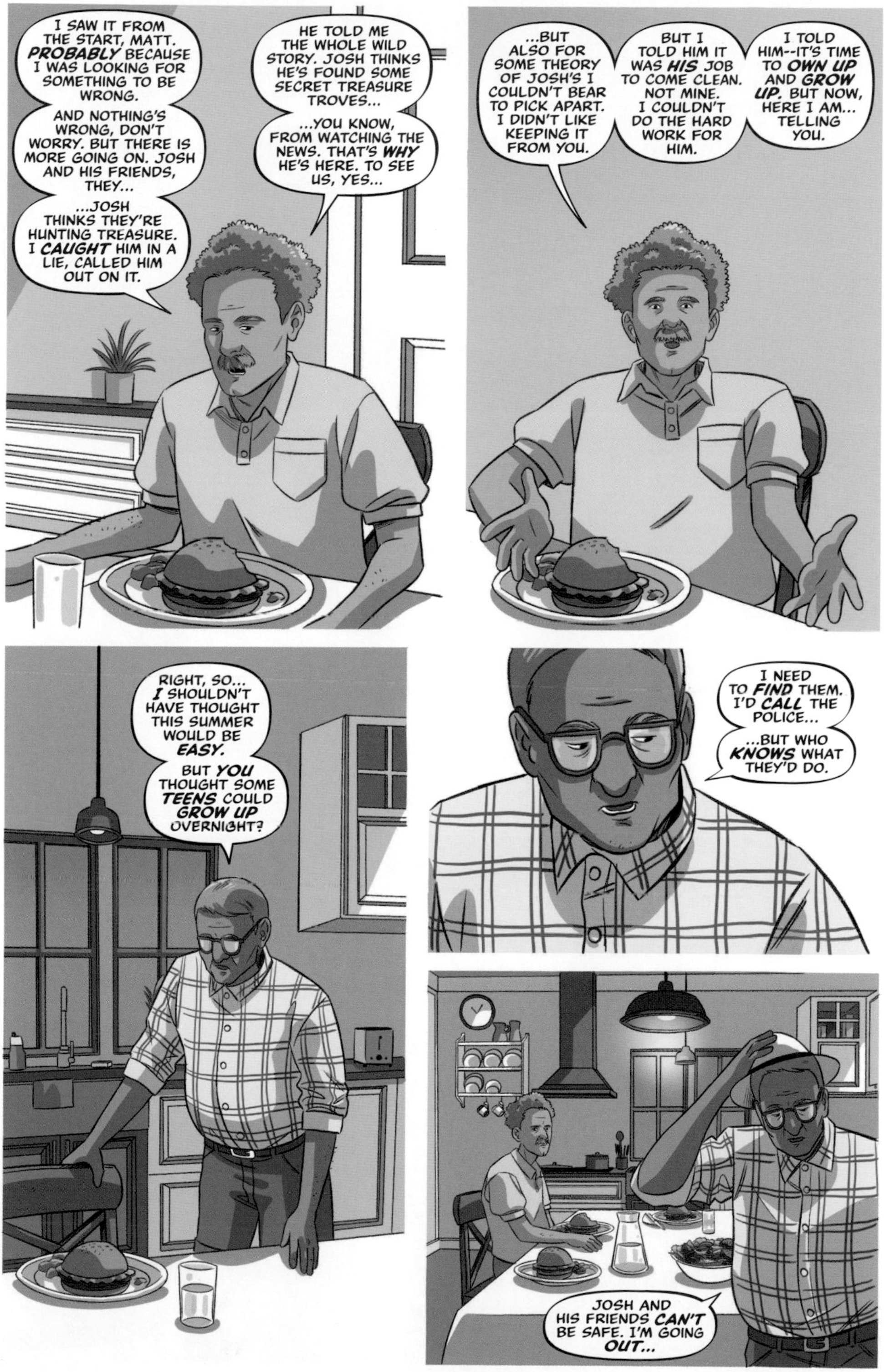
I SAW IT FROM THE START, MATT. PROBABLY BECAUSE I WAS LOOKING FOR SOMETHING TO BE WRONG.
AND NOTHING'S WRONG, DON'T WORRY. BUT THERE IS MORE GOING ON. JOSH AND HIS FRIENDS, THEY...
...JOSH THINKS THEY'RE HUNTING TREASURE. I CAUGHT HIM IN A LIE, CALLED HIM OUT ON IT.
HE TOLD ME THE WHOLE WILD STORY. JOSH THINKS HE'S FOUND SOME SECRET TREASURE TROVES...
...YOU KNOW, FROM WATCHING THE NEWS. THAT'S WHY HE'S HERE. TO SEE US, YES...
...BUT ALSO FOR SOME THEORY OF JOSH'S I COULDN'T BEAR TO PICK APART. I DIDN'T LIKE KEEPING IT FROM YOU.
BUT I TOLD HIM IT WAS HIS JOB TO COME CLEAN. NOT MINE. I COULDN'T DO THE HARD WORK FOR HIM.
I TOLD HIM--IT'S TIME TO OWN UP AND GROW UP. BUT NOW, HERE I AM... TELLING YOU.
RIGHT, SO... I SHOULDN'T HAVE THOUGHT THIS SUMMER WOULD BE EASY.
BUT YOU THOUGHT SOME TEENS COULD GROW UP OVERNIGHT?
I NEED TO FIND THEM. I'D CALL THE POLICE...
...BUT WHO KNOWS WHAT THEY'D DO.
JOSH AND HIS FRIENDS CAN'T BE SAFE. I'M GOING OUT...

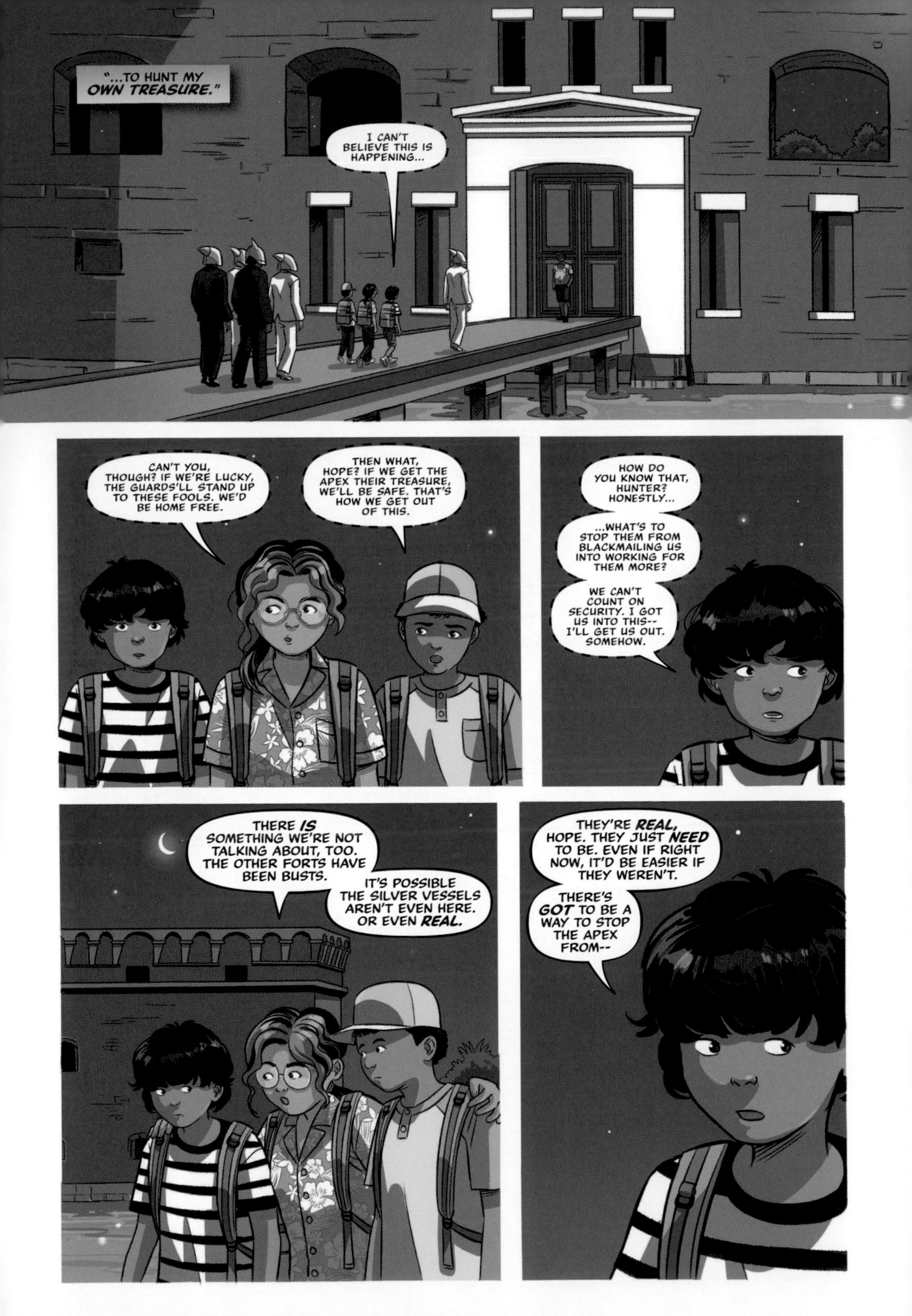
"...TO HUNT MY OWN TREASURE."
I CAN'T BELIEVE THIS IS HAPPENING...
CAN'T YOU, THOUGH? IF WE'RE LUCKY, THE GUARDS'LL STAND UP TO THESE FOOLS. WE'D BE HOME FREE.
THEN WHAT, HOPE? IF WE GET THE APEX THEIR TREASURE, WE'LL BE SAFE. THAT'S HOW WE GET OUT OF THIS.
HOW DO YOU KNOW THAT, HUNTER? HONESTLY...
...WHAT'S TO STOP THEM FROM BLACKMAILING US INTO WORKING FOR THEM MORE?
WE CAN'T COUNT ON SECURITY. I GOT US INTO THIS-- I'LL GET US OUT. SOMEHOW.
THERE IS SOMETHING WE'RE NOT TALKING ABOUT, TOO. THE OTHER FORTS HAVE BEEN BUSTS.
IT'S POSSIBLE THE SILVER VESSELS AREN'T EVEN HERE. OR EVEN REAL.
THEY'RE REAL, HOPE. THEY JUST NEED TO BE. EVEN IF RIGHT NOW, IT'D BE EASIER IF THEY WEREN'T.
THERE'S GOT TO BE A WAY TO STOP THE APEX FROM--

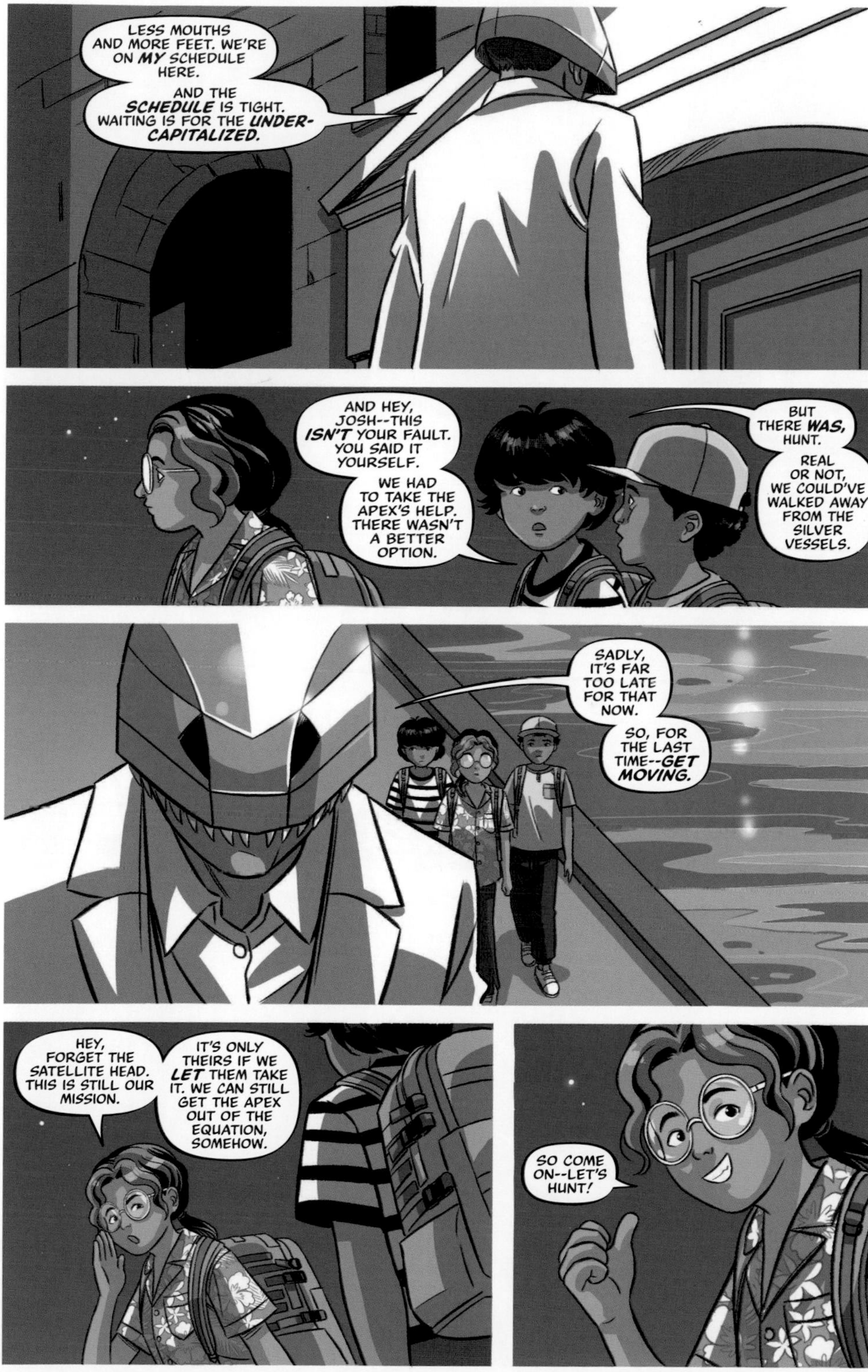

LESS MOUTHS AND MORE FEET. WE'RE ON **MY** SCHEDULE HERE.
AND THE **SCHEDULE** IS TIGHT. WAITING IS FOR THE **UNDER-CAPITALIZED.**
AND HEY, JOSH--THIS **ISN'T** YOUR FAULT. YOU SAID IT YOURSELF.
WE HAD TO TAKE THE APEX'S HELP. THERE WASN'T A BETTER OPTION.
BUT THERE **WAS,** HUNT.
REAL OR NOT, WE COULD'VE WALKED AWAY FROM THE SILVER VESSELS.
SADLY, IT'S FAR TOO LATE FOR THAT NOW.
SO, FOR THE LAST TIME--**GET MOVING.**
HEY, FORGET THE SATELLITE HEAD. THIS IS STILL OUR MISSION.
IT'S ONLY THEIRS IF WE **LET** THEM TAKE IT. WE CAN STILL GET THE APEX OUT OF THE EQUATION, SOMEHOW.
SO COME ON--LET'S HUNT!

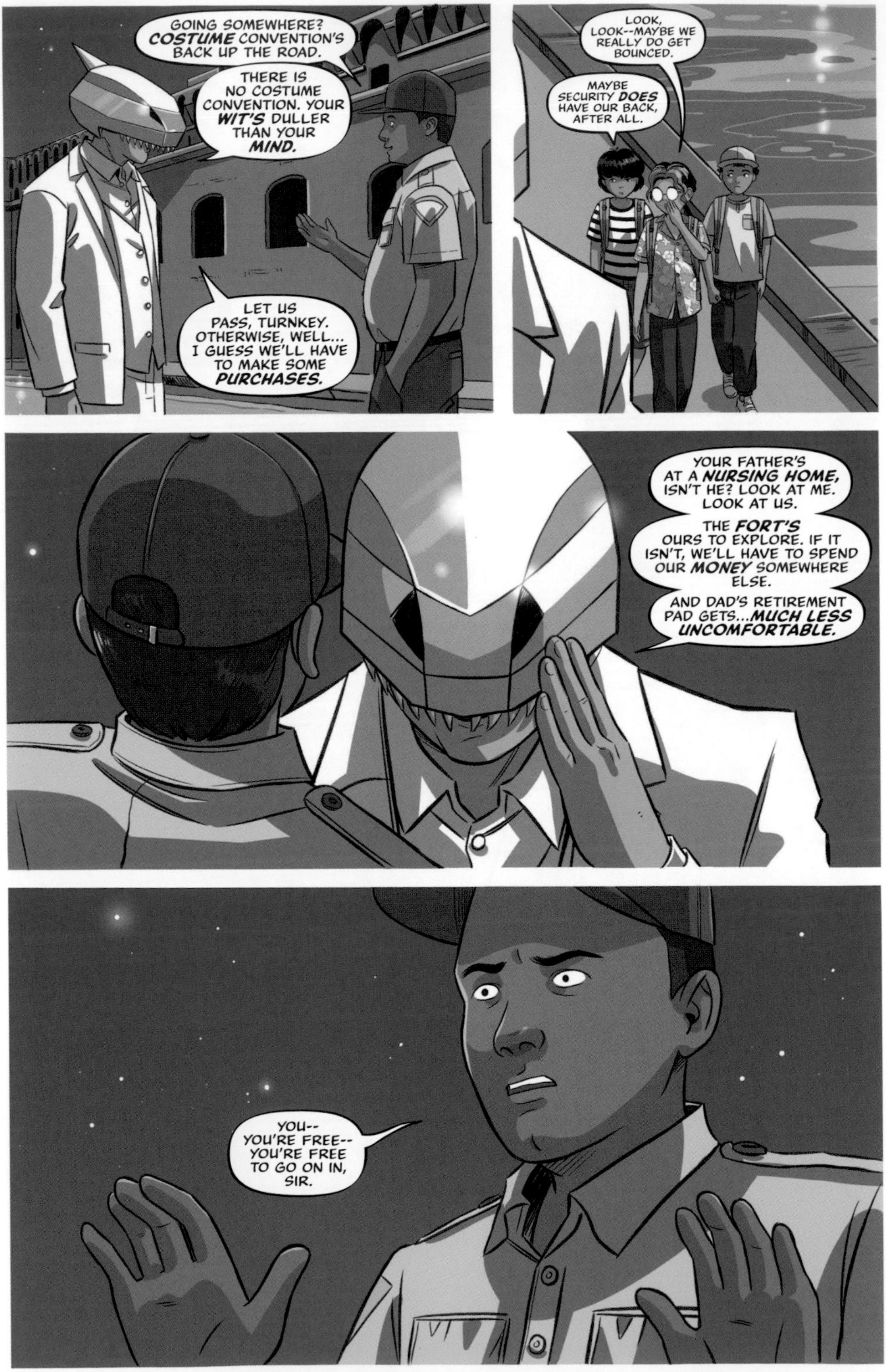
GOING SOMEWHERE? COSTUME CONVENTION'S BACK UP THE ROAD.
THERE IS NO COSTUME CONVENTION. YOUR WIT'S DULLER THAN YOUR MIND.
LET US PASS, TURNKEY. OTHERWISE, WELL... I GUESS WE'LL HAVE TO MAKE SOME PURCHASES.
LOOK, LOOK--MAYBE WE REALLY DO GET BOUNCED.
MAYBE SECURITY DOES HAVE OUR BACK, AFTER ALL.
YOUR FATHER'S AT A NURSING HOME, ISN'T HE? LOOK AT ME. LOOK AT US.
THE FORT'S OURS TO EXPLORE. IF IT ISN'T, WE'LL HAVE TO SPEND OUR MONEY SOMEWHERE ELSE.
AND DAD'S RETIREMENT PAD GETS...MUCH LESS UNCOMFORTABLE.
YOU-- YOU'RE FREE-- YOU'RE FREE TO GO ON IN, SIR.

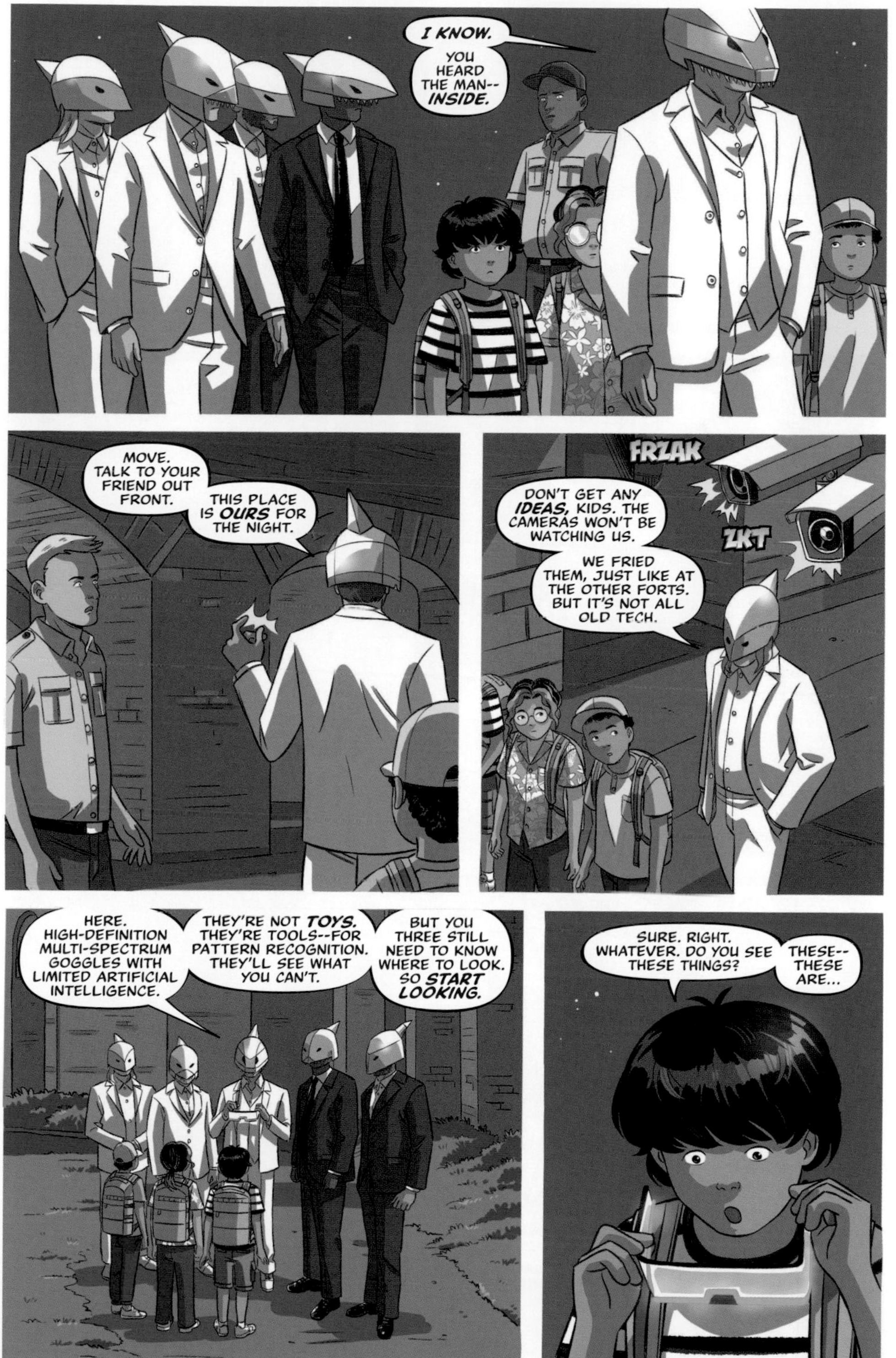
I KNOW.
YOU HEARD THE MAN-- INSIDE.
MOVE. TALK TO YOUR FRIEND OUT FRONT.
THIS PLACE IS OURS FOR THE NIGHT.
FRZAK
ZKT
DON'T GET ANY IDEAS, KIDS. THE CAMERAS WON'T BE WATCHING US.
WE FRIED THEM, JUST LIKE AT THE OTHER FORTS. BUT IT'S NOT ALL OLD TECH.
HERE. HIGH-DEFINITION MULTI-SPECTRUM GOGGLES WITH LIMITED ARTIFICIAL INTELLIGENCE.
THEY'RE NOT TOYS. THEY'RE TOOLS--FOR PATTERN RECOGNITION. THEY'LL SEE WHAT YOU CAN'T.
BUT YOU THREE STILL NEED TO KNOW WHERE TO LOOK. SO START LOOKING.
SURE. RIGHT. WHATEVER. DO YOU SEE THESE THINGS?
THESE-- THESE ARE...

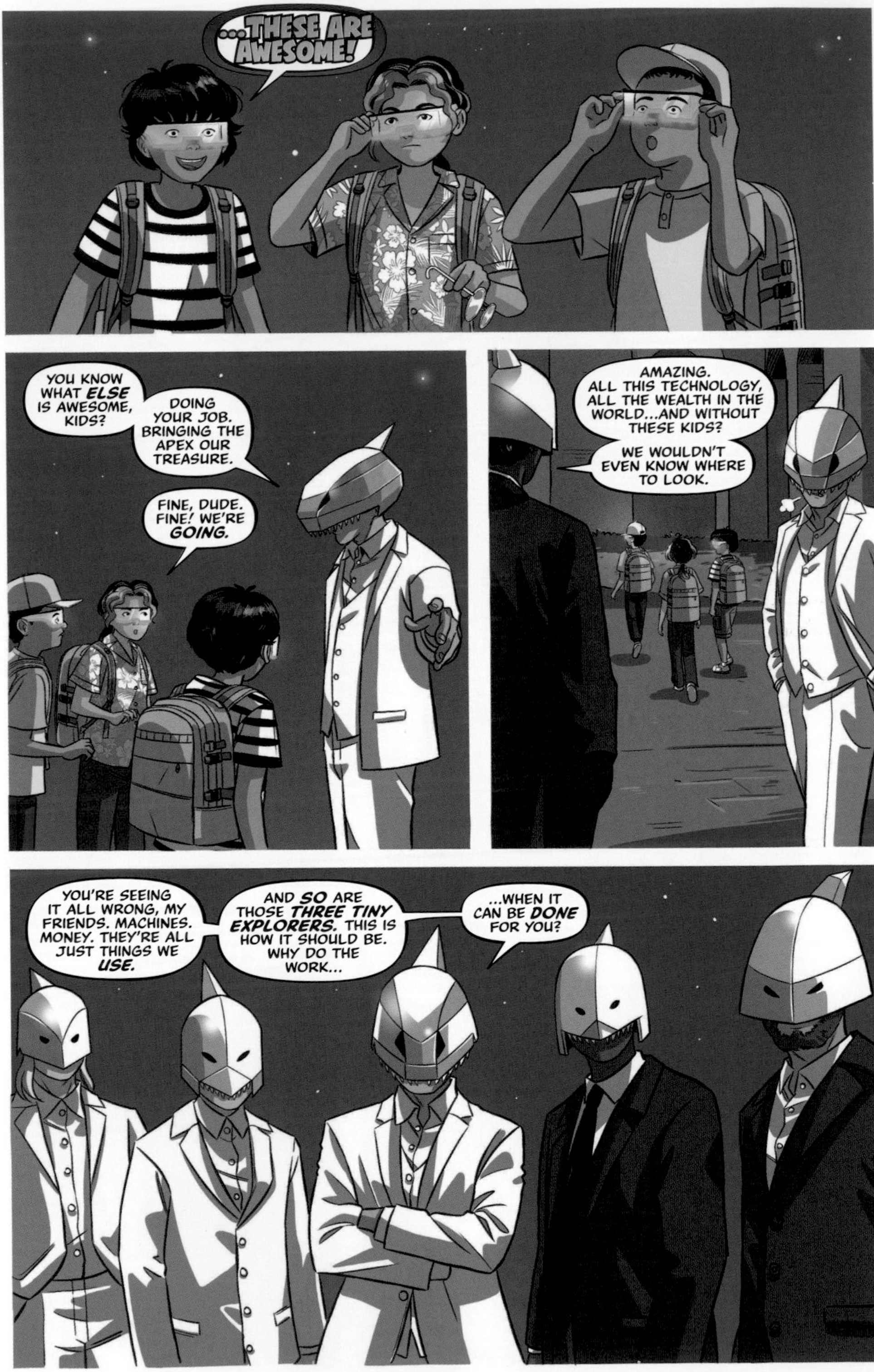
...THESE ARE AWESOME!
YOU KNOW WHAT ELSE IS AWESOME, KIDS?
DOING YOUR JOB. BRINGING THE APEX OUR TREASURE.
FINE, DUDE. FINE! WE'RE GOING.
AMAZING. ALL THIS TECHNOLOGY, ALL THE WEALTH IN THE WORLD...AND WITHOUT THESE KIDS?
WE WOULDN'T EVEN KNOW WHERE TO LOOK.
YOU'RE SEEING IT ALL WRONG, MY FRIENDS. MACHINES. MONEY. THEY'RE ALL JUST THINGS WE USE.
AND SO ARE THOSE THREE TINY EXPLORERS. THIS IS HOW IT SHOULD BE. WHY DO THE WORK...
...WHEN IT CAN BE DONE FOR YOU?

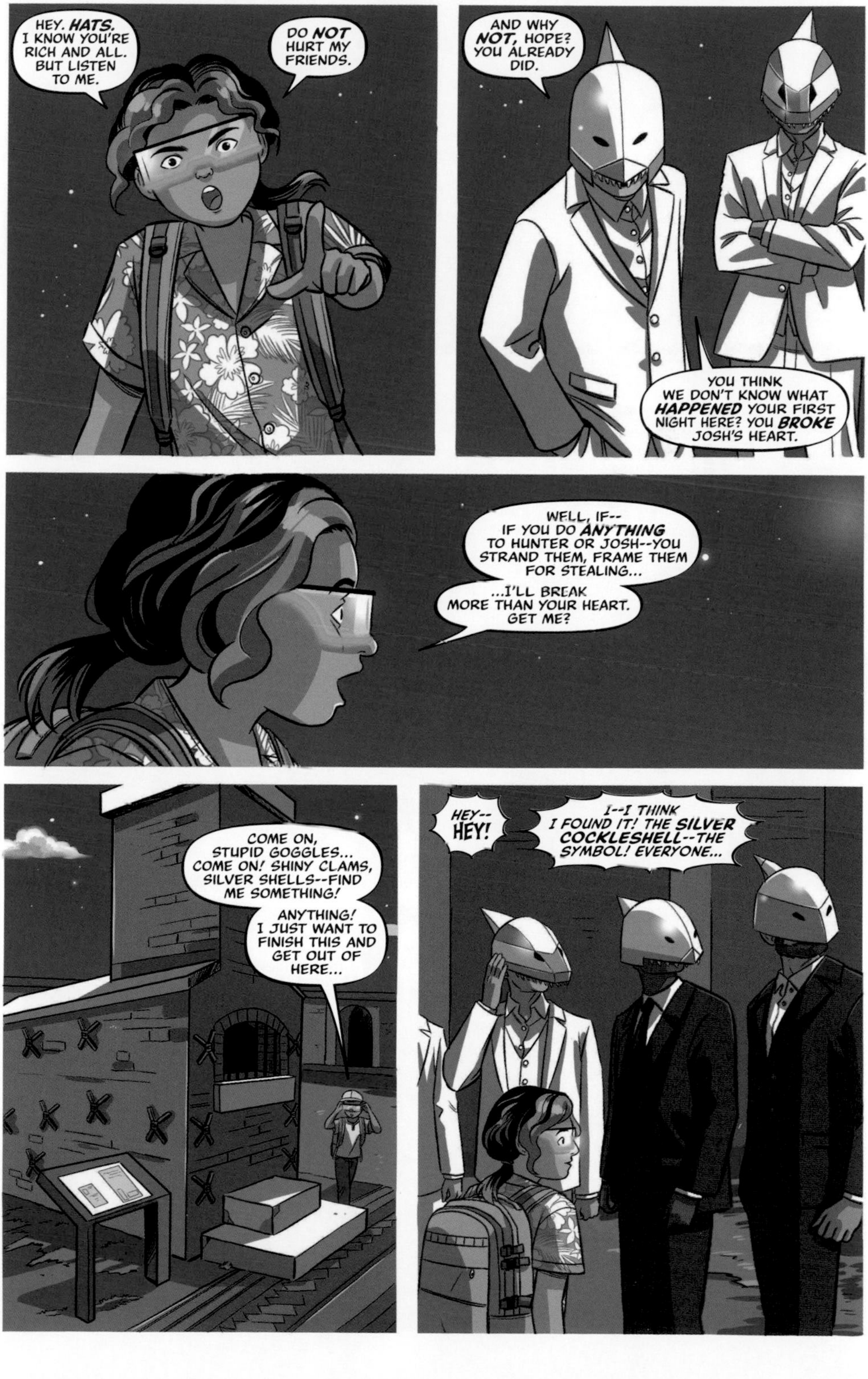
HEY. **HATS.** I KNOW YOU'RE RICH AND ALL. BUT LISTEN TO ME.
DO **NOT** HURT MY FRIENDS.
AND WHY **NOT,** HOPE? YOU ALREADY DID.
YOU THINK WE DON'T KNOW WHAT **HAPPENED** YOUR FIRST NIGHT HERE? YOU **BROKE** JOSH'S HEART.
WELL, IF-- IF YOU DO **ANYTHING** TO HUNTER OR JOSH--YOU STRAND THEM, FRAME THEM FOR STEALING...
...I'LL BREAK MORE THAN YOUR HEART. GET ME?
COME ON, STUPID GOGGLES... COME ON! SHINY CLAMS, SILVER SHELLS--FIND ME SOMETHING!
ANYTHING! I JUST WANT TO FINISH THIS AND GET OUT OF HERE...
HEY-- HEY!
I--I THINK I FOUND IT! THE **SILVER COCKLESHELL**--THE SYMBOL! EVERYONE...

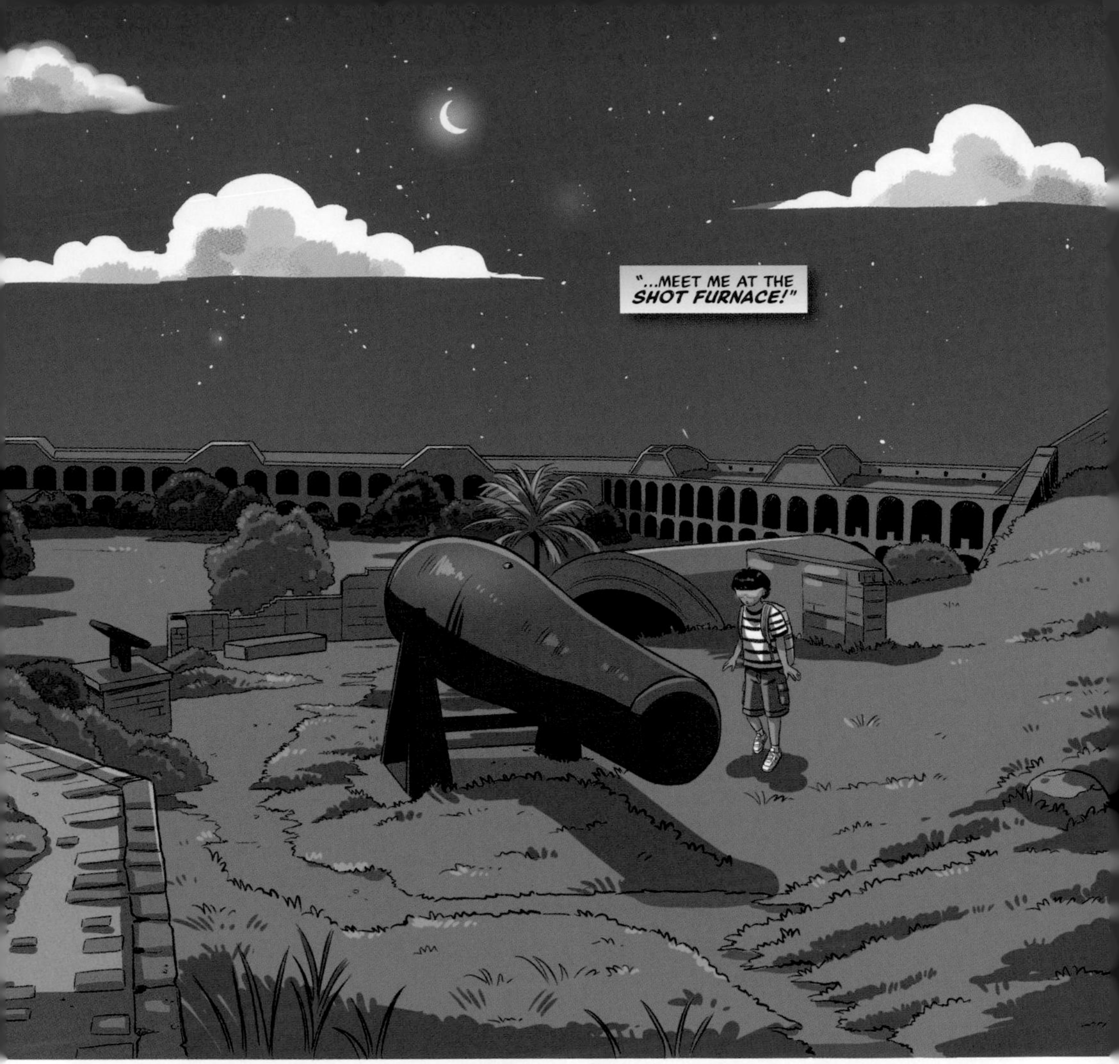
"...MEET ME AT THE **SHOT FURNACE!**"

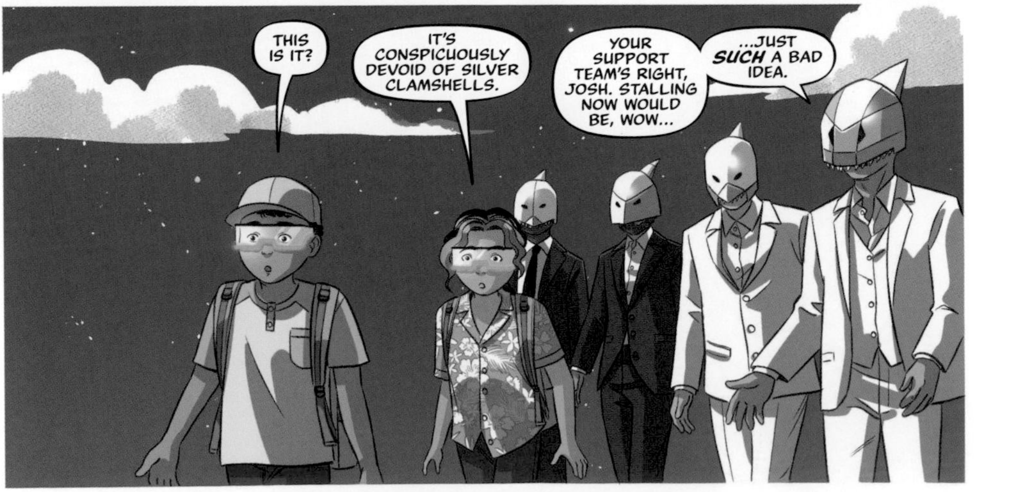
THIS IS IT?
IT'S CONSPICUOUSLY DEVOID OF SILVER CLAMSHELLS.
YOUR SUPPORT TEAM'S RIGHT, JOSH. STALLING NOW WOULD BE, WOW...
...JUST **SUCH** A BAD IDEA.

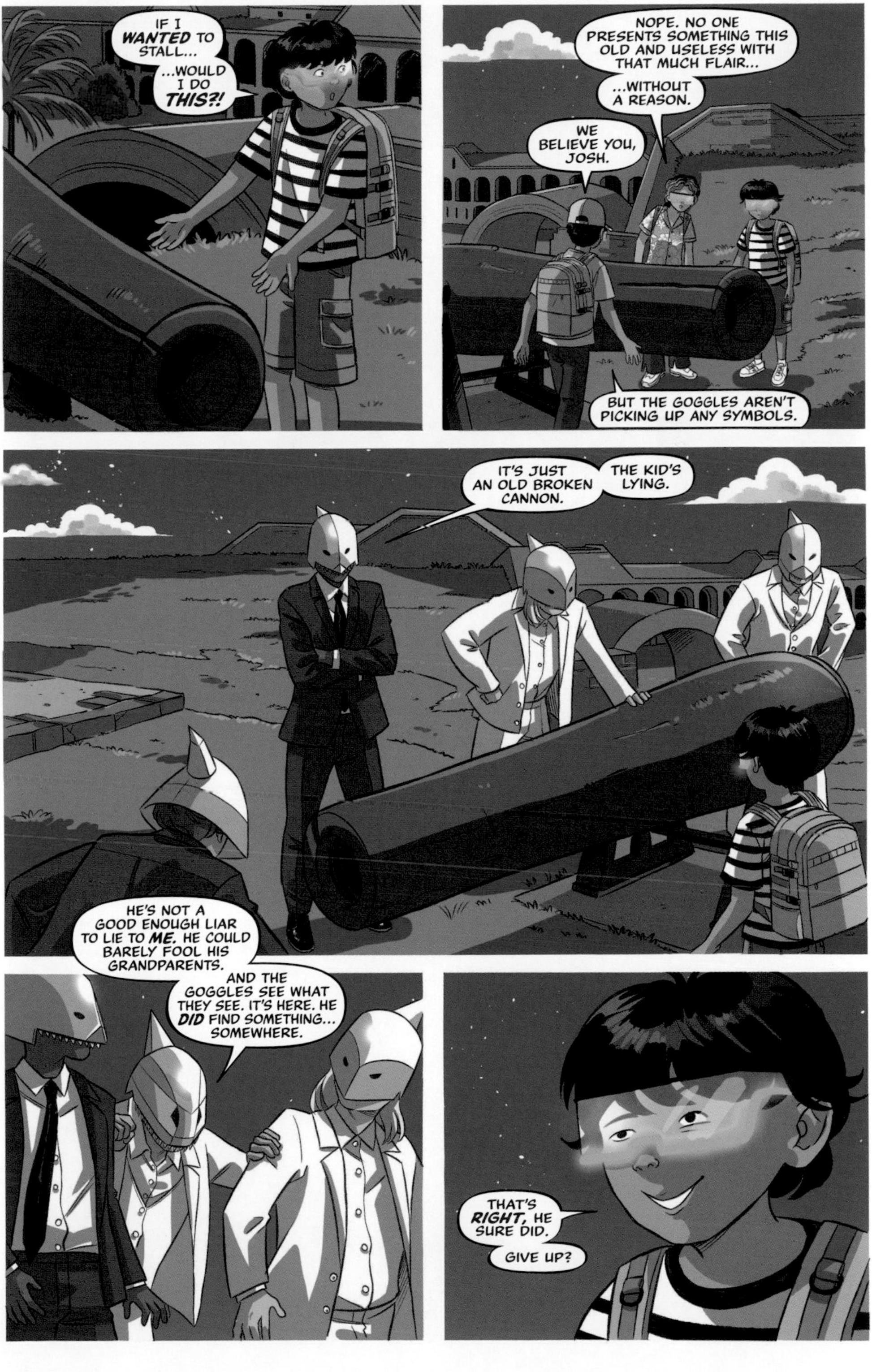
IF I WANTED TO STALL...
...WOULD I DO THIS?!
NOPE. NO ONE PRESENTS SOMETHING THIS OLD AND USELESS WITH THAT MUCH FLAIR...
...WITHOUT A REASON.
WE BELIEVE YOU, JOSH.
BUT THE GOGGLES AREN'T PICKING UP ANY SYMBOLS.
IT'S JUST AN OLD BROKEN CANNON.
THE KID'S LYING.
HE'S NOT A GOOD ENOUGH LIAR TO LIE TO ME. HE COULD BARELY FOOL HIS GRANDPARENTS.
AND THE GOGGLES SEE WHAT THEY SEE. IT'S HERE. HE DID FIND SOMETHING... SOMEWHERE.
THAT'S RIGHT, HE SURE DID.
GIVE UP?

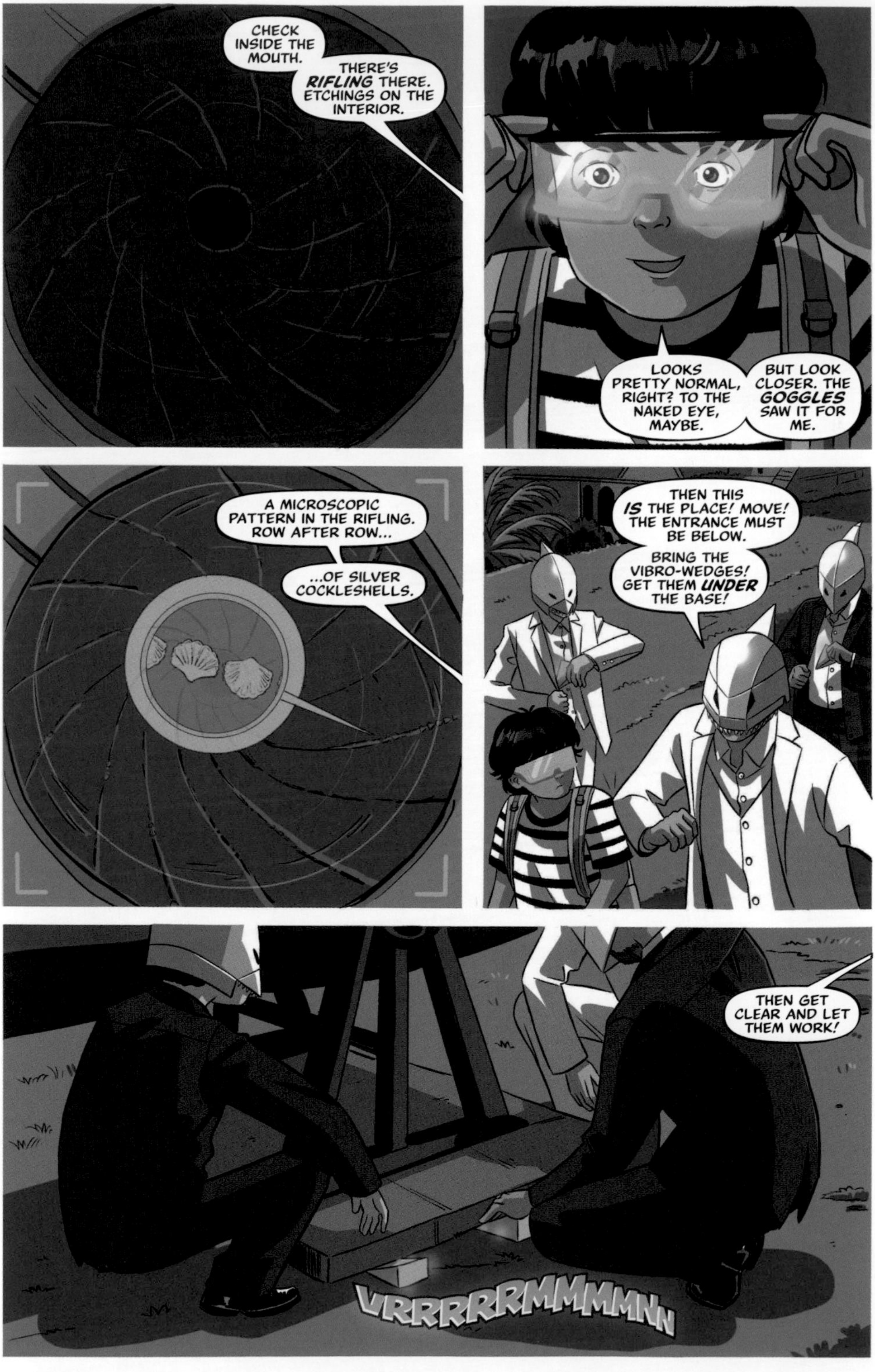

CHECK INSIDE THE MOUTH.
THERE'S **RIFLING** THERE. ETCHINGS ON THE INTERIOR.
LOOKS PRETTY NORMAL, RIGHT? TO THE NAKED EYE, MAYBE.
BUT LOOK CLOSER. THE **GOGGLES** SAW IT FOR ME.
A MICROSCOPIC PATTERN IN THE RIFLING. ROW AFTER ROW...
...OF SILVER COCKLESHELLS.
THEN THIS **IS** THE PLACE! MOVE! THE ENTRANCE MUST BE BELOW.
BRING THE VIBRO-WEDGES! GET THEM **UNDER** THE BASE!
THEN GET CLEAR AND LET THEM WORK!
VRRRRRMMMMNN

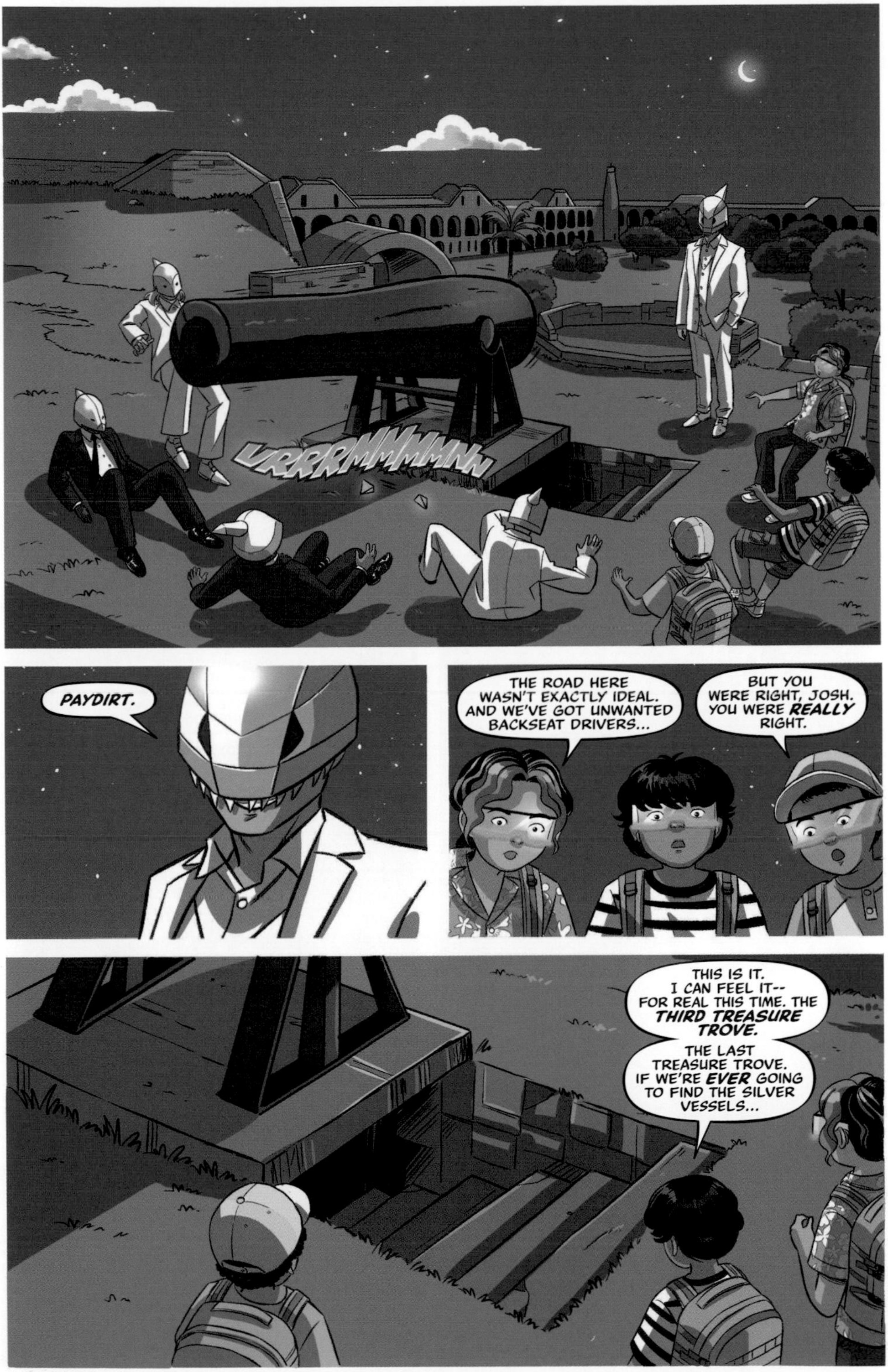
URRRMMMMMNN
PAYDIRT.
THE ROAD HERE WASN'T EXACTLY IDEAL. AND WE'VE GOT UNWANTED BACKSEAT DRIVERS...
BUT YOU WERE RIGHT, JOSH. YOU WERE *REALLY* RIGHT.
THIS IS IT. I CAN FEEL IT-- FOR REAL THIS TIME. THE ***THIRD TREASURE TROVE.***
THE LAST TREASURE TROVE. IF WE'RE ***EVER*** GOING TO FIND THE SILVER VESSELS...

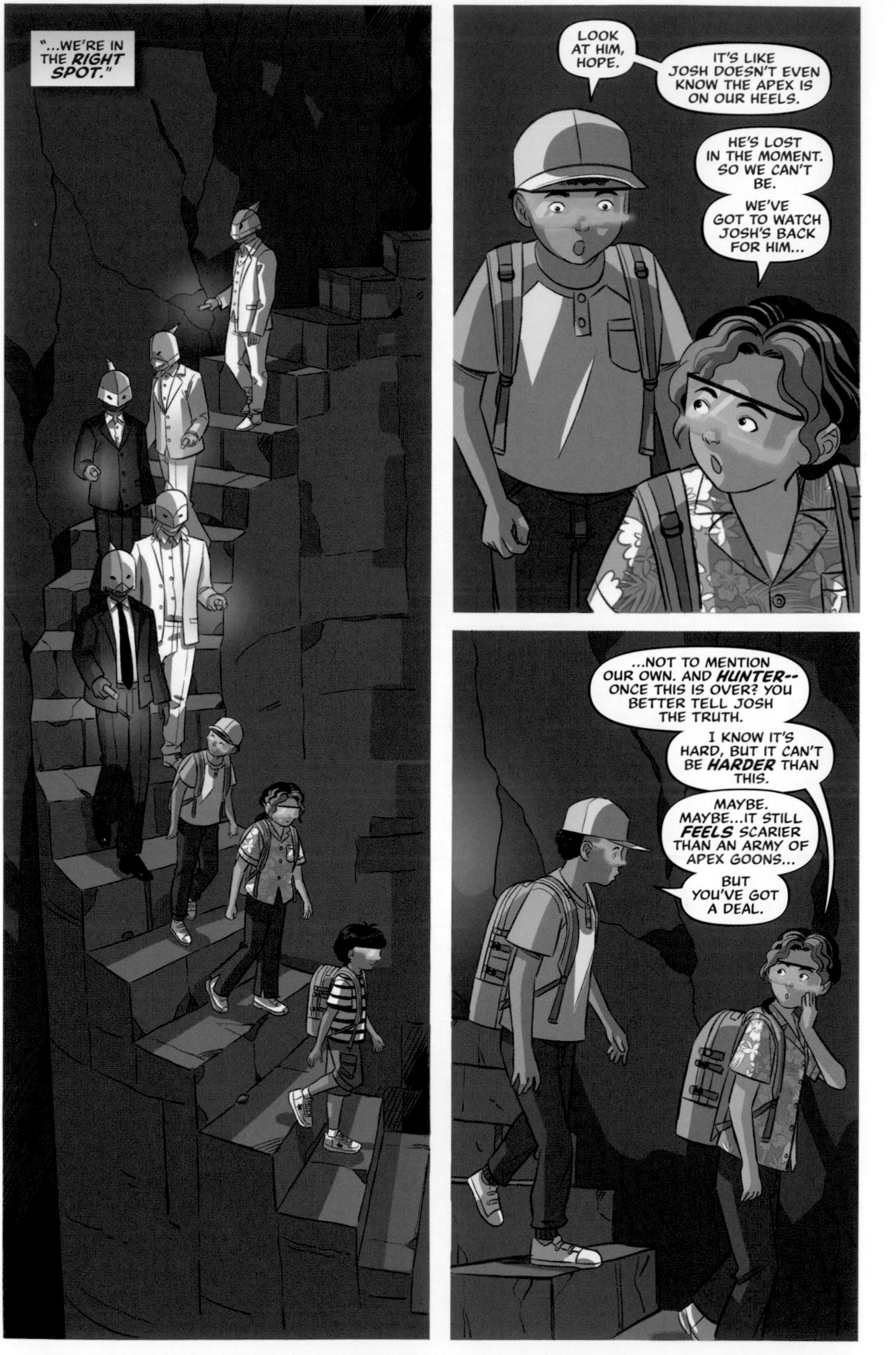
"...WE'RE IN THE *RIGHT SPOT.*"
LOOK AT HIM, HOPE.
IT'S LIKE JOSH DOESN'T EVEN KNOW THE APEX IS ON OUR HEELS.
HE'S LOST IN THE MOMENT. SO WE CAN'T BE.
WE'VE GOT TO WATCH JOSH'S BACK FOR HIM...
...NOT TO MENTION OUR OWN. AND *HUNTER*-- ONCE THIS IS OVER? YOU BETTER TELL JOSH THE TRUTH.
I KNOW IT'S HARD, BUT IT CAN'T BE *HARDER* THAN THIS.
MAYBE. MAYBE...IT STILL *FEELS* SCARIER THAN AN ARMY OF APEX GOONS...
BUT YOU'VE GOT A DEAL.

WE HATE TO ASK, MEG...

...BUT WHAT *ARE* WE GOING TO DO WITH THESE KIDS ONCE THEY RECOVER THE VESSELS?

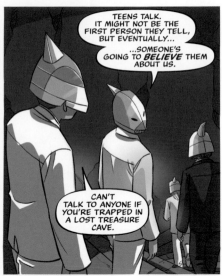

TEENS TALK. IT MIGHT NOT BE THE FIRST PERSON THEY TELL, BUT EVENTUALLY...

...SOMEONE'S GOING TO *BELIEVE* THEM ABOUT US.

CAN'T TALK TO ANYONE IF YOU'RE TRAPPED IN A LOST TREASURE CAVE.

THE SITUATION SOLVES ITSELF.

THMP

TUNNEL'S FLATTENING OUT. AND THE GROUND'S LEVELING, TOO.

WE'RE GETTING SOMEWHERE, AT LEAST.

MORE THAN THAT, HOPE.

DON'T YOU FEEL THE WARMTH? DON'T YOU SEE THE LIGHT?

KLK

KLK

KLK

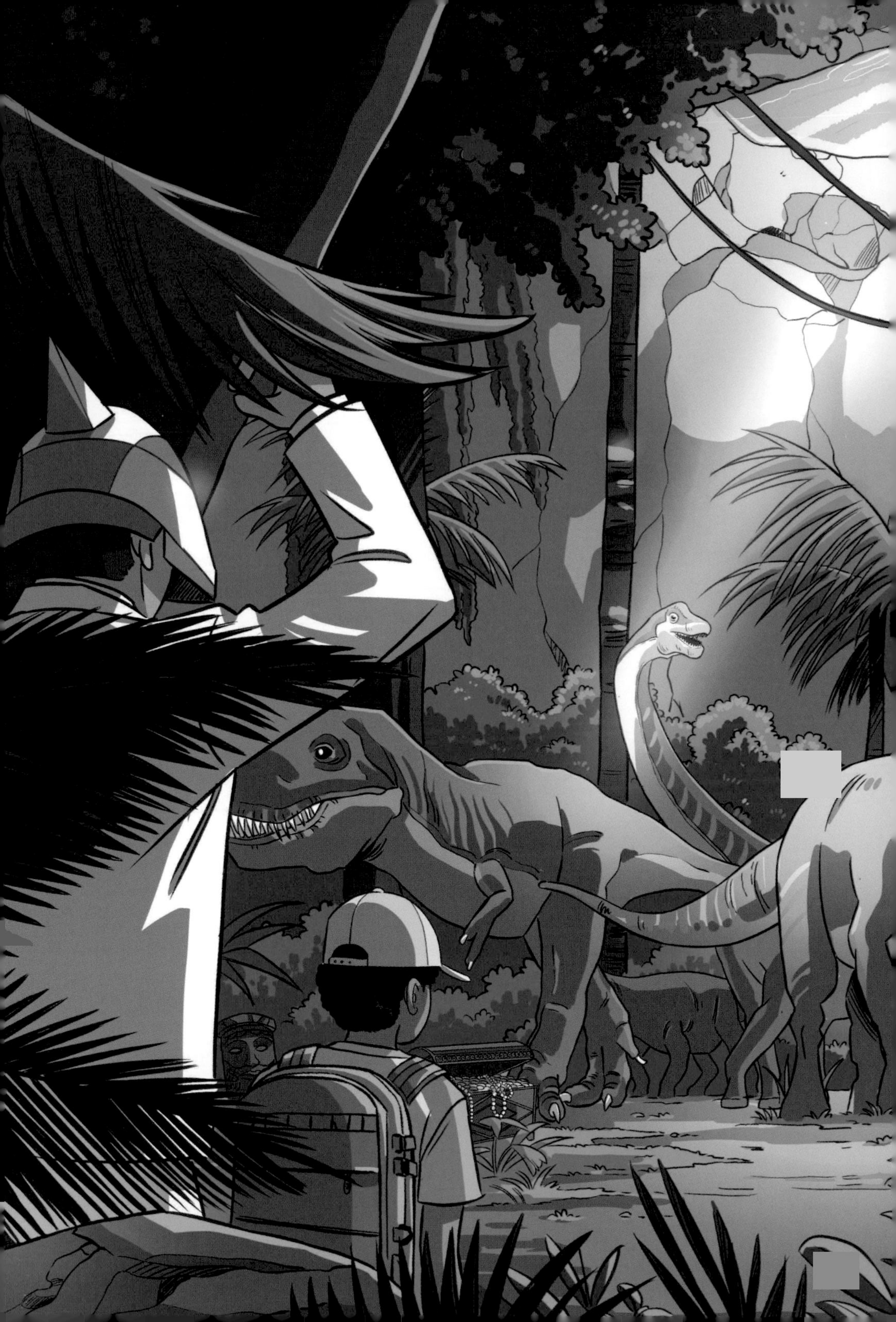

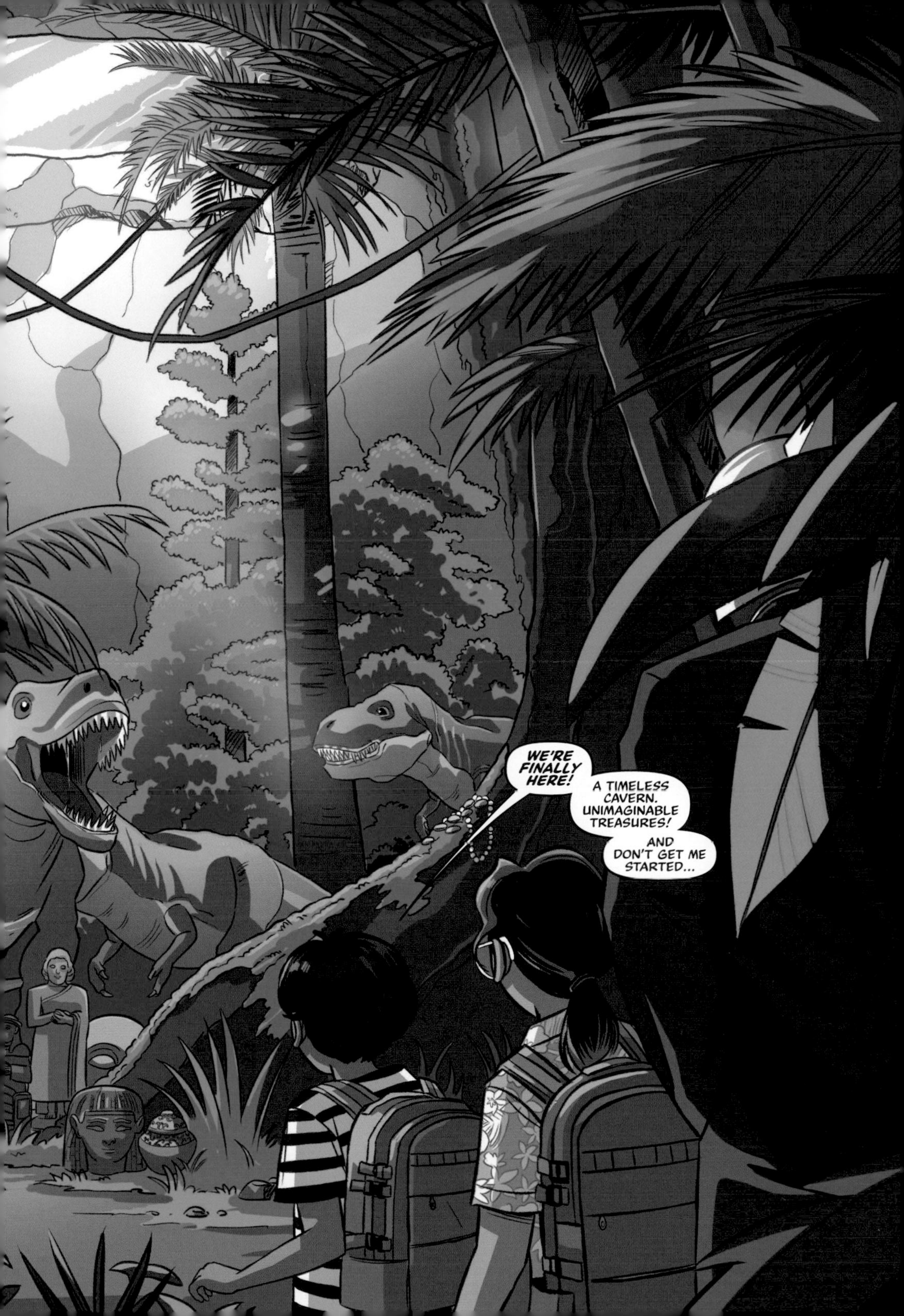
WE'RE FINALLY HERE!
A TIMELESS CAVERN. UNIMAGINABLE TREASURES!
AND DON'T GET ME STARTED...

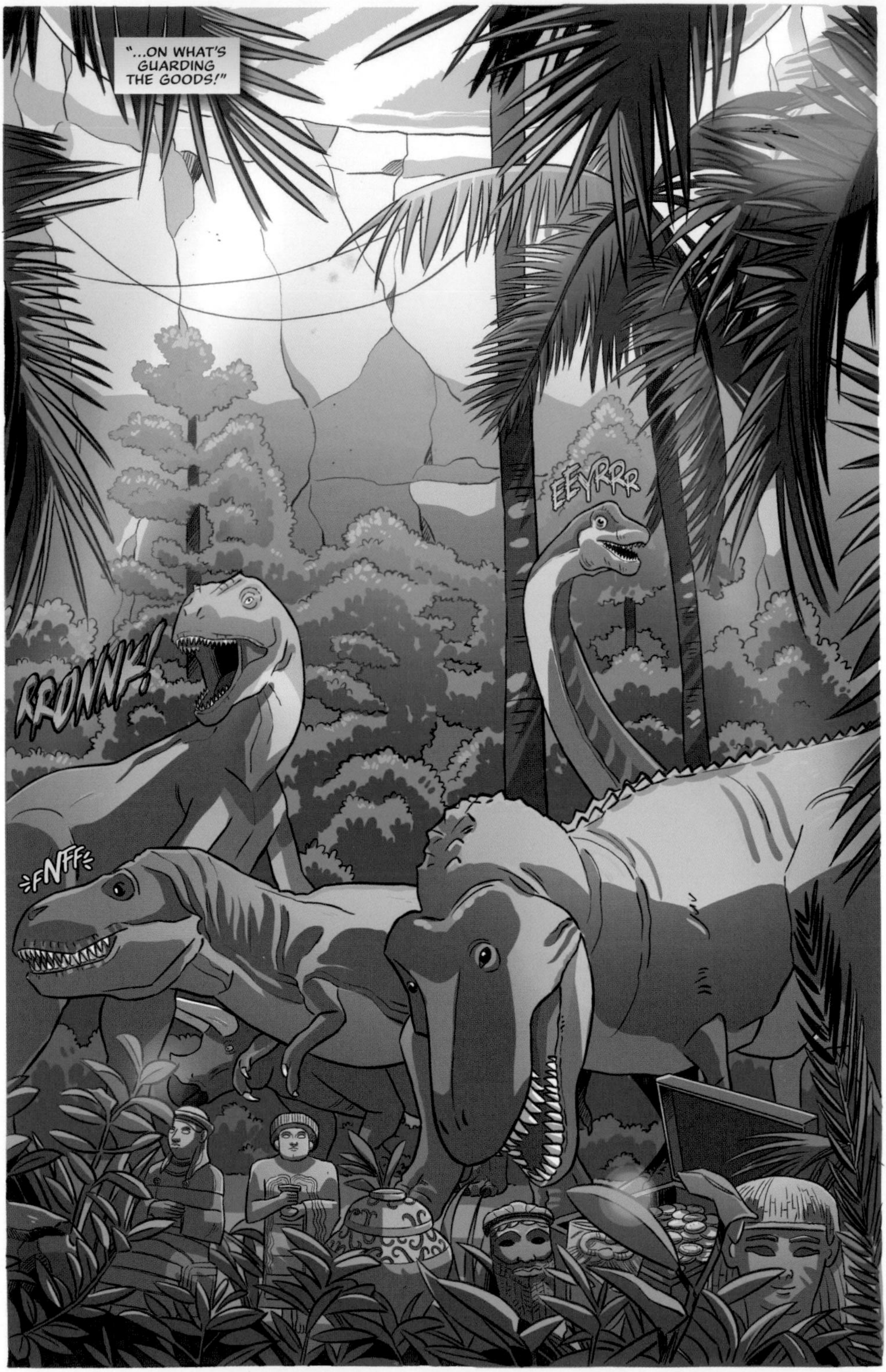
"...ON WHAT'S GUARDING THE GOODS!"
EEYRRR
RRONNK!
FNFF

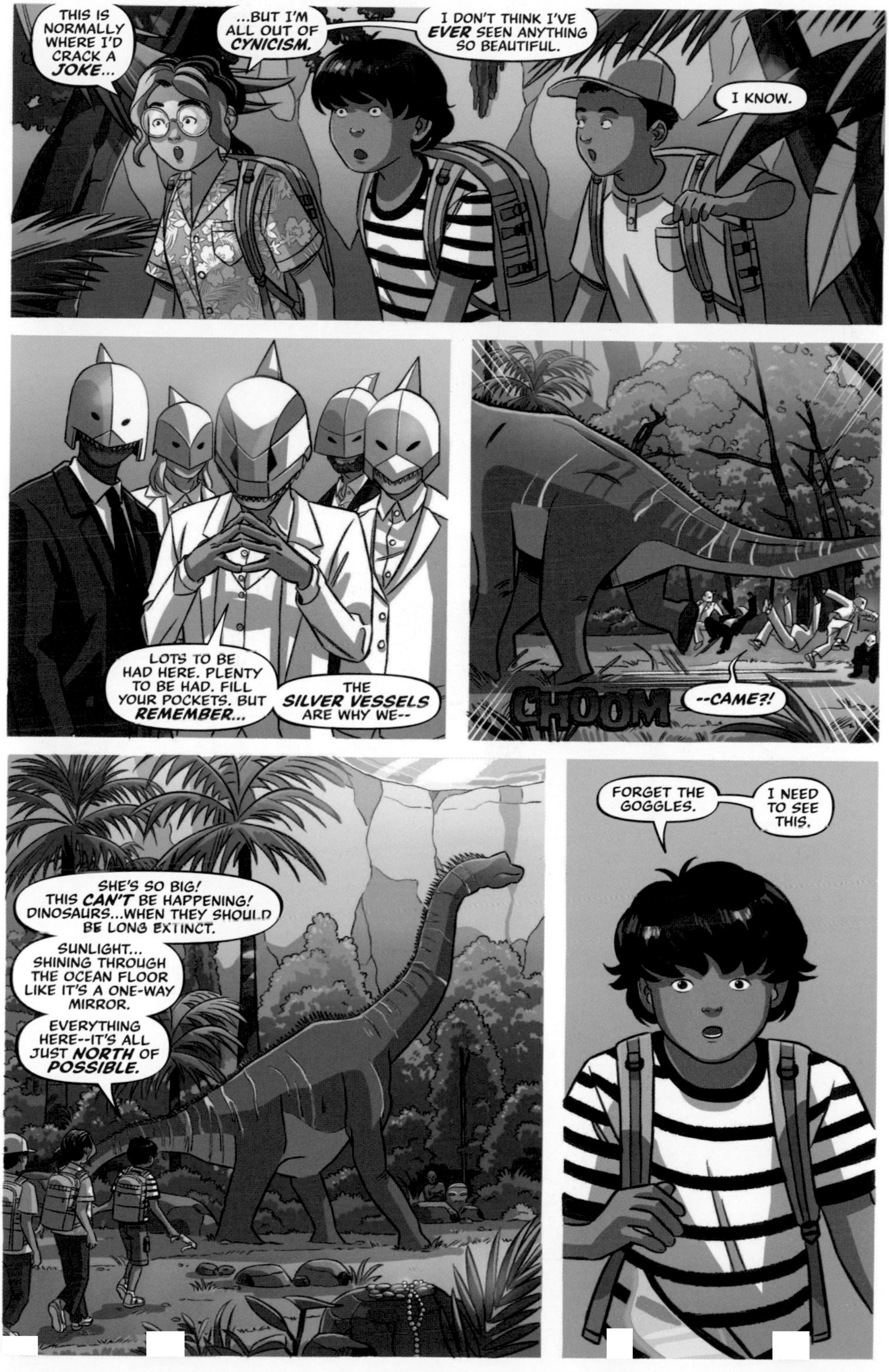
THIS IS NORMALLY WHERE I'D CRACK A JOKE...
...BUT I'M ALL OUT OF CYNICISM.
I DON'T THINK I'VE EVER SEEN ANYTHING SO BEAUTIFUL.
I KNOW.
LOTS TO BE HAD HERE. PLENTY TO BE HAD. FILL YOUR POCKETS. BUT REMEMBER...
THE SILVER VESSELS ARE WHY WE--
CHOOM
--CAME?!
SHE'S SO BIG! THIS CAN'T BE HAPPENING! DINOSAURS...WHEN THEY SHOULD BE LONG EXTINCT.
SUNLIGHT... SHINING THROUGH THE OCEAN FLOOR LIKE IT'S A ONE-WAY MIRROR.
EVERYTHING HERE--IT'S ALL JUST NORTH OF POSSIBLE.
FORGET THE GOGGLES.
I NEED TO SEE THIS.

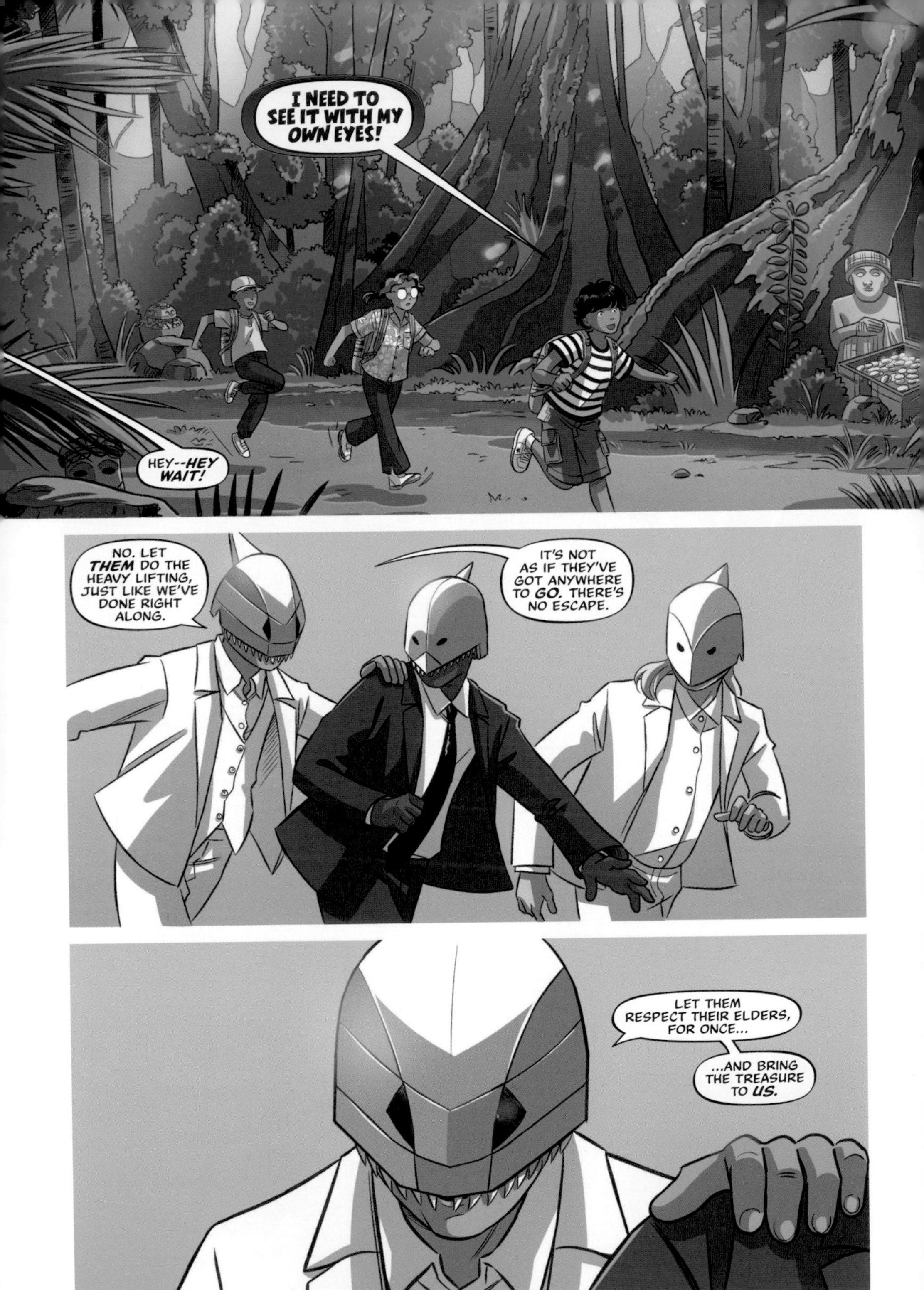
I NEED TO SEE IT WITH MY OWN EYES!
HEY--HEY WAIT!
NO. LET THEM DO THE HEAVY LIFTING, JUST LIKE WE'VE DONE RIGHT ALONG.
IT'S NOT AS IF THEY'VE GOT ANYWHERE TO GO. THERE'S NO ESCAPE.
LET THEM RESPECT THEIR ELDERS, FOR ONCE...
...AND BRING THE TREASURE TO US.

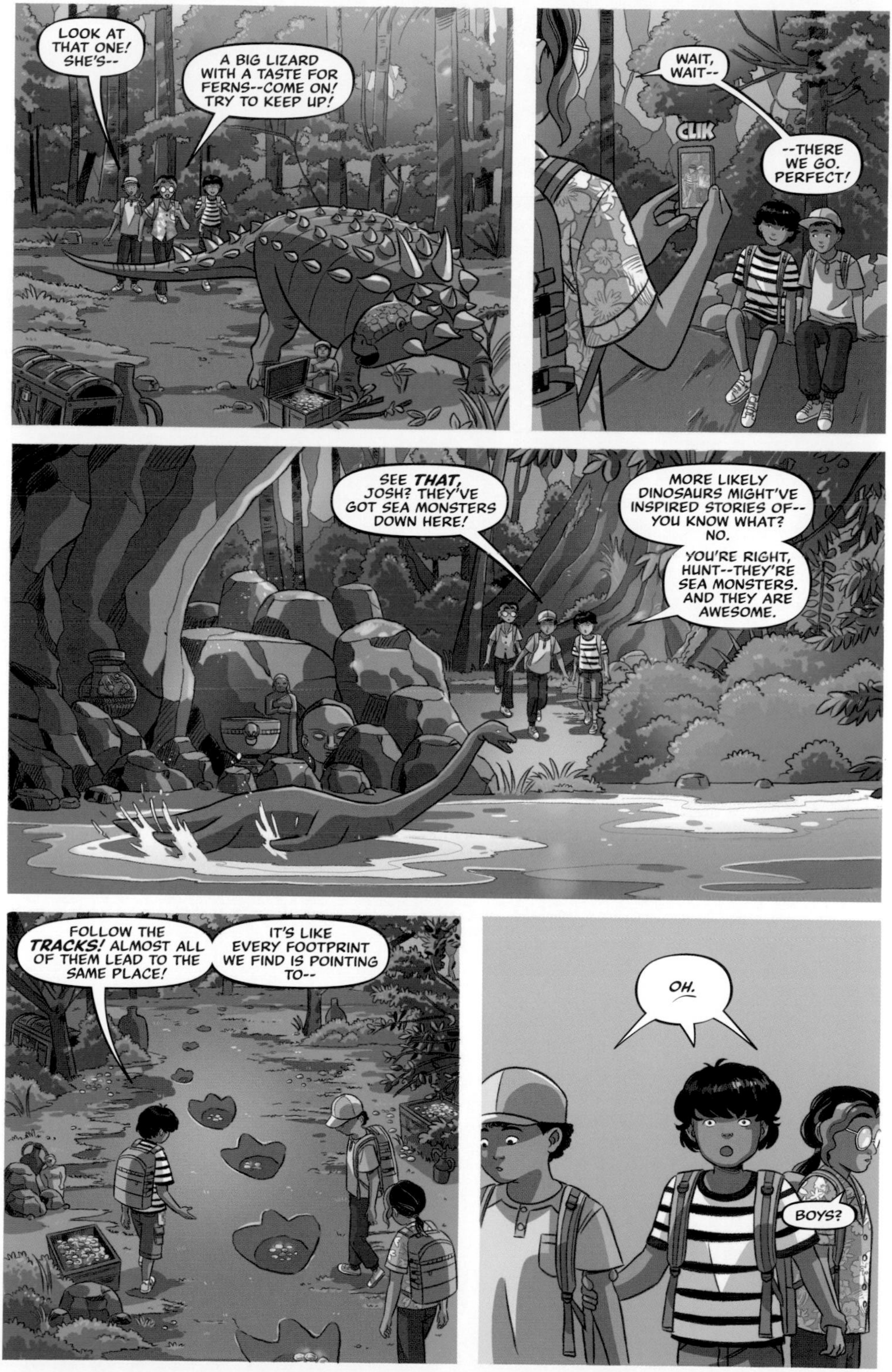
LOOK AT THAT ONE! SHE'S--
A BIG LIZARD WITH A TASTE FOR FERNS--COME ON! TRY TO KEEP UP!
WAIT, WAIT--
CLIK
--THERE WE GO. PERFECT!
SEE THAT, JOSH? THEY'VE GOT SEA MONSTERS DOWN HERE!
MORE LIKELY DINOSAURS MIGHT'VE INSPIRED STORIES OF-- YOU KNOW WHAT? NO.
YOU'RE RIGHT, HUNT--THEY'RE SEA MONSTERS. AND THEY ARE AWESOME.
FOLLOW THE TRACKS! ALMOST ALL OF THEM LEAD TO THE SAME PLACE!
IT'S LIKE EVERY FOOTPRINT WE FIND IS POINTING TO--
OH.
BOYS?

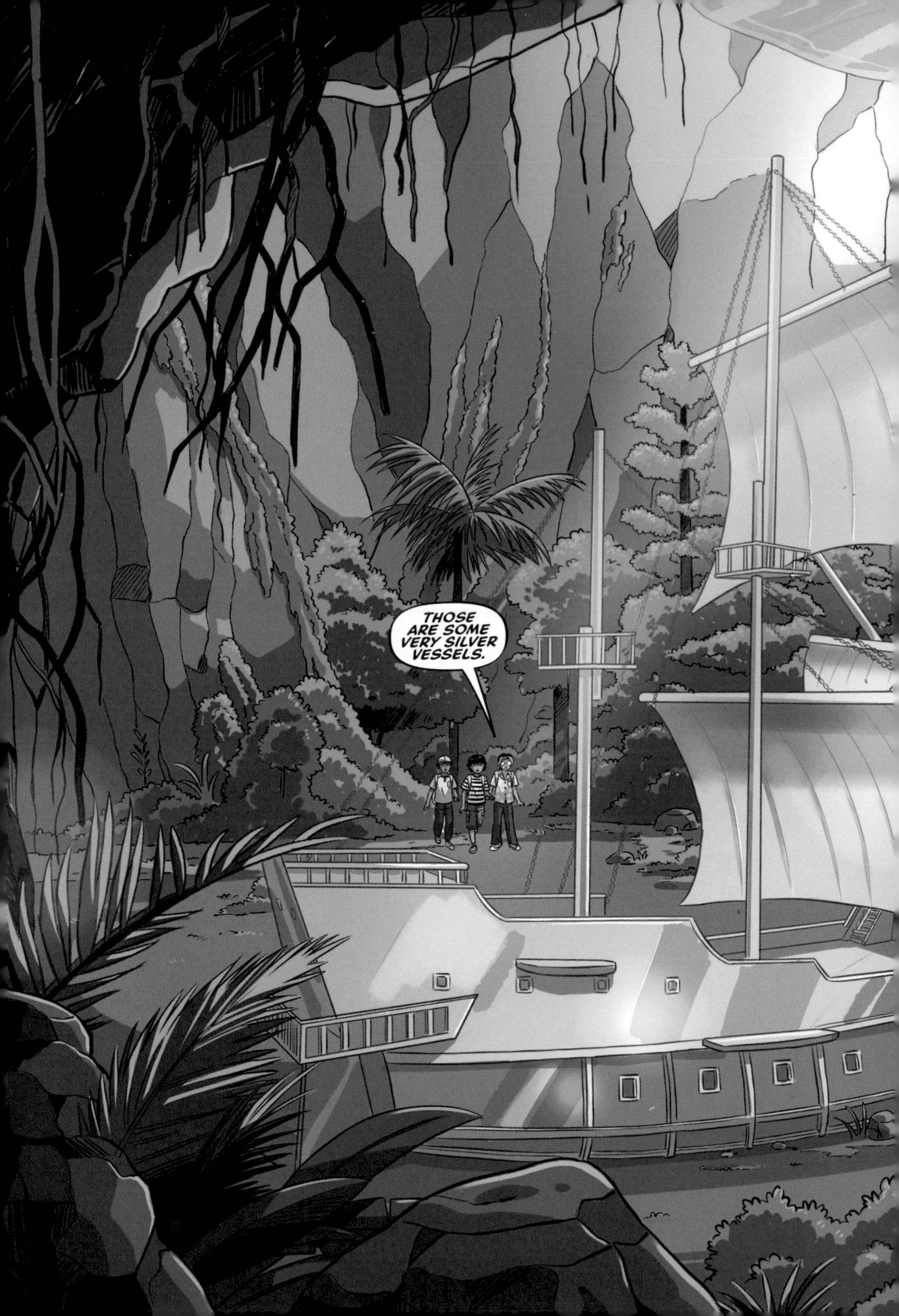
THOSE ARE SOME VERY SILVER VESSELS.

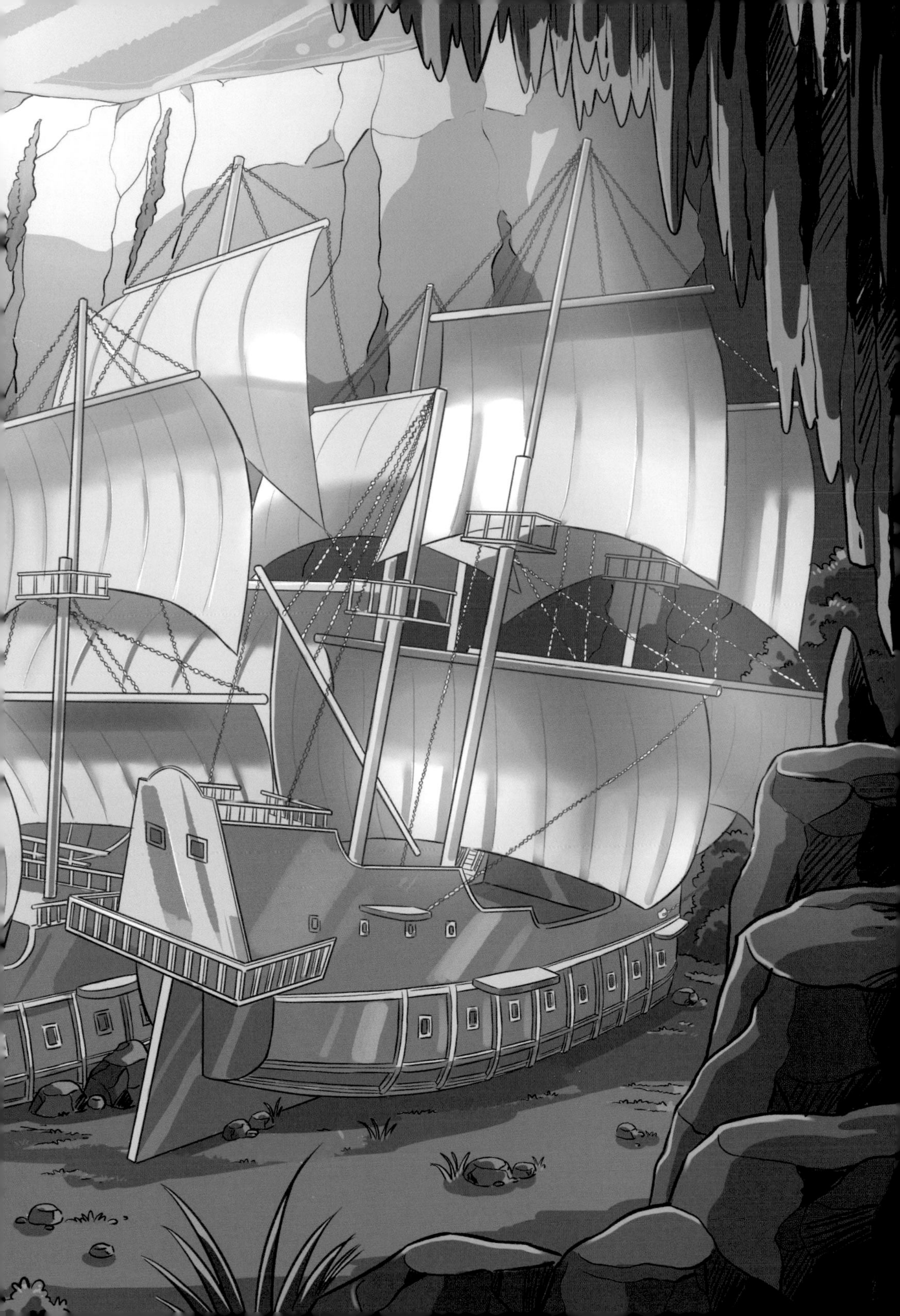

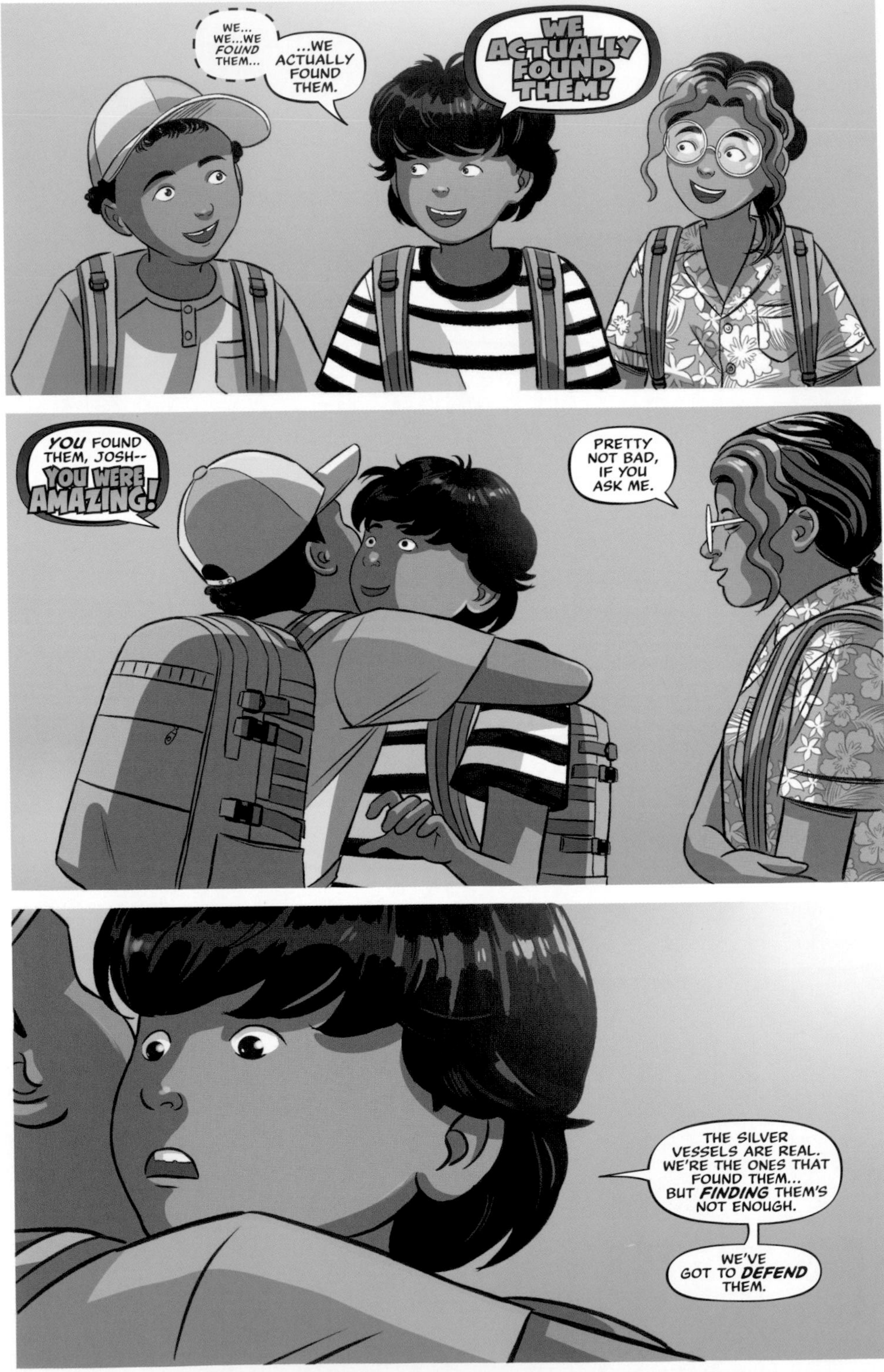

WE... WE...WE *FOUND* THEM...
...WE ACTUALLY FOUND THEM.
WE ACTUALLY FOUND THEM!
YOU FOUND THEM, JOSH-- YOU WERE AMAZING!
PRETTY NOT BAD, IF YOU ASK ME.
THE SILVER VESSELS ARE REAL. WE'RE THE ONES THAT FOUND THEM... BUT *FINDING* THEM'S NOT ENOUGH.
WE'VE GOT TO *DEFEND* THEM.

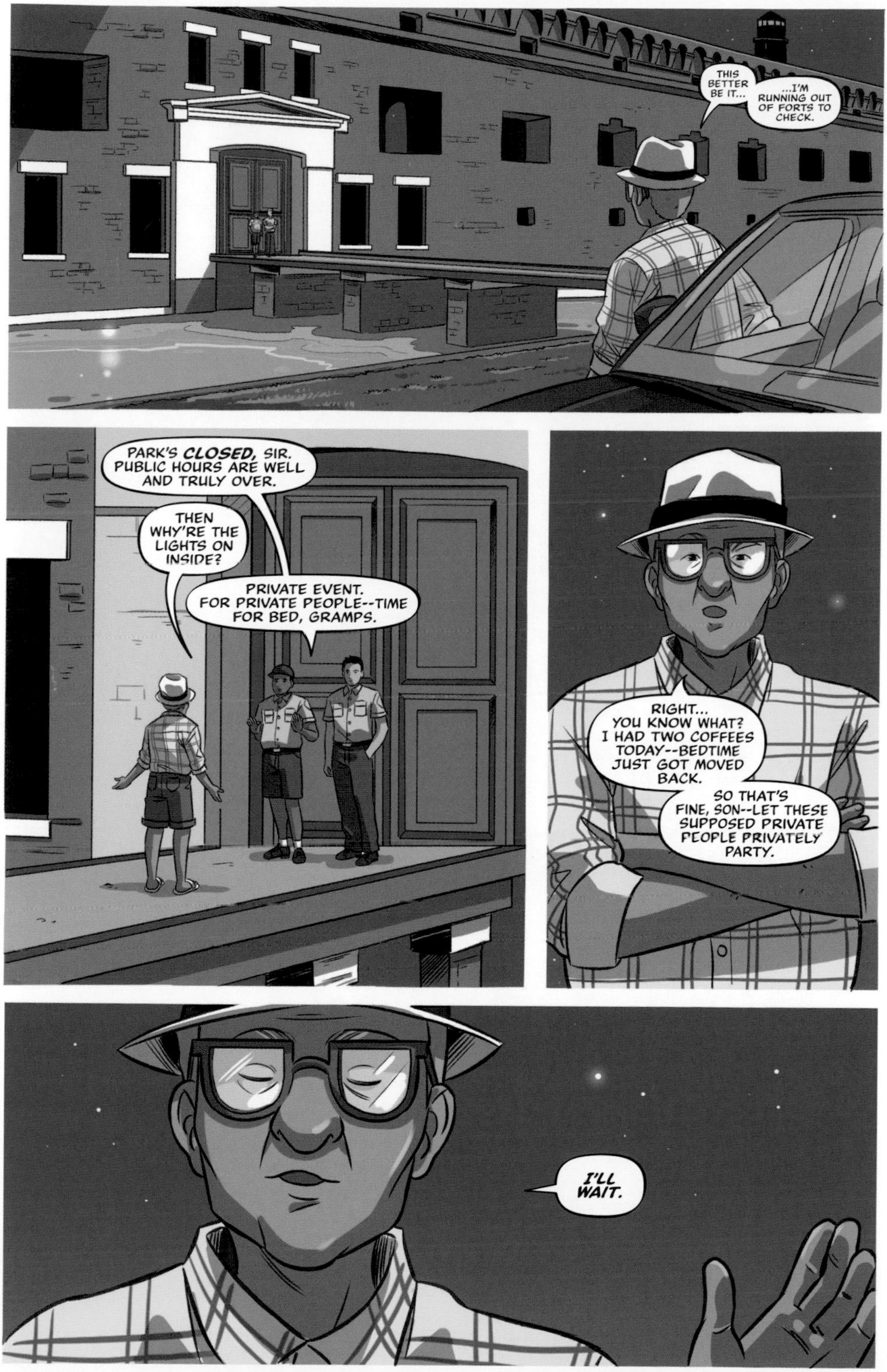
THIS BETTER BE IT...
...I'M RUNNING OUT OF FORTS TO CHECK.
PARK'S **CLOSED,** SIR. PUBLIC HOURS ARE WELL AND TRULY OVER.
THEN WHY'RE THE LIGHTS ON INSIDE?
PRIVATE EVENT. FOR PRIVATE PEOPLE--TIME FOR BED, GRAMPS.
RIGHT... YOU KNOW WHAT? I HAD TWO COFFEES TODAY--BEDTIME JUST GOT MOVED BACK.
SO THAT'S FINE, SON--LET THESE SUPPOSED PRIVATE PEOPLE PRIVATELY PARTY.
I'LL WAIT.

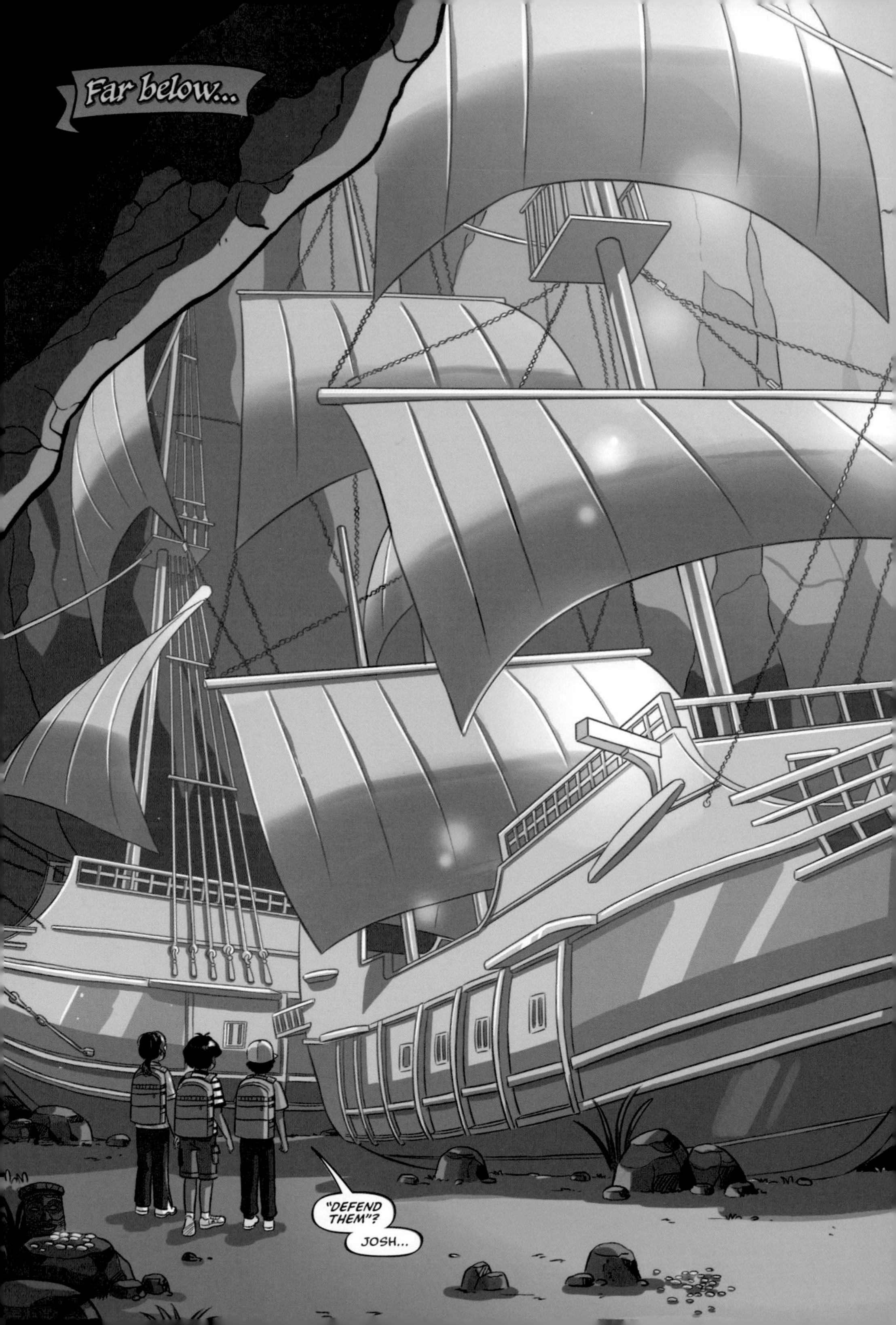
Far below...
"DEFEND THEM"?
JOSH...

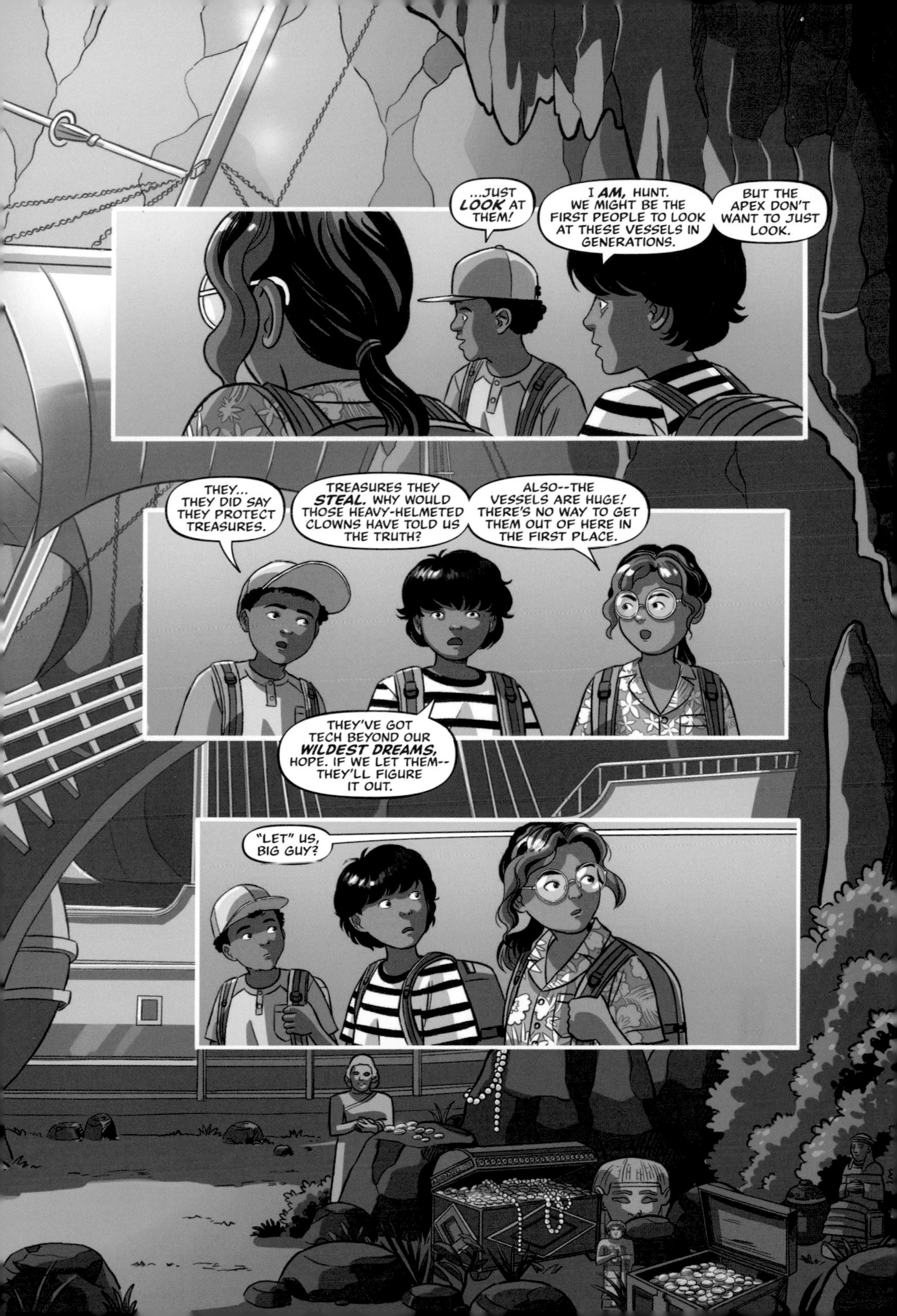
...JUST LOOK AT THEM!
I AM, HUNT. WE MIGHT BE THE FIRST PEOPLE TO LOOK AT THESE VESSELS IN GENERATIONS.
BUT THE APEX DON'T WANT TO JUST LOOK.
THEY... THEY DID SAY THEY PROTECT TREASURES.
TREASURES THEY STEAL. WHY WOULD THOSE HEAVY-HELMETED CLOWNS HAVE TOLD US THE TRUTH?
ALSO--THE VESSELS ARE HUGE! THERE'S NO WAY TO GET THEM OUT OF HERE IN THE FIRST PLACE.
THEY'VE GOT TECH BEYOND OUR WILDEST DREAMS, HOPE. IF WE LET THEM--THEY'LL FIGURE IT OUT.
"LET" US, BIG GUY?

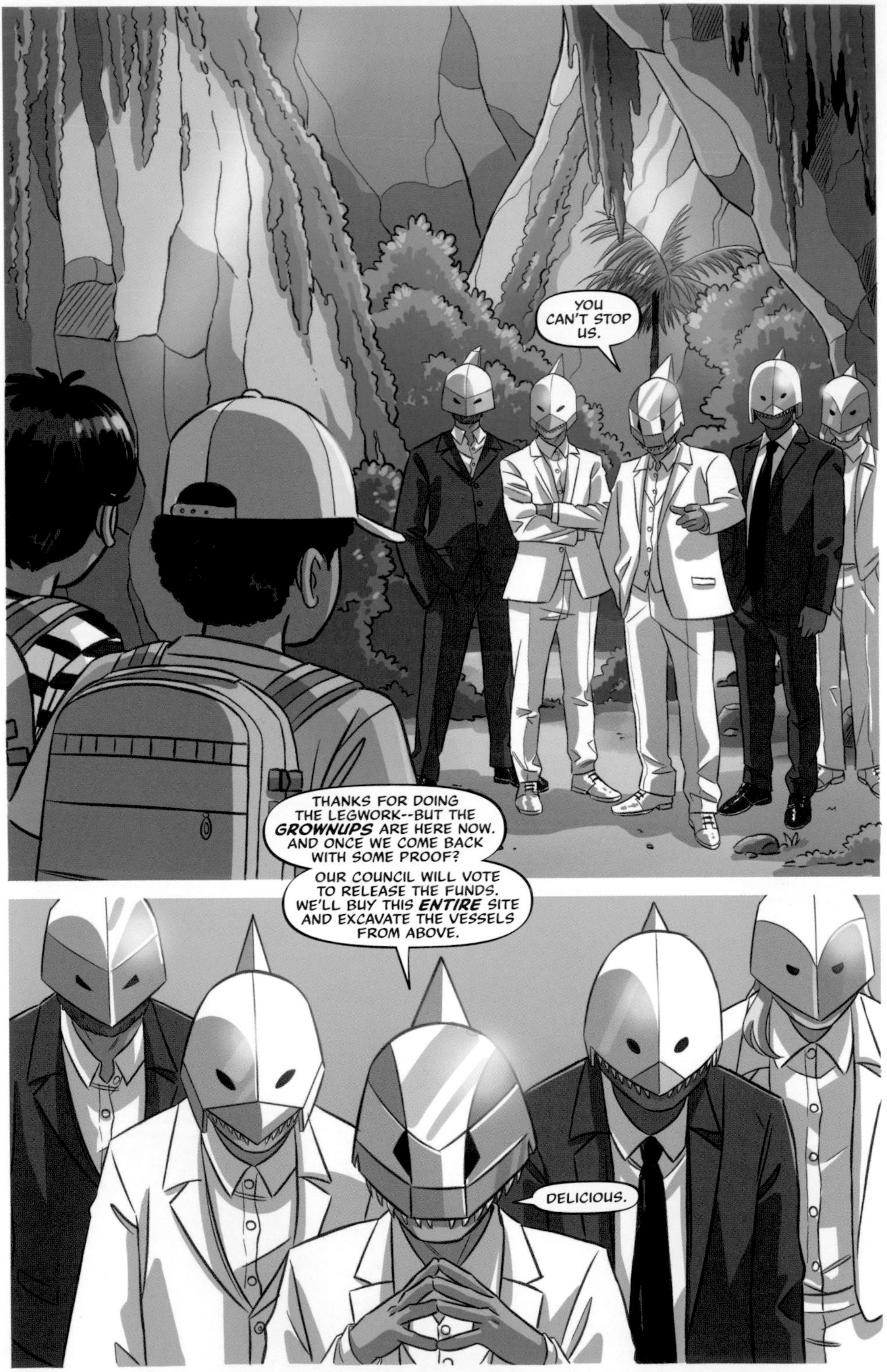
YOU CAN'T STOP US.
THANKS FOR DOING THE LEGWORK--BUT THE GROWNUPS ARE HERE NOW. AND ONCE WE COME BACK WITH SOME PROOF?
OUR COUNCIL WILL VOTE TO RELEASE THE FUNDS. WE'LL BUY THIS ENTIRE SITE AND EXCAVATE THE VESSELS FROM ABOVE.
DELICIOUS.

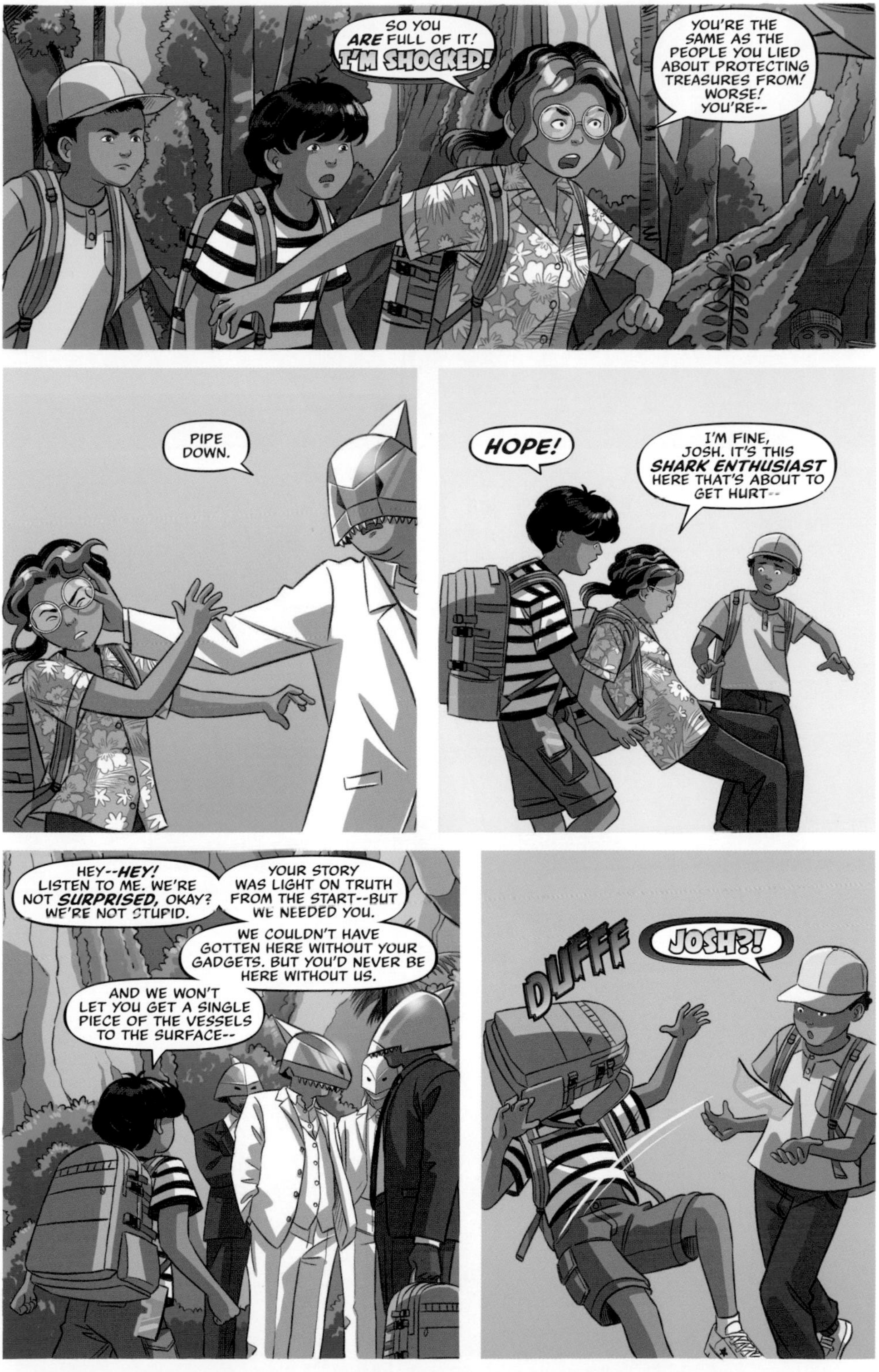
SO YOU ARE FULL OF IT! I'M SHOCKED!
YOU'RE THE SAME AS THE PEOPLE YOU LIED ABOUT PROTECTING TREASURES FROM! WORSE! YOU'RE--
PIPE DOWN.
HOPE!
I'M FINE, JOSH. IT'S THIS SHARK ENTHUSIAST HERE THAT'S ABOUT TO GET HURT--
HEY--HEY! LISTEN TO ME. WE'RE NOT SURPRISED, OKAY? WE'RE NOT STUPID.
YOUR STORY WAS LIGHT ON TRUTH FROM THE START--BUT WE NEEDED YOU.
WE COULDN'T HAVE GOTTEN HERE WITHOUT YOUR GADGETS. BUT YOU'D NEVER BE HERE WITHOUT US.
AND WE WON'T LET YOU GET A SINGLE PIECE OF THE VESSELS TO THE SURFACE--
DUFFF
JOSH?!

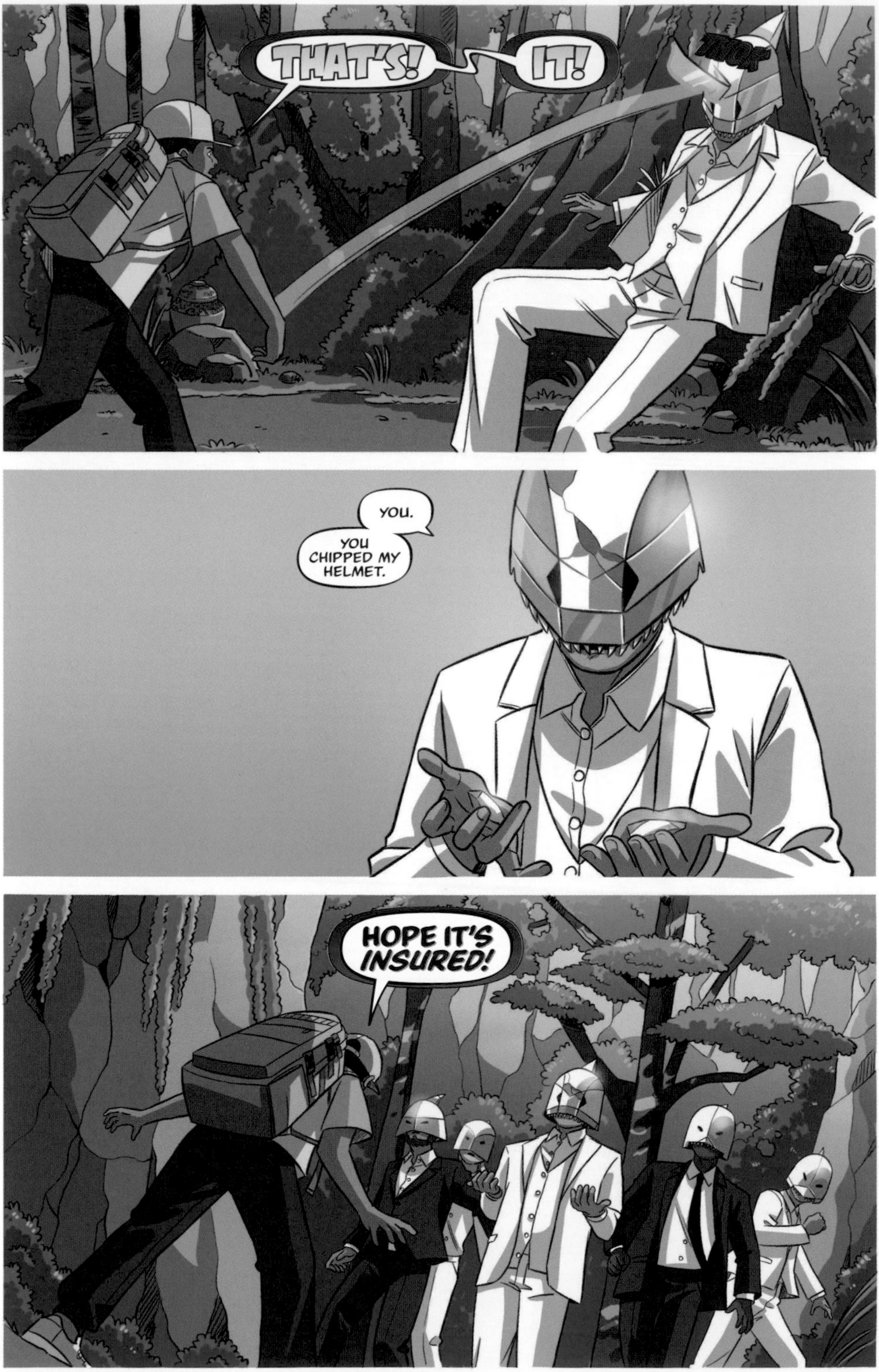
THAT'S!
IT!
YOU.
YOU CHIPPED MY HELMET.
HOPE IT'S INSURED!

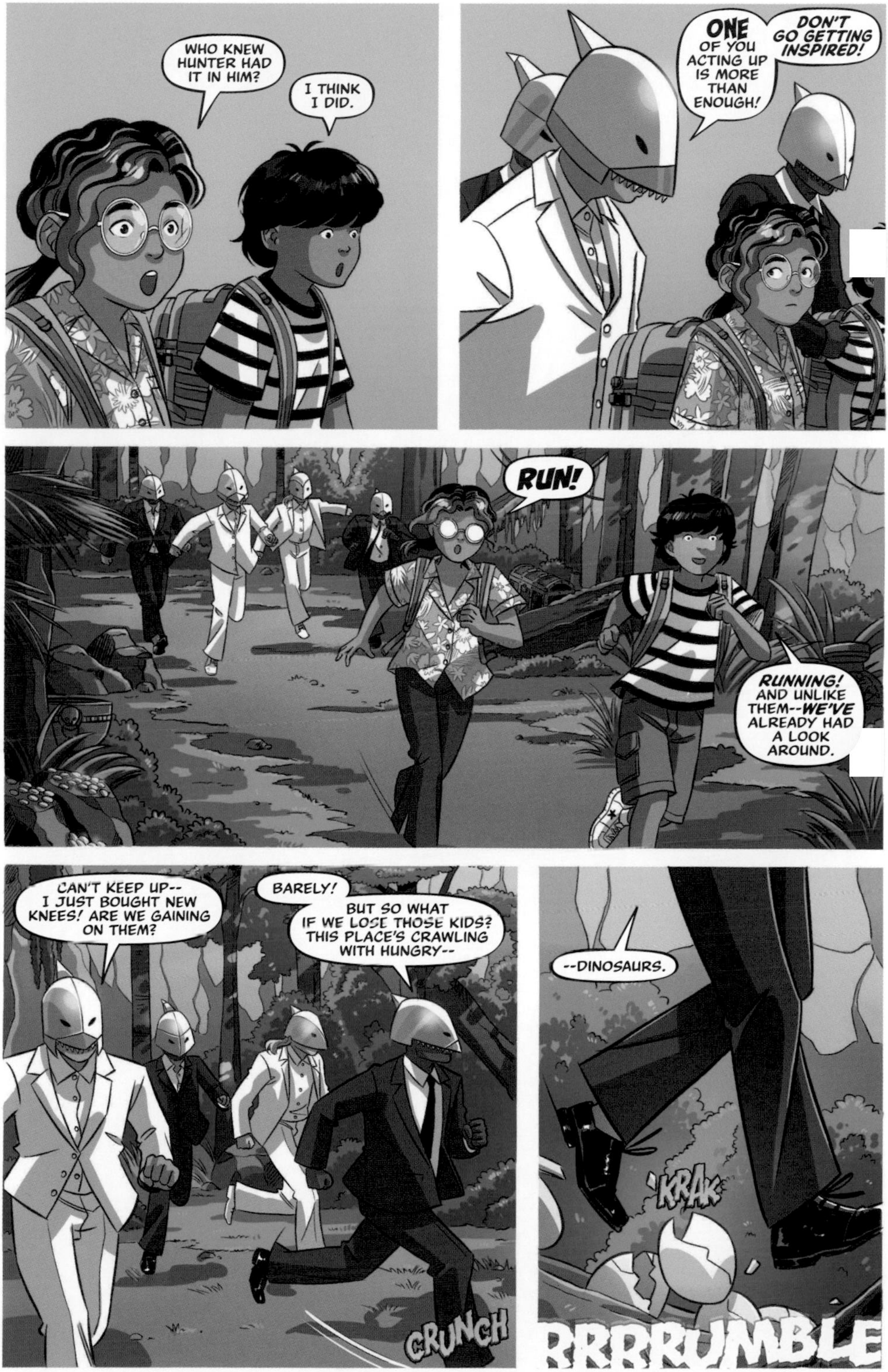
WHO KNEW HUNTER HAD IT IN HIM?
I THINK I DID.
ONE OF YOU ACTING UP IS MORE THAN ENOUGH!
DON'T GO GETTING INSPIRED!
RUN!
RUNNING! AND UNLIKE THEM--WE'VE ALREADY HAD A LOOK AROUND.
CAN'T KEEP UP-- I JUST BOUGHT NEW KNEES! ARE WE GAINING ON THEM?
BARELY!
BUT SO WHAT IF WE LOSE THOSE KIDS? THIS PLACE'S CRAWLING WITH HUNGRY--
CRUNCH
--DINOSAURS.
KRAK
RRRRUMBLE

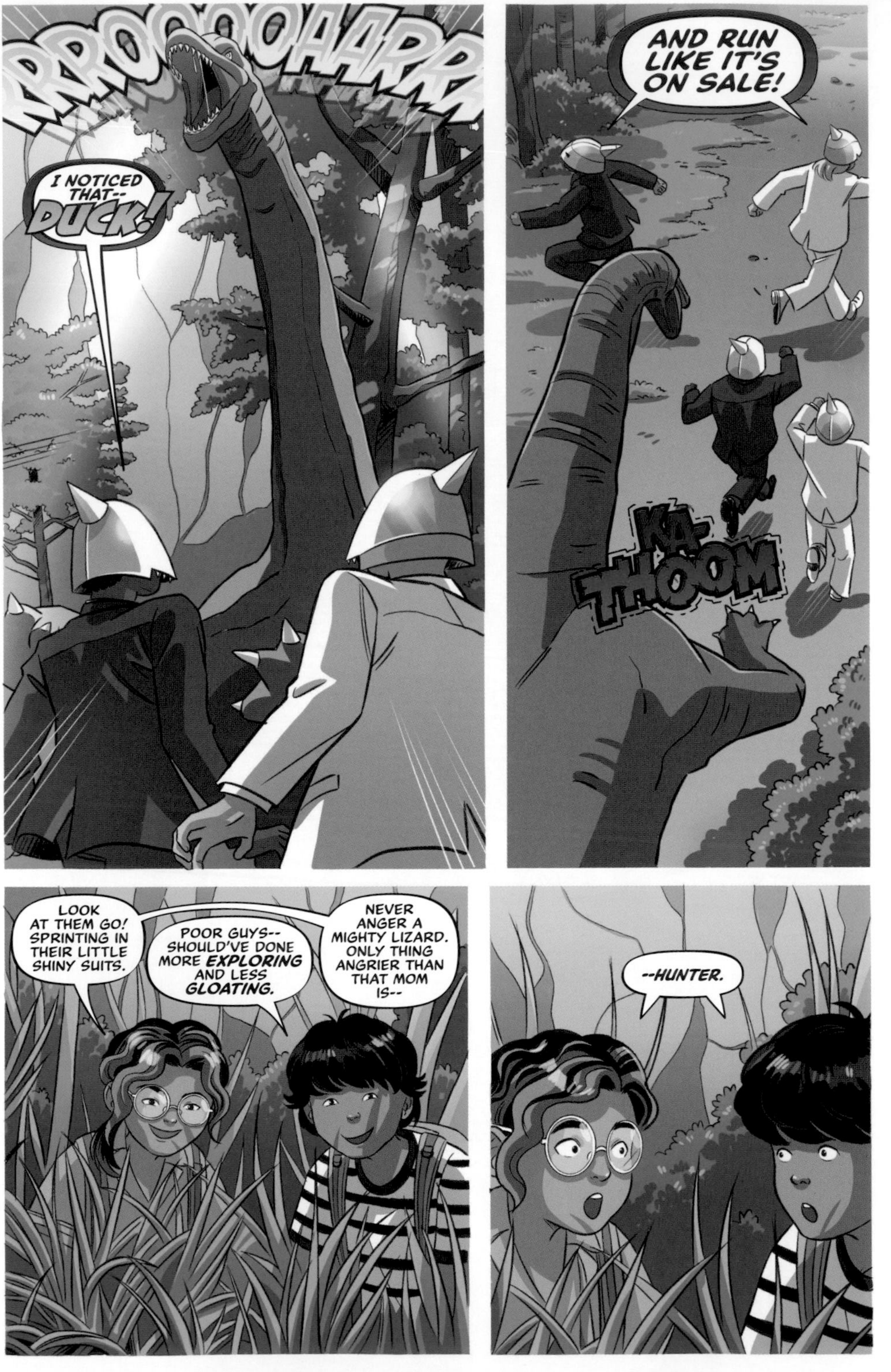
RROOOOAARR
I NOTICED THAT-- DUCK!
AND RUN LIKE IT'S ON SALE!
KA-THOOM
LOOK AT THEM GO! SPRINTING IN THEIR LITTLE SHINY SUITS.
POOR GUYS-- SHOULD'VE DONE MORE EXPLORING AND LESS GLOATING.
NEVER ANGER A MIGHTY LIZARD. ONLY THING ANGRIER THAN THAT MOM IS--
--HUNTER.

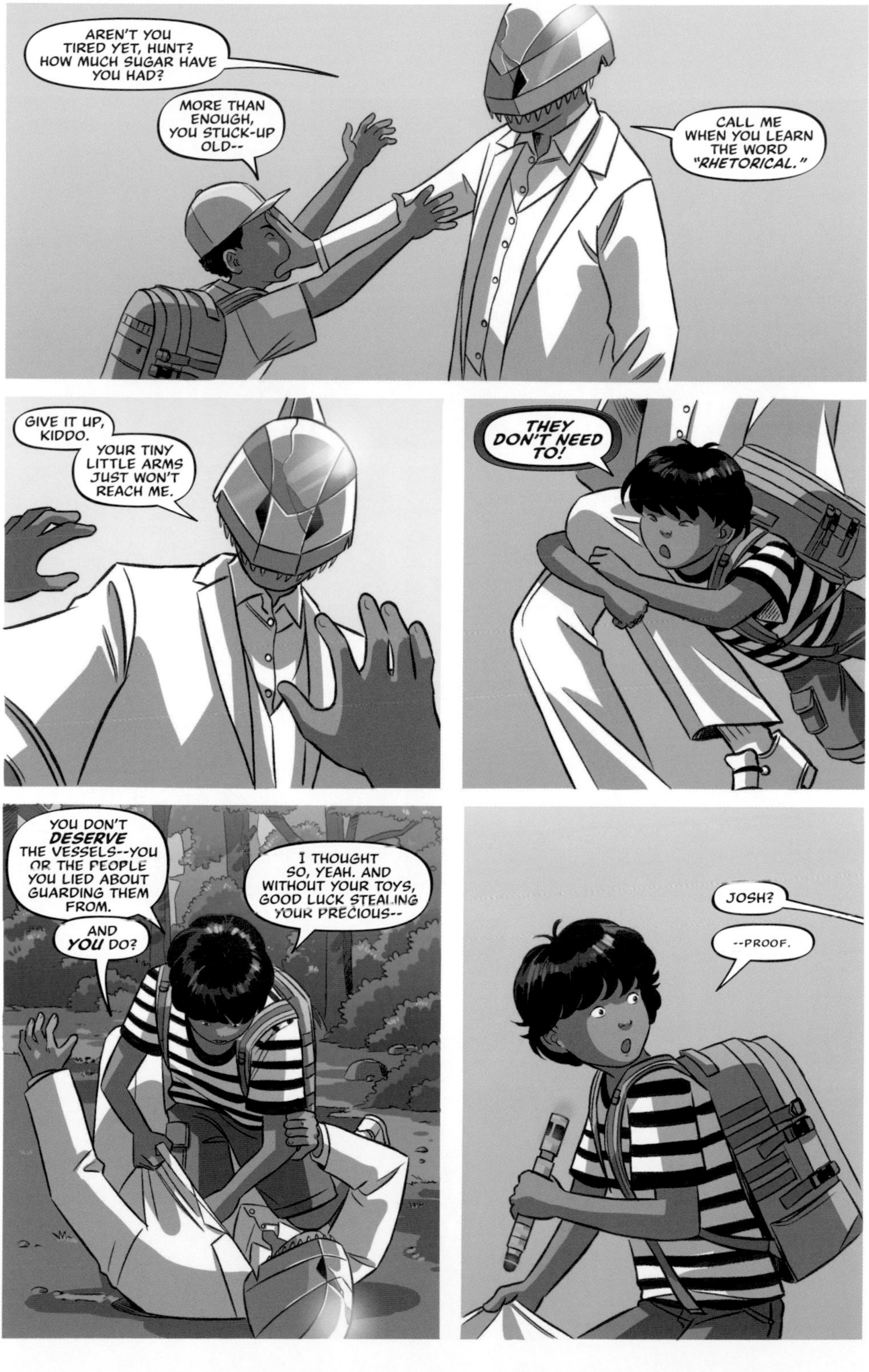

AREN'T YOU TIRED YET, HUNT? HOW MUCH SUGAR HAVE YOU HAD?
MORE THAN ENOUGH, YOU STUCK-UP OLD--
CALL ME WHEN YOU LEARN THE WORD *"RHETORICAL."*
GIVE IT UP, KIDDO.
YOUR TINY LITTLE ARMS JUST WON'T REACH ME.
THEY DON'T NEED TO!
YOU DON'T ***DESERVE*** THE VESSELS--YOU OR THE PEOPLE YOU LIED ABOUT GUARDING THEM FROM.
AND ***YOU*** DO?
I THOUGHT SO, YEAH. AND WITHOUT YOUR TOYS, GOOD LUCK STEALING YOUR PRECIOUS--
JOSH?
--PROOF.

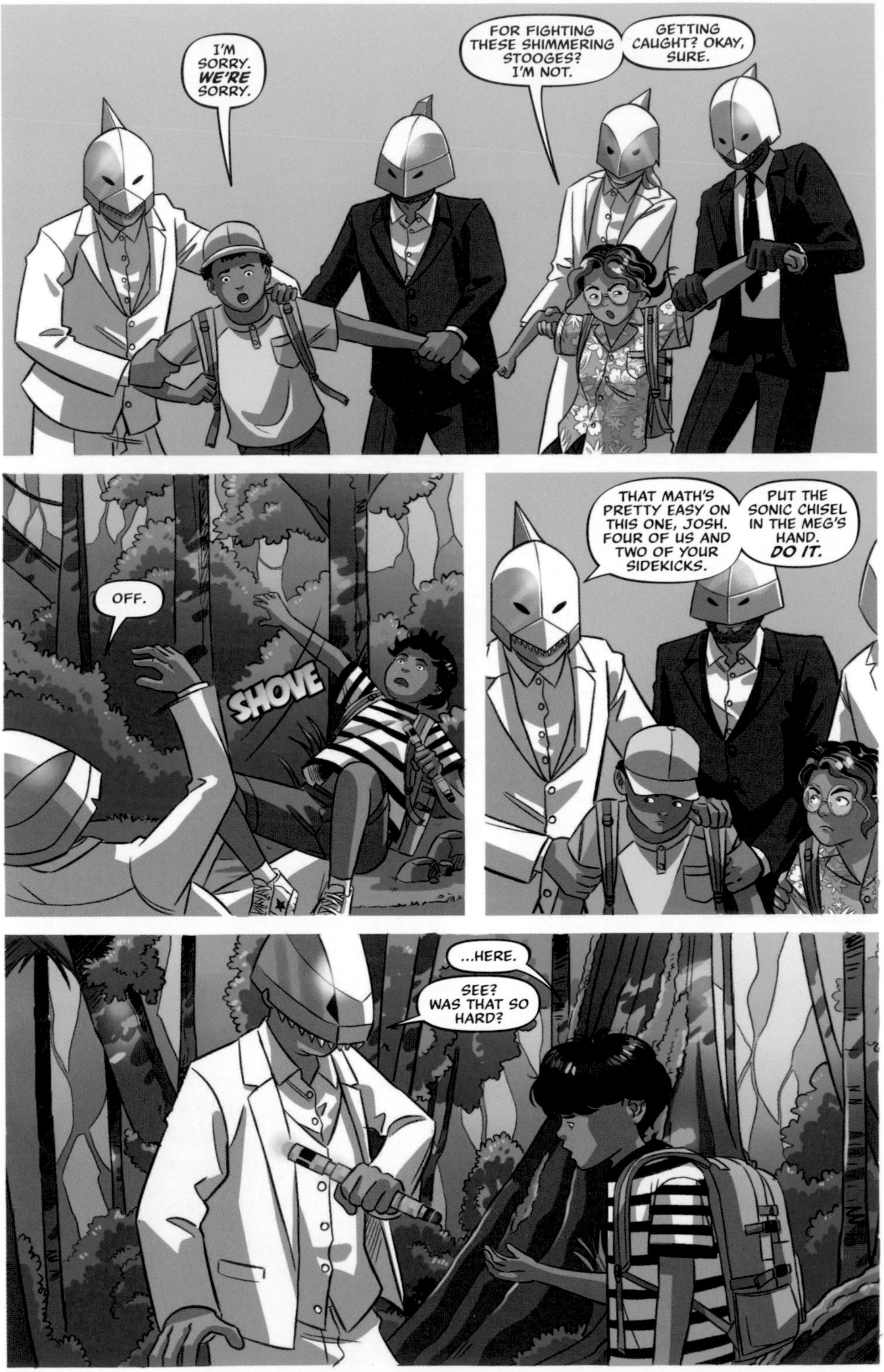
I'M SORRY. *WE'RE* SORRY.
FOR FIGHTING THESE SHIMMERING STOOGES? I'M NOT.
GETTING CAUGHT? OKAY, SURE.
OFF.
SHOVE
THAT MATH'S PRETTY EASY ON THIS ONE, JOSH. FOUR OF US AND TWO OF YOUR SIDEKICKS.
PUT THE SONIC CHISEL IN THE MEG'S HAND. ***DO IT.***
...HERE.
SEE? WAS THAT SO HARD?

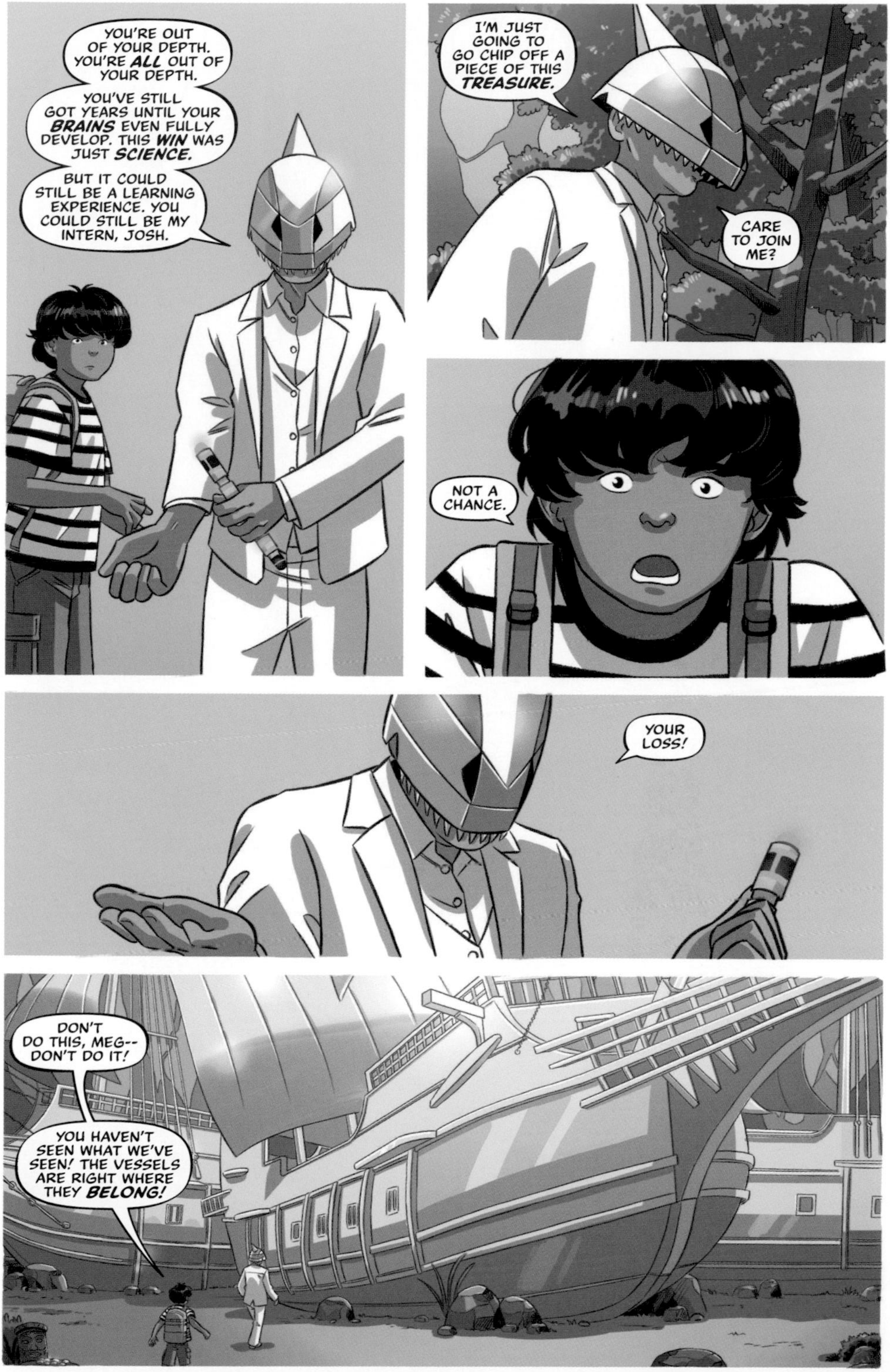
YOU'RE OUT OF YOUR DEPTH. YOU'RE ALL OUT OF YOUR DEPTH.
YOU'VE STILL GOT YEARS UNTIL YOUR BRAINS EVEN FULLY DEVELOP. THIS WIN WAS JUST SCIENCE.
BUT IT COULD STILL BE A LEARNING EXPERIENCE. YOU COULD STILL BE MY INTERN, JOSH.
I'M JUST GOING TO GO CHIP OFF A PIECE OF THIS TREASURE.
CARE TO JOIN ME?
NOT A CHANCE.
YOUR LOSS!
DON'T DO THIS, MEG-- DON'T DO IT!
YOU HAVEN'T SEEN WHAT WE'VE SEEN! THE VESSELS ARE RIGHT WHERE THEY BELONG!

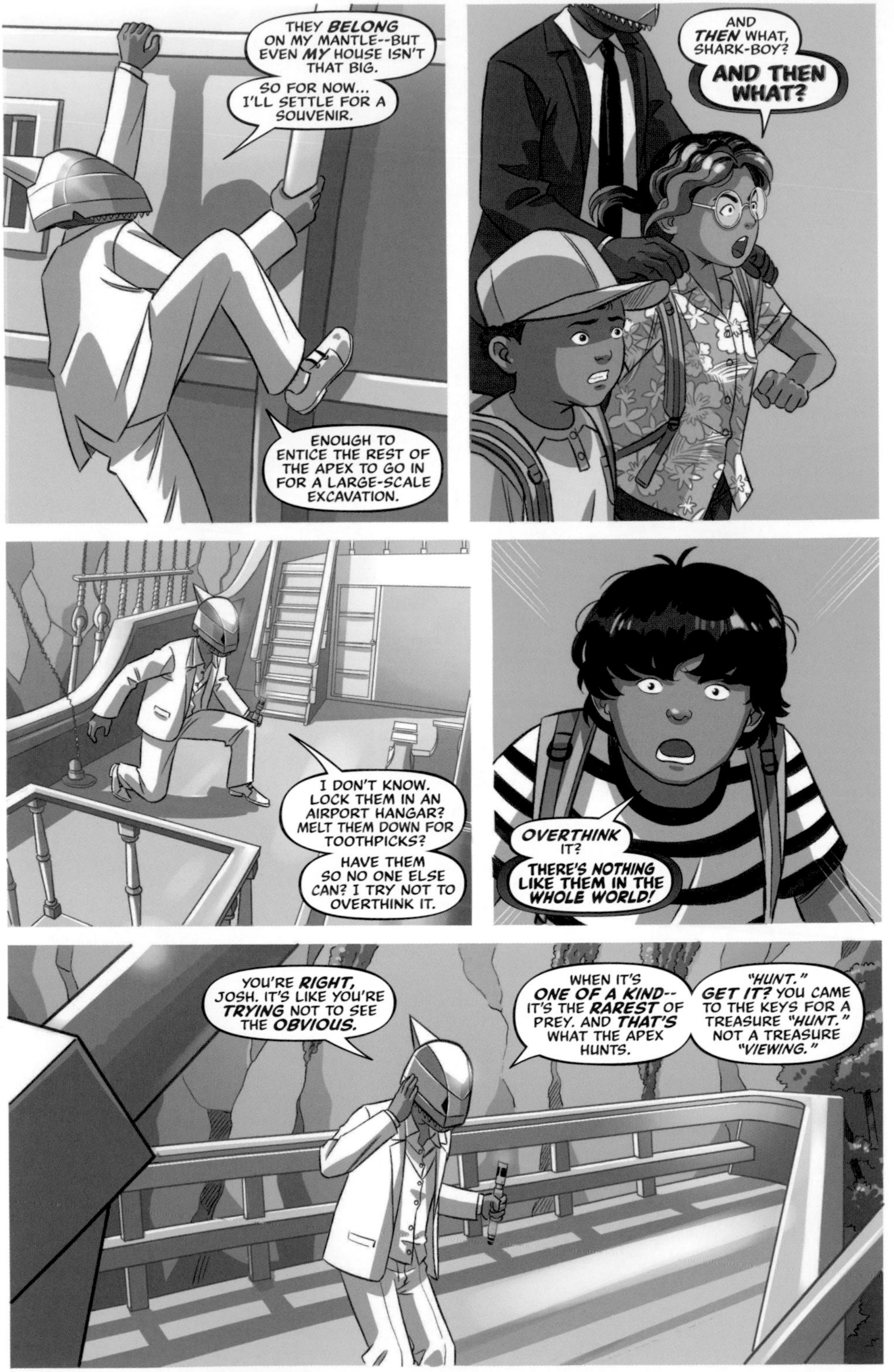
THEY BELONG ON MY MANTLE--BUT EVEN MY HOUSE ISN'T THAT BIG.
SO FOR NOW... I'LL SETTLE FOR A SOUVENIR.
ENOUGH TO ENTICE THE REST OF THE APEX TO GO IN FOR A LARGE-SCALE EXCAVATION.
AND THEN WHAT, SHARK-BOY?
AND THEN WHAT?
I DON'T KNOW. LOCK THEM IN AN AIRPORT HANGAR? MELT THEM DOWN FOR TOOTHPICKS?
HAVE THEM SO NO ONE ELSE CAN? I TRY NOT TO OVERTHINK IT.
OVERTHINK IT?
THERE'S NOTHING LIKE THEM IN THE WHOLE WORLD!
YOU'RE RIGHT, JOSH. IT'S LIKE YOU'RE TRYING NOT TO SEE THE OBVIOUS.
WHEN IT'S ONE OF A KIND-- IT'S THE RAREST OF PREY. AND THAT'S WHAT THE APEX HUNTS.
"HUNT." GET IT? YOU CAME TO THE KEYS FOR A TREASURE "HUNT." NOT A TREASURE "VIEWING."

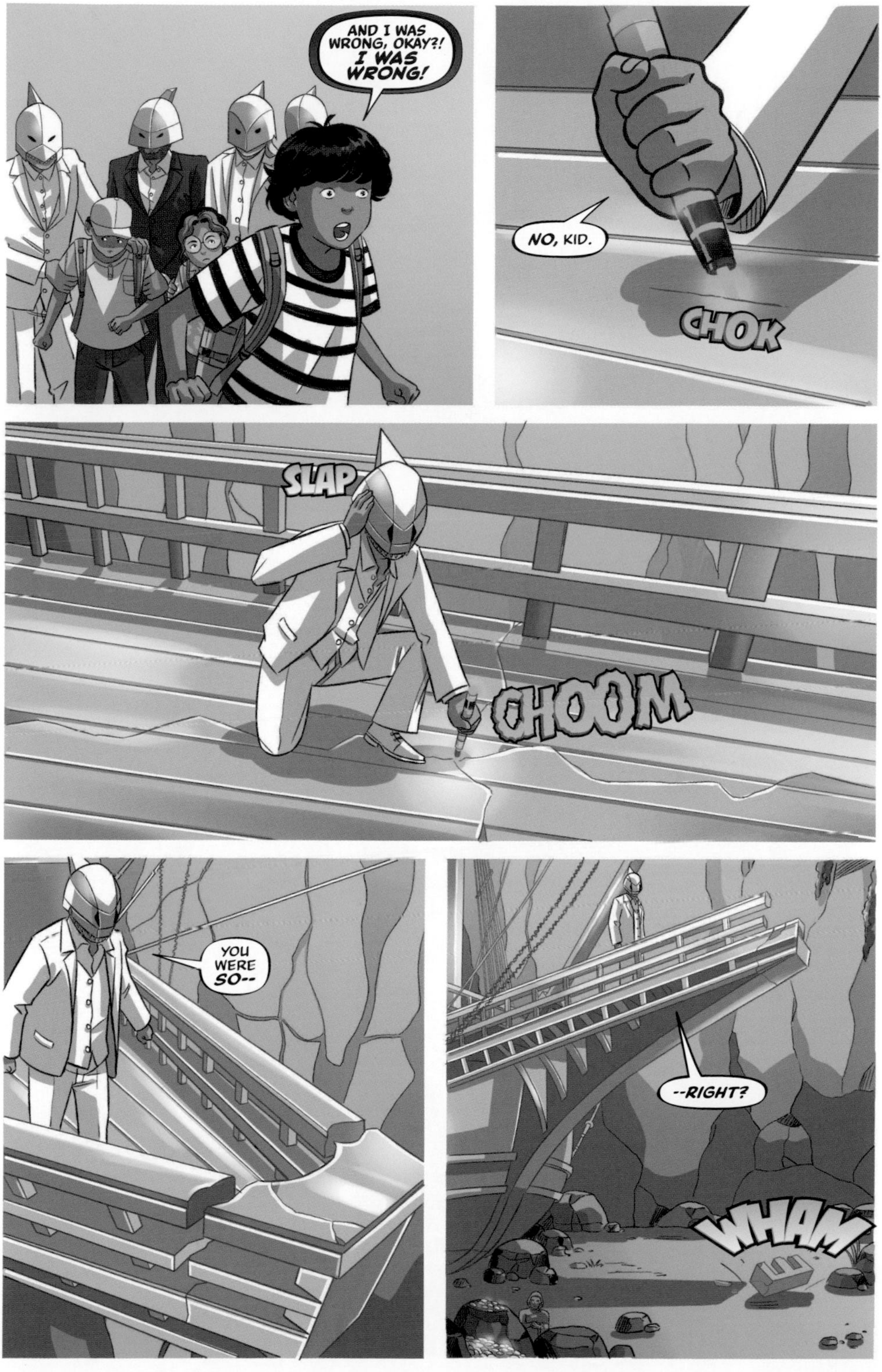
AND I WAS WRONG, OKAY?! I WAS WRONG!
NO, KID.
CHOK
SLAP
CHOOM
YOU WERE SO--
--RIGHT?
WHAM

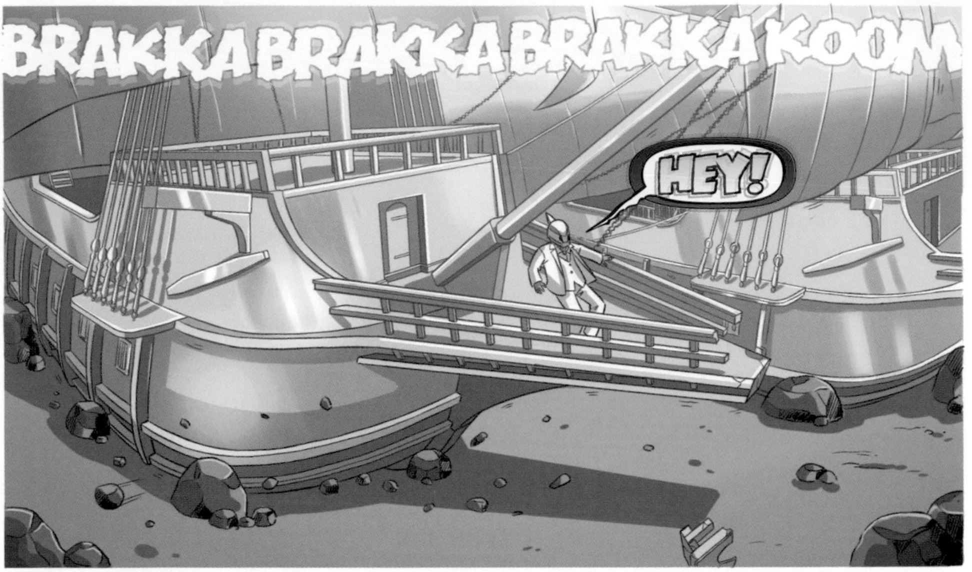
BRAKKA BRAKKA BRAKKA KOOM
HEY!

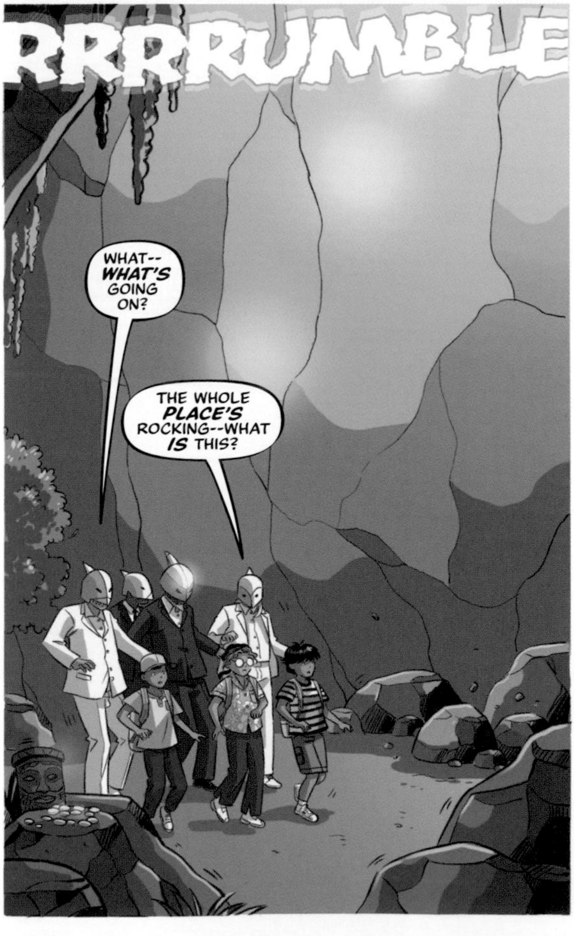
RRRRUMBLE
WHAT-- WHAT'S GOING ON?
THE WHOLE PLACE'S ROCKING--WHAT IS THIS?

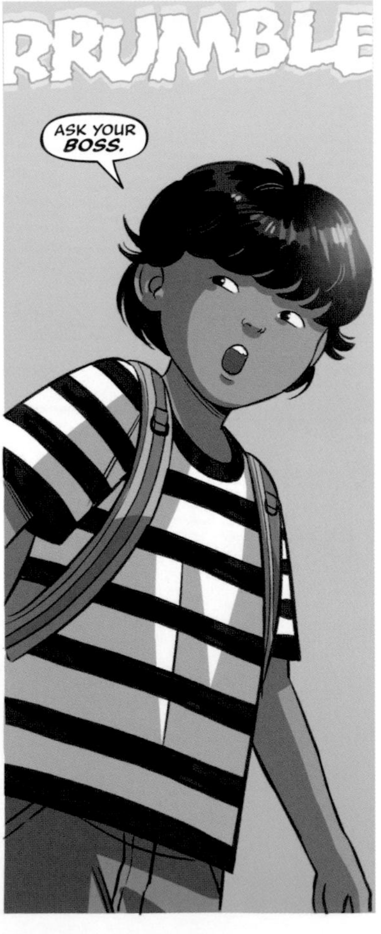
RRUMBLE
ASK YOUR BOSS.

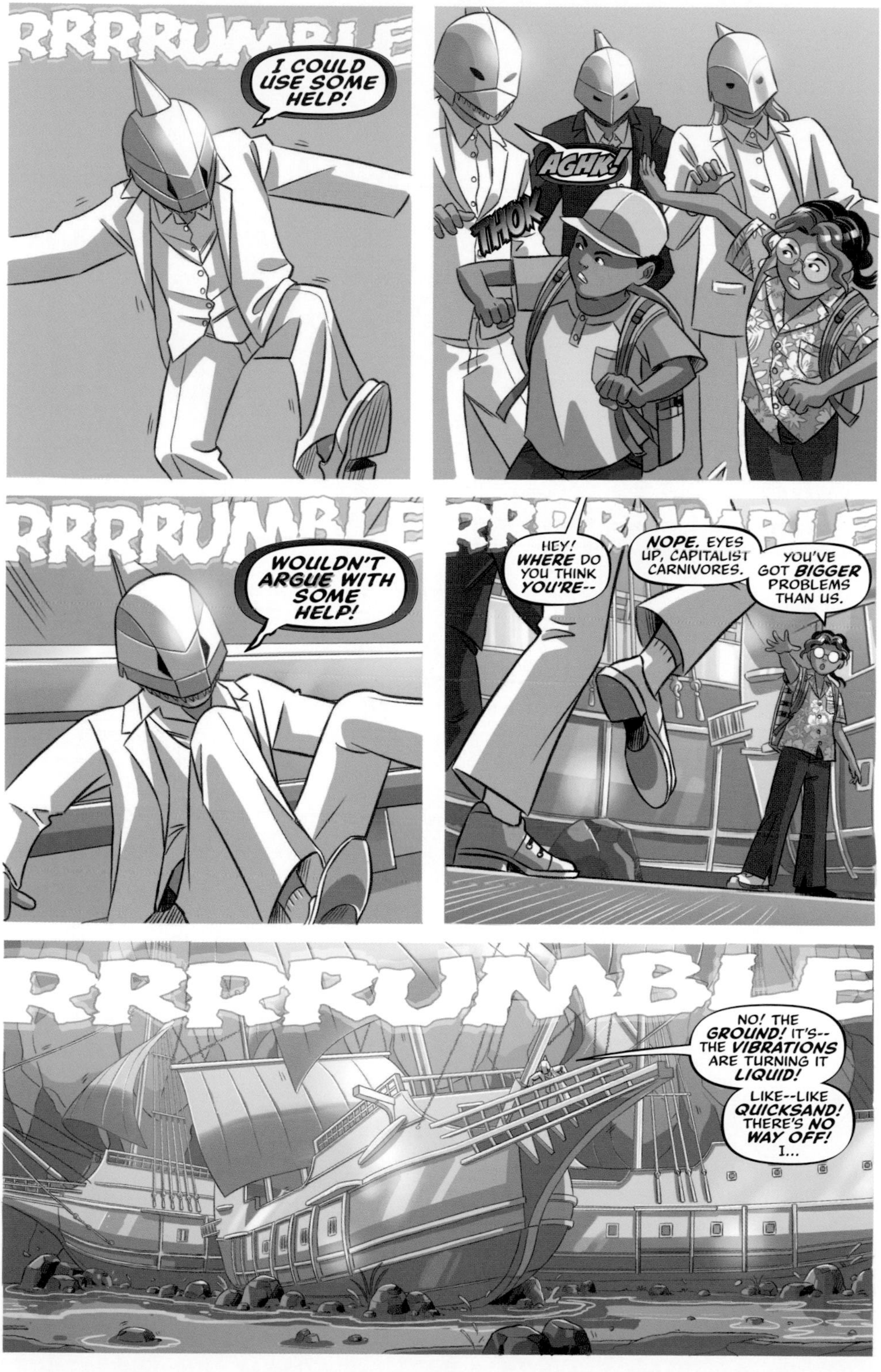
RRRRUMBLE
I COULD USE SOME HELP!
AGHK!
THOK
RRRRUMBLE
WOULDN'T ARGUE WITH SOME HELP!
HEY! WHERE DO YOU THINK YOU'RE--
NOPE. EYES UP, CAPITALIST CARNIVORES.
YOU'VE GOT BIGGER PROBLEMS THAN US.
RRRRUMBLE
NO! THE GROUND! IT'S-- THE VIBRATIONS ARE TURNING IT LIQUID!
LIKE--LIKE QUICKSAND! THERE'S NO WAY OFF! I...

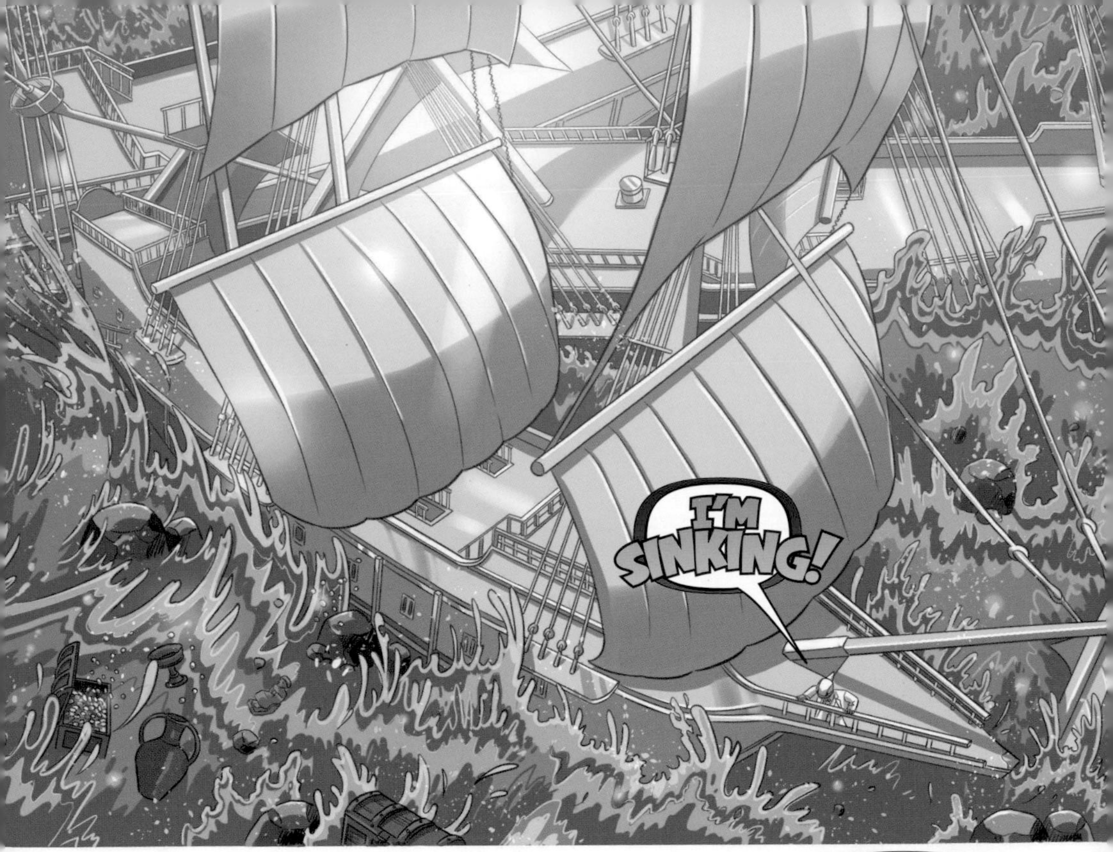
I'M SINKING!

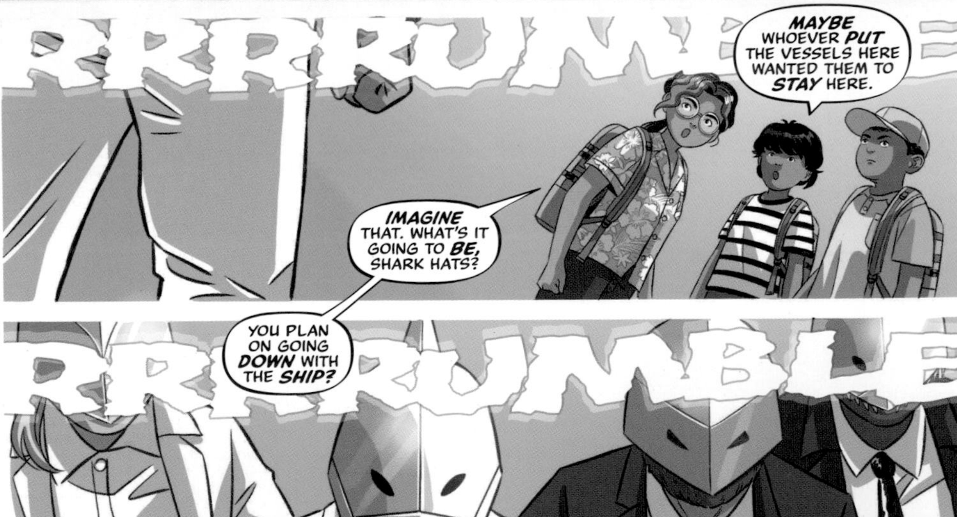
MAYBE WHOEVER PUT THE VESSELS HERE WANTED THEM TO STAY HERE.
IMAGINE THAT. WHAT'S IT GOING TO BE, SHARK HATS?

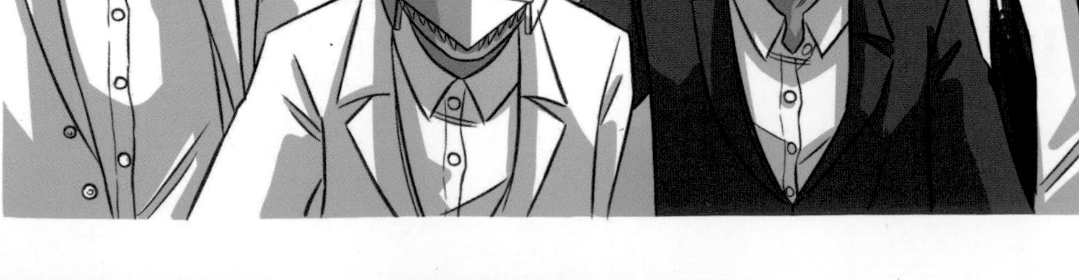
YOU PLAN ON GOING DOWN WITH THE SHIP?
RRRUMBLE

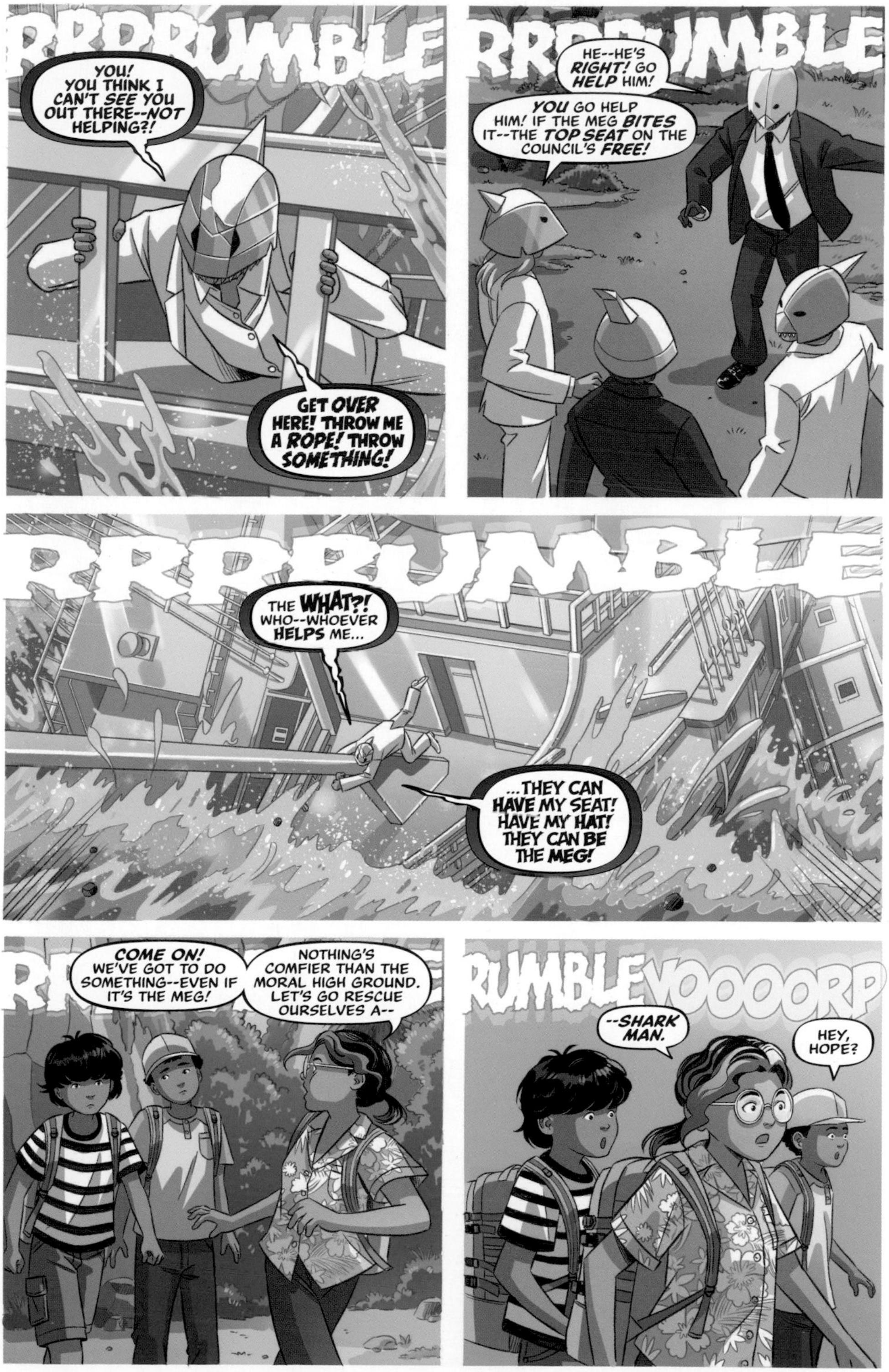
RRRRUMBLE
YOU! YOU THINK I CAN'T *SEE* YOU OUT THERE--*NOT* HELPING?!
GET *OVER* HERE! THROW ME A *ROPE!* THROW SOMETHING!
RRRRUMBLE
HE--HE'S *RIGHT!* GO *HELP* HIM!
YOU GO HELP HIM! IF THE MEG *BITES* IT--THE *TOP SEAT* ON THE COUNCIL'S *FREE!*
RRRRUMBLE
THE **WHAT?!** WHO--WHOEVER **HELPS** ME...
...THEY CAN HAVE MY SEAT! HAVE MY HAT! THEY CAN BE THE MEG!
COME ON! WE'VE GOT TO DO SOMETHING--EVEN IF IT'S THE MEG!
NOTHING'S COMFIER THAN THE MORAL HIGH GROUND. LET'S GO RESCUE OURSELVES A--
RUMBLE VOOOORP
--*SHARK MAN.*
HEY, HOPE?

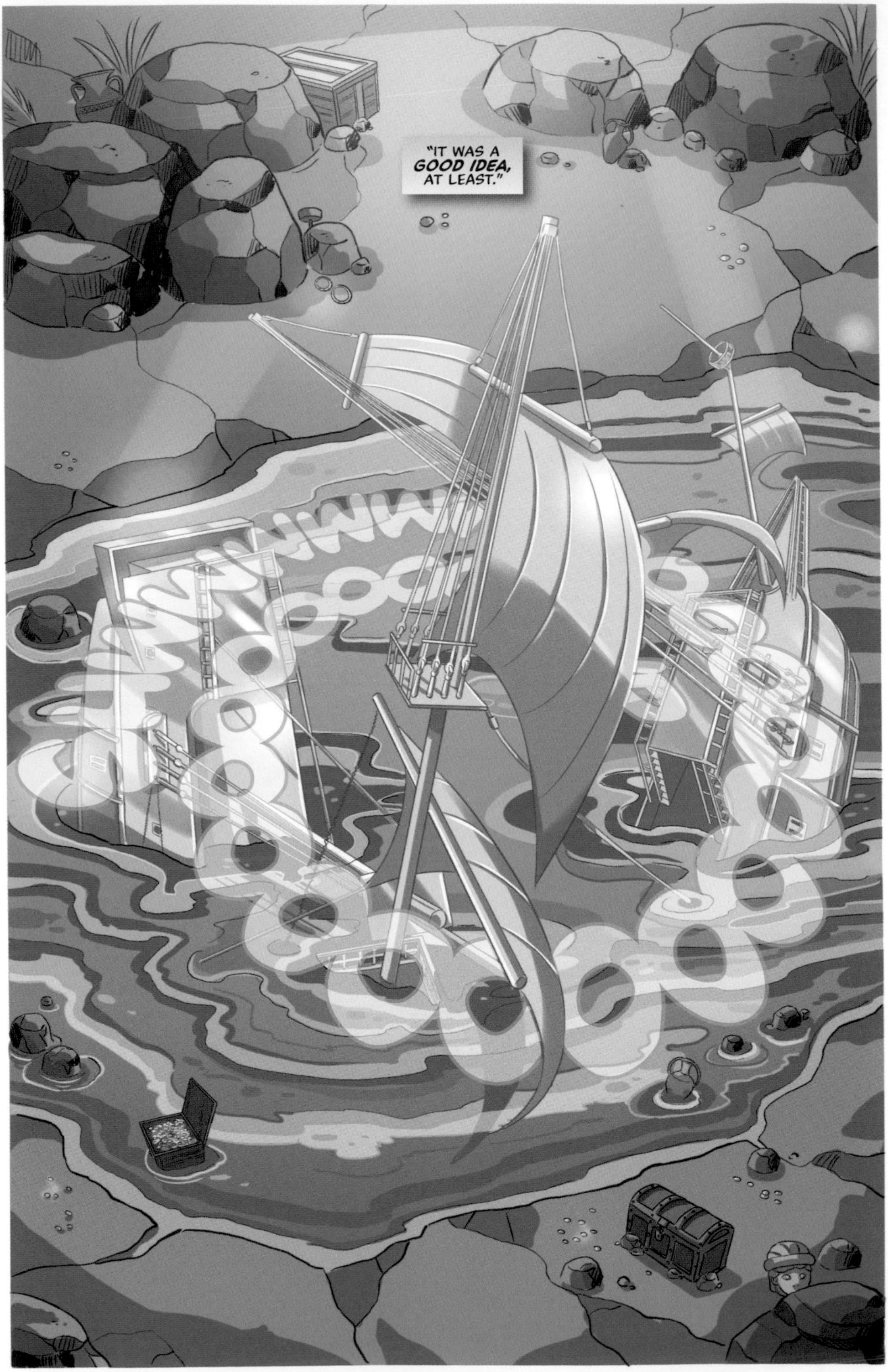
"IT WAS A GOOD IDEA, AT LEAST."

SPLASH

YOU... THINK THE MEG'S OKAY?

HE'S GONE. AND HE TOOK OUR TREASURE WITH HIM.

YOU WANT IT? YOU DIG HIM OUT.

ME? YOU STOOD RIGHT THERE! HE WAS SCREAMING TO YOU FOR HELP!

ME? YOU WERE RIGHT NEXT TO ME! THE MEG LOCKED EYES WITH YOU AND YOU IGNORED HIM!

I WOULD'VE HELPED HIM IF YOU HADN'T BEEN SUCH A COWARD!

WHAT? IF YOU COULD'VE SAVED THE MEG SO EASILY THEN WHY LET ME HOLD YOU BACK?

SO NOW WE'RE NOT A TEAM? WHERE'S YOUR SENSE OF UNITY, YOU--

WAIT--WAIT! JUST SHUT UP AND LOOK AROUND!

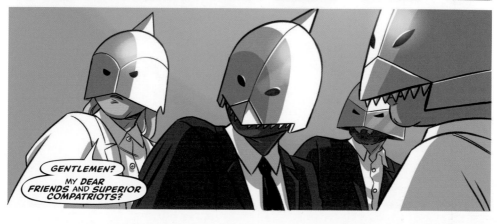

GENTLEMEN?

MY DEAR FRIENDS AND SUPERIOR COMPATRIOTS?

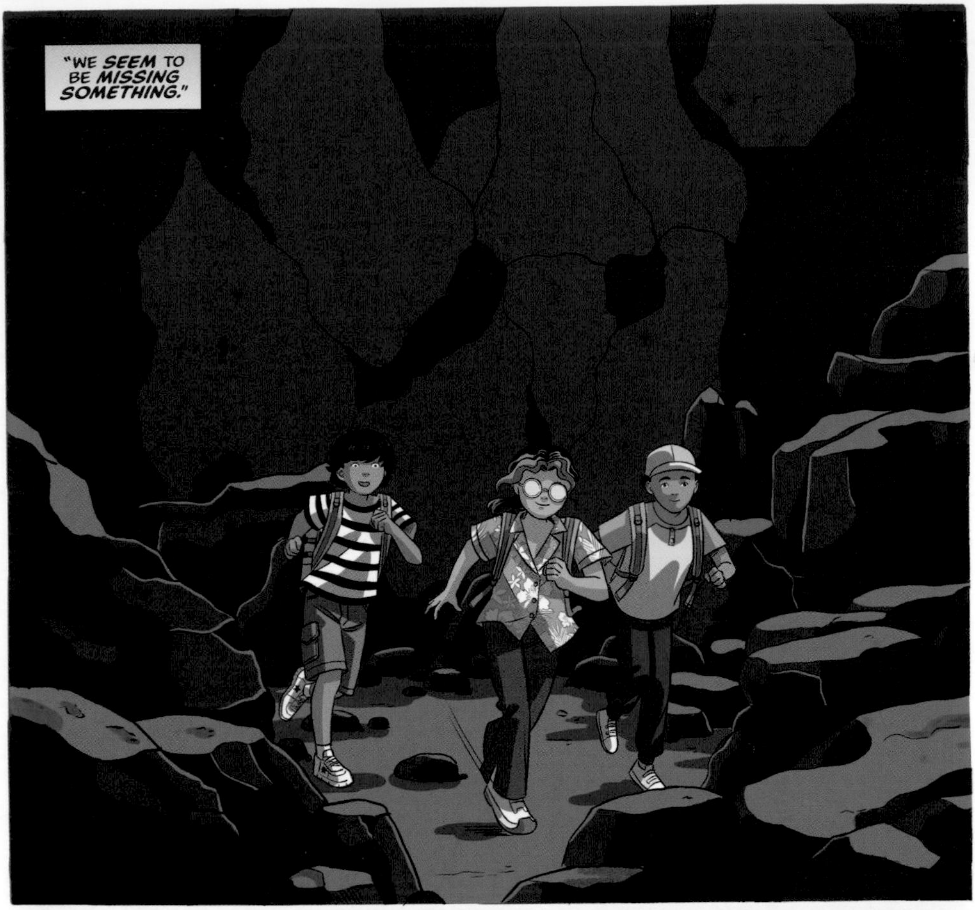
"WE SEEM TO BE MISSING SOMETHING."

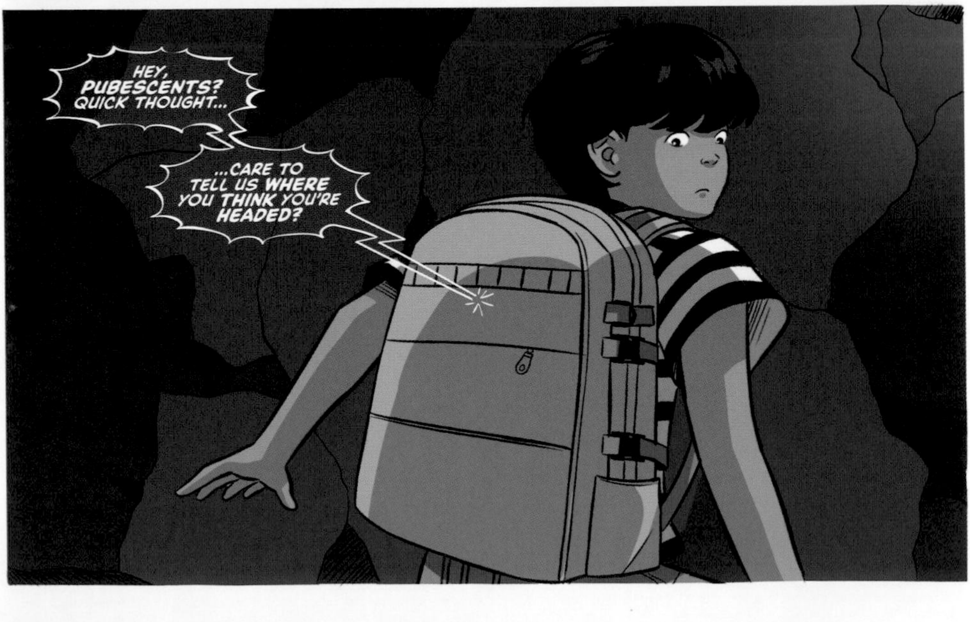
HEY, PUBESCENTS? QUICK THOUGHT...
...CARE TO TELL US WHERE YOU THINK YOU'RE HEADED?

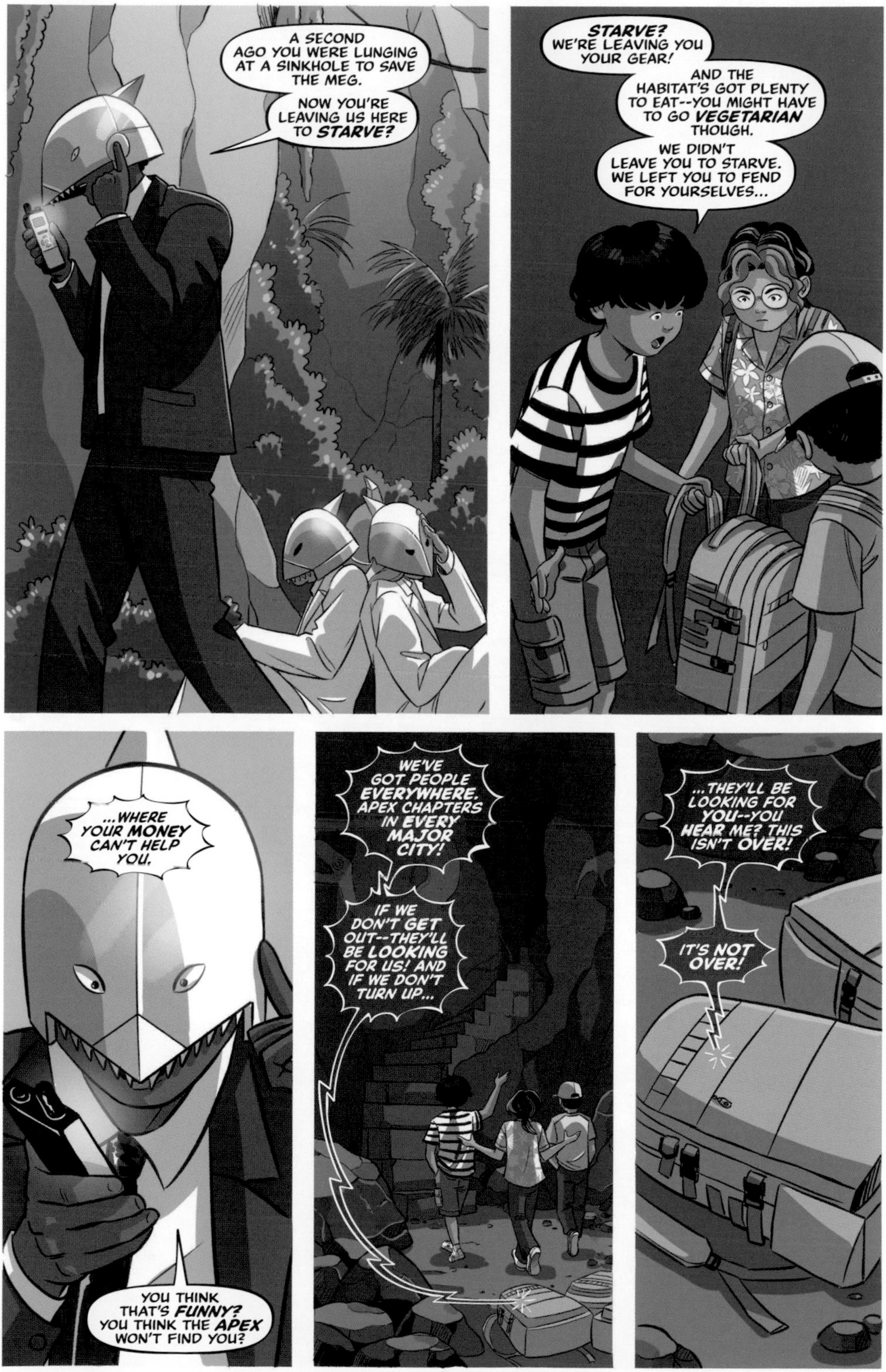
A SECOND AGO YOU WERE LUNGING AT A SINKHOLE TO SAVE THE MEG.
NOW YOU'RE LEAVING US HERE TO STARVE?
STARVE? WE'RE LEAVING YOU YOUR GEAR!
AND THE HABITAT'S GOT PLENTY TO EAT--YOU MIGHT HAVE TO GO VEGETARIAN THOUGH.
WE DIDN'T LEAVE YOU TO STARVE. WE LEFT YOU TO FEND FOR YOURSELVES...
...WHERE YOUR MONEY CAN'T HELP YOU.
YOU THINK THAT'S FUNNY? YOU THINK THE APEX WON'T FIND YOU?
WE'VE GOT PEOPLE EVERYWHERE. APEX CHAPTERS IN EVERY MAJOR CITY!
IF WE DON'T GET OUT--THEY'LL BE LOOKING FOR US! AND IF WE DON'T TURN UP...
...THEY'LL BE LOOKING FOR YOU--YOU HEAR ME? THIS ISN'T OVER!
IT'S NOT OVER!

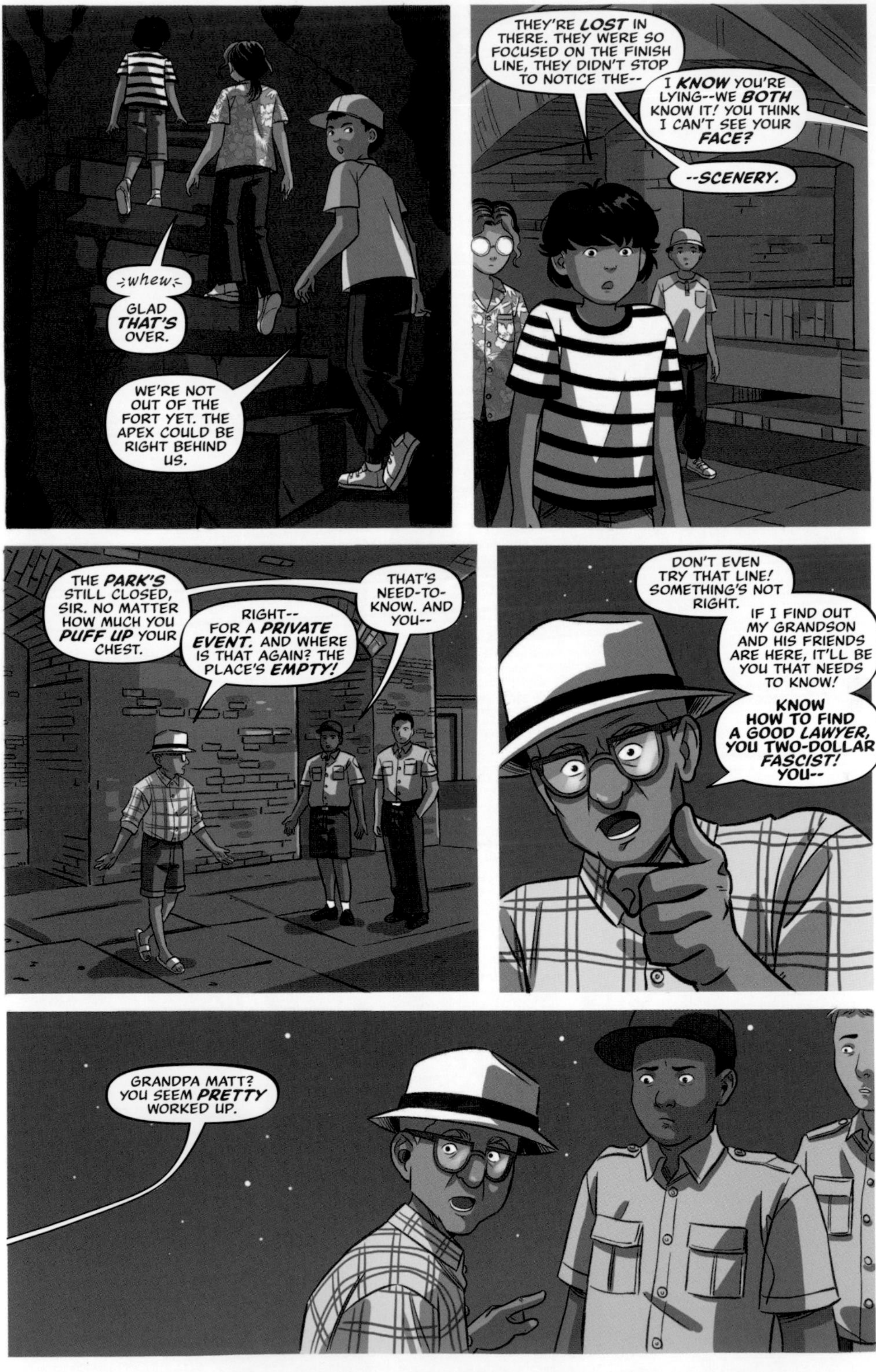

whew
GLAD THAT'S OVER.
WE'RE NOT OUT OF THE FORT YET. THE APEX COULD BE RIGHT BEHIND US.
THEY'RE LOST IN THERE. THEY WERE SO FOCUSED ON THE FINISH LINE, THEY DIDN'T STOP TO NOTICE THE--
I KNOW YOU'RE LYING--WE BOTH KNOW IT! YOU THINK I CAN'T SEE YOUR FACE?
--SCENERY.
THE PARK'S STILL CLOSED, SIR. NO MATTER HOW MUCH YOU PUFF UP YOUR CHEST.
RIGHT-- FOR A PRIVATE EVENT. AND WHERE IS THAT AGAIN? THE PLACE'S EMPTY!
THAT'S NEED-TO-KNOW. AND YOU--
DON'T EVEN TRY THAT LINE! SOMETHING'S NOT RIGHT.
IF I FIND OUT MY GRANDSON AND HIS FRIENDS ARE HERE, IT'LL BE YOU THAT NEEDS TO KNOW!
KNOW HOW TO FIND A GOOD LAWYER, YOU TWO-DOLLAR FASCIST! YOU--
GRANDPA MATT? YOU SEEM PRETTY WORKED UP.

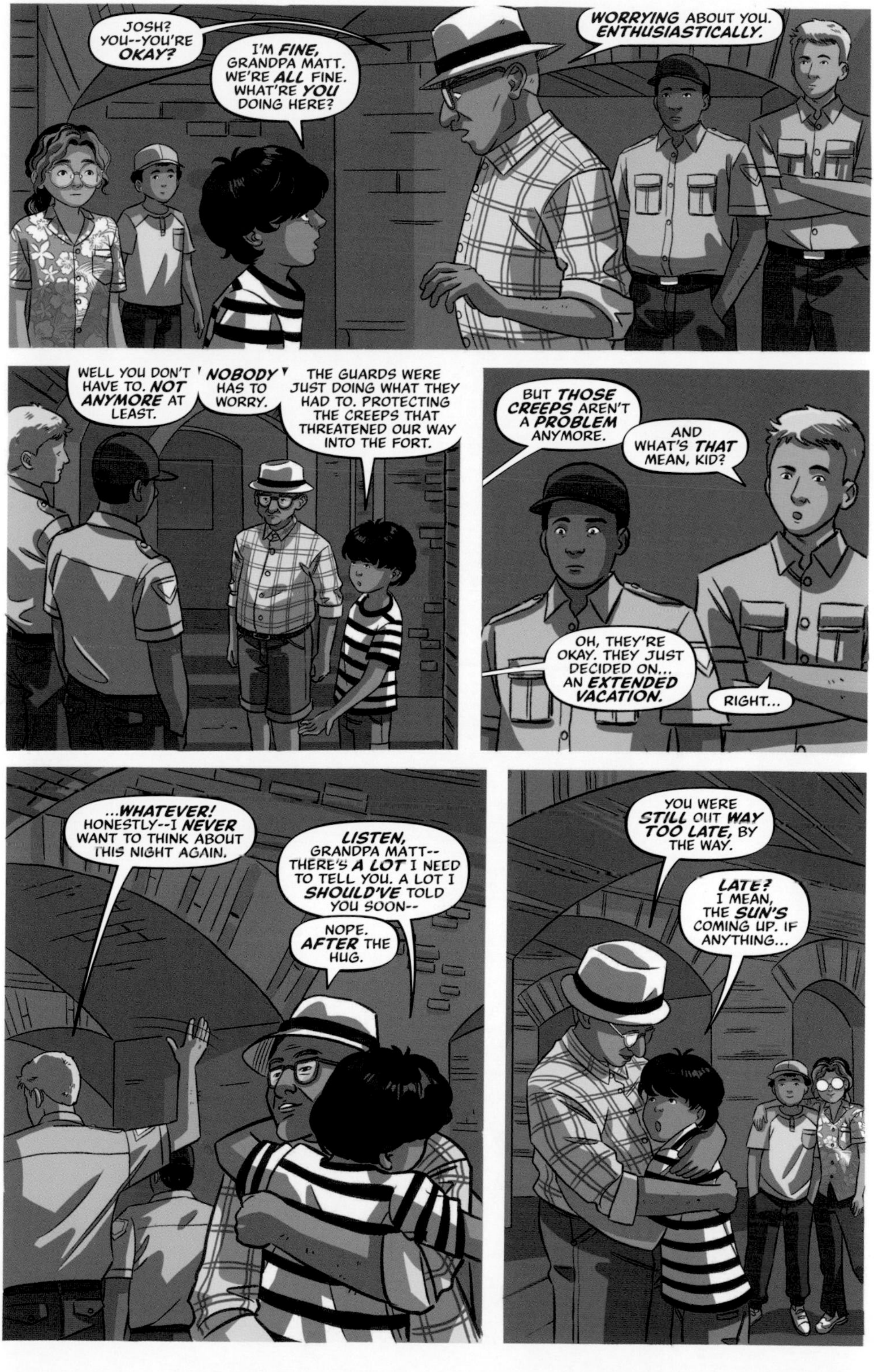
JOSH? YOU--YOU'RE OKAY?
I'M FINE, GRANDPA MATT. WE'RE ALL FINE. WHAT'RE YOU DOING HERE?
WORRYING ABOUT YOU. ENTHUSIASTICALLY.
WELL YOU DON'T HAVE TO. NOT ANYMORE AT LEAST.
NOBODY HAS TO WORRY.
THE GUARDS WERE JUST DOING WHAT THEY HAD TO. PROTECTING THE CREEPS THAT THREATENED OUR WAY INTO THE FORT.
BUT THOSE CREEPS AREN'T A PROBLEM ANYMORE.
AND WHAT'S THAT MEAN, KID?
OH, THEY'RE OKAY. THEY JUST DECIDED ON... AN EXTENDED VACATION.
RIGHT...
...WHATEVER! HONESTLY--I NEVER WANT TO THINK ABOUT THIS NIGHT AGAIN.
LISTEN, GRANDPA MATT-- THERE'S A LOT I NEED TO TELL YOU. A LOT I SHOULD'VE TOLD YOU SOON--
NOPE. AFTER THE HUG.
YOU WERE STILL OUT WAY TOO LATE, BY THE WAY.
LATE? I MEAN, THE SUN'S COMING UP. IF ANYTHING...

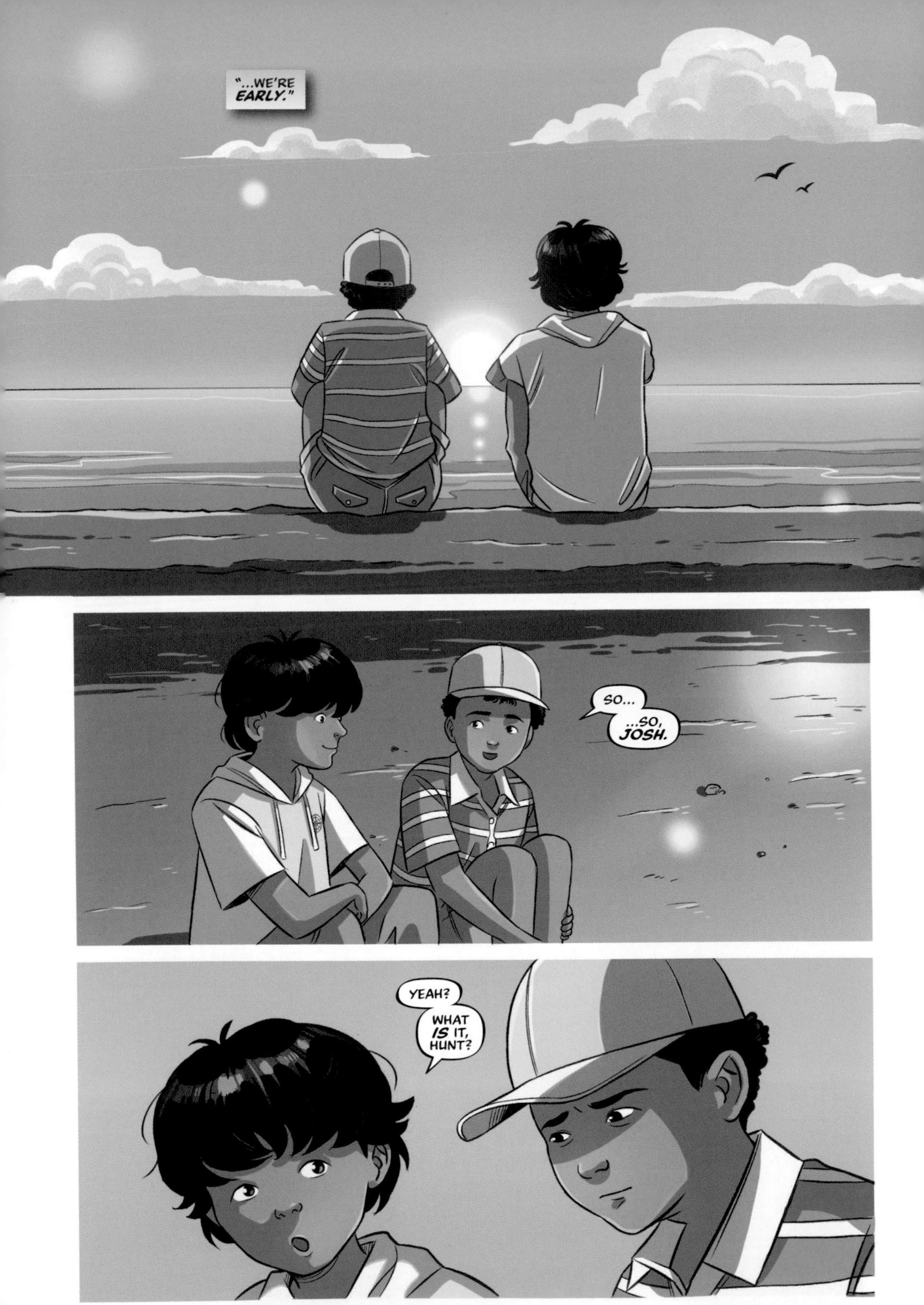
"...WE'RE EARLY."
SO...
...SO, JOSH.
YEAH?
WHAT IS IT, HUNT?

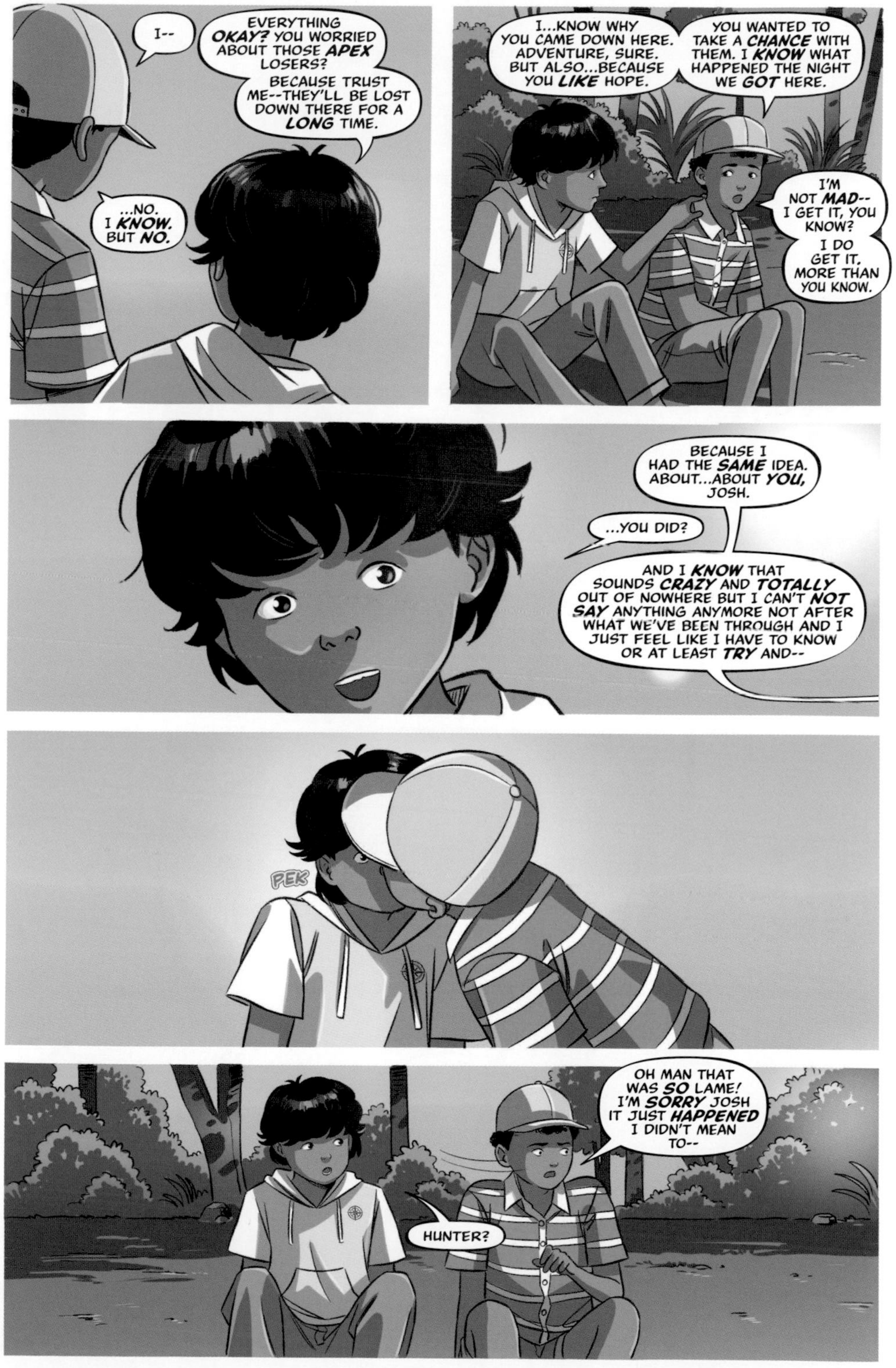
I--
EVERYTHING OKAY? YOU WORRIED ABOUT THOSE APEX LOSERS?
BECAUSE TRUST ME--THEY'LL BE LOST DOWN THERE FOR A LONG TIME.
...NO. I KNOW. BUT NO.
I...KNOW WHY YOU CAME DOWN HERE. ADVENTURE, SURE. BUT ALSO...BECAUSE YOU LIKE HOPE.
YOU WANTED TO TAKE A CHANCE WITH THEM. I KNOW WHAT HAPPENED THE NIGHT WE GOT HERE.
I'M NOT MAD-- I GET IT, YOU KNOW?
I DO GET IT. MORE THAN YOU KNOW.
BECAUSE I HAD THE SAME IDEA. ABOUT...ABOUT YOU, JOSH.
...YOU DID?
AND I KNOW THAT SOUNDS CRAZY AND TOTALLY OUT OF NOWHERE BUT I CAN'T NOT SAY ANYTHING ANYMORE NOT AFTER WHAT WE'VE BEEN THROUGH AND I JUST FEEL LIKE I HAVE TO KNOW OR AT LEAST TRY AND--
PEK
OH MAN THAT WAS SO LAME! I'M SORRY JOSH IT JUST HAPPENED I DIDN'T MEAN TO--
HUNTER?

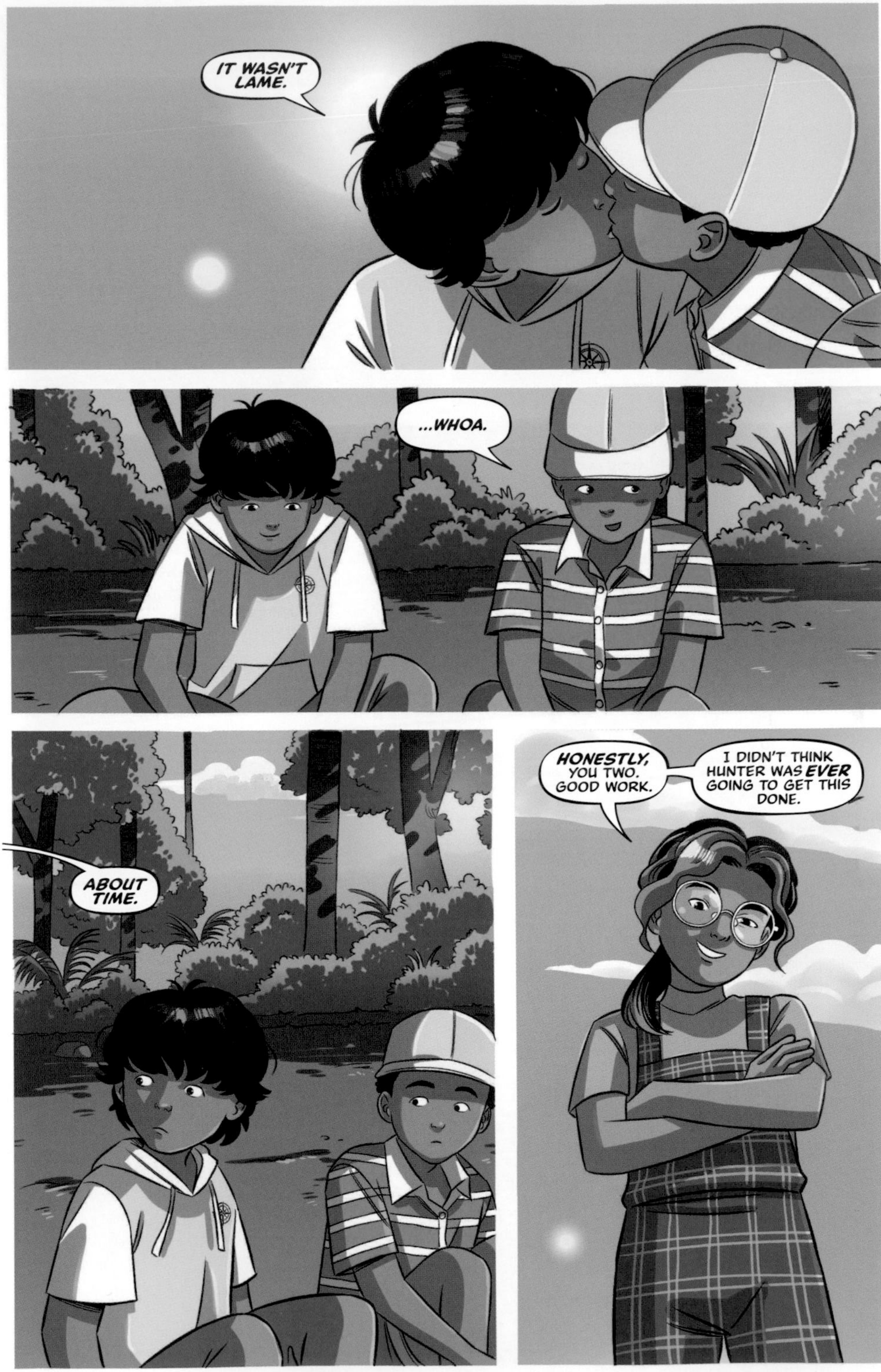
IT WASN'T LAME.
...WHOA.
ABOUT TIME.
HONESTLY, YOU TWO. GOOD WORK.
I DIDN'T THINK HUNTER WAS EVER GOING TO GET THIS DONE.

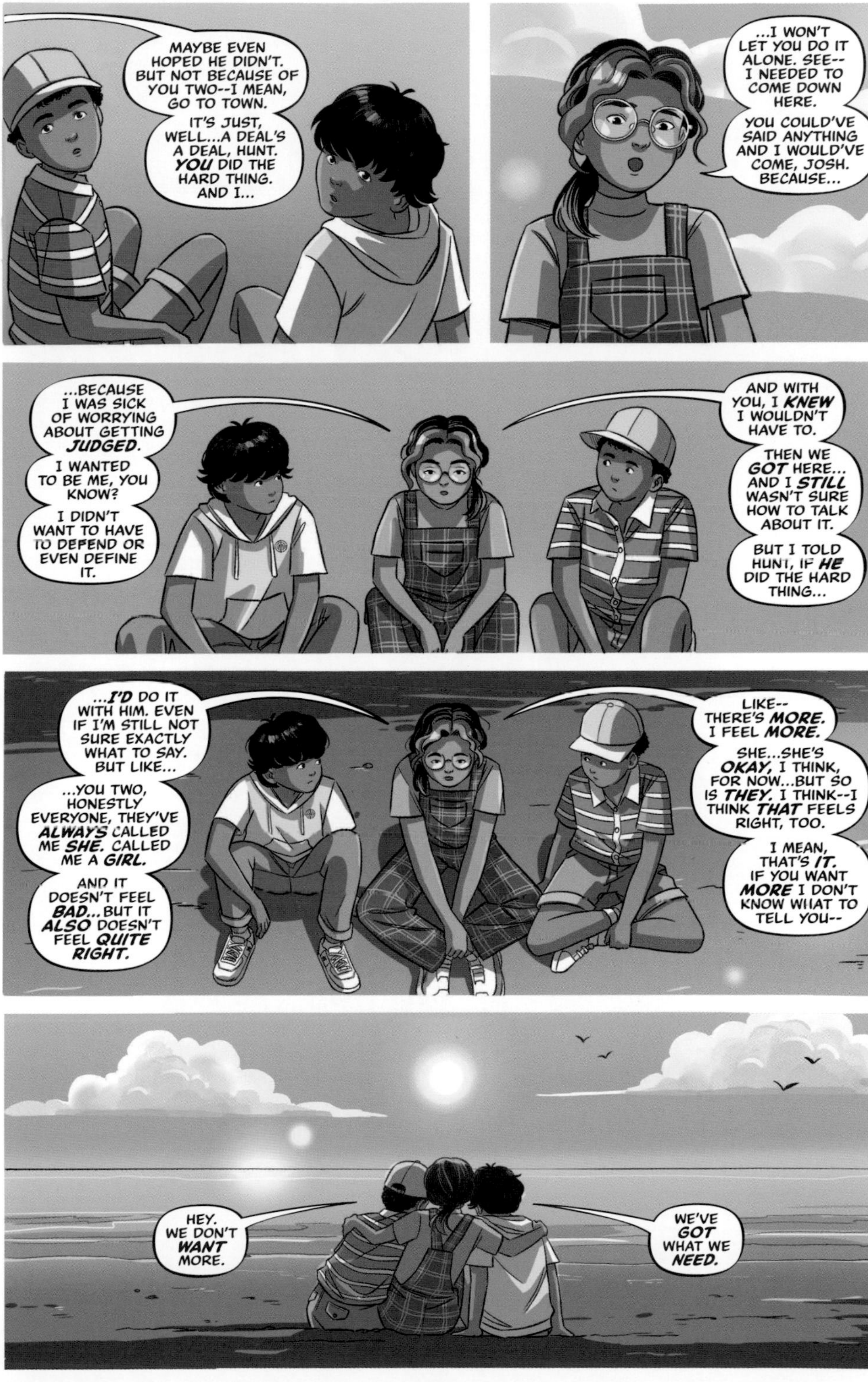
MAYBE EVEN HOPED HE DIDN'T. BUT NOT BECAUSE OF YOU TWO--I MEAN, GO TO TOWN.
IT'S JUST, WELL...A DEAL'S A DEAL, HUNT. YOU DID THE HARD THING. AND I...
...I WON'T LET YOU DO IT ALONE. SEE-- I NEEDED TO COME DOWN HERE.
YOU COULD'VE SAID ANYTHING AND I WOULD'VE COME, JOSH. BECAUSE...
...BECAUSE I WAS SICK OF WORRYING ABOUT GETTING JUDGED.
I WANTED TO BE ME, YOU KNOW?
I DIDN'T WANT TO HAVE TO DEFEND OR EVEN DEFINE IT.
AND WITH YOU, I KNEW I WOULDN'T HAVE TO.
THEN WE GOT HERE... AND I STILL WASN'T SURE HOW TO TALK ABOUT IT.
BUT I TOLD HUNT, IF HE DID THE HARD THING...
...I'D DO IT WITH HIM. EVEN IF I'M STILL NOT SURE EXACTLY WHAT TO SAY. BUT LIKE...
...YOU TWO, HONESTLY EVERYONE, THEY'VE ALWAYS CALLED ME SHE. CALLED ME A GIRL.
AND IT DOESN'T FEEL BAD...BUT IT ALSO DOESN'T FEEL QUITE RIGHT.
LIKE-- THERE'S MORE. I FEEL MORE.
SHE...SHE'S OKAY, I THINK, FOR NOW...BUT SO IS THEY. I THINK--I THINK THAT FEELS RIGHT, TOO.
I MEAN, THAT'S IT. IF YOU WANT MORE I DON'T KNOW WHAT TO TELL YOU--
HEY. WE DON'T WANT MORE.
WE'VE GOT WHAT WE NEED.

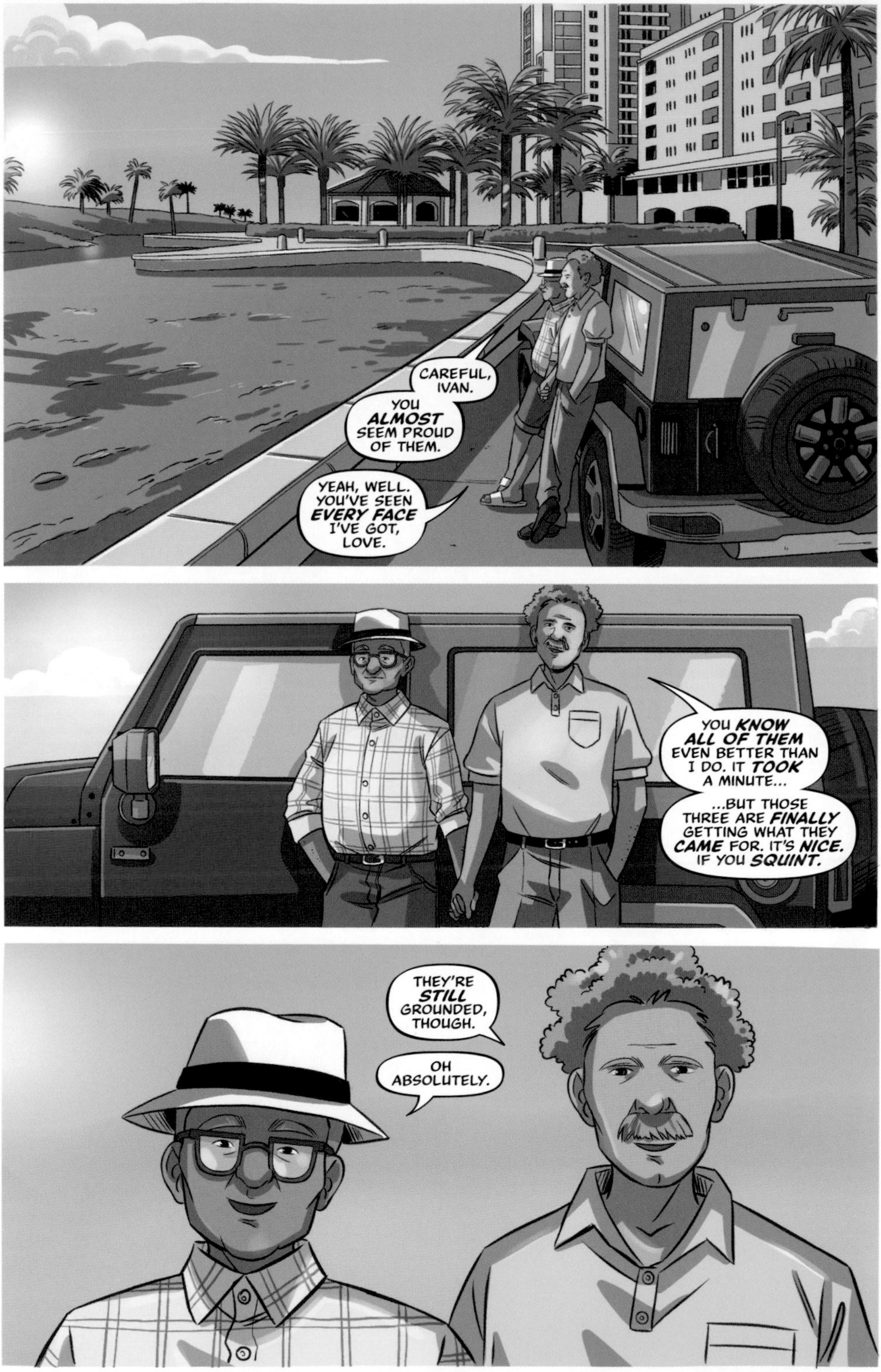

CAREFUL, IVAN.
YOU ALMOST SEEM PROUD OF THEM.
YEAH, WELL. YOU'VE SEEN EVERY FACE I'VE GOT, LOVE.
YOU KNOW ALL OF THEM EVEN BETTER THAN I DO. IT TOOK A MINUTE...
...BUT THOSE THREE ARE FINALLY GETTING WHAT THEY CAME FOR. IT'S NICE. IF YOU SQUINT.
THEY'RE STILL GROUNDED, THOUGH.
OH ABSOLUTELY.

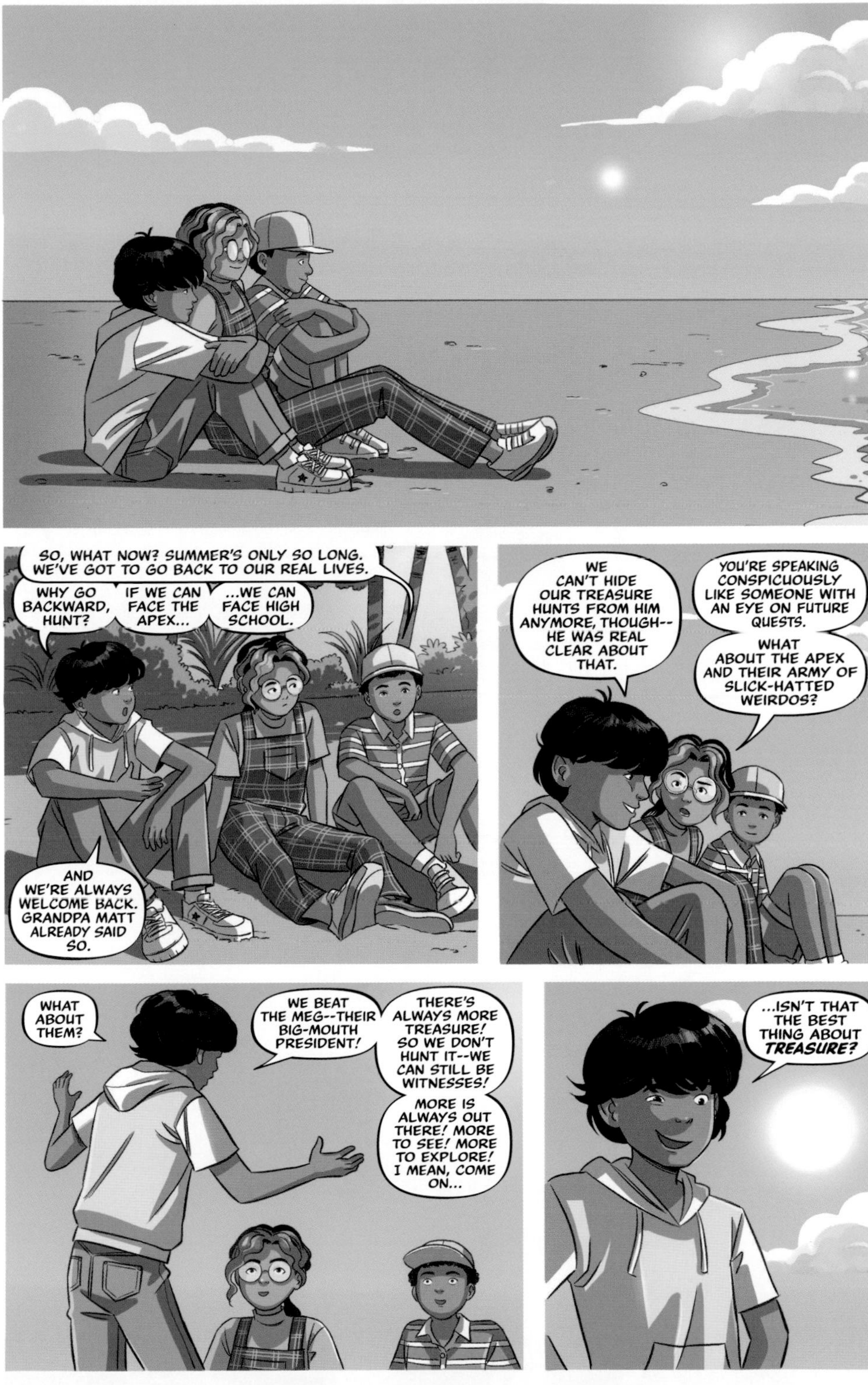
SO, WHAT NOW? SUMMER'S ONLY SO LONG. WE'VE GOT TO GO BACK TO OUR REAL LIVES.
WHY GO BACKWARD, HUNT?
IF WE CAN FACE THE APEX...
...WE CAN FACE HIGH SCHOOL.
AND WE'RE ALWAYS WELCOME BACK. GRANDPA MATT ALREADY SAID SO.
WE CAN'T HIDE OUR TREASURE HUNTS FROM HIM ANYMORE, THOUGH--HE WAS REAL CLEAR ABOUT THAT.
YOU'RE SPEAKING CONSPICUOUSLY LIKE SOMEONE WITH AN EYE ON FUTURE QUESTS.
WHAT ABOUT THE APEX AND THEIR ARMY OF SLICK-HATTED WEIRDOS?
WHAT ABOUT THEM?
WE BEAT THE MEG--THEIR BIG-MOUTH PRESIDENT!
THERE'S ALWAYS MORE TREASURE! SO WE DON'T HUNT IT--WE CAN STILL BE WITNESSES!
MORE IS ALWAYS OUT THERE! MORE TO SEE! MORE TO EXPLORE! I MEAN, COME ON...
...ISN'T THAT THE BEST THING ABOUT *TREASURE?*

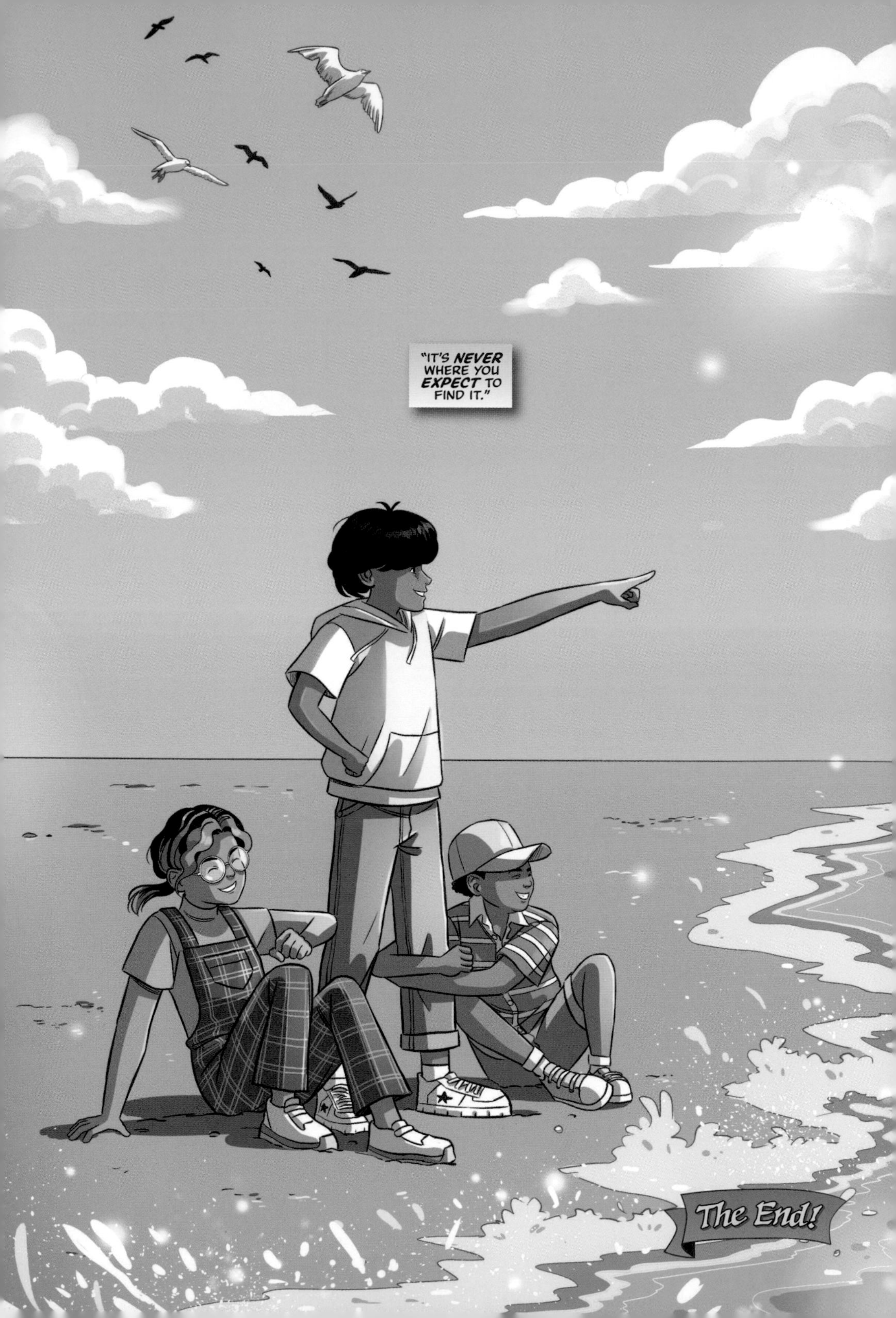
"IT'S NEVER WHERE YOU EXPECT TO FIND IT."
The End!

RESOURCES

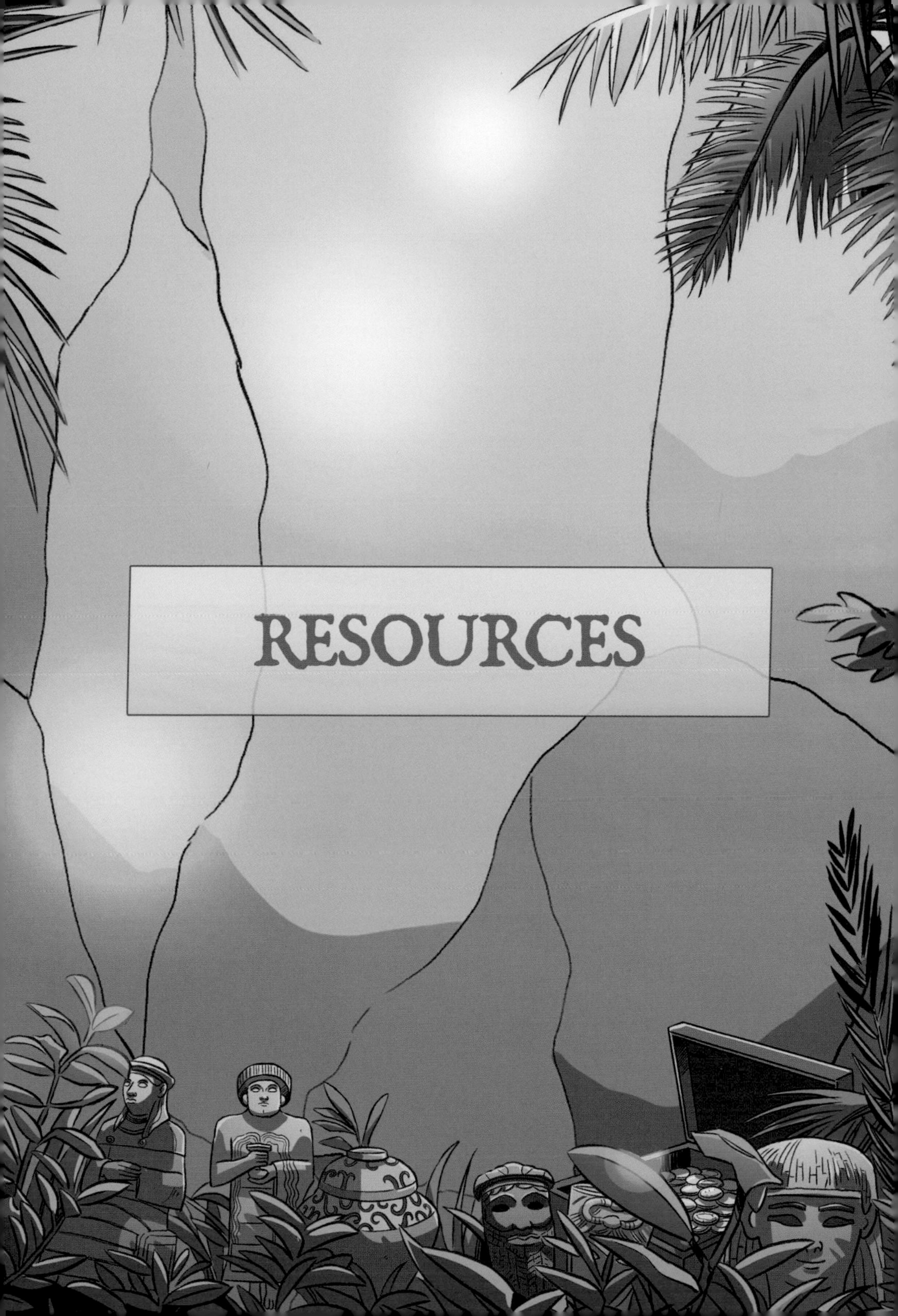

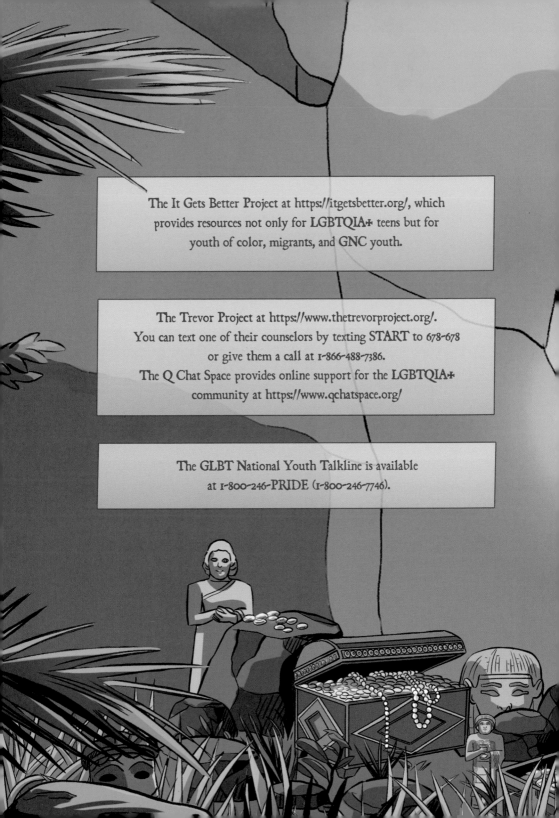

The It Gets Better Project at https://itgetsbetter.org/, which provides resources not only for LGBTQIA+ teens but for youth of color, migrants, and GNC youth.

The Trevor Project at https://www.thetrevorproject.org/.
You can text one of their counselors by texting START to 678-678 or give them a call at 1-866-488-7386.
The Q Chat Space provides online support for the LGBTQIA+ community at https://www.qchatspace.org/

The GLBT National Youth Talkline is available at 1-800-246-PRIDE (1-800-246-7746).

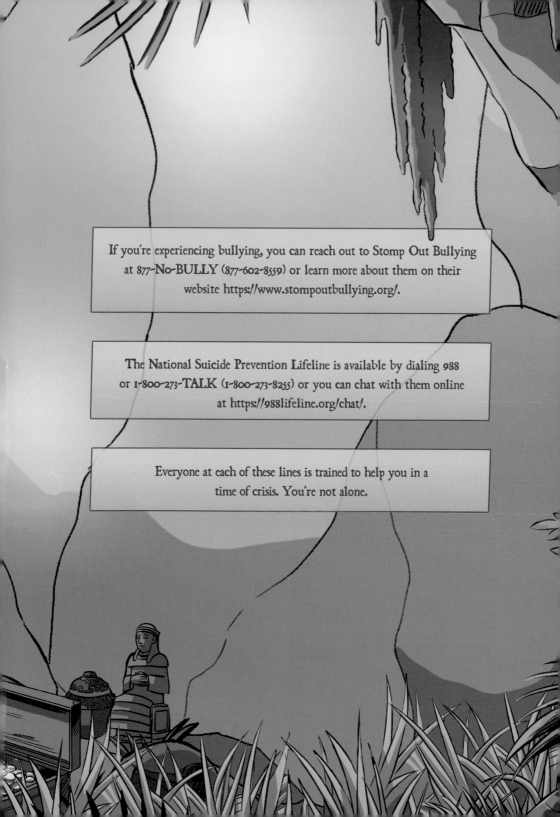

If you're experiencing bullying, you can reach out to Stomp Out Bullying at 877-No-BULLY (877-602-8559) or learn more about them on their website https://www.stompoutbullying.org/.

The National Suicide Prevention Lifeline is available by dialing 988 or 1-800-273-TALK (1-800-273-8255) or you can chat with them online at https://988lifeline.org/chat/.

Everyone at each of these lines is trained to help you in a time of crisis. You're not alone.

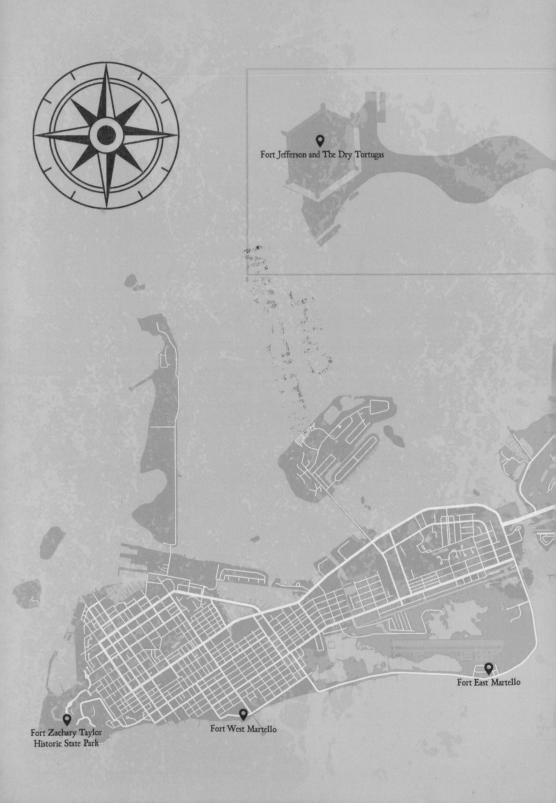

Fort Jefferson and The Dry Tortugas

Fort East Martello

Fort West Martello

Fort Zachary Taylor
Historic State Park